Light and Darkness

Sōseki Natsume (1867–1916) is widely considered the foremost novelist of the Meiji period (1868–1914). After graduating from Tokyo Imperial University in 1893, Sōseki taught high school before spending two years in England on a Japanese government scholarship. He returned to lecture in English literature at the university. Numerous nervous disorders forced him to give up teaching in 1908 and he became a full-time writer for the *Asahi* newspaper. In addition to fourteen novels, Sōseki wrote haiku, poems, academic papers on literary theory, essays, autobiographical sketches, and fairy tales.

Sōseki Natsume
Light and Darkness

Translated from the Japanese
with a critical essay by
V. H. Viglielmo

TUTTLE PUBLISHING
Tokyo • Rutland, Vermont • Singapore

UNESCO COLLECTION OF REPRESENTATIVE WORKS
JAPANESE SERIES
This book has been accepted in the
Japanese Series of the Translations Collection of the
United Nations Educational, Scientific and Cultural Organization (UNESCO)

Originally published in Japanese as *Meian*

Published by the Charles E. Tuttle Company Inc.,
an imprint of Periplus Editions (HK) Ltd,
with editorial offices at 364 Innovation Drive,
North Clarendon, Vermont 05759
and 130 Joo Seng Road #06-01, Singapore 368357
by special arrangement with Peter Owen Limited, London.

First Tuttle edition published 1972

ISBN 4-8053-0652-1 (for sale in Japan only)

Printed in Singapore

Distributed by:

Japan
Tuttle Publishing
Yaekari Building, 3F, 5-4-12 Osaki,
Shinagawa-ku, Tokyo 141-0032.
Tel: (813) 5437 0171;
Fax: (813) 5437 0755;
E-mail: tuttle-sales@gol.com

Asia Pacific
Berkeley Books Pte Ltd
130 Joo Seng Road #06-01,
Singapore 368357.
Tel: (65) 6280 1330;
Fax: (65) 6280 6290;
E-mail: inquiries@periplus.com.sg
www.periplus.com

06 08 10 09 07
1 3 5 6 4 2

TUTTLE PUBLISHING® is a registered trademark of Tuttle Publishing.

In memory of my mother

I

After the doctor had probed the fistula, he helped Tsuda off the operating table.

'The fistula *did* go as far as the intestines, after all. When I probed it before, I found a great deal of scar tissue midway, and I actually thought it didn't go any farther. That's why I said what I did. But today, in scraping at it to drain it properly, I saw it goes quite a bit beyond that point.'

'You say it goes as far as the intestines?'

'Yes. At first I thought it was about an inch, but I find now it's about twice that.'

Faint signs of disappointment were discernible in Tsuda's wry smile. The doctor inclined his head slightly to one side while crossing his arms over his baggy white jacket. This pose could be interpreted as meaning : 'It's too bad, but that's the way things are. A doctor can't lie in his professional life, you know.'

Tsuda retied his obi in silence, and taking up his *hakama*,* which he had thrown over the back of the chair, again turned to the doctor : 'If it goes as far as you say, does that mean it won't heal?'

'No, not necessarily.'

The doctor contradicted Tsuda's words briskly and simply; at the same time he seemed to contradict Tsuda's feelings as well.

'It's just that it won't do merely to clean the opening as I have been doing. The flesh would never join that way, so there's nothing left to do but change the method I've been using and perform a basic operation without delay.'

'What exactly do you mean by "a basic operation"?'

* A kind of skirt worn with the kimono.

1

'An incision. To make an incision and bring the fistula and intestine together. Then the two sides which are now separated should join and heal naturally, so you should really be cured once for all.'

Tsuda nodded but did not speak. Near him, on the table beneath the southern window, was a microscope. Since he was rather intimate with the doctor, upon entering the consultation room earlier, he had been allowed to take a look through it out of curiosity. He had clearly seen under the lens, which magnified objects eight hundred and fifty times, coloured botryoidal bacilli exactly as if they had been minutely sketched.

He finished putting on his *hakama*, and taking up his leather wallet, which he had put on the table, he suddenly remembered those bacilli; the association immediately depressed him. He placed his wallet back in his kimono since he had to leave the consultation room, but he hesitated again even though he had already taken a few steps on his way out.

'If I were tubercular, and you performed the operation you've just mentioned, it wouldn't heal even if you did make that narrow incision all the way to the intestines, would it?'

'If you're tubercular, it's hopeless, since it won't do to treat the opening without probing deep into the fistula.'

Tsuda involuntarily knit his brow.

'I wouldn't happen to be tubercular, would I?'

'No, you're not.'

To determine how much truth there was in the doctor's words, he fixed his eyes on him for a moment.

'How can you know? By the routine examination?'

'Yes, I know just by looking at you.'

At that moment the nurse, standing in the doorway of the room, called out the name of the patient who was to follow. This patient, who had been waiting, immediately appeared behind Tsuda, who then was forced to leave hurriedly.

'Well, when can I have the operation?'

'Any time. When it's convenient for you will be all right.'

After carefully considering his schedule, Tsuda decided to set the date later, and thereupon left the room.

2

On the streetcar he felt somewhat subdued. In the midst of all the passengers, squeezed in so closely as to be unable to move, he could think only of his own affairs as he clung to the leather strap. The acute pain of the previous year rose distinctly in his memory. He could vividly see, in his mind's eye, his wretched form stretched out on the white bed. He could clearly hear his groans like those of a dog unable to break its chain and flee. The gleam of the cold blades, the sound as they touched each other, the dreadful pressure which suddenly squeezed the air out of both his lungs at once, and finally the violent pain which never ended because he could not contract his lungs while the air was being pressed out of them—all of these memories assailed him.

He was depressed. Suddenly his mood changed, and he gazed at his surroundings. But when he saw that those near him were all utterly indifferent to his existence, he continued his musings.

'I wonder why I had to endure such pain.'

He was completely ignorant of the cause of the pain, which he had felt at that time quite suddenly—without any warning—upon his return from cherry blossom viewing at the Arakawa embankment. Its cause lay beyond all imagination. It was more than strange; it was frightening.

'This body of ours can undergo a violent change at any time. What's even worse, right now perhaps some change is taking place inside me, and I know absolutely nothing about it. That's really frightening.'

His thinking having advanced that far, he could not stop at that point. Suddenly he was pushed forward from the rear with a force almost sufficient to knock him down. As if that physical force had been responsible, a thought immediately flashed through his mind :

'In love too it's the same. We don't know when or how our feelings will change. And what's more, I've seen how they change.'

He involuntarily compressed his lips tightly, and turned on his surroundings a glance of wounded pride. The other passengers, however, wholly ignorant of what was taking place within him, paid not the slightest attention to his glance.

His mind, like the streetcar he was riding, moved ahead, running on on its own rails. He remembered a story about the French philosopher Poincaré he had heard from a friend two or three days earlier. In explaining to him the meaning of the word 'coincidence', his friend had told him :

'That's why we often say something's a coincidence, but what we call a coincidence, according to Poincaré's theory, is simply the term we use when the causes are so complex we can't discover them easily. For example, for Napoleon to be born, the combination of a certain special egg and spermatozoon was necessary, but when we try to think a bit further about what conditions were necessary for such a combination to take place, we can hardly imagine them.'

He could not overlook what his friend had said or consider it merely a new fragment of knowledge. He sought instead to apply it exactly to his own case. As he did so, he could imagine some dark, mysterious force pushing him to the left when he had to go right, and pulling him back when he had to advance. And yet he had never before felt that he had been restrained in his actions by anyone. He did not doubt that everything he had said and done had been of his own free will.

'Why did she marry him? Undoubtedly because she wanted to. But still she certainly shouldn't have. And why did *I* marry the woman *I* did? Again undoubtedly because I wanted to. And yet earlier I hadn't wanted to. A coincidence? Poincaré's so-called consummation of complexity? I don't quite know.'

Still thinking about the problem, he got off the streetcar and walked towards his home.

3

As he turned the corner and entered the narrow lane, Tsuda recognized his wife O-Nobu standing in front of their gate. She was looking his way, but as soon as his shadow emerged from the corner she turned to face straight ahead. She then placed her delicate white hands on her forehead as if shading her eyes, and appeared to be looking up at something. She did not change her position until Tsuda had come very close to her.

'Well, what are you looking at?'

As soon as O-Nobu heard his voice, she turned to him in great surprise.

'Oh, you startled me!—But I'm glad you're back.'

As she spoke, she brought together all the brilliance her eyes possessed and cast the full force of it on him. Then she leaned forward somewhat and bowed slightly.

Tsuda half attempted to respond to his wife's coquetry and half held back hesitatingly.

'What on earth were you doing standing there?'

'I was waiting for you.'

'But weren't you looking at something very intently?'

'Yes—those sparrows. They're building a nest in the eaves of the second storey of the house across from us.'

He glanced up briefly at the roof of the house across from them, but he could not see a trace of anything resembling a sparrow. O-Nobu immediately put out her hand in front of him.

'What's that?'

'A cane.'

As if he had noticed it for the first time, Tsuda handed her the cane he was carrying. After taking it, she opened the lattice door of the entrance by herself and let him go in first. Then she followed him into the house.

She made her husband change his clothes, and just as he was sitting down in front of the charcoal brazier, she came out of the kitchen carrying a soap-dish wrapped in a towel.

'Go and take a bath now. If you get settled there it will be a bother.'

'Maybe I'll skip the bath for today.'

'Why? It will refresh you. Go ahead and take one. When you come back I'll give you dinner right away.'

He had to get up again. As he was leaving the room, he turned back briefly towards her.

'On the way home today I stopped at Dr Kobayashi's and had him examine me.'

'Really? And what did he say? You're probably completely recovered, aren't you?'

'Actually I'm not. It's become even more troublesome.'

After that comment, he ignored her questions although she obviously wished to hear more about the matter, and he went out the front way.

When the same subject came up again between them it was night, and the evening meal was over, but he had not yet retired to his study.

'It's unpleasant to be operated on, isn't it? And frightening, too. It wasn't good for you to have let it go for so long.'

'Yes, according to what the doctor says, it's dangerous the way it is now.'

'I don't like it, dear. What if he should make some mistake while he's operating?'

She looked at him, frowning slightly with her thick, well-formed eyebrows. He laughed without responding. Then she asked, as if she had suddenly realized it:

'If you do have an operation, I suppose it has to be on Sunday again, doesn't it?'

They had been invited by relatives for the following Sunday, and it had been decided that they all would go to the Kabuki.

'But since you don't have any seats yet it doesn't matter. You can say no.'

'But that's rude, dear. To say no after they've gone to so much trouble.'

'It isn't at all rude. Since you're doing it for a very good reason.'

'But I do so want to go.'

'Well, if you want to, go right ahead.'

'But why don't you go too? You don't want to?'

He looked at her and gave a forced laugh.

4

Since O-Nobu had a very fair complexion, her well-formed eyebrows stood out even more clearly. She also made a habit of twitching them. Unfortunately her eyes were too narrow, and her one-fold eyelids were rather uninteresting. But the pupils flashing within them were the deepest black, and therefore she used them to very good advantage. Occasionally she even adopted an expression which might almost have been called despotic. At times Tsuda could not help being captivated by the gleam from those small eyes, but at other times, for no reason at all, he was suddenly repelled by it.

When he casually raised his head and looked at her, he felt a kind of weird power dwelling momentarily in her eyes. It was a strange brilliance, utterly out of keeping with the tender words she had just been using. His mind, in attempting to frame an answer to her words, was somewhat confused by this glance. Then she suddenly smiled, showing her beautiful teeth. As she did so, the expression in her eyes disappeared without a trace.

'What I said just now isn't true. It really doesn't matter if I don't go to the theatre. I was behaving like a child.'

Tsuda, remaining silent, still did not take his eyes off her.

'Why are you looking at me so angrily? . . . I've already given up the theatre, so go to Dr Kobayashi this next Sunday and have the operation. That's what you want, isn't it? I'll either drop a card to the Okamotos within the next two or three days or I may actually go there myself to say we can't make it.'

'It's perfectly all right if you go by yourself since they've gone to the trouble of inviting you.'

'No, I'll give it up too. After all, your health is much more important than a play.'

He still had to tell her the details of the operation he had to undergo.

'An operation, you know, isn't as simple a thing as lancing a boil. First of all, they'll give me a laxative to clean out the intestines completely, and then after they finally operate, there may be danger of bleeding, so that I may have to lie still for five or six days with the cut all bandaged up. That's why, even if I go this coming Sunday, it won't be finished that day anyway. On the other hand, if I postpone it beyond Sunday to Monday or Tuesday, it won't make too much difference either; and also if I move it up from Sunday to tomorrow or the day after it's still very much the same thing. Nevertheless, when you think about it, it's not such a terribly serious illness.'

'I don't know about that, dear . . . if you have to stay in bed for a week and aren't able to move.'

She again twitched her eyebrows. Tsuda, as if wholly indifferent to her, rested his right elbow on the edge of the long charcoal brazier between them, and, thinking about some problem, he gazed at the iron kettle on the brazier. From underneath the copper lid came the loud sound of boiling water.

'Well, I suppose you'll have to take about a week off from work in any case, won't you?'

'That's why I think I'll set the date after I've met Mr Yoshikawa and talked things over. It may seem as if it doesn't matter if I take off from work without saying anything, but actually it's not that easy.'

'Well then, dear, it's better if you do talk to him. After all, he's always been very kind to you.'

'If I do speak to him he may say I should enter the hospital tomorrow.'

When she heard the words 'enter the hospital', she quickly widened her narrow eyes.

' "Enter the hospital"? But surely you're not going to enter the hospital, are you?'

'I'm afraid so.'

'But didn't you once say Dr Kobayashi's place isn't a hospital? You said all the patients are only day-patients, didn't you?'

'Well, it isn't really a hospital, but since the upstairs room above the consultation office is open it seems that I could stay there.'

'Is it clean?'

He smiled sardonically.

'It may even be a bit cleaner than here.'

This time O-Nobu was the one who smiled sardonically.

5

Since Tsuda was in the habit of spending one or two hours at his desk before going to bed, he got up shortly afterwards. O-Nobu, still in the relaxed posture of leaning over the charcoal brazier, looked up at him.

'Are you going to study again?'

She would sometimes ask him this when he would get up to go upstairs, and it would always seem to him that there was a certain dissatisfaction in her voice. Occasionally he would be disposed to try to wheedle her out of her attitude but at other times he would, on the contrary, feel great antagonism and want to escape from her. In both cases, however, he inwardly disparaged her in a way that was tantamount to saying : 'I can't be satisfied with merely talking and associating with a woman like you. After all, there are certain important things I have to do.'

When, without answering her, he opened the intervening sliding-door and was about to go into the next room, O-Nobu again called to him from behind.

'Then we're cancelling the theatre now, aren't we? I'll go to the Okamotos and apologize for us.'

He turned around for a moment.

'You go ahead if you want to, because, as I've said, I don't know how things will turn out.'

O-Nobu, still looking down, did not return his glance. Nor did she answer him. Tsuda then made the steep stairs creak as he went up to the second floor.

There was a relatively large Western volume on his desk. He sat down, opened it, and set about reading it at the place where the bookmark had been inserted. But, as an inevitable result of having neglected the book for three or four days, he did not understand the continuity of the passage very clearly. Since, to make sense out of it, he would be forced to re-read the previous section, he was somewhat annoyed, and instead of deciding to read it, he merely ran his fingers along the edges of the pages and wearily contemplated the thickness of the volume. As he did so, he could not help thinking that it would take him a long time to finish it.

He remembered having first looked at the book in the third or fourth month after his marriage. Now that he thought about it, he realized that although more than two months had already passed since then he still had not read even two-thirds of the work. In front of O-Nobu he had always ridiculed as vulgar dunces most men who, upon completing their education and getting a job, immediately give up reading anything serious. A rather large amount of time was thus spent in the upstairs room to make O-Nobu, who often had to listen to this favourite topic of his, realize that he was a true scholar. Therefore, together with the realization that he had a long way to go yet in his reading, a feeling of shame emerged from somewhere and impudently challenged his self-esteem.

And yet the knowledge he was then trying to gain from the volume spread in front of him was not really necessary for his daily work. It was also much too specialized and too esoteric. In fact, even the knowledge he had received from his college lectures was only rarely of any use to him and almost completely unrelated to his present occupation. He merely wanted to store up such knowledge to bolster his self-confidence. He also wanted to acquire it as a kind of adornment to attract people's attention. When he dimly realized the difficulty of his task, he inquired of his vanity : 'It isn't going very well, is it?'

He smoked a cigarette silently. Then, as if he had suddenly thought of something, he placed the book face down on the desk and stood up. He quickly went down the stairs, once again making them creak.

6

'O-Nobu!'

As he called her from the other side of the sliding-door, he quickly opened it and stood at the entrance to the living-room. Upon doing so, he instantly saw the beautiful colours of the obis and kimonos spread in front of her, as she was sitting near the long charcoal brazier. Having come so suddenly from the dark entrance hall into the brightly lit room, the colours stood out even more brilliantly than usual, and he stopped for a moment to look alternately at O-Nobu and the flamboyant patterns.

'What are you doing taking out such things at a time like this?'

O-Nobu, still keeping the edge of a one-piece obi of blackberry-lily pattern on her knee, looked at him distantly.

'I just thought I'd take them out and look at them, that's all. Why, I've never even worn this obi.'

'You mean you're going to wear it when you go to the theatre next time, don't you?'

A certain coldness was mingled with the sarcasm in his words. She looked down, saying nothing in response. And she again twitched her dark eyebrows in her customary fashion. This habit of hers at times strangely stirred him but at others it just as inexplicably irritated him. He silently went out to the veranda and opened the door of the toilet. Afterwards, he was about to go upstairs again when this time it was O-Nobu who called him.

'Yoshio, wait a minute, won't you?'

At the same time she stood up, and blocking his way, she asked him : 'Did you have something you wanted to talk about?'

What concerned him at that moment was rather more important to him than her obis and kimonos.

'A letter hasn't come from Father yet, has it?'

'No, if it did I'd put it on your desk as I always do.'

Since this letter he had been expecting had not been placed there, he had purposely descended the stairs to find out about it.

'Should I have the maid look in the mailbox?'

'No, if it comes, it will be by registered mail, and it would hardly be thrown in the mailbox.'

'I suppose so, but I'll go and have a look anyway just to make sure.'

O-Nobu opened the sliding-door at the entrance and was about to go down to the step where shoes were removed.

'It's no use. Registered mail wouldn't be put in there.'

'But there may be a regular letter even if there isn't a registered one. Please wait a moment while I go and see.'

Tsuda finally went back to the parlour, and since the pillow on which he had sat when he ate supper earlier was still in front of the brazier, he sat down on it cross-legged, and stared at the deep colours of the printed muslins scattered there.

O-Nobu quickly returned from the entrance, carrying in her hand a letter, as she had predicted.

'There *was* one, after all. And it may even be the one from Father, too.'

As she spoke, she held the white envelope in the bright light of the lamp.

'Ah, just as I thought, it *is* from Father!'

'Hm, I wonder why he didn't register it.'

As soon as he got the letter, Tsuda broke the seal and read it through. But after he had finished reading it, and was folding it again before inserting it back in the envelope, his hands merely moved mechanically. He looked neither at his hands nor at O-Nobu. While gazing dully at a rough stripe-patterned garment among her formal clothes, he muttered, as if to himself : 'What in the world do I do now !'

'What happened?'

'It's nothing of any great importance.'

Since he was very much concerned with appearances, he did not wish to talk about the contents of the letter to his wife, particularly since they had been married only briefly. And yet the matter was such that he had to speak to her about it.

7

'He says this month he can't send me the money as he always has done, so I'm supposed to get along without it somehow. There's no telling how old people are going to act. But if he was going to do this, why the devil didn't he say so sooner ! To say so suddenly just at a time when I really need money. . . .'

'But what sort of reason does he give?'

Tsuda removed the letter from the envelope in which he had inserted it and spread it out on his knee.

'He says two of the houses he rents have been vacant since the end of last month. And furthermore it seems the rent from those that are occupied hasn't come in either. He also says, in this connection, that since the garden needed tending and the fences needed repairing, a lot of emergency expenses have piled up and he can't send any money this month.'

He handed the letter, as he had opened it, to O-Nobu, who was across the brazier from him. Without saying anything, she took it, but did not try to read it. He had always feared this cold attitude of hers.

'I certainly don't see why he has to depend on that rent. If he really wanted to send me the money he could manage somehow. After all, how much does it cost to repair some fences? He certainly isn't building any thick brick walls!'

There was considerable truth in Tsuda's statement. Even though his father had no vast wealth, he was not in a position where he had to stint on the monthly allotments to his son and daughter-in-law which made up the deficiencies in their budget. He was, however, an extremely thrifty person. According to Tsuda, he was much too thrifty; and according to O-Nobu, who was far more extravagant than her husband, he was almost senselessly economical.

'Your father undoubtedly thinks we indulge in all kinds of luxuries and spend money recklessly. I'm sure of it.'

'Yes, that's more or less what he was saying when I went to Kyoto last time. Old people always remember how they lived when they were young and they think young people nowadays should live exactly the way they did. I may be thirty the way Father once was, but since everything's changed so completely, I can't manage on what he had. I remember once we went to a meeting together, and when he asked me how much the dues were I told him five yen—you should have seen how astounded he was!'

Tsuda usually feared that O-Nobu would look down on his father; nevertheless he felt he had to make these disparaging remarks about him in front of her. For this was precisely what he felt. Moreover, since he took the initiative in the face of her implied criticism, this action of his was almost the equivalent of an apology on his and his father's part.

'Well, what do we do about this month's bills? In addition to what would normally be lacking, now if you have to be in the hospital a week for the operation we'll have that expense too.'

Her conversation immediately shifted to practical problems since she was somewhat hesitant to express her criticism of her father-in-law in front of her husband. Tsuda did not have a ready answer. After a while he spoke in a low voice, as if to himself:

'If Uncle Fujii had some money, I'd go and see him but. . . .'

O-Nobu looked at him intently.

'Wouldn't it be wiser to ask your father again? And you could also write to him about your illness.'

'It isn't that I can't write to him; it's just that it's annoying to have him make all sorts of complaints again. Once Father gets started he never stops.'

'But if there's nothing else we can do, it can't be helped.'

'That's why I didn't say I won't write. I do intend to explain to him clearly the situation here, but in any event the matter won't be settled right away.'

'I suppose you're right.'

He then looked directly at her, and spoke rather sharply.

'You wouldn't be willing, would you, to go to the Okamotos and have them advance us some money?'

8

'Certainly not! It would be most awkward.'

O-Nobu instantly objected. There was not even a suggestion of faltering. Her refusal, which went beyond all restraint and qualification, was too abrupt for him to assess it. He was jolted as one is when in a speeding automobile which suddenly stops. He was more amazed than hurt by his wife, who seemed to have no sympathy for him. He stared at her.

'Certainly not! It would be most unpleasant to have to go and ask the Okamotos.' She repeated her objection.

'Really? Well then, I surely won't force you. But. . . .'

As he began to speak in this way, she intercepted and cast aside his cold, but nonetheless calm, words.

'Can't you see it would be dreadfully embarrassing for me? Whenever I go there, they keep telling me how happy I should be for having married such a fine husband, that I don't have any worries, and that I don't have any financial problems. Now if I suddenly start talking about needing money they'll certainly think it rather strange.'

He finally understood that the reason she had unqualifiedly rejected his request had been her vanity with regard to the Okamotos rather than any lack of sympathy for him. The cold light in his eyes vanished.

'I don't think it's wise to spread the idea that we're that well off. It's all right to have people think highly of you, but that doesn't preclude the possibility that on certain occasions it may be embarrassing.'

'I don't remember ever having spread such an idea. It's just that they've made up their minds that we are.'

He did not press the point. Nor did she bother to make any further explanations. After that brief digression they returned to practical problems. But since Tsuda until then had never been greatly troubled about finances he did not come up with any particularly good plan. He merely felt his father was being very difficult.

O-Nobu, as if she had just thought about them coincidentally, cast her eyes on her fine kimonos and obis which were still spread about there.

'Shall I do something with these?'

She took the edge of a thick, gold-flecked obi in her hand and held it up to the light of the lamp so that Tsuda could see it. He could not see the significance of her act.

'What do you mean by "do something" with them?'

'I was wondering whether they'd give us some money for them if I took them to a pawnshop.'

Tsuda was astonished. If his young wife, whom he had recently married, was so well acquainted with such schemes for tiding over difficulties, something of which he himself had no previous experience, then this was doubtless for him a surprising and valuable discovery.

'Have you ever had occasion to pawn your clothes or anything?'

'No, never.'

O-Nobu laughingly answered his question in a derisive tone.

'Then you don't know exactly how to go about doing it, do you?'

'No, I don't, but surely it's not the least bit difficult. That is, once you've decided to pawn something.'

He did not wish to have his wife do anything so vulgar, except in extreme circumstances. O-Nobu defended her position.

'Toki knows all about it. She's said that while she's been with us she's often taken bundles to the pawnshop. And I believe she's also said that now if you simply send a postcard they'll come and pick up the articles for you.'

That O-Nobu would offer up her valuable kimonos and obis on his behalf made him happy. But that he would have to force her to do so was most painful to him. He hesitated to act, more in the sense that it was wounding to his pride than that he felt sorry for her.

'Hm, let's think it over for a while.'

He went back upstairs without having arrived at any financial solution.

9

The following day Tsuda went to his place of employment as usual. In the forenoon he accidentally encountered Yoshikawa once on the stairs, but since Tsuda was coming down as Yoshikawa was going up, they merely exchanged polite bows in passing, and he did not say anything.

Shortly before lunchtime he knocked softly on the door of Yoshikawa's office and peered in diffidently. Yoshikawa was then smoking while he was talking to a guest. Of course the guest was someone unknown to Tsuda. When he opened the door halfway, the conversation between the two men, which seemed to have been rather light-hearted, stopped abruptly. Then they both turned towards him.

'Is anything the matter?'

Tsuda, who was spoken to first by Yoshikawa, stood still at the entrance to the room.

'Well, I do actually. . . .'

'Does it concern you personally?'

Of course Tsuda was not someone who had to enter that room often on official business. Rather embarrassed, he answered :

'Yes, if I could just have a minute. . . .'

'If that's the case, please make it later. Right now it's somewhat inconvenient.'

'Yes, of course. Please forgive me, I wasn't aware you were busy.'

After shutting the door noiselessly, Tsuda returned to his desk.

In the afternoon he went twice to the same office, but both times Yoshikawa was not there.

'I wonder where he could have gone.'

As he was going downstairs, he went to inquire of the boy at the entrance. The boy, who was very good-looking, stretched out his hand towards a shaggy brown dog lying at the foot of the stone steps, and whistled as if to induce him to come up the steps by magic.

'Yes, he left earlier with a guest. It's possible he may not come back here at all today.'

This boy, whose sole job it was to check every day on the people who came and went, was, at least on this one matter, a more accurate prophet than Tsuda. Tsuda then left the brown dog, which somebody had brought with him, and the boy who was trying so hard to make friends with it, and went back to his desk. He did his work there as usual until it was time to leave.

When that time came, he left the large building somewhat later than the others. While he was walking as usual towards the streetcar stop, he took his watch out of his pocket and looked at it, as if he had suddenly thought about it. He did this more to determine the direction in which he should walk than to learn the correct time. He was considering whether to stop in at the home of the Yoshikawas, and it was as if he had absent-mindedly consulted his watch on the matter.

He finally jumped on the streetcar running in the opposite direction from his house. Since he knew quite well that the Yoshikawas were very often not at home, he was aware that he might go there and not necessarily be able to see them. He knew further that even if they should be at home, the occasion might be inconvenient for them, and he would only be sent back without seeing them. Nevertheless, he had to pass through the gate of the Yoshikawa home from time to time. He would do this partially out of politeness, partially out of personal interest, and finally out of simple vanity.

'Tsuda is a special friend of Yoshikawa.'

Sometimes he liked to assume this pose and look at himself. He also liked standing before the world thus burdened with so important a friendship. Furthermore, without in the least modifying this characteristic attitude of his, of which he approved, he failed even to recognize the vanity of it. He now stood at the entrance to the Yoshikawa home with that same ambivalence whereby a person, while pushing things into a corner, still wishes to show them to others. Thus he rationalized by telling himself that he had purposely come there on business.

10

The imposing door of the front entrance was closed as always. Tsuda looked casually through the thick lattice, attached as a kind of open work to the upper half of the door. Within, a granite stepping-stone extended over a large area. From the middle of the ceiling hung a blue-black, cast-iron lamp-shade. Since he had never set foot there, he turned aside, and purposely passed beyond it. He then inquired at the side door, which was very near the houseboy's room.

'He hasn't returned yet.'

The answer of the houseboy, kneeling before him in a Japanese duck cloth *hakama*, was brusque and direct. His manner too, which seemed to imply that Tsuda should leave immediately, annoyed him. Finally Tsuda asked him a second question :

'Is Mrs Yoshikawa at home?'

'Yes, she is.'

Actually Tsuda was more friendly with Mrs Yoshikawa than with her husband. While he had been walking there, he had already been thinking that he preferred to meet her.

'Well then, if you would tell her. . . .'

He thus asked another favour of this new houseboy, who was as yet unacquainted with him. The boy went into the house without appearing displeased. When he came out again, he said somewhat ceremoniously, 'Mrs Yoshikawa will see you; please step this way,' and led him into a Western-style parlour.

As soon as Tsuda sat down in one of the chairs there, and even before either the customary tea or cigarette-tray had been brought to him, Mrs Yoshikawa appeared.

'Are you on your way home now?' she asked.

He had to stand again to greet her.

'And how is your wife?' she continued.

Mrs Yoshikawa made a slight bow in response to his greeting, sat down, and instantly asked the latter question. Tsuda forced a smile. He did not know quite how to answer.

'You haven't visited us very much recently, have you? Perhaps that's because you now have a wife.'

There was not the slightest reserve in her speech. She merely saw in front of her a man much younger than she, and one who also was her social inferior.

'I suppose you're still both very happy, aren't you?'

He remained quiet, as one does when a wind gently stirs up sand, and one waits until it settles.

'But it's already quite some time since you were married, isn't it?'

'Yes, over half a year.'

'How time passes! It seems like just the other day. Well then, how are things going these days?'

'There's nothing special to report.'

'You mean you've already passed the happy stage? Don't tell me!'

'It isn't that we've passed it. It's just that there never was any to begin with.'

'Well then, it will start soon. If you didn't have any at the beginning, I'm certain it will begin very soon.'

'Thank you. I'll look forward to it then.'

'By the way, how old are you?'

'Old enough.'

'Don't speak that way. I'm asking seriously, so please tell me honestly.'

'All right, I'll tell you. Actually I'm twenty-nine.'

'Then you'll be thirty next year.'

'I suppose so, if you count properly.'

'And O-Nobu?'

'Twenty-two.'

'Next year?'

'No, this year.'

Mrs Yoshikawa often bantered with Tsuda in this way. When she was in especially good spirits she did so even more. Occasionally he would reply in kind. Often, however, in her attitude, as he judged it, something would emerge which was neither jocular nor serious. He would then be ill at ease in the conversation because he was congenitally opposed to such subtleties. And if the situation allowed, he would dig to the root of the matter in an attempt to discover her real feelings. When, out of a sense of restraint, he was unable to go so far, he would silently study her expression. As a necessary result, a light cloud of doubt would always hover before his eyes. This at certain times made him appear cowardly and at others only cautious. But at still other times it made him seem as if he were giving off sparks from his self-defensive, arrogant nature. And finally an element was included which must be described as 'prudent anxiety'. Whenever Mrs Yoshikawa met him she would always push him that far at least once or twice. And he, while fully aware of what she was doing, would still be dragged in that direction almost before he knew what was happening.

'You're very unkind, Mrs Yoshikawa, aren't you?'

'Why? For having asked you your ages?'

'No, that's not why, but because your way of asking seems to imply something and yet you don't say anything further.'

'There isn't anything further. It won't do for you to probe into things the way you do. Research may be necessary in academic matters, but it simply won't do in social intercourse. If you'd only give up that bad habit of yours you'd become a much better and more likable person.'

He was somewhat pained by these remarks. Yet it was a pain which affected his heart but in no way touched his mind. For he was able with the latter, in the face of this blunt attack, simply to scorn her coldly. Mrs Yoshikawa smiled.

'If you think I'm lying, please ask your wife when you go home. I'm sure O-Nobu will agree with me. And not only O-Nobu either. I'm certain there may be yet another person.'

Tsuda's face suddenly became rigid. His lips moved slightly. He merely cast his eyes down, and did not say anything in response.

'You understand, don't you? There *is* somebody else.'

She asked the question as she peered into his face. Of course he knew perfectly well who that someone was. But he did not have the slightest desire to affirm what she said. When he raised his head again, he turned his silent eyes towards her. She did not understand what those eyes, in their speechlessness, were attempting to convey.

'Please forgive me if I've offended you. I most certainly had no intention of doing so.'

'I thought nothing of it.'

'Really?'

'Yes, I assure you I thought nothing of it.'

'Well then, I feel better.'

She immediately recovered her previous light tone.

'You still have a kind of childish reaction, don't you? When we speak this way, I mean. Men are really amazing, aren't they? The way you spoke just now is a good example. O-Nobu is twenty-two this year, and there's actually quite a difference in your ages, but in her manner she seems, on the contrary, to be the older. Perhaps it sounds rude of me to say that, but I don't quite know how to express what I mean. Well. . . .'

Mrs Yoshikawa, face to face with Tsuda, appeared to be searching for a word to describe O-Nobu's manner. He was awaiting it with a certain amount of curiosity.

'Well, she's so mature. And she's such a remarkably clever person. In fact I don't think I've ever met such a clever person. Take good care of her now, won't you?'

From the tone of her voice there was very little difference between saying 'take good care of her' and 'watch out for her'.

12

At that moment the light hanging above their heads suddenly went on. The houseboy who had previously announced Tsuda entered the room quietly, lowered the blinds noiselessly, and went out just as silently. Tsuda, who since entering had been noticing the deepening colour of the gas heater, looked at the boy's departing figure without speaking. He felt he should then break off the conversation arbitrarily and return home. Attempting to avoid the one slice of lemon floating coldly at the bottom of his teacup, he sipped the remainder of the tea. Then, with that as the signal, he told Mrs Yoshikawa his purpose in coming. It was of course a very simple matter. But it was not of the kind that could be decided immediately merely by her approval or disapproval. She could not know at what point in the month he should take off the week or so that he needed.

'I don't suppose it matters when it is. If only you make the necessary arrangements.'

In a rather casual tone she expressed her kindness towards him.

'Of course I've already done that.'

'Well then, everything's all right, isn't it? Even if you take off beginning tomorrow.'

'Yes, but if I didn't at least ask. . . .'

'Well, when my husband returns I'll speak to him about it. There's absolutely nothing to worry about.'

She accepted the commission willingly. It seemed almost as if she were glad that yet another matter had arisen in which she could be of service to someone. Tsuda was delighted to observe this good-natured and sympathetic woman behave as she did. And the realization that it was his attitude and behaviour which had caused her to act that way made him even happier.

In a certain sense he liked being treated as a child by her. For, by being treated in that way, he was able to enjoy a special kind of intimacy with her. And when he examined this intimacy carefully, he discovered that it was, after all, of a particular kind that could arise only between a man and a woman. Figuratively speaking, it was similar to the pleasant feeling a man receives when he is suddenly tapped on the back coquettishly by a woman at a tea-house.

And yet he possessed in full measure a self which could not be treated in this way by such a person as Mrs Yoshikawa. But he purposely had not forgotten the necessary preparations for hiding this self when he met her. Thus, while on the surface he was reacting rather casually to being teased so unreservedly by her, underneath he was always leaning against the thick and sturdy wall which he himself had built.

When he finished what he had to say and was about to get up from his chair, she suddenly spoke :

'You mustn't cry and groan like a child this time, you know. Try to control yourself.'

He was forced to remember the pain he had had the previous year.

'I was really very weak then. Whenever the sliding-door opened it seemed to affect the painful part of my body so much I almost had to jump up out of the bed. But this time it will be all right.'

'Really? Has someone assured you of this? But I shouldn't think he could be absolutely certain about it. If you boast too much I'll go and make sure myself.'

'It's not the sort of place I'd want you to come and visit me at. It's a dirty, cramped, weird little room.'

'That doesn't matter at all to me.'

He could not determine whether she was in earnest or whether she was bantering again. He was about to say that since the doctor's specialty lay in a certain area unrelated to his own illness it would be better if she did not go near the place, but he hesitated slightly, at a loss for words. She took advantage of the silence, and pressed him hard.

'I'm definitely going. As a matter of fact I have a small matter I'd like to talk with you about, and I really can't mention it in front of O-Nobu.'

'Well then, I'll call again soon.'

She laughed and showed Tsuda, who had risen as if to flee, out of the parlour.

13

He went out into the road, and slowly walked away from the Yoshikawa home. But this did not mean that his mind could withdraw as rapidly as his body from the parlour where he had just been. As he made his way through the relatively deserted evening streets, he could still clearly see the bright interior of the room.

The coldly gleaming texture of the cloisonné vase, the colours of the brilliant pattern flowing on its smooth surface, the round, silver-plated tray which had been brought to the table, the cube sugar and cream containers of the same colour, the heavy curtains of bluish-black fabric with a brown arabesque design, the ornamental album with three of its corners set in gold leaf—these vivid images passed in a disorderly manner before his mind's eye even after he had gone out from under the bright light and was walking in the dark outside.

Of course he also could not forget the figure of his hostess seated amidst this whirlpool of colour. He recalled in fragments the conversation he had just exchanged with her. And when he came to that certain section, he savoured it carefully, just as someone might do who has put a dried bean in his mouth.

'She may actually still want to talk to me a bit about that. But I don't really want to hear it. And yet at the same time I want very much to.'

As he confessed his ambivalence to himself, he blushed on the dark road as if he had suddenly uncovered his weak point. To overcome this, he purposely went on ahead immediately.

'If she wants to talk to me on that subject, I wonder what her real purpose is.'

He could certainly not provide any solution to the problem at that time.

'To poke fun at me?'

He was utterly unable to say. She had always been a woman who enjoyed making fun of others. Moreover the relationship between them was sufficiently close to give her such freedom. Her social position had also unknowingly made her rather reckless in such matters. For the simple pleasure she derived from nettling him she might very easily go beyond the bounds of decorum.

'But suppose it isn't that. . . . Could it be out of sympathy for me? Or because she's attracted to me?'

About this too he could give no answer. Until then she certainly had been kind to him and shown him every favour.

He came to a broad street and took a streetcar from there. Beyond the window panes of the streetcar, as it ran along the moat, he could see only the dark water, the dark embankment, and the dark pines stretching tortuously alongside it.

After he had taken a corner seat and had glanced for a moment through the window at the cold autumn night scene, he was soon compelled to think of other things. For he had to do something about the money matter which he had simply abandoned the previous evening because it was troublesome. He immediately thought of Mrs Yoshikawa again.

'If only I'd told her about the problem a while ago, it would have been so easy.'

As he thought about Mrs Yoshikawa in this way, he began to regret that he had tried so hard to leave her house early. That did not mean, however, that he had enough courage to go to see her again just for that purpose.

When he got off the streetcar and crossed the bridge, he saw a beggar squatting at the base of the dark railing. The beggar lowered his head in front of him as if he were a dark, moving shadow. Tsuda was wearing a light overcoat. He had also just seen the warm flame of a gas heater, being used rather early for the season. And yet there was hardly any way for him to realize the distance separating him from the beggar. For he felt that he himself was in straitened circumstances. And he considered the fact that his father had not sent him his monthly allotment to be thoroughly unpardonable.

14

With much the same mental attitude Tsuda walked to the gate of his home. He was about to put his hand on the lattice door of the entrance, but before he could open it, the interior sliding-door opened swiftly, and the figure of O-Nobu appeared in front of him before he was aware of it. Somewhat surprised, he looked at her lightly made-up face, in profile.

Since their marriage she had often surprised him in this way. At times this habit of hers had the bad effect of taking the initiative away from him, but at other times it created a startlingly sharp and interesting impression. For in the midst of the dull, everyday routine he felt that this dramatic way she had of appearing suddenly before him gleamed sharply like a knife. But while he felt that, though a small thing, it brightened a part of his life, he also sensed something menacing in it.

He suddenly wondered how she had been able to anticipate his return, but he did not wish to ask her about it. To ask the reason and have her make a joke of it would seem like a defeat for him.

He went into the house from the entrance with an air of indifference. He then quickly changed into Japanese clothing. In front of the brazier in the living-room was a black-painted tray, with legs attached, on which lay a table napkin; it seemed to be awaiting his return.

'Did you stop somewhere today too?'

When he did not come home at the regular hour, she would always ask him this. He would be forced to say something in response. But since he was not always late because of business, occasionally there would be something strangely ambiguous in his answer. He then would purposely not look at her face, lightly made up on his behalf.

'Shall I try to guess?'

'Go ahead.'

That day he was extremely easy-going.

'It was the Yoshikawas', wasn't it?'

'You're right.'

'I can usually tell by your manner.'

'Oh can you? Of course, since I said last night I'd decide on the date of the operation only after talking to Mr Yoshikawa, it wasn't very difficult for you.'

'Even if you hadn't said that, I'm sure I'd have known.'

'Really? You're quite clever, aren't you?'

He told her the main point of the matter he had discussed with Mrs Yoshikawa.

'Well, when then will you undergo treatment?'

'As I said, it seems it doesn't matter when I go. . . .'

He was worried about the fact that he would somehow have to raise some money before beginning the treatment. Of course the amount was not so great, but precisely because of this was he even more annoyed at not being able to think of any convenient way of getting it.

He did actually consider for a moment his younger sister, who lived in Kanda, but he certainly did not intend to go there. While on the one hand it had been decided that because of the many expenses after his marriage he should receive a supplement from his father in Kyoto to make up the monthly deficiencies, there had, on the other hand, been attached the condition that he repay a certain amount with his mid-year and year-end bonuses. Because he had been unable, for various reasons, to fulfil that condition during the previous summer, his father's feelings had already been hurt. His sister, who knew this, was also on most matters rather in sympathy with their father. Since from the outset he had felt humiliated at mentioning to her the problem of money in the presence of her husband, with this new situation he was even more opposed to doing so. He thought that there was simply no other way but to do as O-Nobu advised and write another letter to his father explaining the situation. He even thought it would be a good policy if he described his present illness as somewhat more severe than it actually was. Surely merely to put a slight veneer on the actual facts, without going so far as to worry his parents, was something anyone might do without having to endure any pangs of conscience.

'O-Nobu, I'm going to write another letter to Father, just as you said I should last night.'

'Really? But. . . .'

She looked at him as she said this. He did not, however, pay any attention to her, but went upstairs and sat down at his desk.

15

Since he was accustomed to using Western-style stationery, he took out from the desk drawer some lavender paper and an envelope and began offhandedly to write a few lines with a fountain pen. Then he suddenly remembered that his father was usually not too pleased to receive from his son a letter in the colloquial language carelessly written with a straight pen or fountain pen. As he called to mind the face of his father, who was so far away, he smiled wryly and put down the pen. He then felt that even if he sent the letter it would probably not have any very great effect. In the margin of some thick, rough paper resembling charcoal paper he playfully sketched his father's slender face with its goatee, and wondered what he should do.

He shortly made his decision and stood up. He opened the sliding-door, went out to the second-floor landing, and from there called to O-Nobu, who was below.

'O-Nobu, do you happen to have some Japanese-style rolled stationery and envelopes? If so, please lend me some.'

'*Japanese-style* stationery?'

The adjective sounded very strange to her.

'If you want some woman's stationery, I have some.'

A few minutes later he spread out before him a half sheet of brightly patterned paper.

'I wonder if this would please him.'

'So long as he understands the letter, does it matter what kind of paper it is?'

'Well, actually it does. Father's very particular about such things.'

Tsuda was still staring very earnestly at the half sheet of paper. O-Nobu had a faint smile at the corners of her mouth.

'Shall I send Toki out to buy some?'

'I suppose so.'

He gave a noncommittal answer. It was not necessarily true that if he only had some white rolled stationery and unfigured envelopes his hope would be fulfilled.

'Please wait. It won't take a minute.'

O-Nobu immediately went downstairs. Shortly thereafter he heard the side-door being opened and the footsteps of the maid going outside. Until he actually held in his hand the article he required he merely sat at his desk, smoking a cigarette.

His mind simply could not detach itself from his father. His father had been born and reared in Tokyo, and, on the slightest pretext, had made snide remarks about the Kansai* region, but somehow or other he had settled down in Kyoto with the intention of living there permanently. When Tsuda had sympathized with his mother, who was not too fond of that region, and when he had expressed a certain disapproval, his father had shown him the land he had bought and the houses he had built, and had said, 'What do you think I should do with these?' Since Tsuda had been even younger than he was then, he had not even understood very clearly what his father meant. He thought they could dispose of it all in any number of ways. But his father would often turn to him and say, 'These aren't for just anybody, you know. They're all for you.' He would also say, 'Perhaps you can't appreciate such kindness now, but wait till I die. There'll certainly come a time when you will.' Tsuda began to ponder his father's words and his manner as he had said them. His father had been filled with self-confidence and had seemed to hold in one hand his son's future happiness. He seemed to Tsuda to be a prophet who should not be approached. Yet Tsuda wished to tell him, as he saw him with the eyes of his imagination : 'Instead of suddenly appreciating your kindness when you die, how much easier it would be to appreciate it accurately each month little by little.'

About ten minutes later he began to write, on the rolled stationery which would not offend his father's sensibilities, and in a formal epistolary style, the phrases most likely to make him send the money. He felt rather awkward about the whole thing, and when he had finally finished the letter and was reading it over, he was greatly distressed at the clumsiness of his calligraphy. He thought it would not make much difference what he had written since the characters were hardly of a kind to produce a successful outcome. And finally he felt that even if the letter should succeed, the money could not possibly arrive in time.

* Region around Kyoto and Osaka.

After asking the maid to mail the letter, he crawled silently into bed, saying to himself he would face that problem when it arose.

16

On the afternoon of the following day Yoshikawa called him into his office.

'It seems you came to the house yesterday, didn't you?'

'Yes, I called while you were out, and saw Mrs Yoshikawa.'

'You're ill again, aren't you?'

'Yes, somewhat. . . .'

'That's too bad. To be ill so often.'

'Well, actually it's just the continuation of my previous illness.'

Yoshikawa looked somewhat surprised, and removed the small tooth-pick he had just been using. He then searched in his inside pocket and took out a cigar case. Tsuda immediately lit one of the matches which were on the ashtray. Since he was too eager, and lit it too hastily, the first one went out instantly without being of use. He quickly lit a second one, and guided it carefully to Yoshikawa's mouth.

'At any rate, if it's an illness, you just have to accept it. But I think you should take some time off and take care of yourself.'

Tsuda thanked him, and tried to leave the room. Yoshikawa, from amid the smoke, asked him:

'I suppose you've already explained to Sasaki, haven't you?'

'Yes, I've spoken to both Mr Sasaki and the others, and everything has been arranged for me.'

Sasaki was his immediate superior.

'If you're going to take time off I suppose the sooner you do so the better. Take care of yourself right away and get well quickly. Then you should work hard to make up for lost time.'

Yoshikawa's words expressed his personality very well.

'If it's convenient for you, have it done tomorrow.'

'Really?"

Since Yoshikawa spoke to him in this way, Tsuda felt he would have to enter the hospital on the following day.

When he was already half outside the door, Yoshikawa called him back again.

'By the way, Tsuda, how has your father been recently? Is he still as healthy as ever?'

As Tsuda turned around, his nostrils quickly caught the fine aroma of the cigar.

'Oh, he's very well, thank you.'

'He's probably writing poetry and taking it easy. It's a relaxing and pleasant thing to do. Last night I happened to meet Okamoto somewhere, and we talked about him. Okamoto was also envious of him, you know. He too has been less busy lately, but I'm afraid he doesn't behave like your father.'

Tsuda certainly had not thought his father would ever be envied by these two men. He was sure that if someone were to offer to put them in his father's situation they would force a laugh and ask to be left the way they were for at least another ten years. Of course that was nothing more than an observation of Tsuda's deduced from his own character. Yet at the same time it was also one deduced from theirs.

'Since my father's so old-fashioned he's forced to live that way.'

Tsuda had returned again unawares to the middle of the room and was standing in his former position.

'I'd hardly say he's old-fashioned. I'd say rather that he's able to lead that kind of a life because he's ahead of the times.'

Tsuda was forced to make some comment. He felt the burden of his own ineptness of speech by comparison with Yoshikawa's adroitness. Out of a sense of awkwardness he gazed at the slowly disappearing smoke of the cigar.

'Don't worry your father. We know everything about you here, and if something bad happens I'll let him know about it. Is that all right with you?'

After he had listened, with a forced smile, to those words which were spoken as if to a child and which he could not identify as either idle banter or advice, he finally managed to leave the room.

17

On the way home that day Tsuda got off the streetcar and turned a corner at a place somewhat beyond the busy street where the streetcar stopped. Glancing on either side at the shop-curtains of pawn-shops, the signs of *go** clubs, and the lattice-doors behind which it seemed there might be some petty gamblers' den, he pushed open a frosted-glass door in about the middle of the winding alley, and went inside. As the bell, attached to the upper part of the door, gave a sharp ring, he suddenly caught the glances of four or five men, peering from the narrow room facing the entrance. The room was dark as well as narrow, having no windows. Since he had suddenly come in from outside, it almost gave him the feeling of a cellar. He sat down coldly in the corner of a sofa, and looked back at the men who had just been staring at him. Most of

* A Japanese game somewhat like checkers.

them were seated so as to encircle the large porcelain brazier in the centre of the room. Two of them had their arms crossed, two of them stretched their hands over the edge of the brazier, one of them, quite a bit removed from the others, was peering closely at a newspaper, other pages of which lay scattered about there, and the last was stretched out casually, with his legs crossed, at the other end of the sofa in which Tsuda had just sat.

After they had turned towards the door, as if in a group action, at the sound of the bell and had stared at him a moment, they settled down, again as if they had decided on such action together. They all were sitting silently and appeared to be immersed in thought. Their attitude could be interpreted as meaning that rather than not noticing Tsuda's existence, they were, on the contrary, trying to avoid being noticed by him. This same attitude appeared to apply not only to Tsuda, for they shrank from the unpleasantness of being noticed by each other, and turned their eyes the other way.

This gloomy group consisted of men who, almost without exception, had a similar past. While they were waiting quietly in this way in the dark anteroom for their turn to come, it was as if a dark shadow were also cast over them because a portion of their past had been rather too brilliantly coloured. And since they did not have the courage to look at that brightness, they closed themselves in, cowering in the darkness without making a move.

Tsuda placed his arm on the elbow-rest of the sofa, and stroked his forehead with his hand. In this posture of someone offering up a silent prayer to God, he thought about the two men he had unexpectedly met at this doctor's waiting-room since the end of the previous year.

One of them actually had been none other than his younger sister's husband. Tsuda had been surprised upon suddenly recognizing him in this dark room. Although his brother-in-law was relatively indifferent to that sort of thing, he too had appeared to be at a loss for words as a reaction to Tsuda's surprise.

The other person had been a friend. He had been convinced that Tsuda was suffering from the same kind of disease he was, and he had called to him casually from across the room. They had left the doctor's waiting-room together that time, and while they had eaten dinner they had had a serious discussion about the problems of sex and love.

His meeting with his sister's husband had been only a temporary surprise and had ended without any great effect on him, but from the meeting with his friend, which he thought would have ended there, something rather strange had later occurred.

When Tsuda was forced to connect what his friend had said at that time with his friend's present circumstances, he opened his eyes and took his hand away from his forehead, as if he had suddenly received a shock.

At that moment a man of about thirty, wearing a dark blue serge suit, came out of the consultation room, and immediately went over to the dispensary window. As he took his wallet from his pocket and was about to pay, the nurse came and stood at the door of the room. Since Tsuda was well acquainted with her, he called her back just after she had announced the next patient and was about to return to the consultation room again.

'It's bothersome to have to wait my turn, so would you please ask the doctor if it's all right if I come to have the operation tomorrow or the day after?'

The nurse went into the interior of the office but soon her white figure reappeared at the entrance to the dark waiting-room.

'The room upstairs just happens to be empty now, so please come any time it's convenient for you.'

He left the gloomy room as if he were escaping from it. After he had hurriedly put on his shoes and had pulled open the large frosted-glass door, the light suddenly went on in the waiting-room, which until then had seemed extremely dark.

18

Tsuda returned home somewhat earlier than on the previous day, but the autumn days were rapidly becoming shorter, and it was also the time of the year when the chilly, lingering light, which until then had remained only in the streets, disappeared as if it had been swept suddenly away from the earth.

Of course the lights on the second floor of his home were not on. The entrance also was completely dark. Since he had just seen the brightly lit eaves lanterns of the rickshaw-stand on the corner, he felt slightly disappointed. He opened the lattice door brusquely. Even so O-Nobu did not come out. He had not been particularly pleased when at about the same time on the previous day he had been taken aback by her waiting for him as if in ambush, but now that he had actually been made to stand in this way at a pitch-dark entrance with no one to greet him, he somehow felt the previous day's experience had been, after all, a rather pleasant one. While still standing there, he called O-Nobu twice. When he did so, a reply came but unexpectedly from the second floor. Then he heard his wife's footsteps coming down the stairs. At the same time the maid ran out from the kitchen.

'What in the world were you doing?'

There was a slight note of dissatisfaction in his voice. O-Nobu did not say anything. When he looked up at her, however, he was forced to recognize that smile of hers, which as usual was silently attempting to captivate him. Before anything else her white teeth caught his eye.

'But isn't it pitch-black upstairs?'

'Yes, but I was lost in thought and didn't notice you'd returned.'

'Were you lying down?'

'Of course not.'

Since the maid gave a loud laugh just then, the conversation between them was broken off at that point.

Before he went to the bath, O-Nobu said, 'Wait a moment,' and stopped him as he was about to leave his place near the brazier, having taken the soap and towel from her as usual. She turned round, and taking out a flannel-lined silk dressing-gown from the lowest drawer of the double bureau, placed it in front of him.

'Just try it on for a minute. Perhaps it's not pressed very well yet, though.'

Tsuda, with an expression resembling that of someone overwhelmed by smoke, stared at the broad, vertical-striped dressing-gown with a black, unfigured collar. It was not something he had bought nor something he had ordered to be made.

'How in the devil did you get this?'

'I made it myself. For you to use when you go to the hospital. It wouldn't be right for you to be dressed too oddly in such a place.'

'You made it very quickly, didn't you?'

It had been only a few days earlier that he had told her he would be away from home for about a week because of his operation. Furthermore, since then he had never seen her seated in front of the cutting-board with a needle. He naturally was struck with the strangeness of it all. And O-Nobu viewed this surprise of his very much as if it were the reward for her labour. She purposely did not add any explanation or comment.

'Did you buy the material?'

'No, it comes from my old clothes. I'd thought I might wear it this winter, and I'd put it away after taking it apart for washing.'

Of course it was of a pattern that a young woman would wear, for the stripes were broad and the colour also was rather too brilliant. He put it on, and stretching out his hands so as to look somewhat like a kite, glanced rather unpleasantly at O-Nobu as he said :

'I've finally decided to have it done either tomorrow or the day after.'

'Have you? And what am I supposed to do?'

'You don't have to do anything.'

'Can't I go with you to the hospital?'

She appeared to be completely untroubled about the matter of the money.

19

On the following morning Tsuda awoke much later than usual. The interior of the house was very quiet after having been given a light cleaning. After passing through the entrance hall from the parlour and opening the sliding-door to the living-room, he saw O-Nobu sitting composedly near the brazier, reading a newspaper. The iron kettle was making a sound that seemed symbolic of a peaceful household.

'When I let myself go like that, I always oversleep, even though I don't particularly intend to.'

He said this as if it were an apology, and looked at the clock hanging over the calendar. Its hands indicated that it was already nearly ten o'clock.

After washing his face and returning to the living-room, he sat down casually at the customary black-painted tray, which seemed not so much to await his sitting down, as to be tired of waiting for him. As he was about to pick up the napkin placed on top of it, he suddenly remembered something.

'Oh, I mustn't do this.'

He remembered he had been told earlier by the doctor about the precautions he had to take on the day before the operation. But he did not remember those precautions clearly at that moment. He spoke abruptly to O-Nobu.

'I'll go and find out.'

'Right away?'

She looked at him in surprise.

'I mean by phone. That's easy enough.'

He got up, breaking the quiet atmosphere of the living-room, and quickly went out the front way from the entrance hall. He then ran to the public telephone, about a half block to the right of the street with the streetcar tracks. After returning hurriedly, he called to O-Nobu, still standing at the entrance.

'Please get my wallet upstairs for a minute. Or your purse will do.'

'What are you going to do?'

She had no idea what he meant.

'Any amount will do, but please get it quickly.'

He shoved the purse he received from her into his pocket, and swiftly returned to the broad street. Then he boarded a streetcar.

When he came back again about thirty or forty minutes later carrying a rather large package, it was already near noon.

'There was only a small amount in that purse. I thought there was a bit more.'

As he said this, he threw the package he had been carrying under his arm on the living-room *tatami.**

'Wasn't there enough?'

O-Nobu turned on him a glance indicating she could not remain unconcerned even about minor matters.

'No, it isn't that there wasn't enough, but. . . .'

'Well, I haven't the slightest idea what you went to buy. I thought maybe you went to the barber's.'

Tsuda recalled the fact that he had not had a haircut for more than two months. He even remembered that when he did not have his hair cut for a long time his rather small hat would squeak a little every time he wore it and that he had had this new sensation just the previous morning.

'And also, you were in such a hurry I couldn't go upstairs to get the money.'

'Actually there isn't too much money in my wallet either, so there wouldn't have been much difference anyway.'

He felt he had to say this to show that he was not merely disparaging the meagre contents of her purse.

O-Nobu turned on him a glance indicating she could not remain package a can of black tea, some bread, and butter.

'My, are you going to have these? If so, I could have sent Toki to get them.'

'No, she wouldn't understand. I couldn't be sure what she'd buy.'

Shortly thereafter O-Nobu prepared some toast, which gave off a fine aroma, and some steaming oolong tea.

After finishing the very simple Western-style meal, which was neither breakfast nor lunch, Tsuda said, as if to himself:

'I thought today I might go to see Uncle Fujii for a while in the morning since I should tell him about the operation, but now it's too late.'

What he meant was that he would have to make the visit in the afternoon.

20

Fujii was Tsuda's father's younger brother. Tsuda's father, in his life as an official, had been forced to move to various places; he had, for example, spent three years in Hiroshima and two in Nagasaki, and after

* A kind of matting used as floor covering.

considering the inconveniences and disadvantages to Tsuda educationally of taking him with him in his wandering from place to place, he had early entrusted him to that younger brother and had decided to have him look after Tsuda in everything. Tsuda thus had been brought up by this uncle without any difficulty, and consequently the relationship between them went beyond that of the usual one between uncle and nephew. Setting aside differences of temperament and occupation, one would still have judged that they were more father and son than uncle and nephew. If one can speak of a 'second father' and a 'second son', then those words were most appropriate in describing the relationship between them.

This uncle, unlike Tsuda's father, had never left Tokyo. In comparison to Tsuda's father, who for half his life had always liked to move about, there was an extraordinary difference on that one point alone. At any rate, to Tsuda it seemed as if there were such a difference.

'A leisurely traveller through life.'

Tsuda's uncle had previously used this phrase in characterizing his father. Tsuda had inadvertently picked it up, and quickly came to think of his father as that kind of person. Moreover he had not forgotten those words to that day. But just as he had not understood very well the meaning of his uncle's phrase at the time, when his mind had not been well developed, so too did he not understand it very clearly now. It was just that whenever he saw his father he would think of it. The figure of his father, with his wispy beard, like a fortune-teller's, hanging down from the chin of his gaunt, fleshless face, meant the same thing to him as those words of his uncle.

About ten years earlier, his father, like someone who has suddenly tired of his wanderings, had left government circles. He had then begun to work in business. After having spent eight of those ten years in Kobe, he had finally moved two years earlier to some property in Kyoto which he had bought in the interval and where he had done some new construction. Before Tsuda was aware of it, his father had decided on that quiet old capital not only as his place of retirement but also as the place where he would end his days. Upon hearing of this, Tsuda's uncle had crinkled up his nose and said to him:

'Even so it seems that my brother's piled up a great deal of money. He's like a toy balloon that's quietly descended, and it's certainly the weight of money that's pulled it down.'

Fujii himself, however, who would never be affected by the weight of money, had never moved. He had always been in Tokyo and had always been poor. He was a man who could not remember ever having received a monthly salary. It was not so much that he disliked such a salary as that he was so obstinate he would not submit to the work necessary to receive it. He had always been opposed to any regular work, and even after he had become old and his opinion had changed somewhat, the same stubbornness persisted. For he knew very well that if he then changed his principles he would only be despised, and it would not net him any advantage.

Although this uncle, who did not have much experience of living in the practical world nor of grappling with blunt facts, could not but be a rather foolish critic of the world, he was an extremely shrewd observer of it. Moreover, his shrewdness was entirely a result of this foolishness. In other words, because of his foolishness in one area, he said and did quite witty and clever things, in another.

His knowledge was confused rather than extensive. Consequently he liked to speak on many matters. But he could never abandon the attitude of an observer. Such an attitude was not only required of him by his position; his temperament also was conducive to it. He did have a certain intelligence, but he did not have the means of applying it. Even if he did have the means, he chose not to avail himself of it. Literally and figuratively, he always liked to have his hands in his pocket. While he was a kind of student, he had also been born a kind of sluggard; thus he finally became fated to earn his bread by the printed word.

21

For six or seven years Fujii had been leading the kind of peripheral life appropriate to him in a corner of high ground in the northwest part of the city. When he felt that the various houses, continuing to be built year after year on the height which until very recently had been the equivalent of a suburb, were robbing his eyes of the view, he rested the hand which was pushing his pen and thought about his older brother's circumstances. From time to time he felt that he would like to borrow some money from his brother and try to build a house himself. But it appeared very unlikely that his brother would lend him the money. And he too, when he finally came down to it, was not really of a disposition to borrow it. He had characterized his older brother as 'a leisurely traveller through life' but he was actually an economically uneasy traveller through life himself. And, as one sees in the vast majority of such cases, this economic uneasiness became for him nothing more than a certain degree of spiritual uneasiness.

For Tsuda to go from his own house to his uncle's place it was convenient to use a streetcar which followed a river for about half the distance. But since even if he walked the entire way it was a short distance taking less than an hour, he decided that for once in a long while he would take a walk and thereby not need to rely on the trouble-some transportation system.

He left his home a little before one, and after walking in a leisurely fashion along the river, approached his destination. The sky was clear. Sunlight was everywhere. The deep colour of the grove covering the hill across the way appeared as distinct as if it were embossed against the sky.

On the way he remembered the castor oil he had forgotten to buy that morning. Since the doctor had ordered him to take it by about four o'clock that afternoon, he had to stop at a drugstore for a moment to buy the laxative. He thus decided not to turn right at the end of the streetcar line and cross the bridge as usual, but to walk towards a business district in the opposite direction. As he did so, he noticed there was some project for a new extension of the streetcar line, and one section of the street where he was walking was cut off crosswise most abruptly. He stood on a corner of this very rough new road, where the houses had been cruelly demolished and wantonly taken away, and saw a group of people gathered there. Although the group was scattered, it was three to five rows deep and formed a semi-circle around a man of about Tsuda's age.

This man, who was rather stout, had a stiff obi over a kimono and *haori** of double-stranded cotton and was wearing block-like clogs, but he was wearing neither a bamboo hat nor a Western-style one. Using as a shield the one willow tree behind him which had been spared, he was looking around at the group that had gathered, while holding with both hands a large, lined, cotton flannel bag.

'Ladies and gentlemen, I'm going to take an egg out of this bag. I promise you I'll take an egg out of this empty bag and show it to you. Don't be amazed. The whole secret of the trick is in my brain.'

He spoke in a rather disproportionately haughty tone, as such men often do. He then showed each of his clenched hands at his chest, open-ing each of them again as he drew it towards the bag. He then said, 'See, I've thrown the egg in the bag,' as if he were deceiving the crowd. But he did not deceive them, for when he put his hand in the bag there was indeed already an egg in it. He held it between his thumb and forefinger, and after thoroughly showing it to the viewers, still grouped in a semi-circle, he placed it on the ground.

Tsuda craned his neck slightly, with an expression of mixed dis-paragement and admiration. He soon noticed that someone was poking his hips from behind. He turned around, almost as a reflex action to the slight shock he received, and saw his uncle's child standing there laughing, very much like the mischievous boy he was. The school-cap

* A kind of short coat worn with the kimono.

with the insignia, the knickers, and the rucksack he had on his back were enough to tell Tsuda where he had come from.

'Are you on your way home from school now?'

'Uh-huh.'

He did not give a clear-cut affirmative answer.

22

'How's your father?'

'I don't know.'

'He's the same as ever, I suppose, isn't he?'

'I have no idea.'

Tsuda, who had completely forgotten his own psychological state when he was about ten, thought this answer rather strange. He smiled wryly but remained silent as he noticed this peculiarity. The boy, on his part, was paying the closest attention to the magician. The latter, who, judging from his clothing, Tsuda thought was probably an amateur, was at that moment shouting with all his might.

'Ladies and gentlemen, watch closely now as I take out yet another.'

He quickly drew the same bag through each of his clasped hands, and after he had again cleverly feigned throwing something into it, he ostentatiously drew out from the bottom of the bag a second egg. Even so he did not appear to be weary of his work, and this time he turned the bag inside out, unreservedly showing the crowd the slightly soiled cotton flannel striped pattern. But the third egg was drawn out easily with the same gestures. Finally, as if he were handling some precious object, he placed it carefully on the ground.

'How about it, ladies and gentlemen? If I want to take them out in this way, I can take out any number. But since it's boring just to take out eggs, this time I'll take out one live chicken.'

Tsuda turned toward his young cousin.

'Hey there, Makoto, let's go now. I'm going to your house, you know.'

To Makoto the live chicken was more important than Tsuda.

'You go ahead if you want to. I want to watch some more.'

'What he said just now is a lie. He'll never be able to take out a live chicken.'

'Why? Didn't he take out eggs the way he said?'

'Yes, he did, but he'll never take out a chicken. He simply said that so the people wouldn't go away.'

'What will he do then?'

Tsuda also had no idea what he would do thereafter. He had become tired of the whole affair and was about to go on ahead, leaving Makoto behind, when the latter caught his sleeve.

'Please buy me something, won't you?'

Whenever he was so importuned at the boy's home he would always escape by saying that he would buy him something the next time, but since the next time he would always have forgotten to do so, he would again be forced to say in the same tone that he would the time after that.

'All right then, I want a toy car.'

'That costs too much.'

'What do you mean? It's cheap. It's only seven yen fifty sen.'

But even seven yen fifty sen was too large an amount for Tsuda. He began walking without saying anything.

'After all, didn't you say last time and the time before that that you'd buy me something? Aren't you much more of a liar than that man who took out the eggs?'

'He may take eggs out but he certainly won't take out a chicken.'

'Why?'

'I don't know why. He just can't.'

'But you can't buy me a toy car either, can you?'

'Well—that's right. But I will buy you something else.'

'All right then, I want some fine leather shoes.'

Tsuda was taken aback, and before answering he walked a few yards in silence. He then looked down at Makoto's feet. Makoto's shoes were not particularly ugly, but they were of a certain strange colour which was neither brown nor black.

'They were brown but my father stained them black.'

Tsuda laughed. The fact that Fujii would have stained his son's brown shoes black was somehow amusing to him. Fujii had not known the school regulation about the necessity for black shoes, and to conform to that regulation he had blackened the brown shoes which he had already had made. When Tsuda heard the explanation he again wanted to ridicule his uncle's desperate economy measures. And feeling that he would laugh still more, he looked down again at the result of Fujii's cleverness.

23

'But those are good shoes, Makoto.'

'Nobody wears shoes this colour.'

'The colour doesn't matter. Few boys are able to wear shoes their father's stained for them himself. You should be grateful and take good care of them.'

'But everybody makes fun of me and says they're made of dog-skin.'

The juxtaposition of his Uncle Fujii and dog-skin gave rise again to new humour. And yet it also induced a faint sadness.

'It's not dog-skin. I'll vouch for that. It's not dog-skin at all. It's a fine. . . .'

Tsuda could not quite say what exactly was fine. Makoto was not one to let the matter rest there.

'It's a fine what?'

'It's a fine—pair of shoes, I mean.'

If his purse had allowed, he would have liked to buy Makoto the leather shoes he desired. He also thought that this would be a token of gratitude towards his uncle. He computed mentally the amount he had in his wallet, but he hardly had the margin to afford such a purchase. He thought that if the money order were to come from Kyoto he might do it, but he also felt, more selfishly, that before he knew it would arrive he could not possibly endure hardship to show even such a small kindness.

'Makoto, if you want fine leather shoes that much, ask my wife to buy them for you the next time you come to our house. I just don't have the money now, so please make do with something cheaper today.'

He took Makoto's hand as if to persuade him or pacify him, and they walked leisurely down the broad street near the streetcar terminus. Since this street had been pounded down ceaselessly by the footwear of countless people who had to use the streetcars, the shops there were aglow with prosperity. In the show windows here and there items which could never be termed shoddy were attractively displayed. Makoto ran across the way, stood in front of a Korean's candy shop, and then returned to stand underneath the eaves of a goldfish shop. As he ran, the marbles in his pocket jingled.

'I won *this* many today at school.'

He stuffed his hand quickly in his pocket and brought out a palmful of the marbles to show Tsuda. When some of the greenish and purple ones fell out and began to roll in the middle of the street, he ran after them excitedly. He turned around and shouted to Tsuda:

'You pick them up too.'

Finally Tsuda was dragged into a toy shop by this bewildering young cousin of his and was forced to buy him a one yen fifty sen air rifle.

'Sparrows are all right, but you mustn't aim it recklessly at people.'

'I won't be able to hit sparrows with this sort of cheap gun.'

'That's because you can't shoot well. If you're a poor shot, you can't hit them no matter how good the gun is.'

'Well, can you hit them for me with this? Let's go home now and see.'

Tsuda, knowing that if he spoke offhandedly he would be pressed thereafter to put his words into practice, gave a noncommittal answer and tried to change the subject. Then Makoto began freely to list the

names of his friends, such as Toda and Shibuya and Sakaguchi, whom
Tsuda of course did not know, and made disparaging remarks about
them one after another.

'That Okamoto fellow, now. He's really a sneaky one. He made his
father buy him three pairs of shoes.'

The conversation had again returned to shoes. Tsuda mentally compared the Okamoto boy, with whom O-Nobu had a close relationship,
with his young cousin who was now criticizing the other boy in front
of him.

24

'Have you been going to play at Okamoto's place recently?'

'No, I haven't.'

'Have you quarrelled again?'

'No, we haven't.'

'Well then, why don't you go?'

'There isn't any real reason—'

It seemed as if something should follow those words, and Tsuda
wished to know what it was.

'When you go there I suppose they give you quite a few things, don't
they?'

'No, they don't give me that much.'

'Well, I suppose they give you some good things to eat, don't they?'

'I ate some curried rice there the other day but it was too hot.'

Just because the curried rice was hot did not seem to be a reason for
not going to the Okamotos'.

'But that's not why you don't like going there, is it?'

'No, but Dad says I should stop going. And I like to ride on the swing
there too.'

Tsuda inclined his head slightly. He wondered why his uncle did not
wish to have his son go to the Okamotos'. Various reasons quickly came
to his mind, such as the differences in disposition, in family tradition,
and in way of life. Fujii, who was always at his desk and scattering
abroad his printed effusions, was certainly not as powerful in the actual
world as his pen. He secretly was aware of this discrepancy, and this
awareness made him somewhat stubborn. It also made him rather hostile
to strangers. Since, when he ventured out into a world governed by
wealth and power, he feared being made a fool of by others, he always
seemed to be operating out of a sense of caution, for if even a part of
his own special province were attacked by such wealth and power, he
felt it would be unendurable.

'Why didn't you try asking your father why you can't go to the Okamotos', Makoto?'

'I did ask him.'

'And what did he say? I suppose he didn't say anything.'

'Yes he did.'

'Well, what did he say?'

Makoto looked a trifle abashed. After a while, he answered rather seriously, making frequent pauses.

'Well . . . when I go to the Okamotos' . . . Hajime has everything . . . and when I come back home . . . I ask Dad to buy me the same things . . . and he said that's why I shouldn't go there any more.'

Tsuda finally understood. When there is a considerable difference between two men's wealth, this difference appears even in their children's toys.

'Then, you rascal, you always ask only for things that cost a lot, like toy cars and good leather shoes. I suppose you've seen everything Hajime has.'

Tsuda half-jokingly raised his hand and tried to strike Makoto on the back. Makoto had an expression like that of an adult whose true feelings have been embarrassingly exposed. But, unlike an adult, he did not say anything at all to vindicate himself.

'That's not true! That's not true!'

He began to run ahead quickly towards his house while carrying on his shoulder the one yen fifty sen air rifle he had just made Tsuda buy for him. The marbles in his pocket sounded like rosary beads being rubbed violently together. In his rucksack his lunch-box and textbooks could also be heard knocking against each other.

He stopped for a moment at the black wooden fence on the corner, turned to look at Tsuda, and then, like a weasel, quickly darted into the lane and hid himself. When Tsuda had walked down the lane and had passed through Fujii's gate at the end of it, a rifle suddenly sounded a few yards in front of him. He recognized, with a strained laugh, the dark figure of Makoto, carefully aiming at him through the hedge on the right-hand side.

25

When Tsuda heard his uncle speaking with someone in the parlour, he merely glanced through the lattice at the single pair of shoes, obviously belonging to a guest, and purposely not opening the entrance door, went around to the sitting-room veranda. Around the garden, which seemed formerly to have belonged to a professional gardener, there was neither the protection of a wooden gate nor the enclosure of a bamboo fence. By going around the kitchen door of the new house for rent, recently built on the same property, he was able to walk directly to the veranda. After passing the two or three tea trees, still slightly too low to act as a screening hedge, he passed underneath the persimmon tree he remembered so well from his childhood, and saw his aunt standing perfectly still. When he saw her profile reflected in the glass section of the sliding-door, he called out to her.

She immediately opened the sliding-door.

'Hello, how are you?'

She raised a quizzical eye towards him, and did not even thank him for the air rifle he had bought for her son. There was hardly any charm in the personality of this aunt, already three or four years over forty. But in place of this, according to the time and place, she did have a certain naturalness of manner transcending the usual reserve of women of her class. Yet it was a naturalness almost divorced from any feeling of sex. Tsuda would always secretly compare her with Mrs Yoshikawa, and would always be surprised at their difference. The first question that came to mind was why two people, both women, and women not too distant in age at that, could give such different impressions.

'As usual you don't seem very lively, do you?'

'If I did at this age, I'd be a madwoman.'

Tsuda sat down on the veranda. She did not ask him to come in, and continued to move a lightweight iron over a piece of red silk cloth resting on her knee. Then from the next room the maid O-Kin emerged carrying some pieces of clothing which had been taken apart. When she bowed to Tsuda, he quickly spoke to her:

'O-Kin, have they decided yet whom you're going to marry? If not, I'll recommend a fine young man for you.'

O-Kin blushed slightly, giggling good-naturedly, and tried to bring a cushion to the veranda for Tsuda. He put out his hand to stop her and went to sit down in the sitting-room.

'Isn't that so, Aunt Asa?'

'I suppose so.'

She gave this indifferent kind of answer, but when O-Kin began formally to pour some lukewarm dark brown tea for him, she raised her head slightly.

'Go ahead and ask Yoshio, O-Kin. He's kind and really means what he says.'

O-Kin was hesitant but did not try to leave. He was forced to say something further.

'I wasn't joking. I really meant it.'

His aunt did not appear particularly eager to take up the matter. At that moment Makoto's air rifle started popping in the rear of the house, and Tsuda's aunt immediately pricked up her ears.

'O-Kin, please look after Makoto a moment. It's dangerous if he shoots just anywhere.'

She had an expression which all but said that Tsuda had brought her son a troublesome toy indeed.

'It's all right. He's been very clearly warned.'

'No, it isn't all right. I'm sure he's going to shoot at our neighbour's chickens for fun . . . O-Kin, he doesn't really need the bullets, so please go and take *them* away from him, at least.'

O-Kin used this good opportunity to leave by way of the sitting-room. Tsuda's aunt, without speaking, again took up the iron which had been thrust into the brazier. As he unconcernedly watched the thin, wrinkled piece of silk become attractively smooth, he could hear snatches of the conversation in the parlour.

'By the way, who's your guest?'

His aunt, surprised, again raised her head.

'You mean you still don't know? Your ears certainly aren't very keen, are they? Don't you know perfectly well just by listening here?'

26

Tsuda attempted to determine, while sitting where he was, the identity of the speaker in the parlour. Suddenly he struck his knee slightly.

'Ah, I know. It's Kobayashi.'

'Yes.'

Without smiling, his aunt calmly gave the simple answer.

'So it's Kobayashi, is it? I wondered who it was because he was wearing those new brown shoes and trying to look like an important guest. But if it's only Kobayashi, I could have gone in without hesitation.'

He recalled the only too threadbare figure of Kobayashi. His strange costume when Tsuda had met him the previous summer also came to his mind spontaneously. He had been wearing a Satsuma-splashed patterned kimono over an undergarment with a white crepe collar, and this get-up, together with his brown, thin-striped *hakama* and thin silk *haori*, looked precisely like that of an umbrella-shop proprietor, who, on his way back from serving as a local funeral attendant, puts a thin wooden box of ceremonial steamed rice with red beans in his pocket. At the time he had given Tsuda the excuse that his Western clothes had been stolen, and in this connection had also asked him to lend him about seven yen. He said that a certain friend had sympathized with him for having had his clothes stolen. His friend had pawned his own summer clothes and had said that if Kobayashi had the money necessary to redeem them, he would give them to him.

Tsuda smiled and asked his aunt : 'Why did he pick today to sit in the parlour and act like somebody important?'

'He had something he wanted to talk to your uncle about. And it was somewhat difficult to say here.'

'Hm, so Kobayashi too has serious matters to discuss, does he? Is it about money? Or maybe. . . .'

As Tsuda began to speak in this way he suddenly noticed his aunt's serious expression and repressed what was to follow. She lowered her voice a bit, and it harmonized rather well with her calm tone.

'There's also the matter of O-Kin's engagement, you know. But if we say too much about it here, she'll feel embarrassed.'

That was why, as they had been listening in the sitting-room, they had heard Kobayashi speaking in a gentlemanly voice, different from his usual shrill one, and also why Tsuda had been at a loss for a moment as to who it was.

'Has it been decided already?'

'Well, it seems to be going quite well.'

Considerable expectation gleamed in her eyes. Tsuda, in rather high spirits, swiftly added : 'Well, then I don't have to go to the trouble of recommending someone for her, do I?'

She looked at him without speaking. This lighthearted, superficial attitude of his, even if it could not be termed flippant, seemed to be something utterly removed from her own present view of life.

'Yoshio, when you yourself got married did you do so with that kind of an approach?'

His aunt's question was not only sudden, but also Tsuda did not even know in what sense she had asked it.

'Since you're the only one who knows what "that kind of approach" means, and I don't have the slightest idea what you're talking about, I'm afraid I can't answer you.'

'Well, it doesn't matter at all to me whether you tell me or not—but just wait and see when you have to marry off a girl. I assure you it's not a simple matter.'

Four years earlier, when their elder daughter had married, they had not had enough money to make all the preparations and had had to borrow a considerable amount. Just when they had finally cleared up the debt they then had to arrange the marriage of their second daughter. Therefore, if O-Kin's engagement was now decided upon, it would indeed mean the third such expense. Even though she was not their daughter and they tried to economize as much as possible, it would nevertheless surely add a rather painful burden to their present manner of living.

27

If Tsuda had then been able of his own free will to undertake to pay even half of the expenses, this would certainly have been a satisfactory recompense to them for having helped him over the years. The sympathy he could give them in financial terms at that time, however, was at best limited to buying Makoto the fine leather shoes he wanted so much. And even for that he had to consult the condition of his purse. Still less did he consider showing them the kindness of applying to his father for a substantial loan to ease their financial situation somewhat. For he had already decided that even if he were to tell his father of the Fujiis' condition his father would not be moved, and even if he should be, his uncle was not one to borrow money from him. Moreover, Tsuda was too much involved in his own hopes that a money order would soon arrive for him, and he did not appear to be very much affected by what his aunt said. She then began to speak to him again : 'Yoshio, tell me, what kind of attitude did you have when you got married?'

'Well I certainly didn't do it in a joking manner. I'm not very happy being considered merely a trivial person, even if I may appear rather lighthearted at times.'

'Of course you were serious. Yes, I'm sure you were, but still there are various degrees of seriousness.'

Depending on the person who said them, those words of hers could have been interpreted by him as an insult, but instead he listened to them with curiosity.

'Well then, how do I appear to you? Please tell me frankly.'

She looked down, and fussing with the disassembled pieces of clothing,* gave a slight laugh. Perhaps because her face was hidden from him, he suddenly felt uneasy. But he did not in the least wish to retract the question.

'Actually, when the occasion demands I think I can be very serious indeed.'

'Of course you're a man, and if you didn't have something solid in you, you wouldn't be qualified to go to your office every day. But even so. . . .'

She began to say something, but then quickly added, as if she had changed her mind : 'All right, let's forget it. It won't do any good to mention it at this late date.'

She neatly piled up the red silk cloth she had just ironed, and began

* Traditional Japanese clothing is taken apart at the seams for cleaning, and then reassembled.

to put it away in a dark tan folding paper-case. She then looked at Tsuda's face, detecting in it a trace of an uneasiness caused somehow by disappointment at her not telling him what she really thought. She then spoke as if she had suddenly made a discovery.

'Yoshio, I think you're much too extravagant.'

Tsuda was accustomed to her telling him this ever since he finished school. He also firmly believed that what she said was true, but he did not think it was such a very grave fault.

'Yes, I am a bit extravagant.'

'I don't mean only in your dress and food. The really bad thing is that your entire being is made up of flamboyance and extravagance. You're like a person who's forever looking around restlessly to see whether there's a feast somewhere.'

'Well then, far from being extravagant, I sound like a beggar.'

'No, you're not a beggar; you're a person who's neither natural nor serious enough. It's a great achievement for a man to be composed and relaxed at will.'

The image of his aunt's daughter suddenly passed through his mind. This cousin of his was already married with two children. After her marriage, four years earlier, she had gone to Formosa with her husband, and was even then living there. The second daughter, who had been married very recently at about the same time as Tsuda, had gone to Fukuoka immediately after the ceremony. Fukuoka was also the place where the Fujiis' elder son, Mayumi, had that year enrolled at the university.

Neither of these cousins, whom Tsuda could easily have married if he had so desired, had seemed in any way suitable for him. The whole matter had thus ended without his becoming involved. Thinking over the attitude he had taken at that time, in the light of his aunt's present statements, he still could not discover any special feeling of guilt and he therefore watched her behaviour in a detached manner. She, on her part, suddenly stood up, opened the lid of a Chinese suitcase, and placed inside it the folding paper-case she held in her hand.

28

Makoto, who had for some time been having O-Kin help him review his lessons in the small room at the back, suddenly snatched away the French reader, which O-Kin did not understand at all. While Tsuda was being amused by the unnatural tone of a second-grader reading out loud, and purposely making long pauses after every single word, in phrases such as *Je suis poli* or *Tu es malade*, the wall clock over his head struck the hour. He quickly took the castor oil out of his pocket, and looked at the colour of the syrupy oil that seemed so unpleasant to take. Then he heard his uncle, who also seemed to have been affected by the sound of the clock, speaking in the parlour.

'Well then, let's go over there.'

His uncle and Kobayashi entered the sitting-room by the veranda. Tsuda, after changing his sitting position slightly to greet his uncle, quickly turned to Kobayashi.

'Kobayashi, you seem quite prosperous. You've had a splendid suit made, haven't you?'

Kobayashi was wearing a jacket of rough texture that looked like homespun. Since the crease of his trousers, contrary to his usual practice, was not as yet in any way blunted, they could only appear to anyone's eye as brand-new. He sat down in front of Tsuda so as to hide behind him his rather strangely coloured socks.

'Come on now, stop joking. You're the one who's looking prosperous.'

Having seen the price-tag attached to a three-piece suit set up in the show window of a certain department store, Kobayashi had then been able to order his new suit to be made for exactly the same price.

'This cost only twenty-six yen, and that's very cheap. I don't know what someone with your expensive tastes may think, but for someone like me this is quite enough.'

Tsuda did not have the courage to criticize Kobayashi in front of his aunt again. He silently took a teacup and drank his castor oil, frowning. Everyone observing his behaviour thought it strange.

'What in the world is that? You certainly take strange stuff. Is it medicine?'

His uncle, who had never once had a serious illness, was indeed extraordinarily ignorant about medicine. Even when he heard the term castor oil he did not know why Tsuda was taking it. When Tsuda used such words as 'operation' and 'hospitalization' to explain to him his present condition, his uncle, who had had almost no contact with any disease, was not in the least moved.

'Then I suppose you came here purposely to tell us about this, didn't you?'

His uncle stroked his grizzled beard as much as to say that he was sorry for him. That beard, of which it would have been more appropriate to say that it merely grew rather than that he cultivated it, made his face look as slovenly as an untended garden.

'I tell you, young people nowadays are no good at all. They're forever having silly illnesses.'

Tsuda's aunt looked at him and gave a broad grin. Tsuda, knowing how his uncle had recently begun using the words 'young people nowadays', returned the grin. When he recalled that for quite a long time his uncle had been telling him rather proudly that mental and physical illnesses come from the same source and that all ailments are the result of man's evil, and when he realized that these statements merely indicated pride in his uncle's not having contracted any disease himself, Tsuda considered him even more comical. He laughed softly as he looked again at Kobayashi. Kobayashi immediately began to speak. But he said something completely different from what Tsuda expected.

'What do you mean by saying young people always get sick? Some don't. I haven't been sick at all recently. If you ask me, I think people don't become sick when they don't have any money.'

Tsuda showed that he thought the statement ridiculous.

'How can you be so stupid!'

'No, I really mean it. You've been sick so often recently because you have the financial margin to allow you to be.'

This illogical conclusion made Tsuda laugh even more because the speaker was so serious. And then this time his uncle agreed with Kobayashi.

'That's right. The day I become sick on top of everything else I don't know how in the world I'll manage.'

His uncle's face appeared dimmest in the dimly lit room. Tsuda stood up and turned on the electric light.

29

Before Tsuda realized it, his aunt, who had gone out towards the kitchen and had been clattering dishes and bowls as she worked with O-Kin and another maid, peered into the sitting-room again.

'Yoshio, it's been a long time since we've seen you, so why don't you stay and have dinner with us?'

Tsuda, concerned about his operation at the hospital on the following day, declined, and decided to return home.

'Since you came just when we were expecting Kobayashi to have dinner with us, there may not be quite enough food, but I think we can manage anyway,' his uncle interposed.

Since Tsuda was unaccustomed to having his uncle ask him to stay for dinner, he felt rather strange, and sat down again.

'Is there something special about today?'

'Yes, there is. Kobayashi's now—'

His uncle broke off with that and looked a moment at Kobayashi. The latter grinned as if he were rather proud of himself.

'Kobayashi, have you done something?'

'No, it's nothing at all. When it's finally decided I'll call on you and tell you all about it.'

'But I'm entering the hospital tomorrow, you know.'

'That doesn't matter. I'll come and visit you, and tell you about it.'

Kobayashi followed this up by asking the location of the hospital and the name of the doctor as if they were some necessary pieces of information for himself. Upon learning that the doctor's name was the same as his, he said, 'Ah, well then, it's that fellow Hori's. . . .' but quickly fell silent. Hori was the name of Tsuda's younger sister's husband. Kobayashi knew very well that because Hori had contracted a certain special disease he had been going to the same doctor, whose place was very near where they then were.

Tsuda wished to ask further about the matter concerning Kobayashi. He thought it might be the problem of O-Kin's marriage, about which his aunt had previously spoken. But it also might not be. His curiosity was greatly piqued by this mystifying attitude of Kobayashi, yet even so he did not clearly invite him to visit him at the hospital.

Tsuda said that because of the preparations for his operation he could not touch either the meat or the side dishes or even the rice with mushrooms that he had always especially liked, all of which his aunt had expressly made for them. Thus, as he would have expected of her, she felt sorry for him and asked O-Kin to go and buy some bread and milk which he would be able to take. Tsuda secretly disliked the local bread, which always stuck between his teeth, but since he was slightly afraid of being called extravagant again, he merely watched without protest as O-Kin left the sitting-room.

After O-Kin had left, Tsuda's aunt said to his uncle in front of all of them : 'I suppose that girl too will be very happy when her marriage is finally settled.'

'Don't worry, it will be.'

Tsuda's uncle answered in a rather carefree manner.

'It seems to me an extremely fine match.'

Kobayashi's comment also was made rather lightly. The only ones who remained silent were Tsuda and Makoto.

When Tsuda learned the name of O-Kin's prospective husband he felt sure he had met him once or twice at his uncle's home but he did not have any clear recollection of those occasions.

'Does O-Kin know him?'

'She knows what he looks like but she's never spoken to him.'

'And I suppose he's never spoken to her either.'

'Naturally.'

'It's amazing that even so people do get married.'

Tsuda thought he had sufficient reason to comment on the matter in this way, and in order to show this to everybody he assumed an expression which indicated that he considered arranged marriages strange rather than ridiculous.

'Well then, how do you think things should be done? Are you trying to say everybody should behave the way you did when you got married?'

Tsuda's uncle turned to him in a tone that seemed to show that he was a bit offended. Since Tsuda had intended his remark for his aunt, he was slightly disappointed that it had missed its mark.

'I didn't mean that. I certainly didn't intend to imply that if O-Kin's marriage takes place that way it's at all improper. In fact I think it's fine, no matter how it happens, as long as it turns out all right.'

30

Even so a chill was cast over the gathering. The conversation, which until then had been flowing along pleasantly, was suddenly stopped as there was no one who took up Tsuda's remarks or in any way made further comment on them.

Kobayashi pointed to his glass of beer in front of him, and in a low voice, as if he were saying something private, asked Makoto, who was next to him:

'Makoto, do you want me to give you some? Try drinking a little.'

'It's bitter; I don't like it.'

Makoto swiftly rejected the offer. Kobayashi, who had never really intended to make him drink any, took that opportunity to give a hearty laugh. Makoto, then thinking he had made a good friend, suddenly asked him:

'I have a one yen fifty sen air rifle. Do you want me to bring it and show it to you?'

He instantly stood up and ran into the small room at the back; when he returned to the sitting-room carrying his new toy, Kobayashi was forced to admire the shiny air rifle. Tsuda's uncle and aunt as well had dutifully to add a word or so of appreciation on behalf of their child, who was so happy.

'This boy's forever badgering his poor father to buy him a watch or a fountain pen, and I'm quite worn out. Still I think we're rather lucky that somehow or other he's at least finally become resigned to not having a horse.'

'A horse is really quite cheap, you know. If you go to Hokkaido you can get a splendid one for only five or six yen.'

'Don't talk as if you've actually been there.'

Thanks to the air rifle, they all began speaking to each other again. For the second time marriage became their topic of conversation. This was doubtless a continuation of what had earlier been interrupted. But they all gradually began to fall into a mood somewhat different from the previous one.

'I think this is rather strange : when two people who've never seen each other and don't know each other at all marry, it doesn't necessarily mean it will be an unsuccessful marriage; yet when two people who are head over heels in love marry, it doesn't necessarily mean they'll live happily ever after.'

It was inevitable that Tsuda's aunt should speak this way when she came to sum up honestly the institution of marriage as she saw it. Her attempt to place the marriage of O-Kin safely within a corner of this broad generalization was explanatory rather than defensive. Yet for Tsuda such an explanation was most incomplete and even dangerous. He could only think that it was indeed his aunt who, having shown by her manner of speaking that she doubted his seriousness regarding marriage, was herself lacking in basic seriousness on that point.

She began again, by saying to him, 'What you've been talking about, Yoshio, are the doings of people who are well off. Can people like us speak about such extravagant things as courtships and engagements? We simply have to think ourselves lucky if there's someone who'll say he'll marry the girl or wants her as a wife.'

Out of regard for everyone present, Tsuda did not wish to comment on O-Kin's case. He did not have a very close relationship with her nor did he have any interest in her, but since, to reject his aunt's criticism of him as not being serious, he felt compelled to expose her own lack of seriousness, he could not remain silent. Inclining his head and appearing to be thinking deeply, he said :

'I have no intention of commenting on O-Kin's case, but I wonder whether marriage is after all something one should think about so lightly. I have the feeling you're the one who's somehow not being serious, and I don't approve.'

'But after all if the girl who becomes the bride does so seriously and if the man who marries her also is serious about it, how can there possibly be any lack of seriousness, Yoshio?'

'I suppose the problem is whether someone can become serious so quickly in that way.'

'Of course they can. When I came as a bride here, wasn't I doing precisely that?'

'Yes of course you were, but young people nowadays. . . .'

'Nowadays or in the past—do human beings change? They've all made their important decision.'

'When that day comes there certainly won't be any need for discussion.'

'Even without discussion it's quite clear my position will win out over yours any day, Yoshio. I think people like me are much, much more serious than those who are so particular in their choice of a bride and who even after they're married are still dissatisfied and can't settle down.'

Tsuda's uncle, who for some time had been stimulated by the discussion, lifted his eyes from his plate as if he had arrived at the point where he was forced to speak.

31

'It's become quite heated, hasn't it? Just listening to you one wouldn't think it was conversation between aunt and nephew.'

Tsuda's uncle entered the conversation between them but was really acting neither as umpire nor as judge.

'Somehow you both seem angry with each other. Have you actually had a quarrel?'

His question was simply a warning in an interrogative form. Kobayashi, who was rolling marbles with Makoto as his adversary, stole a glance at the group. Both Tsuda and his aunt fell silent at once. His uncle was finally forced to speak as an arbiter.

'Yoshio, perhaps it's a bit difficult for a young person like you to understand now, but I assure you your aunt isn't lying. When she first came here she didn't know me at all and yet she'd already made her decision to be a good wife. She was really just as serious before she came as she was after.'

'I'm already quite aware of that.'

'But you think the problem is to learn why she made such a great decision, don't you?'

His uncle had gradually begun to feel the effects of alcohol, and like a man who feels he has to apply some water to his flushed face, he took up his glass again and gulped down some beer.

'Actually I haven't ever told anyone why till today, but how about telling you all now?'

'Go right ahead.'

Tsuda was half serious in his response.

'Well, to tell the truth, your aunt here had taken a fancy to me. In other words, from the outset she wanted to marry me. That's why even before she came here she was already quite determined to be a good wife.'

'Don't make up such foolish stories! Who in the world could have taken a fancy to an ugly man like you?'

Both Tsuda and Kobayashi burst out laughing. Makoto, who alone stared in wonder, turned towards his mother.

'Mama, what does "take a fancy" mean?'

'Your mother doesn't know; go ahead and ask your father.'

'All right then, Father, what does "take a fancy" mean?'

His father laughed and rubbed the middle of his bald head carefully. To Tsuda, perhaps because of his uncle's feeling at the moment, that bald pate appeared somewhat redder than usual.

'Well, Makoto, "to take a fancy" means—it means in effect—well, it means "to have a liking for"!'

'Hm, well then, isn't that something good?'

'Nobody said it was bad, did they?'

'But didn't everybody laugh?'

Since O-Kin returned right in the middle of that exchange, Tsuda's aunt quickly made Makoto's bed and sent him into the bedroom. The conversation begun by Tsuda's uncle, which had enlivened the gathering, only proceeded to develop further.

'There were love affairs in the past, you know. No matter how much O-Asa here seems to disagree with me, I assure you there were. But it's strange that there's one aspect of the matter young people nowadays can't understand. It's simply that in the old days women would fall in love but men never would—isn't that so, O-Asa?'

'I have no idea, I'm sure.'

She sat down at the place Makoto had left, and briskly helping herself to some rice with mushrooms, began to eat.

'It won't do any good to become angry that way. There's truth in what I say and also a kind of philosophy. I'll now explain to you what I mean by it.'

'I can get along perfectly well without listening to anything so boring.'

'All right then, I'll tell it only to the young people. Yoshio and Kobayashi, both of you listen carefully to what I say because it may be useful to you some day. Now, let me ask you: What do you think someone's daughter is?'

'I think she's a girl.'

Tsuda purposely answered in this way, half out of malicious intent to interrupt his uncle's talk.

'I thought you would. You think she's only a girl and not a daughter, I suppose. That's quite different from what men like me think. We've never once looked at someone's daughter as merely a girl independent of her parents. No matter where we see a girl, from the beginning we consider that she's attached to her parents, or, so to speak, her "owners". That's why, no matter how much we may want to fall in love, there's this restriction making it impossible. If you ask why, I'll show you: to become infatuated with a girl, or for two people to fall in love, means in effect that the man must possess, or "own", the girl completely. But to put forth one's hand to take someone who's already "owned" is to act like a thief, isn't it? That's why men in the old days who had this strict sense of family never fell in love. Of course women certainly did. Actually even O-Asa there, who's eating her rice with mushrooms, really did fall in love with me. But I don't remember ever having loved her before we were married.'

'It's all right now, so serve the plain boiled rice whenever you're ready.'

Tsuda's aunt called back O-Kin, who had gone to tuck in Makoto, and told her to dish out the rice into everyone's bowl. Tsuda alone, however, was forced to gnaw on the gluey, tasteless bread.

32

The conversation after dinner was no longer very lively. Nor did it settle down in any particularly confidential direction either. As when the pillar of conversation supporting people's common interests collapses, they realized, after each had spoken on topics of special interest to him, that no one would make the effort to bring the conversation into focus.

Tsuda's uncle, having drunk too much, put both his elbows on the tea-table and yawned twice in succession. Tsuda's aunt called the maid and had her take the remaining food back to the kitchen. Tsuda for some time had gradually been feeling the effect of the rather oppressive atmosphere, and his uncle's words that evening from time to time had cast a light shadow over his heart, as does a floating cloud in passing over the moon. On such occasions he would try to chase after and pin down, as if they had some deep meaning, words which, if heard by someone else, would instead have seemed as insubstantial as the foam on a glass of beer. And when he realized what he was doing he could not help becoming unhappy.

He also could not but recall the verbal exchange with his aunt. During it he had been continually restraining himself and trying very hard not to show what he really felt. His feelings taught him only too well that in this behaviour, together with his pride, there had also been latent a kind of unhappiness.

Tsuda, who judged this long-delayed visit, which had used up the leisure of more than half a day, merely according to the amount of pleasure or displeasure it gave him, quickly contrasted the lively Mrs Yoshikawa and her attractive parlour, with the scene in front of him. Then the face of O-Nobu, who had finally begun to wear her hair in the round chignon of a married woman, also came to his mind.

He got up from his seat and turned around to look at Kobayashi.

'Are you staying?'

'No, I have to leave too.'

Kobayashi quickly stuffed into one of his trouser pockets the remainder of the pack of Shikishima cigarettes he had been smoking. As they were on the point of leaving, Tsuda's uncle again began to speak, almost coincidentally.

'How's O-Nobu been recently? I've always been thinking of going to see her, but I haven't because, as they say, there's no rest for the poor. Please remember me to her. She'll probably be bored with too much free time while you're at the hospital. I wonder how in the world she does spend her time.'

'She certainly doesn't have anything special to do.'

Tsuda answered casually in this way, and then quickly added, as if he had thought of it just then :

'Although she jokes about wanting to go to the hospital with me, she still can be even stricter than my aunt here in keeping after me to have my hair cut and to take baths.'

'Don't you admire her for it? Where else could you find someone able to take such care of a dandy like you?'

'Yes, I know I'm lucky.'

'What about the theatre? Does she go frequently?'

'Yes, she goes occasionally. Recently she was invited by the Okamotos, but unfortunately we have to settle this matter of my operation first.'

At that point Tsuda looked at his aunt for a moment.

'How about it, Aunt Asa? Shall I take you to the Imperial Theatre one of these days? It's a tonic to go to such places once in a while, you know. It really cheers you up.'

'Well, thank you. But I'm afraid being taken there by you—'

'Would it be unpleasant for you?'

'No, it wouldn't be unpleasant. It's just that I hardly know when it will happen.'

Tsuda purposely braved the full force of this answer of his aunt, who actually was not too fond of the theatre, and scratched his head in perplexity.

'Well, if that's as much as you trust me, it may indeed never happen.'

She then gave a little laugh.

'It really doesn't matter about the theatre, Yoshio. But how have things been in Kyoto recently?'

'Have you had some news from there?'

With a rather serious expression Tsuda turned from his aunt to his uncle. But neither of them said anything in response.

'Actually they haven't sent me any money this month, and Father's told me I have to get along as best I can. Don't you think that's quite severe of him?'

Tsuda's uncle merely laughed.

'I suppose he's angry.'

'I don't think O-Hide should keep telling him all those things she does.'

Tsuda seemed slightly annoyed as he mentioned his sister.

'O-Hide isn't at fault. It's quite clear you, Yoshio, are to blame from the beginning.'

'That may well be, but where in the world is there a fellow who returns the money he's received from his father down to the last penny?'

'Well then, you shouldn't ever have promised to do so. And in addition. . . .'

'All right, I understand, Aunt Asa.'

Tsuda stood up, showing by his expression that he felt it was quite useless to talk to them. Because of his defeat, however, he did not forget to drag Kobayashi along, and to leave from the front entrance with him, to add some liveliness to his hasty departure.

33

Outside there was not even a breeze. The air touched their cheeks coldly as they walked at a brisk pace. It even seemed as if invisible or transparent dew were falling softly from a sky where stars twinkled distantly. Tsuda stroked the shoulder of his overcoat. After clearly ascertaining with his fingertips the damp, chilly sensation penetrating to the underside of it, he turned to Kobayashi.

'During the day it's still warm but at night it's already quite cold, isn't it?'

'Yes. No matter what anyone says, it's autumn already. It's really cold enough to want an overcoat.'

Kobayashi was not wearing anything over his new three-piece suit. His manner of striding noisily in his grim-looking American-style shoes, which were particularly thick and square-toed, and of purposely waving about his thick cane, seemed to be that of a political demonstrator defying the cold air.

'Whatever happened to that overcoat you had made when you were at school and which you were so proud of?'

He suddenly asked Tsuda this rather strange question. Tsuda was compelled to recall the time when he had flaunted that overcoat before Kobayashi.

'I still have it.'

'Do you still wear it?'

'No matter how poor I am, do you really think I'd still be wearing an overcoat I wore during my schooldays?'

'Really? Well then, that's just fine. Give it to me.'

'If you really want it, I shall.'

Tsuda answered rather coldly. It seemed slightly inconsistent for a man who had bought even new socks to want to have someone's old overcoat. It gave evidence, however, of the vicissitudes of that person's economic life. After a while Tsuda asked Kobayashi : 'Why didn't you have an overcoat made at the same time as that suit?'

'You shouldn't think of me the way you do of yourself.'

'Then how did you manage to get that suit and those shoes?'

'The way you ask that question is a bit too crude. After all, I didn't steal them, so don't worry.'

Tsuda immediately stopped talking.

The two came out at the top of a large hill. The small hill which could be seen across the intervening broad valley stretched darkly like the back of some monster. In the autumn night the points of light here and there gave forth a small amount of warmth.

'Hey, why don't we have a drink somewhere on our way back?'

Before Tsuda answered he first glanced over at Kobayashi, and then tried to evade the question. On their right was a high embankment, covered completely by a luxuriant bamboo grove. Since there was no wind, the bamboos were not rustling, but the tops of the leaves, which seemed to be sleeping, sufficed to give Tsuda a feeling of loneliness appropriate to the season.

'This certainly is a gloomy place, isn't it? It's the back of some nobleman's estate, and I suppose it's been left in this condition forever. I do hope they clear it soon.'

Tsuda spoke this way, attempting to evade the question he had been asked. But such things as bamboo groves were far removed from Kobayashi's mind.

'Hey, aren't you coming? It's been a long time since we've gone drinking together.'

'But haven't you just been drinking?'

'What are you talking about? What I had doesn't even begin to count as real drinking.'

'But didn't you say you'd had enough when they offered you more?'

'I had to say that simply because I'm on my good behaviour with the Fujiis, and I can't get drunk. If I hadn't drunk anything it wouldn't have mattered, but to drink only a little bit is actually bad for you. Now if I don't drink enough to get drunk it will really tell on me.'

Kobayashi, who had constructed this convenient logic to please himself and was trying to drag Tsuda with him, was a most annoying companion. Tsuda asked him half-jokingly :

'Are you treating me?'

'I don't mind.'

'And where do you intend to go?'

'Anywhere will do. Even an *oden** shop's all right, isn't it?'

They went down the hill without speaking.

34

If they had followed their normal routes, Tsuda would have turned to the right there and Kobayashi would have proceeded straight ahead. But Kobayashi peered at Tsuda, who put his hand to his hat in an attempt to say goodbye politely, and said to him : 'I think I'll go that way too.'

In the direction they were going there was a district of two or three blocks where they could find some convenient place to eat and drink. When they saw the glass doors of a well-lit place looking like a bar, in about the centre of that district, Kobayashi abruptly came to a halt.

'This place is fine. Let's go in here.'

'I don't like it at all.'

'Around here there aren't any high-class places you'd approve of, so why don't we make do with this one?'

'I'm sick, I tell you.'

'That doesn't matter. I'll take care of you—don't worry.'

'Don't joke with me. I don't like this place, I tell you.'

'Everything's going to be all right. I'll explain it all to your wife.'

Tsuda became annoyed, and leaving Kobayashi behind, tried to go on ahead quickly. Kobayashi then turned to walk right next to him, and pressed him in a slightly different tone : 'Is it that unpleasant for you to have a drink with me?'

Tsuda, for whom it actually was that unpleasant, immediately stopped when he heard those words. He then spoke in complete contradiction to his inner feelings.

'All right, let's have a drink.'

The two quickly pulled open the bright glass doors and went inside. There were only five or six customers other than themselves, but since the place was not too large, it seemed relatively crowded. They chose a corner where they could find seats easily, and sat down opposite each

* A cheap dish of boiled bean-curd and fish.

other; while waiting for their order, they looked with curiosity at their surroundings.

Among their fellow-customers they did not see even one who, judging from his dress, appeared to them to have any social position. One, who seemed to be on his way back from the public bath and had a wet towel slung over the shoulder of his striped workman's livery, and another, who wore a stiff sash over a cotton garment and who purposely had placed an imitation nephrite stone in the middle of the flat braid of his *haori*, were rather in the upper stratum. One, much more disreputable, appeared to be only a rag-man. And there was also one who was wearing a workman's waistcoat and close-fitting trousers.

'How about it here? Isn't it wonderfully plebeian?'

Kobayashi said this as he poured saké for Tsuda. His brand-new, gaudy suit, which was such as to cancel out those words of his, was instantly reflected in Tsuda's knowing eyes, but he himself seemed wholly unaware of the contrast.

'Unlike you, you know, I have a great deal of sympathy for the lower classes.'

Kobayashi acted very much as if they were all his own brothers and sisters, and he looked around at everyone.

'Look around you. They all have much better faces than the bourgeoisie.'

Tsuda did not have the energy to respond to that remark, and instead of looking around at everybody, scrutinized Kobayashi. The latter swiftly gave way.

'Well, at least they're able to get magnificently drunk.'

'The bourgeoisie can do that too, you know.'

'Yes, but their way of doing it is different.'

Tsuda proudly did not ask about the difference between the two. Nevertheless Kobayashi kept filling up his saké-cup without becoming in the least disheartened.

'You despise this sort of people, don't you? You've always looked down on them as not worthy of sympathy.'

As soon as he had said this, without even waiting for Tsuda's answer, he called to a young man across from them who looked like a milkman.

'You agree with me, don't you?'

The young man who had been thus suddenly called turned his burly neck and looked at them for a moment, whereupon Kobayashi swiftly thrust a saké-cup at him.

'Come on, young fellow, have a drink.'

The young man grinned. Unfortunately there was a distance of about two yards between him and Kobayashi. Since he did not feel he had to stand up to get the saké-cup, he only smiled and did not move. Nevertheless, Kobayashi appeared satisfied. He drew back the saké-cup he had offered, and bringing it to his own mouth, said to Tsuda again :

'You see, it's just as I said. There isn't a single person here who's haughty the way the bourgeoisie is.'

35

A small man, wearing an Inverness cloak, passed, on his way in, the man with the square-cropped head who was wearing workman's livery, and took a seat at a place slightly removed from the two of them. After he had given one quick look around him, while still wearing a hunting-cap with the visor pulled far down, he put his hand in his pocket. He then took out of it and opened a small, thin notebook, which he looked at fixedly as if he were either reading it or pondering it. He never tried to take off his old Inverness cloak. His cap too remained on his head. His notebook, however, did not remain open for very long. After returning it carefully to his pocket, he began, as he drank, to look searchingly at the other customers but in a way that seemed as if he were not doing so. From time to time he would put out his hand from underneath the wings of his undersized cloak and stroke his thin moustache.

When the line of vision of the two men, who had for some time been noticing this behaviour rather offhandedly, crossed that of the newcomer, Tsuda and Kobayashi turned away and looked into each other's faces. Kobayashi was the first to comment.

'Who do you think he is?'

Tsuda did not change his previous posture. He answered in a tone that indicated he thought the question hardly worth a response.

'How in the world should I know?'

Kobayashi lowered his voice even further.

'That fellow's a detective.'

Tsuda did not answer. He could drink more than his companion and had in fact done so, yet he was much less affected by the alcohol. He silently drained the saké-cup in front of him. Kobayashi immediately filled it to the brim.

'Look at the expression in his eyes.'

Tsuda gave a slight laugh and finally spoke.

'If someone keeps on, as you have, criticizing the bourgeoisie, he'll soon be mistaken for a socialist. Be a bit more careful.'

'A socialist?'

Kobayashi purposely shouted and looked pointedly at the man with the Inverness.

'Don't make me laugh. No matter what I may seem to be, I'm only a fellow who sympathizes with the good-hearted masses of the poor.

Compared to me, people like you who are forever putting on airs and keeping up appearances are much worse. Try thinking about which of us deserves to be hauled off by the police.'

Since the man with the hunting-cap was looking down silently, Kobayashi had no choice but to fall upon Tsuda.

'Maybe you've never really had the intention of treating this kind of day-labourer and coolie as human beings.'

Kobayashi began to speak this way again, and looked around him, but unfortunately nowhere were there any day-labourers or coolies. Even so, this did not bother him, for he continued his tirade.

'You wouldn't understand how they naturally have a more human and nobler spirit than you or any detective. It's just that their warm human beauty is concealed by poverty and dirt. In other words, you think they're dirty just because they can't take baths. How can you be such a fool!'

Kobayashi's tone sounded more like one of defending himself than of defending the poor. Tsuda, however, purposely avoided discussion because he was worried that, by heedlessly disputing with him, his own dignity might be impaired. Nevertheless Kobayashi still kept after him.

'You aren't saying anything, but you don't believe me, do you? You certainly look as if you don't. If so, I'll explain what I mean. I suppose you've read some Russian novels, haven't you?'

Tsuda, who had never read even one Russian novel, still said nothing.

'People who've read Russian novels, particularly Dostoyevsky's, should certainly know what I mean. Everybody should know that no matter how lowly people may be, and no matter how uneducated they may be, occasionally there may flow from their mouths, as from a fountain, precious, and wholly unaffected, utterly pure, utterly innocent feelings that bring tears to one's eyes. Do you think that's nonsense?'

'Since I've never read any Dostoyevsky, I'm afraid I wouldn't know.'

'If you ask your uncle, he'll say it's a lie. He'll say it's nothing more than a device whereby the author purposely invests humble people with such noble emotions to arouse the reader sentimentally; in other words, he says that because Dostoyevsky was successful in this, many writers have imitated him, and it's nothing more than a kind of artistic technique that's been absurdly cheapened. But I don't think so. When I hear your uncle say such things, I become furious. He doesn't understand Dostoyevsky. No matter how old he is, it doesn't mean he really knows anything about these matters. And no matter how young I may be. . . .'

Kobayashi's words had gradually acquired force. Finally he showed that he could no longer control his emotions, and his tears fell on the table-cloth.

36

Unfortunately Tsuda was not sufficiently affected by his drinking to be drawn into his companion's feelings. His eyes, viewing this agitated state of Kobayashi's from beyond the bounds of empathy, were instead critical. He wondered whether it was the saké or his uncle that had made Kobayashi cry. He also wondered whether it was Dostoyevsky or the lower classes of Japanese society that had so affected him. Whichever it was, he looked upon it as something without too much relation to himself. It was of no consequence to him. But it still made him uneasy. He was merely annoyed as he observed the traces of the tears shed in front of him by this highly emotional person.

The man Kobayashi had thought was a detective again took out his thin notebook from his pocket, and began very intently to note something down in pencil. His manner, which not only was as quiet as a cat's but also was cat-like in that he seemed to notice everything, gave Tsuda a strange feeling. Kobayashi's drunkenness, however, had already passed beyond that point. Such things as detectives no longer concerned him. He brought one of his arms abruptly to the point of Tsuda's nose to show him his new suit.

'When I'm wearing a dirty suit you despise me for being dirty, don't you? And when occasionally I have on some clean clothes you then despise me for being clean. Well then, what in the world am I supposed to do? How should I behave to be respected by you? For God's sake tell me! Because despite everything, I still want you to respect me.'

Tsuda smiled grimly, pushing back Kobayashi's arm. Strangely enough there was no resistance in it. As if its earlier force had suddenly spent itself, it returned meekly to its former position. But his mouth was not so docile as his arm. As soon as he withdrew his arm he began speaking.

'I know perfectly well what's in your mind. You want to laugh at me because you think that even though I show this much sympathy towards the lower classes and I myself am poor I've had a new suit made. And you think this is being inconsistent, don't you?'

'No matter how poor you are, it's quite natural that you'd have at least one suit made. If you didn't, you'd have to walk the streets stark naked. I'm glad you've had it made. No one's thinking anything of it.'

'But actually that's not so. You think I'm only getting myself decked out. You interpret it as a kind of foppishness, and that's rotten of you!'

'Really? If so, I'm sorry.'

Since Tsuda, who felt he could no longer tolerate Kobayashi, had finally realized the convenience of capitulating, he began arbitrarily to modify his tone, as a result of which Kobayashi's tone, too, naturally changed.

'No, I'm really bad too. It was wrong of me. I admit I want to get all dressed up once in a while. Even I am quite aware of that. I'm aware of it, but still you wouldn't know why I had a suit made at this time.'

Of course Tsuda could not be expected to know the particular reason. Nor did he want to know it. But he was forced by the circumstances to ask him. Kobayashi spread out his arms on either side of him, and as he looked around at his suit, answered rather forlornly :

'Actually I'm going to be leaving Tokyo very soon in these clothes. I'm running off to Korea.'

Tsuda for the first time looked at Kobayashi with a startled expression. After he had interrupted him to remark that his necktie was twisted to one side, something that had been disturbing him for some time, and had made him adjust it, he continued to listen to his story.

Kobayashi had for a long time been working as an editor and proofreader of Tsuda's uncle's magazine at the same time that he had been writing his own articles and taking them around to various places which were likely to pay him for them; indeed he seemed to be forever busy, but finally, unable to bear such a life in Tokyo any longer, he had almost decided to go over to Korea and work there for a certain newspaper company.

'No matter how much I've tried to put up with this Tokyo life, I just can't because it's simply too dreadful. I really can't stand living in a place with no future.'

Although he said that the future seemed to be all ready and waiting for him in Korea, immediately thereafter he contradicted himself.

'Maybe a fellow like me is after all just someone born to wander through life. I can't ever settle down. And it's terrible that even if I want to, the world won't let me. There's nothing for me to do but become a kind of runaway from life, is there?'

'You're not the only one who can't settle down. I don't seem to be able to relax either.'

'Don't say such asinine things! The fact that you can't relax is a luxury. The fact that I can't is painful, and means I'm forced to go chasing after my bread until I die.'

'But not being able to settle down is a universal feature of modern man. You're not the only one who's suffering.'

Kobayashi did not seem to derive the slightest comfort from Tsuda's words.

37

The waitress, who had for some time been observing the behaviour of the two men, came without warning, and in a rather unnatural manner began to clear the table-top. As if that were the signal, the man wearing the Inverness quietly stood up. The two men, who had stopped drinking quite a while before and who were then merely talking, were also unable to overlook her action. Tsuda seized this opportunity, and immediately got up. But before Kobayashi got up from his chair he picked up Tsuda's pack of M.C.C. cigarettes which lay between them. He then took out one of the new gold-tipped cigarettes, lit it, and put the pack down. This action of his, which seemed to be his parting thrust at his companion, irritated Tsuda greatly as he picked up the pack of cigarettes and put it in his pocket.

Even though it was not so very late, the streets on that autumn night were strangely quiet. Streetcars were running somewhere in the distance, making a noise one could not have heard in the daytime. The dark shadows of the two men, each of whom was involved in his own private thoughts, moved along the edge of the river without yet separating.

'About when will you be going to Korea?'

'It may even be while you're in the hospital.'

'Are you leaving that soon?'

'No, not necessarily. I won't know for certain until your uncle meets the editor-in-chief from over there again.'

'Do you mean you're not yet certain about the day you're leaving, or of going at all?'

'Yes, well—'

His answer was a trifle vague. When Tsuda did not pursue the matter further and began walking ahead swiftly, Kobayashi spoke again.

'Actually, I don't particularly want to go, you know.'

'Does my uncle say you have to?'

'Of course that's not it.'

'Well then, why don't you give it up?'

To the extent that Tsuda's words contained a logic self-evident to anyone, they were the equivalent of cruelly wounding his companion, who seemed to be starving for sympathy. After going on a few steps, Kobayashi suddenly turned towards him.

'Tsuda, I'm very lonely.'

Tsuda did not respond. The two continued walking silently. As the trickle of water flowing in the middle of the shallow river-bed disappeared darkly underneath the dimly seen bridge it murmured faintly in the intervals between the noise of passing streetcars.

'I will go to Korea after all. I certainly think it's better.'

'Well then, go ahead.'

'Yes, I'm definitely going. It's much, much better to go to Korea or Formosa than to stay here and be made a fool of by everybody.'

His voice was quite shrill. Tsuda suddenly felt the necessity of using a calm tone in his voice.

'You shouldn't be so pessimistic. If a person's young and healthy, he should be able to make out quite well wherever he goes, shouldn't he? . . . Before you leave I'll give you a going-away party to cheer you up.'

This time it was Kobayashi who did not make an appropriate answer. Tsuda again felt he had to say something to suit the occasion.

'If you go, it will be rather hard for O-Kin when she gets married, won't it?'

Kobayashi, who until then had not been thinking of his younger sister, suddenly looked at Tsuda as if he had remembered something.

'Yes, it's too bad for her, but it can't be helped. She'll resign herself to it and think how unlucky she is to have such a good-for-nothing for a brother.'

'If you're not here, I suppose my uncle and aunt will do something for her.'

'Well, I'm afraid it can't be any other way. Of course she could turn down this marriage and work forever as a kind of maid at your uncle's house—but as for that, well, I suppose it's about the same as the other. But I'm indebted to your uncle in yet another way. If it turns out that I do go, I'll have to borrow the money for the travel expenses from him.'

'Won't they give it to you over there?'

'It doesn't seem so.'

'Well, couldn't you somehow make them do it?'

'I wonder.'

When Kobayashi broke the one-minute silence which followed, he again spoke as if to himself.

'I'll borrow the travel money from your uncle, I'll get an overcoat from you, and I'll abandon my only sister—everything's so very simple.'

This was the last speech to come from Kobayashi that evening. The two men finally parted. Tsuda hurried towards his home without even looking back.

38

The main gate of his house was locked as usual. He then tried the side gate, but that night it did not open either. Thinking it might not have opened because it was off its runners, he tried two or three times more to open it but finally, when he pulled at it with all his might, he heard inside the heavy, dull sound of the resisting bolt, and he had to give up the struggle.

He cocked his head in perplexity at this unforeseen event, and for a while simply stood in front of the gate. He did not recall ever having spent the night out since his marriage, and even if he had occasionally returned home late at night, he had never yet had this happen to him.

That day, from the time it had become dark, he had wanted to return home early. The reason he had eaten dinner, a dinner in name only, at his uncle's house was simply that he had been forced to do so. His having drunk some saké, which he had not really wanted, was also nothing more than a kind of duty towards Kobayashi. After it had become dark he had done these various things away from home but always with the image of O-Nobu in his mind. When he returned from the chilly out-of-doors he was indeed longing for the warm lights of his home, and it was as if he had been directing his steps with them as his object. Thus, at the same time that his body was checked, like a horse before a wall, his expectations too were suddenly blocked by the gate. And it certainly was now not a minor problem for him to determine whether it was O-Nobu or an accident that had blocked them.

He raised his hand and pounded loudly twice on the side gate which he could not open. The sound, which seemed to be demanding 'Why did you lock this?' rather than 'Open up!', echoed in the gradually increasing darkness of the street. There then came a long drawn out 'Yes' from within. And the voice which struck his eardrum almost as swiftly as the echo of his pounding was not that of the maid but of O-Nobu. He quickly calmed down and listened intently from his side of the gate. He distinctly heard the turning of the switch of the entrance light, which was customarily used only when needed. The lattice-door was soon opened with a clatter. He was certain that the hinged door of the entrance had not yet been closed.

'Who is it?'

When her footsteps had come very near on the other side, O-Nobu first challenged him in this way. He felt even more impatient.

'Open up right away! It's Yoshio.'

O-Nobu exclaimed, 'Oh, my goodness! Is it you? I'm so sorry.'

64

After she had noisily released the bolt and let him in, he saw she was slightly paler than usual. He quickly went on ahead from the entrance into the living-room.

The living-room, as always, was neatly arranged. The iron kettle was humming as usual. In front of the long brazier a thick muslin cushion was spread as usual, as if it were awaiting his return. Across from it, where O-Nobu customarily sat, was placed a woman's inkstone case, near her cushion. The mother-of-pearl lid of the case with its inlaid plum blossom pattern had been taken off and placed to one side, and the small inkstone that was inserted in the pear-skin lacquer interior of the case glittered wetly. As evidence that its owner had left her seat hurriedly, the thin tip of the writing-brush was causing Indian ink to blot the rolled paper, and it was smudging the end of the letter, of which seven or eight lines had already been written.

O-Nobu, who had seen that the doors were fastened and had come in after Tsuda, sat down abruptly while still wearing an everyday *haori* thrown over her nightgown.

'I'm really very sorry.'

Tsuda raised his eyes and glanced at the wall clock. It had just struck eleven. Although it was unusual, it was certainly not the first time since their marriage that he had returned at such an hour.

'Why did you lock me out? Did you perhaps think I wasn't coming back any more?'

'No. For quite a while I was waiting, wondering when you'd ever come back. Finally, since I was so lonely I couldn't stand it, I began writing a letter home.'

O-Nobu's parents, like Tsuda's, lived in Kyoto. Tsuda observed this partially written letter from a distance. But he still could not understand the matter of the side gate.

'But why did you lock the side gate just because you were waiting? Did you perhaps feel it was unsafe?'

'No. . . . I didn't lock the side gate.'

'But, as you know, it actually *was* locked, wasn't it?'

'Toki undoubtedly left it locked from last night. I'm sure of it. The forgetful girl!'

As she said this, O-Nobu twitched her eyebrows in her customary manner. The explanation that in the morning they had forgotten to release the bolt of the side gate was certainly not an unreasonable one.

'What's Toki doing?'

'I already let her go to bed.'

Since he did not feel any necessity of going so far as to awaken the maid and investigate the person responsible, he let the matter of the side gate drop at this point, and went to bed.

39

On the following morning, before Tsuda had even washed his face, he was startled by a strange sight which he had in no way anticipated when he went to bed the night before.

He had arisen at about nine o'clock. He had as usual gone through the entrance hall and was about to go into the kitchen from the living-room. But there was O-Nobu, fascinatingly and brilliantly dressed, sitting smugly. He was taken aback. She gave a smile and seemed to be satisfied with her husband's reaction, which was as if water had been thrown into his still sleepy face.

'Are you just getting up now?'

He blinked, and looked at her elaborate chignon with its red silk chignon-band, the pattern of her intricately embroidered neckband, and between them her white, carefully made-up face, with a new expression as if he were beholding some very rare sight indeed.

'What in the world have you done? And so early in the morning, too.'

'Why, I haven't done anything. . . . After all, today's the day you're going to the doctor's, isn't it?'

Both his *hakama* and *haori* which he had taken off and thrown there the night before were folded and placed in careful alignment on the tan paper.

'Do you intend to go there with me?'

'Yes, of course I do. Will it bother you if I do?'

'No, it isn't that but. . . .'

He again looked penetratingly at his wife's attire.

'You're dressed a bit too extravagantly, aren't you?'

He quickly recalled the scene of the gloomy waiting-room where he had recently been. The group of patients who had been sitting there and this resplendently dressed-up young matron in no way harmonized.

'But today's Sunday, my dear.'

'Even so, it's a bit different from going to the theatre or cherry-blossom viewing.'

'But I. . . .'

As far as Tsuda was concerned, Sunday was even worse because it just meant that there would be a great number of patients waiting from the morning on.

'For both of us to go to the doctor's with you so gaudily decked out seems to me to be a bit. . . .'

'Ostentatious?'

O-Nobu's choice of that difficult word suddenly struck him as humorous, and he began to laugh. She twitched her eyebrows a little, and instantly used a rather coaxing tone.

'But to change my clothes now would take quite a bit of time and be rather troublesome. Since I purposely put these clothes on, please try not to mind just for today, won't you?'

He finally acknowledged defeat. As he was washing his face he heard her hurriedly directing the maid to order two rickshaws, very much as if she herself were pressed for time.

Since he was not having his usual meals, breakfast took hardly five minutes. He got up without even using a toothpick, and was about to go upstairs quickly.

'I should get together the things I'm taking to the hospital.'

As he spoke, O-Nobu swiftly opened the closet behind her.

'I've already gathered them here. Please look at them a minute.'

Tsuda, who had to be considerate of her since she was wearing her best clothes, pulled out of the closet by himself the rather heavy suitcase and the small cloth-wrapped bundle. In the bundle there were only the aforementioned dressing-gown which he had earlier tried on and the flat, blind-stitched belt of his nightclothes, but from the suitcase there emerged in a jumble such things as toothpicks, tooth-paste, the lavender writing-paper he was in the habit of using, envelopes of the same colour, a fountain pen, small scissors, and tweezers. When he took out the large Western volume, the heaviest and bulkiest item, he turned to O-Nobu.

'I'll leave this behind.'

'Really? But it's always on your desk with a bookmark stuck in it, so I thought you'd read it, and I put it in.'

Without saying anything, he placed on the *tatami* this German volume of economics he had not yet been able to finish in over two months.

'It's heavy and won't do for reading in bed.'

Although he knew it was a suitable reason for leaving behind the ponderous tome, he did not feel very good about it.

'Oh, is that so? Well, since I don't know which ones you'll need, please select the ones you like by yourself.'

He brought down two or three light novels from upstairs and packed them in the suitcase in place of the economics volume.

40

Since the weather was fine, they left the house with both the hoods of their rickshaws folded, and they put the suitcase in one and the cloth-wrapped bundle in the other vehicle. When they had turned the corner of the lane and had gone one or two blocks down the street with the streetcar line, O-Nobu's rickshaw-man suddenly called out to Tsuda's. Both rickshaws immediately stopped.

'Oh, how dreadful! I've forgotten something.'

Tsuda turned around in his rickshaw and stared at O-Nobu without saying anything. He was not the only one who was fascinated by these urgent words from this elaborately dressed young woman. The rickshaw-men too turned their curious gaze towards her, while still holding the shafts. Even the people passing by in the street had to glance at the couple.

'What's the matter? What have you forgotten?'

O-Nobu looked preoccupied.

'Please wait a moment. It won't take long.'

She made only her own rickshaw turn back. Tsuda, who was left behind in the psychological state of hanging in mid-air, silently watched her retreating figure. Once her rickshaw, after having been hidden in the lane, appeared again, it ran with considerable speed to the place where he was waiting. When it had stopped in front of him, O-Nobu took from her obi a steel chain, about a foot in length, and dangled it before him. On the end of the chain was a ring, and five or six keys of various sizes were hanging from it. As she held the chain up high to show it to him, a jangling sound struck his ear.

'These are what I forgot. I'd left them lying out on the bureau.'

As a precaution, when both of them went out, leaving only the maid in the house, it was necessary to lock up the valuable things and take the keys with them.

'You take care of them.'

O-Nobu again inserted the jangling objects in her obi, and as she struck it with the palm of her hand, she smiled at Tsuda.

'It's all right now.'

The rickshaws once again began to move.

They arrived at the doctor's somewhat later than the appointed hour. But they were not so late as not to be on time for the morning consultation hours. Since it was rather embarrassing for them to go and sit down in the waiting-room as a couple, when Tsuda came in he immediately went to the dispensary window.

'I suppose it's all right if this patient goes upstairs immediately, isn't it?'

The boy in the dispensary called from the rear to the nurse, whom Tsuda knew by sight. The nurse, who was still not more than sixteen or seventeen, smiled effortlessly and bowed to Tsuda, but when she saw the figure of O-Nobu standing near by, she felt somewhat overwhelmed by the latter's imposing appearance, and showed by her expression that she wondered where in the world such a bird of paradise had come from. Since O-Nobu took the initiative from her, and greeted her with 'I'm sorry to trouble you', the nurse also bowed as if she had noticed her for the first time.

'Take this for me, will you?'

Tsuda handed over to the nurse the suitcase he had received from the rickshaw-man, and turned towards the foot of the staircase leading to the second floor.

'It's this way, O-Nobu.'

O-Nobu, who had been standing at the entrance to the waiting-room and had been peering into the room where the patients were, quickly followed him, and climbed the stairs.

'That's a very gloomy room down there, isn't it?'

Fortunately, however, the upstairs room, which opened on the southeast, was bright. She opened the sliding-door and went to the veranda, and after looking at the clothes driers of the Western-style laundry which was only a few inches away from her, she turned around to Tsuda.

'Unlike downstairs, here it's cheerful. And it's rather a nice room, isn't it? The *tatami* are dirty, though.'

The second floor of the clinic, which had been done over from a place that had been the apartment of some contractor's mistress, somehow still retained its lively character from the past.

'It's old, but it may even be better than the upstairs of our own house.'

Tsuda, looking, with a sense of the autumn season, at the whiteness of the laundry gleaming in the sun, said this, and turned around to look at the ceiling and the alcove pillars, somewhat smoke-stained with age.

41

The same nurse as before brought them up a tea-tray, and poured them some tea.

'We'll get things arranged soon, but please be patient.'

They were forced to sit opposite each other politely as they drank the tea.

'I don't know why, but I'm nervous and can't seem to calm down.'

'It's exactly as if we'd come as guests, isn't it?'

'Yes.'

O-Nobu took out a woman's watch from her obi, and looked at it. Tsuda was more concerned about the operation he was shortly to undergo than he was about the time.

'I wonder about how many minutes it will take. Even if I don't see it, if I just hear the sound of that blade I feel rather odd.'

'Oh, it *frightens* me. Just to see that sort of thing.'

O-Nobu actually twitched her eyebrows as if she were frightened.

'Why don't you wait here then? There's no need at all for you to come near the operating table and watch such an unpleasant thing.'

'But in this sort of situation it wouldn't be right if some relative weren't present.'

He noticed her serious expression, and began to laugh.

'That's only at times of really serious illnesses when it's a matter of life or death. Who'd ask anybody to watch this kind of minor operation !'

Tsuda was a man who disliked revealing anything unpleasant to women. He particularly disliked showing them any unpleasant aspects of himself. And even more than that, he felt unusual discomfort in being forced to look at his own unpleasant aspects.

O-Nobu said, 'Well then, I won't,' and took out her watch again.

'I suppose it will be over by noon, won't it?'

'I think so. At any rate, now that we're here, it doesn't really matter when it's over, does it?'

'Yes, that's right, but even so. . . .'

O-Nobu did not finish her sentence. Nor did Tsuda ask her what she meant.

The nurse again appeared at the top of the stairs.

'Everything's ready, so please come now.'

Tsuda immediately stood up. O-Nobu started to get up at the same time.

'Didn't I tell you to wait right there?'

'Oh, I'm not going to the consultation room. I just want to use the phone here for a moment.'

'Where do you have to call?'

'It's not very important—I just thought I'd call O-Hide and let her know about your operation.'

Tsuda's younger sister's house was in the same ward not very far from there. Tsuda, who had not been thinking very much about his sister in connection with his present illness, stopped O-Nobu as she was about to stand up.

'Oh that's all right. You don't have to let her know. If you tell O-Hide and the others, it will seem too important. Besides, if she comes here and annoys me, it won't be very pleasant.'

He considered this sister, who differed from him in temperament, in a certain sense a rather difficult person to deal with, even though she was younger than he.

O-Nobu answered while still in a half-rising posture.

'Even so, if she says something to us afterwards about not having been told, I'll feel embarrassed.'

Since he could not find any special reason for restraining her, he was forced to say : 'Well, it doesn't matter if you phone, but it certainly doesn't have to be now, does it? She lives just near here, so she'll surely come right away. Since I'll just have had my operation and my nerves will be on edge too, it really won't be very pleasant to have her come here and start telling me what I should do and saying all sorts of things about Father as well.'

O-Nobu laughed faintly so as to show that she was concerned about being heard downstairs. But the white teeth which she exposed clearly told Tsuda that rather than feeling any sympathy for him she simply felt he was amusing.

'All right then, I won't telephone O-Hide.'

As she said this, she finally stood up beside him.

'Are you phoning somewhere else?'

'Yes, to the Okamotos. I did promise them I'd phone before noon. It's all right if I do, isn't it?'

They descended the stairs singly, and at the foot of the staircase they went their separate ways. While one was standing in front of the telephone, the other was seated in the chair of the consultation room.

42

'You did take the castor oil, didn't you?'

As the doctor asked Tsuda this question his newly-laundered, white operating gown rustled from its heavy starch.

'Yes I did, but it didn't seem to have as much effect as I thought it would.'

Actually on the previous day Tsuda had not even had the time to notice its effect. His mind had been busily taken up with one thing after another so that not only had the psychological effect of the laxative been almost nil, but physiologically as well it had been unexpectedly slight.

'Well then, I'll give you another enema.'

The enema too did not have much effect.

Tsuda climbed up on the operating table just as he was, and lay on his back. When the cold waterproof cloth touched his skin directly, he shuddered instinctively. Since the rays of light streamed directly down on his head, resting against the hard, attached pillow, like anyone lying down facing a light he could not possibly relax. He blinked many times and looked at the ceiling just as often. The nurse then brought something looking like a square, shallow, nickel tray, on which had been placed the instruments for the operation, and since she passed by his side he noticed its white metallic glitter. Lying as he was, face up, however, it only caught his eye for a moment in passing. His feelings intensified, for he had caught a glimpse of those unpleasant instruments he was not supposed to see. At that moment the ringing of the telephone in the front office suddenly sounded in his ears. He quickly remembered the presence of O-Nobu, whom he had forgotten until then. When her telephone call to the Okamotos was finally over, his operation had at long last begun.

'I'll do it with cocaine only. I don't think it will be very painful. If the injection does no good, I intend to insert some drugs way inside. I think that will probably take care of it.'

The doctor spoke this way as he disinfected the affected area, and Tsuda listened to his words with a feeling that was a strange mixture of fear and unconcern.

The anaesthetization of the affected part was successful. Tsuda, who was looking hard at the ceiling, scarcely knew what was happening in the area below his waist. He only felt from time to time that someone, at a point deep within his body, was applying pressure. He also felt a dull resistance at that point.

'How does it feel? It doesn't hurt, does it?'

The doctor seemed to have considerable confidence in himself as he asked these questions. Tsuda answered, still looking at the ceiling :

'No, it doesn't hurt. I only have a heavy feeling.'

He did not know how to describe the feeling, but he suddenly imagined that the insensate earth might very well have such a feeling when dug up by human hands.

'It's a very strange feeling. It's hard to explain.'

'Is that so? Can you stand it?'

The words of the doctor, who seemed to be worried that Tsuda might have an attack of cerebral anaemia during the operation, made Tsuda uneasy when he had not been particularly concerned. He had no idea whether they would make him drink some wine or what they would do to prevent the anaemia, but in any event he did not want to receive any such special treatment.

'It's all right.'

'Are you sure? It will soon be over.'

In the manner of the doctor, moving his hands ceaselessly as he conversed with his patient, there seemed to gleam a skill which only a man of experience could possess. The operation, however, took longer than he had indicated it would.

From time to time Tsuda heard the sound of the instruments touching the plate. The sound of the scissors cutting dully through the flesh assailed his eardrums, greatly exaggerated. He could imagine at such times the raw, red stream of blood which had to be wiped away with the gauze. He had of course been made to lie perfectly still, but his nerves were so taut he found it painful to do so. It was as if crawling insects had crept stealthily into his arteries and were making his whole body uneasy.

He opened his eyes wide, and looked at the ceiling. In the room immediately above, O-Nobu was waiting. He had no idea what she was then thinking or doing. He was just about to give a loud cry and try to call her, but at that moment, from near his feet, the doctor spoke.

'It's finally over.'

After experiencing the ticklish sensation of being crammed with an inordinate amount of gauze, Tsuda was once again spoken to by the doctor.

'Since the scar is harder than I expected and there's danger of bleeding, you'll have to lie still for a while.'

With this last word of advice, Tsuda was finally taken down from the operating table.

43

As he was leaving the consultation room, the nurse followed him, and asked :

'How are you feeling now? You don't feel too bad, do you?'

'No—I suppose I'm quite pale, though, don't you think?'

Since Tsuda was rather concerned about himself, he could not help asking that in return.

The fact that the incision had been stuffed with as much gauze as possible made him far more uncomfortable than anyone could imagine. He was forced to walk very slowly. Nevertheless, as he climbed the stairs, he felt his rent flesh and the gauze rubbing together.

O-Nobu was standing at the top of the stairs. When she saw him, she immediately called to him from above.

'Is it over? How are you feeling?'

He entered the room without giving a clear answer. There, as he had expected, were the quilts lined with the white sheeting, spread out and awaiting him. As soon as he had taken off his *haori*, he stretched out. O-Nobu, who had intended to help him on with the flannel-lined, grey silk dressing-gown, and had held up the collar with both hands, gave a strained laugh of disappointment, folded it again, and placed it at the foot of the bed.

'Shouldn't he take some medicine?' She turned and asked the nurse, who was near by.

'It's perfectly all right if he doesn't take any internal medicine. I'm just now preparing his meal, and I'll bring it up right away.'

The nurse began to leave. Tsuda, who had lain down without saying anything, suddenly spoke :

'O-Nobu, if you're going to eat something, you should ask the nurse about it.'

'I suppose so.'

O-Nobu hesitated.

'I wonder what I should do.'

'After all, it's past noon, isn't it?'

'Yes, it's twelve-twenty. Your operation took exactly twenty-eight minutes.'

O-Nobu opened the lid of her watch, and told him the precise time. While Tsuda, like a fish on a chopping board, had been patiently enduring the operation on the operating table, O-Nobu, on her part, above the very ceiling at which he had had to gaze fixedly, had been measuring the time as if she had been having a staring contest with her watch.

He again asked her a question.

'There's no point in going home now, is there?'

'I suppose not.'

'Well then, why don't you have a Western-style meal here?'

'Well, I suppose I should but. . . .'

Her answers continued to be very unclear. The nurse finally went downstairs. Tsuda closed his eyes, as does a tired person trying to avoid the glare of the light. When O-Nobu spoke to him as she bent over his head, he was forced to open his eyes again.

'Are you feeling bad?'

'No, I'm all right.'

O-Nobu had just wanted to make sure, and quickly added :

'The Okamotos send their regards. They say they'll come to see you soon.'

'Really?'

Tsuda gave just a casual answer, and then tried to close his eyes again. O-Nobu, however, would not let him.

'By the way, about the Okamotos . . . they insist that I absolutely must go with them to the theatre today. But of course you say I shouldn't.'

All at once her entire behaviour since that morning flashed through his keen mind. Her dress, too flamboyant for accompanying him to the hospital, her special mention, before leaving the house, that it was Sunday, and, after arriving at the clinic, her nervous attitude in telephoning the Okamotos—everything could be explained by the one word 'theatre'. Viewing the matter in that way, he felt that even her motive in measuring precisely the time of his operation became open to question. He looked aside, without saying anything. In the raised alcove, such things as envelopes, writing-paper, scissors, and books, all piled up together, caught his eye. They were the things he had earlier packed in the suitcase and brought there.

'I thought I'd ask the nurse for a small desk and place them on it, but she still hasn't brought it, so I put them there that way for the time being. Why don't you look at a book?'

O-Nobu immediately stood up and took one down.

44

He did not touch the book.

'You told the Okamotos you couldn't go, didn't you?'

When, with an expression of displeasure rather than distrust, he rolled over on his side, the upstairs floor, which was not too sturdily constructed, groaned heavily, as if to complement his feelings.

'Yes I did.'

'Do you mean to say they insisted you go even though you said you couldn't?'

He then looked at her for the first time. But nothing he had anticipated was expressed there. Instead, she smiled.

'Yes, they did insist that I go even though I said I couldn't.'

'But. . . .'

He was at a slight impasse. Although he still had something to say, his mind did not operate as rapidly as he could have wished.

'But—if you said you couldn't, how could they possibly have insisted that you should?'

'But I tell you they did. The Okamotos are very obstinate.'

He fell silent. He had no idea how to pursue the conversation.

'Somehow or other you still doubt me, don't you? Well, I don't at all like being suspected by you in that way!'

She twitched her eyebrows, greatly displeased.

'I'm not doubting you. It's just that it's rather odd, that's all.'

'All right then, tell me what you think is so odd. I'll explain anything you want me to.'

Unfortunately he could not say very clearly what he thought was so odd.

'You see, you do suspect me after all, don't you?'

He had the feeling that if he did not distinctly say he did not suspect her it would somehow affect his standing as a husband. Nevertheless, he also felt no inconsiderable annoyance at being thought too indulgent by a woman. But even while both desires competed with each other for mastery of his mind, he would have seemed relatively calm to an impartial observer.

'A-ah.'

O-Nobu let out a faint sigh and stood up quietly. She opened again the sliding-door, which had been shut, and went out on the veranda, which faced south; she placed her hand on the railing and looked abstractedly at the high, clear, autumn sky. The shirts and sheets, hung without interval on the clothes driers of the neighbouring laundry, were, as she had seen them earlier, blowing in the dry wind as they absorbed the strong sunlight.

'My, but it's fine weather.'

When he heard her say this in a low voice as if to herself, he suddenly felt as if he had heard the pleading cry of a small caged bird. He felt rather sorry that he was tying a weak woman to himself. He wanted to speak to her, but he found it very difficult to find something to say. She still leaned against the railing, and did not return to the centre of the room right away.

At that point the nurse came up from downstairs, carrying the meals for the two of them.

'I'm very sorry to have kept you waiting.'

On Tsuda's tray there were only two eggs, a small amount of soup, and some bread. It had been decided, without his knowledge, that the amount of bread too should be limited to a few ounces.

As Tsuda, still lying in bed on his stomach, munched his food, he found his opportunity, and spoke to her.

'Are you or aren't you going?'

She immediately rested the hand holding the fork.

'It's entirely up to you. If you say I should go, I shall, but if you say I shouldn't, I won't.'

'You're very obedient, aren't you?'

'I'm always obedient. . . . As for the Okamotos, they said that if, when I asked you, you said it was all right, they'd take me to the theatre. That is, of course, if your illness proved to be not too serious."

'But you were the one who telephoned them, weren't you?'

'Yes, that's right. I'd promised I would. Of course I'd already declined once, but they said that since, depending on your condition, I might be able to go, I was to let them know again by phone by noon of that day.'

'Did you get a letter to that effect from them?'

'Yes.'

She had not, however, shown the letter to him.

'Well, to come to the point, how do you feel about it? Do you or don't you want to go?'

'Well of course I want to go.'

'So you've finally confessed, have you? All right then, go ahead.'

The two finished their lunch at the same time as they finished their conversation.

45

When she finally saw her husband resting quietly after the operation and went downstairs by herself, O-Nobu was already very late for her appointment. She simply told the rickshaw-man the name of the theatre to indicate her destination, and immediately got into the vehicle. The rickshaw, which had been made to wait in front of the hospital, was the newest of the four or five at the corner rickshaw-stand.

Once the rubber wheels had left the lane, they ran only along the street with the streetcar tracks. The rickshaw-man's brisk trot, which had no particular meaning except that it seemed to indicate he was increasing his speed as he headed towards the business district of the city, communicated itself to her. As her body, on the full, thick seat, was rapidly bobbing up and down, in her mind too there arose a kind of soft, pleasant oscillation. It was the delightful feeling of going to her desired destination by relentlessly cutting across the active lives of the people milling around her.

In her rickshaw she did not have time to think about domestic matters. Since the mental image of Tsuda, whom she had just put to bed comfortably in the upstairs room of the hospital, gave her the guarantee that she could with impunity forget him for the rest of that day, she was not in the least troubled about her husband either. Only the future immediately awaiting her seemed to be keeping pace with her rickshaw. Since she had never really had any great taste for the theatre itself, she was more concerned about arriving there quickly than she was about being late for the performance. For in the same sense that it was really stimulating for her to be travelling in a new rickshaw, it was even more stimulating to arrive there.

The rickshaw stopped in front of a tea-house. She swiftly responded with 'The Okamotos,' to the greeting and question of the woman attendant, as her eyes were dazzled by the lanterns, the shop-curtains, and the red and white artificial flowers. When she got down from the rickshaw, she was immediately guided along a corridor from the tea-house to the theatre before she even had time to sort out these images of colour and shape, and she abruptly made her appearance within the theatre, which was like a sea, over the length and breadth of which had been woven patterns many times more intricate and many times richer than those of the scene outside. This was her feeling when the man from the tea-house opened the door from the corridor and said, 'This way,' and when she saw through the crack the scene far in front of her. Since she particularly liked going to such places, such a feeling was not especially strange and yet it was one which was eternally new for her. Therefore one could almost have said that it *was* an eternally strange feeling for her. She opened her eyes like a person who has come through the dark and suddenly entered the light. Moreover, since she occupied a corner of this atmosphere and had become a part of the large, moving, living pattern in front of her, her excited mind distinctly sensed that her every action was from then on being woven into it.

Mr Okamoto was not in his seat. Since there were only three people, Mrs Okamoto and her two daughters, there was quite enough space for O-Nobu to sit down. Nevertheless, the elder daughter, Tsugiko, concerned lest she block O-Nobu's view, turned around, and, leaning over obliquely, asked:

'Can you see? Shall I change places with you for a while?'

'No thank you. This is fine.'

O-Nobu shook her head in refusal.

Since the fourteen-year-old younger daughter, Yuriko, sitting immediately in front of O-Nobu, was left-handed, she was holding a pair of small, light, ivory opera glasses in her left hand, and with her left elbow still placed on the red, cloth-covered railing, turned around.

'You're late, aren't you? I thought maybe you'd gone home.'

Since she was still quite young she did not yet possess the social grace to make some polite comment to O-Nobu about Tsuda's illness.

'Did you have something you had to do?'

'Yes.'

O-Nobu gave only a simple answer, and looked at the stage. This was the direction in which the mother of the two sisters had been staring earnestly for quite some time, without even looking to the side. When she and O-Nobu first saw each other, they merely exchanged polite nods, and did not say a word to each other until the wooden clappers sounded.

46

'I'm so very glad you could come. I was just speaking with Tsugi here about how it might be rather difficult for you to come today.'

After the curtain had been drawn, Mrs Okamoto for the first time was able to relax, and she finally began to speak to O-Nobu.

'See, didn't I tell you? Isn't it just as I said?'

Tsugiko looked at her mother as she said this triumphantly, and then immediately turned to O-Nobu to add further:

'I made a bet with Mother. As to whether you'd come today or not. Since Mother said you might not and I knew you certainly would, I took her up on it.'

'Oh, did you really? Are you reading oracles to predict the future again?'

Tsugiko owned a small oracle box, two and a half inches in length and a half-inch in width. On the black-painted lid of the box were written in gold the ancient seal-style characters meaning 'sacred oracle', and within it were exactly one hundred numbered tallies, exquisitely made of planed strips of ivory. She would often say, 'Shall I look at one for you?' and as if she were handling a small toothpick-case she would draw out a long thin ivory tally, and then open up and examine a folding copybook of sayings, of the same size as the box. Moreover, to read the characters written there, as minute as a fly's head, she would take out of a printed cotton bag lined with *habutae* silk the small magnifying glass which was attached as an accessory to the box, and would pore over the book self-importantly. When O-Nobu had gone on a trip to Asakusa with Tsuda they had bought this elaborate gift in one of the arcaded street shops, paying for it the too high price of almost four yen, but for Tsugiko, who the following year would be twenty, it was an innocent adornment which dramatically added a dash of mystery to her girlish imagination. Occasionally she would even take it from her desk while it was still in its case, insert it in her obi, and go out with it.

'Did you bring it today too?' O-Nobu jokingly asked her.

Tsugiko smiled wryly, and shook her head. Her mother, near her, spoke as if she were answering for her.

'Today's prediction has nothing to do with the oracle box. It's much greater than any oracle.'

'Is that so?'

O-Nobu wanted to hear more, and looked from mother to daughter.

When Mrs Okamoto began with 'Well actually, Tsugi. . . .' her daughter instantly and emphatically stopped her.

'Please stop, Mother! It's wrong to say that sort of thing here.'

Yuriko, the younger daughter, who until then had been listening silently to the conversation of the three women, began to giggle.

'I can tell you what it is.'

'Stop it, Yuriko. Don't be so mean. All right then, if you do, I won't go over your piano lessons with you any more.'

Their mother laughed softly so as not to attract the attention of people near by. O-Nobu also thought it amusing but she still wanted to find out the reason for the quarrel.

'Please tell me. It doesn't matter if Tsugiko gets angry at you. I'll stick by you, so it's all right.'

Yuriko looked at her sister, and purposely jutted out her chin. This action, together with her crinkling up her nose somewhat, was intended to impress her opponent with her having gained the right to talk or not.

'All right, Yuriko. Go ahead and do as you like.'

As soon as Tsugiko said this, she rose, opened the door in the rear, and went out into the corridor.

'Tsugiko's angry, isn't she?' said Yuriko.

'She's not angry. She's embarrassed.'

'But it isn't something to be embarrassed about, is it? Just to have said that sort of thing.'

'That's why you should tell me.'

O-Nobu had observed the childish psychological state of Yuriko, who was about six years younger than her sister, and had tried to exploit it skilfully. But since Tsugiko, in unexpectedly leaving her seat, had already upset Yuriko, O-Nobu's persuasion had no effect. The mother of the two girls finally had to shoulder the responsibility for everything herself.

'Oh, it's really nothing at all. It's just that Tsugi said she was certain you were coming today because she thinks Yoshio's that sort of tender and considerate person and does everything you want him to.'

'Really? Tsugiko thinks Yoshio's *that* considerate a husband, does she? I'm very glad to hear that. I'll have to thank her for saying it.'

'And then Yuriko said that if that's the case, Tsugi should also marry a man like Yoshio. And since Tsugi was embarrassed at having that said in front of you, she acted the way she did, and ran off.'

'My, my!'

O-Nobu uttered that weak exclamation rather sadly.

47

It suddenly occurred to O-Nobu that Tsuda was extremely egotistical. She normally harboured the suspicion that although she earnestly and with the best intentions showed him every kindness there seemed to be no limit to the sacrifices he demanded of her, but such a suspicion came to her mind abruptly then in deeper hue. With the realization that the sole person who could clear up the matter for her was then right in front of her, she looked at Mrs Okamoto. O-Nobu, whose parents lived in distant Kyoto, had only this one aunt to rely upon in all of Tokyo.

'I wonder whether a husband's merely a kind of sponge existing only to soak up affection from his wife.'

This was the problem which O-Nobu wished to discuss with her aunt. But unfortunately she had a kind of innate pride. And it was this pride, which, according to the way one looked at it, could be interpreted as either a strained endurance or a kind of conceit, which strongly checked her in approaching her aunt on this one point. In a certain sense, when she and Tsuda privately viewed their relationship, very similar to that between *sumō* wrestlers facing each other in the ring every day, they felt that it was of a kind where she was always his opponent and occasionally even his enemy; and yet once they faced the world outside, O-Nobu felt that unless she thoroughly supported him she would be openly exposing the weakness of two people bound together as husband and wife, and she could not but be ashamed of such an exposure. Therefore, even when she felt she simply had to speak to someone or complain about something, upon meeting her aunt, whom she had after all to include in that category of other people termed 'the world', this sensitive O-Nobu could not say anything, for fear it would be considered rather scandalous.

In addition, she had always been apprehensive lest the fact that her husband did not return her kindness as she had anticipated he would, be interpreted by others as a result of her own ineptness. Among all possible criticisms, the one she recoiled from most instinctively, as she might from fire, was that of being called stupid.

'There are a lot of young women who can easily turn around their little fingers even men who are much more difficult than Tsuda, so the fact that you can't manipulate him as you wish, even though you're already twenty-two, must really mean you're not intelligent enough to do it.'

For O-Nobu, who considered intelligence and virtue practically synonymous, to be spoken to by her aunt in this way would have been the most painful thing imaginable. To confess that, as a woman, she had no skill in handling a man would have wounded her self-respect, and she considered it an indignity tantamount to confessing that she was worthless as a human being. Thus, even if she had not been at the theatre, where both the time and the circumstances did not allow such a personal conversation, she still would have had to remain silent. She did look significantly at her aunt for a moment, but she then quickly turned away.

The curtain, which hung over the entire stage, billowed a bit, and from a slightly torn place in a seam someone looked out at the spectators. Since O-Nobu somehow felt that that person was looking at her, she turned her eyes in yet another direction. Below, a general stir had suddenly begun, with some people leaving their seats, others returning to them, and still others just walking about. Even the great majority of them, who remained seated, changed their positions by leaning forwards or backwards, or to the right or left, as they wished, and did not sit still even for a moment. The numberless black heads seemed like a whirlpool. The movement of the brilliant attire of certain of the spectators intermittently gave her a pleasant, though nervous, sensation.

When she looked away from the pit of the theatre, she casually began to examine the opposite side, separated from her as if by a valley. Yuriko, who had just then turned around, suddenly spoke to her.

'Mrs Yoshikawa's over there. You've seen her, haven't you?'

O-Nobu, slightly startled, looked in the direction Yuriko had indicated, and easily discovered a woman resembling Mrs Yoshikawa.

'You have very keen eyes, Yuriko, don't you? When did you discover her?'

'I didn't discover her. I knew all along she was there.'

'Did your mother and Tsugiko know too?'

'Yes, everybody knew.'

O-Nobu finally realized she was the only one who did not, and as she was still staring that way from behind Yuriko, she suddenly saw that the opera glasses which Mrs Yoshikawa held were directed at her own seat.

'I don't like that at all—to be looked at in that way.'

O-Nobu shrank back as if to hide. Nevertheless the opera glasses from across the theatre continued to be aimed at her.

'All right then, if that's the case, there's nothing to do but escape.'

O-Nobu immediately went out into the corridor to look for Tsugiko.

48

The scene outside, which O-Nobu surveyed, was also very lively, as one would have expected of such a place. People she did not know were ceaselessly coming and going on the removable openwork board flooring, which had been placed over the real floor. Standing in a corner of the corridor, she half leaned against a pillar. It took her quite some time before she found Tsugiko, but when she recognized her standing in front of one of the stalls lined up on the opposite side of the theatre, she quickly went down the stairs. Walking lightly on the board flooring, she then crossed over towards her destination.

'What are you buying?'

O-Nobu asked this while peering from behind, and when Tsugiko turned around in surprise, they practically touched each other, and smiled.

'I'm having some trouble right now. Hajime said I have to buy him some souvenir, so I've been looking for one, but unfortunately there isn't anything at all—at least nothing that would make *him* happy.'

Tsugiko, who had made a mistake in trying to buy a toy for a boy, was really quite perplexed, as she had one item after another lined up for her without being able either to buy or to give up the idea completely. She stood hesitantly in front of floral hairpins with designs of crests connected with famous actors, wallets, and hand towels, and turned to O-Nobu with an appealing glance, as much as to ask her what she ought to do. O-Nobu immediately scolded her.

'Those won't do at all! If it's not a pistol, or a wooden sword, or something he can pretend he's murdering someone with, he won't like it. And that sort of thing can't be found in a stylish place like this.'

The man at the stall began to laugh. O-Nobu took Tsugiko by the hand.

'At any rate, why don't you buy it after speaking to your mother? . . . We're very sorry. We'll be back later perhaps.'

With that she began to walk away briskly, almost dragging Tsugiko along with her as far as the end of the corridor, since Tsugiko still seemed a bit reluctant to leave the stall. There they stood and talked again, with one of the eaves pillars as a shield.

'What happened to your father? Why isn't he here today?'

'Oh, he will be. And very soon too.'

O-Nobu was surprised. If such a large man was going to be added in a place already crowded with four women, it must surely be an important event.

'If your father comes too, a tiny person like me will be crushed to death.'

'You can change places with Yuriko.'

'Why?'

'Well, it would be much more convenient that way. And after all, it doesn't matter whether Yuriko's there or not.'

'I see. Well suppose Yoshio weren't ill, and had come with me, what would you have done then?'

'We'd probably have thought of something if the situation had arisen. Either we'd have taken another box, or else we'd have gone in with the Yoshikawas.'

'Did you make arrangements with them earlier?'

'Yes.'

Tsugiko did not say anything further. O-Nobu, who did not think that the Okamoto and Yoshikawa families were that close, looked somewhat incredulous and wondered whether there might be some special significance to the occasion, but since there was ample reason for viewing it as merely one of those social engagements that might easily arise among people of leisure, she did not ask any further questions. Their conversation merely touched on Mrs Yoshikawa's opera glasses. O-Nobu purposely even went so far as to imitate her.

'She had them pointed *this* way directly at me. Can you imagine such a thing?'

'That was quite brazen of her, I suppose. But that's the Western-style way, Father says.'

'You mean to say in Europe or America it doesn't matter if you do that? Then it's all right for me to stare at her that way too, I suppose. I wonder whether I should try it.'

'Go right ahead. She'd probably like it, and say you're very smart and stylish.'

As the two young women were laughing together, a young man came from somewhere, and stood near them a moment. As soon as this young gentleman, who had a two-coloured crest on his single-coloured *haori* and was wearing an undivided serge *hakama*, saw them, he silently made a polite gesture as if to say 'Pardon me' in passing, moved along the board flooring, and crossed over to the other side. Tsugiko blushed.

'Let's go back in now.'

She quickly urged O-Nobu to go with her, and they went back in.

49

The atmosphere within the theatre had not changed at all from when they had been there earlier. O-Nobu and Tsugiko observed the forms of the men and women walking in the pit of the theatre confusedly, very much as if they were crossing over their heads. Everywhere people were gesturing exaggeratedly, as they tried to attract as much attention as possible. These gestures then suddenly disappeared as, in the next instant, they gave way to other colourful movements. This small world was merely one of agitation in the eyes of O-Nobu and Tsugiko; it was disorderly but it was always brilliant.

From behind the relatively quiet stage the sound of the hammers being used by the scene-shifters resounded from time to time within the theatre so as to arouse the general expectation. At odd moments the sound of the wooden clappers being struck behind the curtain could be heard as if it were a kind of alarm to focus the scattered attention at one point.

The spectators were indeed strange, for they did not in the least complain about the long intermission during which there was nothing at all to do. Without showing a trace of their previous boredom, they were tranquilly absorbing desultory sensations in their vacant minds, and were being swept along frivolously with the passing moment. They appeared drunk from the very breath which they breathed on one another, and when they had recovered a bit from it, they would immediately turn their eyes and observe someone's face; they then would just as quickly discover therein a certain intoxicating substance. They appeared to be able to acclimatize themselves instantly to their companions' feelings.

The two young women returned to their seats and surveyed their surroundings happily. They then looked in the direction of Mrs Yoshikawa, about whom they had just been gossiping, as if they had agreed upon it. But the lady's opera glasses were no longer aimed at them. Instead, the owner of those opera glasses had gone off somewhere.

'Oh my, she isn't there.'

'Yes, you're right.'

'Do you want me to find her for you?'

Yuriko immediately put her own opera glasses, which she had in her hand, to her eyes.

'She's not there, she's not there. She's gone off somewhere. Since she's as fat as two women I'd find her right away, but, you're right, she's not there.'

Yuriko put down the ivory glasses as she spoke. Since, even though she was dressed as a young lady with a high obi which almost hid the pretty printed silk pattern on her back, she had spoken in a most informal and even slightly ill-bred manner, her elder sister, displaying a dignity befitting her greater age, yet attempting to suppress a smile, scolded her.

'Yuriko!'

Yuriko did not seem the least affected by the rebuke. As usual she crinkled up her nose a little, and looked pointedly at Tsugiko, as if to say that she had said nothing amiss.

'I want to go home already. I hope Father comes soon.'

'If you want to, go right ahead. It doesn't matter if Father's not here yet.'

'I've changed my mind—I think I'll stay.'

Yuriko therefore did not move. As if by contrast to this rather petulant performance, which only a child could have given, O-Nobu turned to her aunt and showed a discretion appropriate to her age.

'Shall I just go over and say hello to Mrs Yoshikawa? It seems wrong to sit here without saying anything.'

She actually did not like Mrs Yoshikawa very much. She also thought Mrs Yoshikawa disliked her too. Moreover she vaguely sensed that this unhappy relationship had arisen between them because Mrs Yoshikawa had disliked her from the outset. She was also quite confident that Mrs Yoshikawa had begun to dislike her without O-Nobu's having given her any cause. When the opera glasses had been directed at her earlier, she had already realized that she should go and exchange greetings with her, but she could not summon up the courage to do it right away; thus, as she was expressing her secret uneasiness in the form of a question to her aunt, she inwardly was hoping to perform that duty easily by having her aunt accompany her.

Her aunt immediately answered.

'Ah, that would be fine. Go right ahead.'

L.A.D.—D

'But she's not there right now.'

'Oh, she's undoubtedly just stepped out into the corridor. If you go there you'll find out where she's gone.'

'But—well, I will go, but won't you please come with me?'

'You want me?'

'You mean you won't come?'

'Well, I suppose I could. After all it will soon be time to eat, and since we're supposed to eat together I was thinking of going over there then anyway.'

'My, so you've made those arrangements, have you? I knew nothing at all about it. Who's going to be eating with whom?'

'Everybody will be eating together.'

'And I too?'

'Yes of course.'

O-Nobu was overwhelmed, and spoke again after a brief pause.

'If that's the case, I'll wait and speak to her then.'

50

Okamoto came shortly thereafter. After the man from the tea-house had opened the door to their box for him, Okamoto peered through the crack and called Yuriko out into the corridor. The two of them stood and spoke there in low voices so as not to disturb everybody, and after they had exchanged two or three words, Yuriko quickly left the theatre, as she had promised, accompanied by the tea-house man. Okamoto then entered the box in place of her, and seated himself uncomfortably. Since he was so stout it seemed troublesome for him even to change his position slightly in such a small place. After sitting down he turned halfway around, as if he had suddenly realized something.

'O-Nobu, shall I change with you? It must be annoying to have such a huge person blocking your view.'

O-Nobu, who had indeed felt as if a mountain had suddenly appeared in front of her, was concerned about the people around her, who were absorbed in what was happening on the stage, and did not move. Okamoto, who never wore the usual Japanese woollen underwear next to his skin, crossed his bare, hairy arms, and turned his gaze in the direction in which everyone was looking, as if to say that this is what is meant by social intercourse. On the stage a strange, pale-looking man was walking restlessly under some willows. Since this young gallant, who was fashionably though casually dressed in a rough, striped kimono and was purposely sporting a Hakata obi rather low on his waist, and was wearing leather-soled sandals without socks, every time he walked an unpleasant clattering sound assailed Okamoto's ears. This young man looked around at the bridge, near the willows, and at the whitewashed storehouses, lined up on the other side of the bridge, and in the process turned his gaze towards the spectators. As he did so the faces of the spectators became tense. As if there were some extraordinarily important meaning in the movements of this young man who came and went on the stage, clattering his sandals, the entire theatre was as still as death, and not a cough could be heard. Perhaps because for Okamoto, who had suddenly entered the theatre from outside, it was difficult to attune himself to this special atmosphere right away, or perhaps because he thought the scene foolish, after a while he again turned halfway around rather uncomfortably, and began to speak to O-Nobu in a low voice.

'How's it been? Has it been interesting? . . . And how's Yoshio?'

He asked her three or four simple questions one after another, and after hearing the answers one at a time, finally asked her another question, with a significant glance.

'How did it go today? Didn't Yoshio say something about your coming here? He probably complained, didn't he? He probably said something about how terribly outrageous it was for you to be going to the theatre while he's lying sick in bed. Didn't he? I'm sure he did.'

'No, he didn't say anything about its being terribly outrageous.'

'But he did say something, didn't he? At least something about my being rather demanding, I'm sure. Your manner on the phone was very strange.'

Since with no one else talking around them, even in a low voice, it seemed improper for her to give lengthy answers, she merely smiled.

'It really doesn't matter. I'll talk to you about it later, so try not to worry about it,' her uncle began again.

'But I tell you I'm not worrying.'

'Really? But I think you are a trifle upset. To have hurt your husband's feelings so soon after marriage.'

'It's all right. I tell you I didn't hurt his feelings at all.'

O-Nobu twitched her eyebrows in an annoyed way. Okamoto, who had been half teasing her, became rather serious.

'To tell the truth, the reason we asked you to come today was not only to see the play; it was quite necessary to have you. That's why we had to make you come even though Yoshio's ill. But I'll explain everything to him afterwards, so it doesn't matter. I assure you I'll explain everything to him carefully.'

O-Nobu's eyes suddenly turned from the stage.

'What are you talking about?'

'I can't tell you right now. I'll tell you afterwards.'

O-Nobu had to remain silent. But Okamoto added :

'Today we're going to have dinner with the Yoshikawas at the restaurant. Did you know that? Look, Yoshikawa's come in over there.'

O-Nobu suddenly saw the figure of Yoshikawa, which she had not noticed until then.

'He came with me. From the club.'

Their conversation was broken off at that point. O-Nobu again began to look earnestly at the stage. Before about ten minutes had passed, however, her attention was again disturbed by the man from the tea-house opening the door behind her quietly. The man whispered something to her aunt, who immediately leaned over towards her husband.

'Since the Yoshikawas say they've made the preparations for dinner, they want us to go to the restaurant during the next intermission.'

O-Nobu's uncle swiftly relayed his answer to the man.

'Tell them that's all right with us.'

The man quietly shut the door again, and went out. While O-Nobu wondered what was going to happen thereafter, she silently awaited the hour of the dinner engagement.

51

It was nearly one hour later that O-Nobu got up from her seat, followed her aunt and uncle, and together with Tsugiko walked towards the narrow restaurant in a corner of the second floor. She spoke softly to her cousin as they walked down the corridor shoulder to shoulder.

'What in the world's going to happen now?'

'I don't know.'

Tsugiko lowered her eyes as she answered.

'Are we just going to eat dinner?'

'I suppose so.'

Since O-Nobu felt that the more she asked the vaguer Tsugiko's answers became, she said nothing further. Perhaps Tsugiko was shy because her parents were in front of her, or perhaps she actually did not know anything. Or it was not impossible that even if she did know, she did not want to talk to her about it, and therefore purposely only gave brief answers in a low voice.

The crowd of people they met in the corridor, who liked to cast sharp glances on them as they passed, all looked more at Tsugiko than O-Nobu. All of a sudden the contrast between Tsugiko and herself flashed through O-Nobu's mind. Since even though she excelled Tsugiko in her dress she certainly had to take second place to Tsugiko's general appearance and facial features, she looked with slight jealousy at this cousin who seemed to be forever childishly shy and so naïvely constituted as not to have the slightest anxiety, and who glowed with a maiden freshness. Even though in O-Nobu's attitude there was a note of condescension towards Tsugiko for being so innocent, there was also a strong feeling of envy, such that she would have liked to exchange places with her. O-Nobu thought :

'I wonder if before I was married there was a time when I too had such a fresh, innocent attitude.'

Fortunately or unfortunately she could not recall such a time. Since she normally lived without constantly comparing herself with Tsugiko she had thought nothing of it, but now that she was rubbing shoulders with her and standing in a corridor brightly lit by glittering chandeliers, she was struck by a kind of sadness she had never felt before. It was a mild thing, yet of a kind that could easily turn into tears. It was also of a kind that made her want to grasp tightly the hand of the very person she had just been looking at enviously. In her heart she cried out to Tsugiko :

'You're much more innocent than I ever was. You're so innocent I envy you. And yet your innocence won't be of any use to you at all in your marriage. Even if, like me, you treat your husband perfectly, he certainly won't appreciate it as you think he should. And you'll soon have to lose that pureness of yours to preserve his love. But even if you do make such a sacrifice, and exert yourself for him, he may still treat you unkindly. I envy you, but I also feel sorry for you, because you now have, without realizing it, a precious gift you'll soon have to lose. Fortunately or unfortunately I've always been utterly lacking in those qualities you have, so I can truthfully say my loss wasn't so great. But you're different. As soon as you marry your innocence will be taken away from you. You're really more pathetic than I.'

The two young women were walking rather slowly. When they could not see Mr and Mrs Okamoto, who had gone ahead, because they were blocked by other people, O-Nobu's aunt purposely turned back.

'Hurry up. Why are you lagging behind so? The Yoshikawas have already gone on ahead and are waiting for us.'

Her aunt's glance was directed only at Tsugiko. Her remarks also were particularly directed towards her. But when O-Nobu heard the name Yoshikawa, it was like a wind suddenly blowing away the mood she had been in until then. She immediately recalled this Mrs Yoshikawa whom she did not like very much and who did not seem to like her very much either. O-Nobu would have to show as much charm and politeness as possible when she met the lady, who was an important man's wife, from whom her husband had always received exceptional favours. Since O-Nobu felt a certain tenseness in the midst of her calm, she assumed an impassive expression and followed everybody into the restaurant.

52

As her aunt had said, it seemed that Mr and Mrs Yoshikawa had arrived at the appointed place slightly ahead of them, and the lady who was O-Nobu's concern was standing facing the entrance, talking to her uncle. The first thing O-Nobu saw was her very large form which extended even beyond the large figure of her uncle, who had his back to O-Nobu. At the same time Mrs Yoshikawa too, whose fleshy cheeks were swollen with smiles, instantly turned her eyes on O-Nobu. But since the sudden electric spark she emitted from those eyes disappeared almost as soon as it was made, the two women finally did not take note of each other until they exchanged greetings formally.

As she cast that one glance at Mrs Yoshikawa, O-Nobu could not but see the young gentleman standing near her. Since he was undoubtedly the man who had, without speaking, surprised her when she had been with Tsugiko in the corridor earlier and they had been half-jokingly criticizing, but in a rather ill-mannered way, Mrs Yoshikawa's opera glasses, O-Nobu could not help shuddering slightly.

As simple greetings were being exchanged by everyone, O-Nobu was standing modestly behind the group, and when it shortly became her turn, this unknown man was introduced to her merely as Miyoshi. The one who introduced him to her was Mrs Yoshikawa, but since her words were precisely the same as those she had used towards O-Nobu's uncle, her aunt, and Tsugiko, O-Nobu still did not learn who Miyoshi was.

When they took their seats, Mrs Yoshikawa sat next to O-Nobu's uncle. Miyoshi was made to sit on the other side of him. O-Nobu's aunt's seat was at a corner of the dining-table. Tsugiko's was in front of Miyoshi. O-Nobu, who was thus forced to sit down in the one remaining seat, was slightly hesitant. Next to her was Mr Yoshikawa. But in front of her was his wife.

'Please sit down.'

Mr Yoshikawa looked up at O-Nobu from the side as if to urge her.

'Yes, please do,' said Mrs Yoshikawa lightly as she looked at her directly.

'Please sit down, and don't be so reserved. Everybody's already seated.'

O-Nobu was forced to take her seat in front of Mrs Yoshikawa. She immediately decided that she would have to behave so as to have her attitude interpreted as true reserve resulting from politeness. When she observed, further down the table, Tsugiko's innocent manner, diametrically different from her own, she was strengthened in her decision.

Tsugiko was even more submissive than usual. As she spoke little and kept her eyes lowered at her place, a certain element almost akin to pain could be perceived in her behaviour. After O-Nobu had given her a glance which seemed to express pity, she rapidly turned her eyes, which possessed a charm peculiar to her, towards Mrs Yoshikawa, who was in front of her. Mrs Yoshikawa too, thoroughly familiar with social intercourse, was not one to remain silent. O-Nobu and Mrs Yoshikawa exchanged a few words of polite conversation. But since the subject was one that could not develop further, it stopped abruptly at that point. O-Nobu thought that she might make Tsuda, who was of interest to both, the subject of the conversation, but while she was still hesitating to mention him, Mrs Yoshikawa had already left her to turn to Miyoshi, who was farther away.

'Speak up, Miyoshi. Tell Tsugiko some interesting story about your stay abroad.'

Miyoshi had just finished saying something to Mrs Okamoto, and turned to speak softly to Mrs Yoshikawa.

'All right, I'll tell her anything she wants to hear.'

'Good. Tell her anything. You mustn't keep quiet.'

These peremptory words made everybody laugh.

'Why don't you tell us again the story about escaping from Germany?' Yoshikawa immediately made his wife's command concrete.

'But I've repeated that story so many times. Now it's even more boring to me than it must be to others.'

'We'd still like to hear it again. I suppose even a rather calm person like you must have been a bit excited.'

'A bit of excitement wouldn't have been too bad, but I was almost out of my mind with fright. Actually I don't clearly remember everything.'

'But I don't suppose you thought they'd kill you, did you?'

'Well, I didn't really know.'

While Miyoshi was recalling the episode, Yoshikawa quickly spoke again, from his seat right next to O-Nobu.

'I'm sure he didn't think he'd be killed—particularly this fellow.'

'Why? Because I'm too mean to die?'

'Not exactly. But because you want so much to live.'

Tsugiko giggled, while still looking down. O-Nobu had learned only that Miyoshi had had to leave Germany about the time the war had begun.

53

The talk about foreign travel, centring around Miyoshi, became rather lively for a time. O-Nobu, silently observing the skill of Mrs Yoshikawa, who at intervals would insert adroit phrases to draw out the conversation further, perceived with what efforts she was attempting to push forward this unknown young gentleman in front of the four of them. This young man, who was simply not talkative rather than quiet, did not realize this himself, and while he was being cajoled by Mrs Yoshikawa, he was in effect being presented by her to all of them in the most flattering perspective.

In the course of this conversation O-Nobu was hardly given the opportunity to insert a word. Since she was thus forced to become a silent and attentive listener, her critical faculty was free to operate most efficiently. As she observed step by step Mrs Yoshikawa's technique, which yet in no way seemed to be technique, and which contained many elements of frankness and even bluntness, and as she saw how it succeeded steadily, she could not but recognize the extraordinary distance separating her own disposition from that of Mrs Yoshikawa. Yet she felt that this was not a vertical but a horizontal distance. Nevertheless it would certainly not have been true to say that therefore it was not enough to inspire fear in her. Somewhere in O-Nobu's heart she had a sense of danger, for she felt that, in addition to Mrs Yoshikawa's peremptory attitude, which seemed to arise from her special position at that time, there might emerge from her a fearful destructive force.

'But maybe I'm simply imagining it all.'

As O-Nobu was thinking in this way, the very person about whom she was thinking turned her attention to her.

'You're probably amazed, aren't you, Nobuko, that I talk so much?'

O-Nobu drew back, surprised. Although in Tsuda's presence she previously had never been at a loss for words, she suddenly did not know how to behave. Only a faint, hollow smile filled the void of the moment. But it was nothing more than a false charm serving no purpose at all.

When O-Nobu later added, 'No, I was listening with great interest,' even she herself realized that her comment had been made too late. Moreover, the rather bitter feeling that she had bungled welled up in her. Her eagerness to ingratiate herself with Mrs Yoshikawa on that occasion was suddenly paralyzed. Mrs Yoshikawa then changed her tone so quickly as to seem cruel, immediately turning to Okamoto.

'It's been a long time since you returned from abroad, hasn't it, Mr Okamoto?'

'Yes, it certainly was a long, long time ago.'

'But exactly how long ago was it? About what year?'

'Let's see, it was about. . . .'

'The time of the Franco-Prussian War?'

'Don't be ridiculous. I'm not *that* old. After all, I remember acting as a guide for your husband around London.'

'Then you weren't caught in the siege of Paris, were you?'

'Stop your nonsense.'

Mrs Yoshikawa, who had thus halted for a time the talk about Miyoshi's trip abroad, swiftly turned the topic in another direction, but one having a close connection with the previous one. And naturally Yoshikawa was forced to become Okamoto's partner in the conversation.

'At any rate, it was at the time automobiles were still very new, and when they passed, everyone turned his head to look.'

'Yes, it was when those terribly slow old buses were still the only real way of getting around.'

Despite the fact that for the others, who had no memory of those slow buses as a means of transportation, the reference meant absolutely nothing, as the two men recalled those times, they too seemed to feel a certain gentle nostalgia. Okamoto turned from Tsugiko to Miyoshi, and then, smiling wryly, said to Yoshikawa :

'We're both getting old, aren't we? Even though I usually don't notice it, and think I'm still rather young, as I forever run around keeping busy, when I sit down near my daughter Tsugiko this way, I'm afraid I have to reconsider.'

'In that case you should always be sitting near her.'

Mrs Okamoto quickly turned towards her husband in this way. The latter immediately responded :

'You're quite right. Now when I came back from my trip abroad, she was still. . . .' he began to say, and then after thinking a bit, added, 'Just how old was she?' Since his wife remained silent, with an expression that seemed to indicate that she was not required to answer such an easy-going, forgetful person, Yoshikawa began to speak again.

'Now I'm afraid the time has almost come when you're going to be called Grandpa. You'd better be prepared.'

Tsugiko blushed and looked down. Mrs Yoshikawa quickly looked at her husband.

'Mr Okamoto's better off since he has a living clock to tell his age. But as for you, since you don't have any such device to make you reflect a bit, you're simply too much to handle.'

'Now of course we all know that *you* are forever young, don't we?'

Everybody laughed heartily at that.

54

The other groups of customers, not so numerous and consequently relatively quiet, would look from time to time at O-Nobu's group, which seemed to be engaged only in pleasant conversation, very much as if it were on another stage in the same theatre. Even though the time came when the others, who had purposely taken a light meal to save time, were gradually beginning to leave without even drinking their coffee, new dishes were still being placed, one after another, in front of O-Nobu and her group. They could not simply throw down their napkins half-way. Nor did they seem particularly to want to behave in such a restless way. They all seemed to have the leisurely attitude of having come to relax at the playhouse rather than having come to see a play.

'Has it begun again already?'

O-Nobu's uncle looked around at the restaurant, which had suddenly become quiet, and asked this question of the white-uniformed waiter. As the waiter placed a hot dish in front of him, he answered politely :

'It's begun just now.'

'Even so, I don't care. On an occasion like this our mouths are more important than our eyes.'

He immediately began to attack a chicken leg still in its skin. Yoshikawa, opposite him, also seemed quite indifferent to what might be happening on the stage. He immediately followed Okamoto's example, and also talked about something completely unrelated to the theatre, food.

'You still seem to enjoy your food, don't you? . . . Mrs Okamoto, have you heard the story about your husband riding pickaback on a foreigner's shoulders? And he was eating more and much fatter than he is now, too.'

Mrs Okamoto had not heard it. Yoshikawa then asked the same question of Tsugiko. She too had not heard it.

'Is that so? Well, I'm sure he's keeping it secret because after all it isn't very edifying.'

'What isn't?'

Okamoto finally took his eyes from his plate, and looked at Yoshikawa strangely. Mrs Yoshikawa then spoke.

'You probably were too heavy and crushed the poor foreigner.'

'If that had happened he'd have been proud of it, but instead he merely hung on to this large man's shoulders, in the middle of a London crowd, while everyone was staring at him amazed. He did it to see the procession.'

Okamoto still did not laugh.

'What story are you cooking up? When in the world is this supposed to have happened?'

'At the time of the coronation of Edward VII. You were standing in front of the Mansion House trying to see the procession. But, unlike us, people over there are all much taller than you, so out of desperation you asked the owner of the boarding-house who'd gone with you if you could get on his shoulders.'

'Don't tell such silly stories. It was somebody else. I know perfectly well the fellow who did that. It was that Monkey-face.'

Okamoto's explanation was given rather seriously, but when the word 'Monkey-face' suddenly emerged in the midst of his serious account, they all laughed.

'Of course if it was Monkey-face, then he fits the story very well. I did think that no matter how large Englishmen are supposed to be, if it was you he had on his shoulders, it still seemed impossible. . . . And Monkey-face was rather a dwarf too, wasn't he?'

Whether Yoshikawa had known all along and had merely pretended to make a mistake in the person, or whether he had not really known the true facts of the case, when he spoke as if he had finally understood, he still repeated the nickname 'Monkey-face' so as to cause a ripple of laughter throughout the group. Mrs Yoshikawa took a half-curious, half-reprimanding attitude.

'But who in the world *is* this Monkey-face you're talking about?'

'Oh, he's someone you don't know.'

'Don't worry, Mrs Yoshikawa. Even if Monkey-face were seated right here, he's the sort of person we don't have to be afraid of calling Monkey-face to his face. And it doesn't matter either when he calls me Pig-face, as he often does.'

While this rather absurd conversation was being exchanged, O-Nobu was quite unable to do her share as a member of that social group. The opportunity to force herself on Mrs Yoshikawa never seemed to come. Mrs Yoshikawa paid no attention to her. Or rather she avoided her. Then she began talking particularly to Tsugiko, who was one seat over from O-Nobu on the same side of the table. Even if O-Nobu's cousin was the centre of attention for only a minute, it was abundantly clear that Mrs Yoshikawa was trying to draw her out in front of everyone. Every time Tsugiko, who did not know how to take advantage of this opportunity, unreservedly expressed annoyance rather than gratitude, O-Nobu would immediately compare her with herself, and feel waves of envy.

'If only I were in her position. . . .'

She often felt that way in the course of the dinner engagement. And she would then secretly pity her unsophisticated cousin. Finally there arose also a feeling of disdain at Tsugiko's pathetic state.

55

They got up from their seats about the time nearly one inch of white ash had collected on the after-dinner cigars the men had begun to smoke. The fact that someone then said, 'I wonder what time it is,' accidentally caused a change in O-Nobu's position. For Mrs Yoshikawa seized the moment before they got up to begin speaking to her suddenly.

'How's your husband making out, Nobuko?'

She said this abruptly, and, without waiting for O-Nobu's answer, immediately added herself :

'I've been intending to ask you this all along, but somehow I spoke only about things that concerned me—'

O-Nobu secretly considered this excuse a lie. This was not a suspicion caused by Mrs Yoshikawa's manner of speaking or her attitude at that time but rather a hypothesis with a somewhat more profound basis. O-Nobu remembered very well the words she had used when she had greeted Mrs Yoshikawa upon entering the restaurant. She had spoken on behalf of Tsuda rather than herself. As soon as she had seen Mrs Yoshikawa, she had bowed respectfully, and had said, 'Thank you for your many kindnesses to my husband.' But Mrs Yoshikawa at that time had not said a word about Tsuda. Despite the fact that O-Nobu was the last member of the group with whom she had exchanged greetings, and she therefore had not had so much time to speak, she had turned away immediately. Moreover, she appeared to have forgotten completely about the visit she had had from Tsuda a few days earlier.

O-Nobu did not interpret this behaviour of Mrs Yoshikawa as resulting solely from Mrs Yoshikawa's dislike of her. She thought there was still another reason. If there had not been, she thought that even Mrs Yoshikawa would not have assumed an air of particularly avoiding Tsuda's name in front of his wife. O-Nobu knew very well that Mrs Yoshikawa was quite fond of Tsuda. But why, simply because she was partial to him, should she hesitate to make him the subject of conversation with his wife? O-Nobu did not understand the reason. Even though she had attempted in the course of the dinner to start a conversation with her about Tsuda, who could be considered the only point in common between them, so as to display before her her own charming womanly personality, which had always been appreciated by others, she had failed completely; for this attempt had been obstructed from the outset by Mrs Yoshikawa's cold response. When the time finally came for them to leave their seats, and Mrs Yoshikawa began talking to her again, O-Nobu was not satisfied with simply suspecting that Mrs Yoshikawa's explanations were lies. She wondered whether Mrs Yoshikawa, who at that late hour began to ask about Tsuda's illness, might not be thinking of something other than the inevitable social formalities.

'He's doing very well, thank you.'

'Has he had the operation already?'

'Yes, today.'

'Today? And even so you were able to come here?'

'It isn't such a very serious illness.'

'But I suppose he is in bed, isn't he?'

'Yes, he's in bed.'

Mrs Yoshikawa then showed by her manner that she wished to ask O-Nobu why she was not more concerned about her husband. At least her silence seemed to indicate this to O-Nobu. O-Nobu thought that Mrs Yoshikawa, who behaved in an unreserved and rather masculine way towards others, was an entirely different person with her.

'Is he in a hospital?'

'It's not really worthy of being called that. Since the upstairs room of the doctor's office happened to be empty, he's being allowed to stay there for five or six days.'

Mrs Yoshikawa asked the name and address of the doctor. Even though she said nothing at all about intending to visit him, O-Nobu wondered whether she had not actually brought up Tsuda's name on purpose for this reason, and for the first time she felt that she had been able to understand somewhat what Mrs Yoshikawa meant.

Yoshikawa, who, unlike his wife, had seemed from the beginning not to be thinking too much about Tsuda, then spoke about him for the first time.

'When I spoke to Tsuda himself, he said this illness of his was a continuation of one from last year. It's really unfortunate that he has to be sick so often while he's still so young. But he doesn't have to limit his stay in the hospital to only five or six days. Please tell him to take care of himself until he's completely recovered.'

O-Nobu thanked him.

The seven of them left the restaurant, and separated again into two groups in the corridor.

56

O-Nobu spent the remainder of the time with her aunt's family, and there were no disturbances at all. The image of Tsuda, lying in his nightclothes and wearing the dressing-gown she had made for him, suddenly appeared in her mind, however, as she was staring intently at the stage. This image seemed to put face down the book it had been reading until then, and to observe her sitting there, from a distance. But as soon as she tried to return its look pleasantly, it reprimanded her with a glance which meant : 'No, you mustn't misunderstand me. I just came for a moment to see what you were doing. It isn't that I really have anything to say to you.' O-Nobu was deceived, and felt rather foolish; whereupon Tsuda's image immediately disappeared, like a ghost. The second time it came, O-Nobu was the one to say : 'I was no longer thinking about you.' When for the third time his image appeared before her, she wanted to click her tongue in annoyance.

Since before she had entered the restaurant she had not been thinking about her husband, she could only consider that this compulsive functioning of her mind was simply another result of the dinner engagement. She compared her mental states before and after that event. And she could not but repeat to herself the name of Mrs Yoshikawa as the person responsible for this startling change. She somehow felt that had she not had dinner that night at the same table with Mrs Yoshikawa this strange phenomenon of conjuring up Tsuda would certainly not have arisen. But when it came to asking what particular aspect of Mrs Yoshikawa had become the fermenting element to brew this bitter liquor and in precisely what way it had been poured into her mind, she could give no clear answer at all. She had only unclear data. But she had arrived at a relatively clear conclusion. Since she did not have any doubts as to the insufficiency of the data, she could not be expected to wonder whether her conclusion was defective. She firmly believed the cause of everything lay with Mrs Yoshikawa.

O-Nobu feared that when the play was over and they went back to the tea-house for a while she would meet Mrs Yoshikawa there again. And yet she felt that if she did meet her she wanted to probe her a bit. Although she had already resigned herself to the fact that at the confusing moment of their hurried departure there would be no such opportunity, this feeling of curiosity from time to time would rear its head from behind the other feeling of desiring to avoid her.

Fortunately they went to different tea-houses. Mrs Yoshikawa was nowhere to be seen. As Okamoto threw over him a heavy-looking

Japanese-style coat with a fur collar, he turned to look at O-Nobu, who was putting on her coat.

'Won't you come and stay at our house tonight?'

'It's kind of you to ask me.'

O-Nobu gave this vague sort of answer, and looked at her aunt with a smile. Her aunt then looked at her husband with an expression as if to say : 'I'm really amazed at how imperceptive you are.' But whether he did not realize what he was asking O-Nobu to do, or whether he did and was indifferent to it, he repeated his offer in a more serious tone than before.

'If you want to stay with us, please do. There's no need to be shy about it.'

'But don't you realize, my dear, that you're asking O-Nobu to stay with us when there's only one maid at her house and she's waiting for her to return? It's too much to ask of her.'

'Oh yes, of course. It's not safe with just one maid staying at her home.'

He then showed by his expression that it was all right for O-Nobu to decline, and of course he had simply asked without being overly concerned about the kind of answer he would receive.

'Now that I think about it, since we've been married I've never once yet stayed overnight with you.'

'Oh, that's true, isn't it? Well, your conduct is most admirable and irreproachable.'

'Don't flatter me so. . . . Actually Yoshio hasn't stayed out overnight either.'

'That's splendid. Both of you then are behaving most properly, and that's—'

'The source of married bliss.'

Tsugiko, in a low voice, completed her father's statement by using an actor's speech which she had just heard used onstage, and then, as if she herself were astonished at its boldness, blushed slightly. Her father purposely spoke in a loud voice.

'What was that you said?'

Since Tsugiko was embarrassed, she pretended not to hear, and walked swiftly towards the front entrance. They all followed her, and went outside.

As they were getting in their rickshaws, O-Nobu's uncle spoke to her.

'It's all right if you can't stay at our place tonight, but do come sometime within the next two or three days, won't you? There's a small matter I'd like to talk to you about.'

'I too have something I must speak to you about, so I'll definitely call on you soon—and also to thank you for your kindness to me today. If I can arrange it, I may even call tomorrow.'

'All right,' her uncle answered, using the English expression.

The rickshaws for the four of them began to move as if those English words were the signal.

57

Since the Okamoto home, which was in about the same direction as Tsuda's, was rather more distant than the latter, O-Nobu's rubber-wheeled rickshaw, which had followed after the three of theirs, had been able to come with theirs as far as the familiar corner where it turned into the lane. When they parted there, O-Nobu called out, from within the hood of her vehicle, to those going on ahead. But before she could know whether they had heard her, her rickshaw had already cut across the street with the streetcar tracks. In the quiet lane she was suddenly overwhelmed by a kind of loneliness. Like someone who has been going around in a group formation and who, involuntarily getting out of step, is the only one to be thrown out of the circle, O-Nobu entered her home with the slight but perceptible feeling of having lost her main support.

Even though the maid heard the sound of the lattice-door, she did not come out. In the living-room only the lamp was burning brightly, and even the iron kettle did not give forth its usual pleasant sound. She looked around the room, completely unchanged from when she had seen it that morning, with an eye which had, however, changed considerably from that morning. A chilly feeling began to be added to her loneliness. When that moment passed, and mere loneliness began to change into uneasiness, she was about to throw down her pleasantly tired body in front of the long brazier, but she suddenly turned in the direction of the kitchen door, and called the maid twice by name. At the same time she opened the door of the maid's room, adjacent to the kitchen.

O-Toki, who had spread out her sewing in the middle of her two-mat room and who had flung herself down childishly on top of it, instantly raised her head. Then, as soon as she saw O-Nobu, she gave a clear response in place of her previous casual one, and stood up. Since as she did so she hit her head, with its dishevelled Western-style hair-do, against the lampshade, which she had purposely lowered in order to do her sewing, the light bulb, flying off at an angle, confused her even further.

O-Nobu did not laugh. Nor did she wish to scold her. She did not even think of the contrast between O-Toki and herself in this situation.

In the mood she was then in she was grateful for even sleepy O-Toki's being there with her.

'Shut the front door right away and go to bed. I've already locked the side-gate.'

O-Nobu sent the maid to bed ahead of her, and then without even changing her clothes, sat down again in front of the brazier. She mechanically stirred up the ashes, and added new charcoal to the dying embers. She then boiled some water as if it were absolutely indispensable for her home. And yet as she strained her ears to the sound of the iron kettle whistling in the deepening night a feeling of loneliness pressing in on her from somewhere gathered even greater force than when she had returned earlier. Since, in comparing it with the lonesomeness she usually felt as she grew tired of waiting for Tsuda's late return, she found it was far deeper, she could not help but consider with nostalgia the figure of her husband lying in bed at the hospital.

'I have to admit it's all because you're not here.'

She said this to her husband, whose figure she drew in her mind. She then thought that on the following day, no matter what she would have to leave undone, she would first go to visit him at the hospital. And yet in the next instant her mind was no longer attuned to her husband's. Something got caught between them. The closer she tried to draw to him the more the obstacle between them irritated her. Also Tsuda, as she imagined him, was unconcerned and nonchalant about it. And then even she, who had grown rather obstinate, wanted to say that if that was the case it was all right with her. Indeed she even wanted to turn her back on him.

When she reached this point, her imagination was abruptly forced to jump to Mrs Yoshikawa. O-Nobu's feeling, which she had already had at the theatre, was only strengthened that she would never have had such unpleasant thoughts about her beloved husband if she had not met her that evening.

Finally she wanted to unburden herself to somebody somewhere. Thinking she might write the continuation of the letter to her family she had begun the night before, she took up her writing-brush. She knew, however, that she could never write her real thoughts on the rolled paper and would say merely that her family should not worry since she and Tsuda were living together happily. This was what she always wanted very much to say to her parents. But that night those words seemed extremely inadequate. Exhausted from trying to bring order to mind, she finally threw down her writing-brush. At last she went to bed, leaving her kimono there as she had taken it off. For a long time scenes from the theatre fragmentarily assumed many times brighter colours than in actuality, stimulating her already excited brain, and, like a person who is irritated by a certain problem, she could not fall asleep.

58

From her pillow she heard the clock strike one. She also heard it strike two. And then she opened her eyes to the morning light, which somehow confused her. That light, streaming in from a crack in the shutters, clearly told her she had slept later than usual.

By that light she looked at her clothing from the previous evening which she had scattered near her pillow. Since her outer garments, underclothes, and long undergarment were all in disorder on the *tatami* together, just as they had been thrown off, there was only a confused pile of colour without distinction of upper or lower, front or rear. From underneath the pile of colour a gold-threaded blackberry-lily-patterned obi, with its narrowly folded edge showing, extended to within an arm's length of her bed.

She observed this disorderly scene with a rather astonished expression. She had always held that neatness was an important womanly virtue, and therefore when she realized that this was what she herself had done she even felt somewhat ashamed. Since her marriage she did not remember ever having shown Tsuda such an example of untidiness, but when she saw that he was not then sleeping in the same room with her, she heaved a sigh of relief.

She had been negligent not only of her clothing. She realized that if Tsuda had not entered the hospital, and had instead been at home as usual, she would never have allowed herself to sleep so late, no matter how late she had been up the night before; and she could not but despise herself for being a thorough sluggard in not jumping up out of bed as soon as she opened her eyes.

Even so she did not get up easily. Satisfied at hearing in the kitchen the footsteps of O-Toki, who had arisen earlier without O-Nobu's knowing it, perhaps because she had wished to atone for her carelessness of the night before, O-Nobu lay nestled in the warm and snug bedclothes for a long time.

As she lay there, the feeling she had had upon awakening, of being conscience-stricken, gradually receded. She began to think that no matter how much of a woman she was there was nothing wrong if once or twice a year she did that sort of thing. All of her limbs began to relax. In this unusual leisurely mood, she enjoyed, with gratitude, a freedom such as she had never known since her marriage. Upon realizing that this too was after all a result of Tsuda's absence, she even felt it was a blessing that she was then alone for a while. Then she was amazed that the rigidity of her life, which, as she lived day by day with her husband, she had simply not perceived, and had until then overlooked, should be for her such an extraordinarily heavy burden. And yet this momentary awakening, which had occurred accidentally, did not of course last very long. When, with her mind's eye which had for a time been liberated, she observed with derision her over-anxious state of the previous evening, and finally got up from her bed, she was already governed by a different mood.

She efficiently, albeit tardily, performed her duties as a housewife as she had always done. Since Tsuda was not there, she saved herself a great deal of trouble, and without even bothering the maid, folded her clothes by herself. She then dressed simply, and immediately went outside; without even stopping on her way, she went into the new self-operating telephone booth which was about half a block from the main street.

There she made three separate telephone calls. The very first person she selected was, despite everything, Tsuda. But she was forced to hear only indirectly, from someone else, the news of his condition since he was lying down and unable to come to the telephone himself. Her expectation, however, that there could not be anything particularly wrong with him was proved correct. After she had been assured, by a person who sounded like the nurse, that everything was going well and that there were no complications, she had the nurse ask him whether he cared if she did not visit him that day, so as to learn to what extent he was waiting for her. Tsuda then had the nurse ask her back why she could not come. Since O-Nobu could not know either his expression or tone of voice, she turned her head to one side at the telephone, at a loss to know what to do. In such a situation Tsuda was not one to demand that she go. But he was one who would be offended if she did not. And yet this did not mean that he would be happy if she did go. It was not impossible that he would force her to show him this kindness and then look at her smugly as if to indicate that her action was only a woman's duty towards her husband. As she suddenly thought about this, she expressed at the telephone an attitude towards him which she considered similar to the one Mrs Yoshikawa had had towards her on the previous evening.

'Please tell him I won't go there today, since I have to go to the Okamotos'.'

Thus, after completing her call to the hospital, she quickly rang up the Okamotos, and inquired whether it was all right for her to visit them shortly. Then, to Tsuda's sister, whom she called last, she merely conveyed perfunctorily the news of his condition, and returned home.

59

When she sat down for her meal, a combination of breakfast and lunch, and was served by O-Toki, this too was the first such experience for O-Nobu since her marriage. While these changes which had occurred because of Tsuda's absence gave her the new feeling of being a queen, the freedom which, contrary to everyday habit, she was then able to enjoy seemed, paradoxically, to confine her more than usual. Since her mind was as unsettled as her body was relaxed, she turned to O-Toki, and commented :

'Somehow it's strange when my husband isn't here. Don't you agree?'

'Really? You're probably lonely.'

O-Nobu had not yet made her point.

'This is the first time I've overslept so.'

'Yes, but since you're always up so early, it's good to have breakfast and lunch together for a change.'

'I suppose you're thinking that when my husband isn't here I'll always behave this way, aren't you?'

'Of course not.'

This rather unnaturally loud answer of O-Toki pierced O-Nobu much more cruelly than if O-Toki had been honest. O-Nobu immediately fell silent.

About half an hour later when she put on the clogs for formal wear which O-Toki had lined up in the entrance hall, and went out again, O-Nobu turned to speak to O-Toki, who was seeing her out :

'Take good care of everything, now. If you go to bed the way you did last night it's not safe, you know.'

'Will you be returning late tonight too?'

O-Nobu had not thought at all about when she would return.

'I don't intend to stay out so very late.'

Nevertheless O-Nobu somehow felt she wanted to have a leisurely visit with the Okamotos on this rare occasion of Tsuda's absence.

'I'll try to return as early as possible.'

She said this as she went out into the road, and immediately turned towards the Okamotos' house.

Since the Okamoto home was in approximately the same direction as the Fujii home, for part of the way she was able to take the familiar streetcar that ran along the river. She got off at the last or next to last stop before the terminus, crossed over the small wooden bridge which had been built there, and walked a bit down the street on the other side. The street was the one down which Tsuda and Kobayashi had walked two or three nights earlier after they had left the bar, and down which the two men, each with involved feelings arising from their differing circumstances and temperaments, had discussed Kobayashi's going to Korea and the problem of O-Kin's forthcoming marriage. Since O-Nobu had not heard about that discussion from Tsuda, she did not give a thought to either of them, and after walking mechanically in the opposite direction, she began to climb the long and narrow hill which led to her uncle's house. But she then coincidentally met Tsugiko coming from the opposite direction. Tsugiko spoke first :

'Hello. I was so glad you could come yesterday.'

'Where are you going now?'

'To practise.'

Her cousin had finished at a girls' higher school the previous year, and she was then taking lessons in various things in her spare time. Since O-Nobu knew her habit of trying her hand at many things, such as piano, the tea ceremony, flower-arrangement, water-colours, and cooking, when she heard the word 'practise', she was tempted to laugh.

'To practise what? Toe-dancing?'

They were so intimate they could indulge in this kind of private joke. But even though this joke, as far as O-Nobu was concerned, was not without a slight element of sarcasm directed at the fact that Tsugiko had more leisure than she, Tsugiko, who was the object of it, did not seem to feel the slightest sting in the remark.

'Certainly not.'

She answered simply, laughing good-naturedly. And no matter how discerning O-Nobu was, she had to admit that her laugh was innocence itself. But Tsugiko did not tell her where she was going or what she was practising, after all.

'You shouldn't make fun of me.'

'Have you begun something else?'

'Well, since I seem to be so greedy to learn new things, I don't know what I might begin.'

It was an open fact at Tsugiko's home that she had been dubbed greedy in the matter of taking lessons. This unpleasant adjective, which had first been used by her younger sister and then had quickly spread throughout the family, had recently been used by Tsugiko herself without thinking anything of it.

'Wait for me. I'll be back right away.'

As O-Nobu turned back to look at the figure of Tsugiko descending the hill with a brisk light step, she again had the usual feeling towards her of mingled respect and disdain.

60

When she arrived at the Okamoto residence, she again coincidentally found her uncle in front of the entrance. He was not even wearing a *haori*, and with his waistband sagging loosely and his arms clasped behind him at the knot, he was saying something eagerly to the gardener, who was hoeing near by, but as soon as he saw O-Nobu he called to her from a distance.

'You came after all, didn't you? I'm just pottering about the garden.'

On one side of the gardener a large akebia vine, still entwined, had been pulled out and thrown on the ground.

'I've just been saying that I want to make this vine climb on the entrance gate to the garden. It's a good idea, don't you think?'

O-Nobu looked from the adze-hewn pillars supporting the miscanthus-thatched gate in about the centre of the wickerwork bamboo fence to the log beams on top of the gate.

'My, you've taken out the low fence, haven't you?'

'Yes, and in place of it I've put a solid *meseki* bamboo fence with beading.'

Since her uncle had recently had considerable free time and had built a new home in accordance with his own specifications, his vocabulary of architectural terms had quite suddenly increased. O-Nobu, having merely heard the words '*meseki* fence' and not seeing the Chinese characters, had no idea what they meant, and could only give an exclamation of surprise in response to his comment.

'It's good as after-dinner exercise, isn't it? It helps you digest.'

'What are you talking about? I haven't had lunch yet.'

He pulled O-Nobu along, and purposely entering the living-room from the garden, shouted her aunt's name, 'Sumi, Sumi.'

'I'm terribly hungry. Give me something to eat right away.'

'Well, why didn't you eat with everybody earlier?'

'But the whole world doesn't run to suit your convenience, you know. Will you ever realize there are certain times to do certain things?' he retorted.

While O-Nobu's aunt's attitude towards her rather self-satisfied husband was one of smugness, her uncle's responses were also as obstinate as ever. O-Nobu felt that for the first time in a long while she was breathing the air of her old home, and she could not help secretly comparing this elderly couple with her husband and herself, who were still at the threshold of a new life after less than a year of marriage. It was a kind of riddle insoluble to young O-Nobu's intelligence and imagination whether they too, if only they lived long enough, would naturally become like her uncle and aunt, or if, no matter how long they lived together, their temperaments would forever differ and they would forever have to oppose each other. O-Nobu was not satisfied with her husband at that time. And yet she could not think that even in the future she would, like her aunt, be able to make the best of an unsatisfactory situation. If such a situation was indeed her destiny stretching into the future, she would attempt to continue, as long as possible, the illusion of romance existing at present, so that she would one day have to accept the cruel blow of disillusionment all at once. For, to her young mind, to lose her womanly qualities and still to exist in the world as a woman could only be considered a truly frightening existence.

Her uncle, who could not possibly have imagined what distant thoughts were milling about in this young wife's mind, looked at her, as he sat cross-legged facing his low dining-table placed in front of him.

'Hey there, why are you so absent-minded? You're forever thinking about something, aren't you?'

She immediately replied, 'Let me wait on you. I haven't for so long.'

Since unfortunately there was no rice-bucket, she tried to get up from her seat, but her aunt stopped her.

'Even if you want to serve him rice, I'm afraid you can't because he's having bread with this meal.'

The maid brought some dark brown toast on a plate.

'O-Nobu, a dreadful thing has happened to me. Your poor uncle can't eat rice any more, even though he was born in Japan.'

Since he had diabetes, he had been strictly forbidden by his family doctor to take any starch other than the prescribed amount.

'So I'm now eating only bean-curd, as you can see.'

On his low dining-table there was indeed so much white, uncooked bean-curd it seemed impossible for one man to eat it all.

When O-Nobu saw her very stout uncle's purposely self-pitying expression, not only did she not feel very sorry for him, she wanted, on the contrary, to laugh.

'Isn't it better if you cut down on your food a bit? Anyone would be uncomfortable being as fat as you.'

He turned to her aunt.

'O-Nobu always did say nasty things, but since she's been married she's become even more expert at it, hasn't she?'

61

Having grown up under his charge from childhood, O-Nobu knew better than anyone her uncle's peculiarities and the various aspects under which they appeared.

He had a nervous temperament, which did not accord with his stoutness, but there was an open-hearted element in it. Although he had the habit of occasionally going into his room and staying there for about half a day without speaking to anybody, at other times, if he just saw someone he would not stay still an instant without speaking to him about something. Indeed many occasions arose when he would show personal consideration to put his conversational partner as much at ease as possible, rather than be at a loss for a place to express his good spirits. Since with a guest he would try to avoid his own awkwardness of merely talking at random, in his conversation on matters other than important business there would always emerge a kind of interesting core, which would captivate his listeners. Often this most socially advantageous art of story-telling, which had made no small contribution to his success, gave off an even more brilliant lustre because of the sense of humour which he possessed as an innate gift. And this gift had passed, without their being aware of it, to O-Nobu, who had always been close to him since her childhood. When she had been in particularly good humour it had become effortless second nature for her to make some witty rejoinder and even turn the tables on him. After marrying Tsuda, however, she had swiftly changed. The witty remarks she had restrained out of discretion did not reappear at all even after two or three months had passed. She had finally become a different person from the one she had been when she lived with the Okamotos, and had to face her husband as such. She was dissatisfied with this change. At the same time she could not help feeling she was deceiving Tsuda. When she occasionally saw her uncle, who had not changed, there was a certain something in him which would make her recall her former freedom. She looked wistfully at his droll face, as if it were a memento of the past, as he sat cross-legged in front of his uncooked bean-curd.

'But didn't I learn all those nasty remarks from you, Uncle? I certainly don't recall having learned them from Yoshio.'

'Hm, that may be true.'

He used a slang Tokyo expression, and then looked mischievously at his wife, who thoroughly disliked such words and often said she would not allow them in the house. But since she knew very well that if she was there paying attention to him he would want to use them even

more, she acted as if she had not heard him and did not take him up
on it. Then, having missed his mark, he turned again to O-Nobu.

'Is Yoshio then such a stern person?'

O-Nobu merely grinned, and did not answer.

'Ah-ha, you're smiling again. That makes me happy.'

'Why?'

'Don't pretend you don't know why. You know perfectly well. . . .
But, tell me, is Yoshio really so very stern?'

'I don't really know. But why are you asking me in such a serious
way?'

'I have a little scheme—depending on your answer.'

'Oh, that's a bit frightening! All right, I'll tell you. Yes, it's as you
suppose : Yoshio *is* stern. And now, what are you going to do?'

'Are you telling the truth?'

'Yes. My, but you're obstinate.'

'Well then, I'll tell you quite simply the conclusion I've come to.
That is, of course, if Yoshio really is stern, as you say. In effect he isn't
suited for someone like you who's so clever at making nasty remarks.'

As he said this, he jutted out his chin at O-Nobu's aunt, who was
sitting there silently.

'Now if your aunt were married to him, maybe he'd suit her just
perfectly.'

A lonely feeling suddenly passed over O-Nobu's heart, like a breeze
from afar. She was amazed at how easily she had been seized by this
sad mood.

'I'm glad to see you're as light-hearted as ever, Uncle.'

When she laughed at her uncle's teasing remark, made on the
assumption that she and Tsuda were a couple who got along extremely
well together, and treated it merely as a random statement uttered for
the sake of entertainment, O-Nobu sensed a very large gap between
what she was feeling and what she could say. Furthermore, since she
thought she had to close that gap as much as possible and show herself
to others as a woman who had a husband without a single flaw, she
could not reveal to her uncle anything of what she really felt. At the
point where tears were just about to gather in her eyes, she covered up
her feelings by blinking several times.

'No matter how perfectly I may suit him I'm afraid it's no use at this
age. Don't you agree, O-Nobu?'

When her aunt, always able to appear much younger than her years,
spoke and turned towards O-Nobu her fresh, lustrous eyes, O-Nobu did
not say anything. But she did not forget to exploit this first opportunity
to conceal her emotions. She merely laughed charmingly.

62

O-Nobu secretly liked her uncle, who was only an uncle by marriage, more than her aunt, who was a blood relation, and as a reward she always had the conviction that she was especially favoured by him. Since she understood very well his innate fun-loving yet nervous disposition, and since she easily moulded her own behaviour, which displayed both these aspects, in exact conformity to what he desired, for she had always had a youthful flexibility of personality, she pleased her uncle almost without effort, and also was able to give herself satisfaction. Since she considered that he turned appreciative eyes on her as he watched her every movement, at times she even marvelled that her aunt should be so stolid and rigid.

O-Nobu had in this way learned only from her uncle how to treat the opposite sex, and believed that no matter whom she married she would succeed if she applied this particular method, precisely as it was, to her husband. When she had married Tsuda, for the first time she had felt somewhat out of her element, and had looked upon this completely new experience with considerable astonishment. She often met with situations where she had to choose between attempting to change Tsuda into a person like her uncle and transforming her own already crystallized personality to conform to Tsuda's. Her love was of course directed towards him. But her sympathies were rather with people of her uncle's type. There were often occasions when she thought that if Tsuda had been her uncle he would have made her happy. And then a natural force ordered her to tell her uncle about this in detail. But she was obstinate enough to go against this compulsion, and she finally was unable to confess what she had somehow managed to endure until then without telling anyone.

Having in this way deceived her uncle and aunt, she was also confident that they had been completely taken in by her. At the same time she was alert enough to know quite well that her uncle too wished to confess to her, and yet was unable to, the fact that he had, with regard to Tsuda, a secret of the same degree as hers. O-Nobu was convinced, as she looked clearly into her uncle's heart, that he certainly did not like the man who was closer to her than anyone in the world. This was a hypothesis which was not too difficult to conceive of if she tried to compare the two men and examined the differences in temperament. At any rate, after her marriage O-Nobu had quickly noticed this. But she possessed additional data on which to base her opinion. Her uncle, who appeared rough when he was really delicate, who seemed indifferent when he was sensitive, and who spoke brusquely when he was at heart really kind, had already seemed to dislike Tsuda basically from the time he had first met him. When she had felt that behind the question he had then asked her, 'Do you really like that kind of man?' there had seemed to be implicit the words 'Well then, you dislike men like me, don't you?' she had been taken aback. But when she had asked him in return what his opinion was, he had already passed beyond that unpleasant stage.

'Marry him, if you feel you want to, and don't worry about what anyone will say,' he had told her affectionately.

But she had one more piece of evidence concerning his real feelings. She had been able to learn from her aunt of his blunt appraisal of Tsuda, although he had said nothing to her about it directly.

'Doesn't that fellow look as if he thinks all the women in Japan should fall in love with him?'

Strangely enough, this remark did not surprise O-Nobu at all. She was convinced she was able to love Tsuda with all her heart, and she was also confident that he would return her love. Since her first reaction to her uncle's words had been that she felt he was making one of his usual cutting remarks, she had merely laughed. And then she had been elated when she secretly interpreted his remark as issuing from jealousy. Her aunt had joined her by saying, 'He's already forgotten his own conceit when he was young.'

As she sat facing her uncle she could not help recalling those events of the past. And then she even felt there might be some deep significance in his trivial remark about whether she suited 'stern' Tsuda as a wife or not.

'Isn't it as I say? If not, I'm glad. But if there should be something, or even if there isn't now, if there should be in the future, you mustn't hesitate to tell me.'

She could even read those kind words in her uncle's eyes.

63

She had laughed away her pensive mood, and to escape from the pain of such concealment she immediately asked her aunt and uncle about the matter which had perplexed her.

'What in the world was yesterday's dinner party all about?'

She had to seek for an explanation from her uncle, who had promised one to her. But instead of giving her an answer, he in turn asked her a question.

'Well, what do *you* think about it?'

He put special emphasis on the word 'you', and then, with a glance that O-Nobu could easily read, he looked at her fixedly.

'I'm sure I don't know. You shouldn't ask me that question point-blank. Don't you agree, Aunt Sumi?'

Her aunt snickered.

'Your uncle feels that a dullard like me wouldn't understand, but that you, O-Nobu, certainly would. He keeps saying you're much more perceptive than I.'

O-Nobu could do nothing but give a hollow laugh. She of course had a certain vague notion about what the previous day's events had meant. But she was not so deficient in breeding as to attempt to appear clever, and mention it, even though she was not forced to do so.

'I really don't know, I tell you.'

'Well, try to guess. You'll most likely figure it out.'

After she understood that her uncle really wanted her to say something first, and they had wrangled several times, she finally revealed what her guess had been.

'Wasn't it a *miai*?'*

'Why? . . . Did it look that way to you?'

Before he confirmed O-Nobu's guess, he asked her a few questions in succession. Finally he gave a loud laugh.

'You guessed it, you guessed it! It's just as I said. You *are* more clever than Sumi.'

Both O-Sumi and O-Nobu poked fun at this light-hearted man, who made distinctions between them on this basis.

'If that's all it is, I'm sure Aunt Sumi could have guessed it just as well.'

'And I'm sure you're not too happy to be praised by your uncle in this way, are you, O-Nobu?'

'No, not in the least.'

O-Nobu again thought of Mrs Yoshikawa and her officious manner as she had dominated the entire group.

'I certainly thought that was what it was. That lady was always trying so very hard to set off both Tsugiko and that young man Miyoshi to good advantage.'

'But actually in Tsugiko's case there were many instances when she wouldn't be drawn out. The more Mrs Yoshikawa tried to show her off, the more she seemed to withdraw. She was just like a cat with a paper bag on its head. In such a situation someone like you, O-Nobu, would do very nicely. At least you'd react in a positive way.'

'You mean because I'd take her up rather brazenly, I suppose. Somehow I'm not sure whether I'm being praised or criticized. Whenever I

* An arranged meeting between prospective bride and groom.

see a well-behaved girl like Tsugiko I wish I somehow could become like her.'

O-Nobu answered in this way, and pondered with unhappiness and dissatisfaction the gathering of the previous evening where she had not been given the opportunity to display what her uncle had called 'a positive reaction', and which consequently, as far as she was concerned, had ended in failure.

'But why was my presence necessary?'

'You're Tsugiko's cousin, aren't you?'

If the only reason was that she was a relative, many people other than O-Nobu would have had to be present. Moreover, on the side of the prospective groom there had been only Miyoshi himself, and apart from Mr and Mrs Yoshikawa, who had introduced him, there had been no one to represent him.

'But it's still rather strange. Because in that case, if Yoshio hadn't been ill, that would have meant he too, as a relative, would have had to attend.'

'That's another matter. That would mean something entirely different.'

One of her uncle's objectives had been the considerate one of using the previous evening's gathering to have Tsuda and O-Nobu become even better acquainted with Mr and Mrs Yoshikawa. When her uncle clearly told her about this, she thought that his personality, as she had always judged it to be, was well expressed in such an act, but while she secretly was grateful for his kindness, she regretfully wondered why he had not behaved so as to have her become more intimate with Mrs Yoshikawa. Of course he had made them sit at the same dining table, but he had seemed wholly ignorant of the special psychology by which, as a result, things were, instead, worse than before they had come together. O-Nobu felt inclined to observe that, no matter how attentive to details a man might be, he was after all a man, lacking a woman's finesse in such matters. But thereafter she felt more lenient, and sighed, as she realized that if one had not known the kind of subtle relationship existing between her and Mrs Yoshikawa, one would not have been able to do anything about the situation.

64

O-Nobu then cast aside the problem, and tried to clear up the remaining important matter which she simply could not understand.

'Of course it did have that meaning. I must thank you for having thought about it. But there's still something else, isn't there?'

'There may have been, but even if there hadn't, I think there was sufficient reason in what I've just said for asking you to be present.'

'Yes, I agree.'

She had to answer that way. But even so she inwardly felt that the way she had been induced to attend had been a trifle too crude. Her uncle had kept the last thing to himself but now disclosed it.

'Actually I thought I'd ask you to pass judgment on the young man. I'm asking your advice because you can see through people very well. Well, what do you think of the fellow? Is he good or bad as O-Tsugi's future husband?'

Judging from her uncle's usual manner, O-Nobu was slightly at a loss to know to what extent this was a serious request.

'My, what a very important task you've given me! I'm greatly honoured.'

She laughingly spoke in this way, and looked at her aunt, by her side, but since her aunt seemed unexpectedly cool, she quickly changed her tone.

'It's rather impertinent for someone like me to pass judgment on him. I was only seated there with him about an hour. Who in the world would be able to say anything? That is, unless he possessed some special psychic power.'

'That's just it. You *do* seem somehow to have some psychic power. That's why everybody wants to ask your opinion.'

'Don't make fun of me.'

O-Nobu purposely pretended she was offended and was not speaking to her uncle. Yet inwardly she had the pleasant sensation of being flattered. It was simply the result of the realization that she seemed to be considered a most perceptive person. But it was also of a kind to be blotted out by some disappointing facts. For she was quickly forced to think of her own husband in connection with the matter as an immediate example. The confidence, which before marriage she had always had, of being able to see through his character with a kind of second sight, had already, since their marriage, been marred here and there by traces of misunderstanding and misjudgment, just as dark sunspots emerge on the bright sun. In the final analysis she had to bow her head to the sad truth that her intuition concerning her husband was perhaps something which had to be corrected and modified by her long experience. Therefore, even though she was urged by her uncle, she did not immediately feel up to making observations on Miyoshi's character.

'But, Uncle, you can't possibly understand a person unless you've had considerable contact with him, you know.'

'Anybody knows that. We hardly need you to tell us.'

'That's what I mean. Having just met him once, I can't possibly say anything about him.'

'That's what a man would say. But even if a woman sees someone at a glance, doesn't she always say something? And doesn't she often say something quite clever too? That's why I'm now asking you to make some comment just so I'll have a judgment to go by. You needn't worry that I'm trying to make you share some of the responsibility.'

'But it's unreasonable to ask me. I can't make that kind of prophecy. Don't you agree, Aunt Sumi?'

Her aunt did not side with O-Nobu the way she usually did. But even so, this did not mean she became her husband's ally. Although she did not seem to want to force O-Nobu to comment, she also did not stop her husband's insistent prodding. She also seemed to be saying that if O-Nobu could provide material for assessing the future husband of her dear eldest daughter, the first of her children to marry, then no matter how slight it might be, there was sufficient reason for her to listen. Thus O-Nobu could not but make one or two harmless and inoffensive statements.

'Well, isn't he a fine young man? And he's quite poised for being so young, isn't he?'

Since O-Nobu did not say anything more, even though her uncle was waiting for her to speak further, he prodded her again.

'Is that all?'

'But I tell you I wasn't even seated next to him, and I couldn't even see his face clearly.'

'Well, maybe it was wrong to seat our prophet in such a place. . . . But you still have something rather keen to say, don't you? I mean something where you show your perceptiveness more clearly. Just one word neatly revealing Miyoshi's vulnerable spot. . . .'

'That's quite difficult. . . . I repeat, it's impossible having seen him just once.'

'But suppose you had to say something after having seen him just once. I think you'd surely say something then.'

'No, I wouldn't.'

'You wouldn't? Well then, has your intuition ceased to be effective recently?'

'Yes, since I've been married it's gradually been worn away. Recently I've not only not had second sight, I've not even had first sight.'

65

While she was engaging in this kind of drawn-out conversation with her uncle, O-Nobu's mind was ceaselessly occupied with quite another matter.

She did not doubt that her uncle considered Tsuda and her a good example of marital harmony. But she also knew very well that he had not liked Tsuda from the very first encounter and that he had had no reason to change his opinion thereafter. Therefore she felt certain he was always looking rather sceptically at the seemingly harmonious pair. To express the matter differently, beneath her uncle's amazement at how a woman like O-Nobu was able to love Tsuda there was always latent his own confidence concerning his own attractiveness to women of her type. It seemed that the conviction that it was not he but rather O-Nobu who had misjudged people was always present deep within him, awaiting the opportunity to come to the surface.

'But why is it, I wonder, that you're so insistent on hearing my opinion of this young man, Uncle?'

O-Nobu could not understand his objective. Since he already secretly considered her someone who had misjudged her own husband, she did not have the courage, with the awareness of this fact, to respond readily to his demand. Finally there was nothing for her to do but remain silent. But for her uncle, who had for so many years been accustomed to her being so unreserved, her silence on this occasion was nothing short of amazing. He turned from her to his wife.

'This child's personality seems to have changed somewhat since she's been married, hasn't it? She's become quite timid. I wonder whether this too is her husband's influence. It's very strange.'

'That's because you tease her so. Anyone would be annoyed if she's constantly being prodded into saying something.'

Her aunt's attitude became more one of defending O-Nobu than of reproving her husband. O-Nobu, however, had become too full of her own reflections to be pleased by this.

'But isn't this first of all Tsugiko's problem? I think it should be settled by her opinion alone. And no one like me should have anything to say.'

O-Nobu could not help recalling the time when she had chosen her husband herself. She had fallen in love with Tsuda upon first meeting him. And therefore she had immediately disclosed to her guardians her desire to marry him. Furthermore, as soon as she had received their permission she had actually done so. From beginning to end she had always been mistress of her own affairs. And she had been thoroughly responsible for her actions. She did not remember ever having wanted to set aside her own ideas and defer to someone else's opinion.

'But what actually did Tsugiko say?'

'She didn't say anything. She's even more timid than you are.'

'Well, if that's the way the person most directly involved behaves, there's nothing much to be done about it, is there?'

'Yes, it's really hopeless if she's that timid.'

'She's not timid—she's well-behaved.'

'Well, whichever it is, it's hopeless, since she doesn't say anything at all. Or perhaps she can't say anything. She may not have enough on which to base a judgment.'

O-Nobu doubted very much whether, if Tsugiko and Miyoshi were united in this passionless way, a true marital relationship could develop between them. For she instantly realized that even her own marriage had not turned out entirely satisfactorily. Since she could not in this case say that her own marriage resembled what was happening between Tsugiko and Miyoshi, she could only see their prospective marriage as being as joyless as the previous evening's meeting. She did not think they were foolish so much as she felt frightened by the whole affair. And she wondered how they could be so carefree.

She turned to her uncle, casting her narrow eyes intently on him. He then spoke to her:

'It's no use. Since Tsugiko from the outset hasn't wished to say anything. And, to tell the truth, that's why we wanted you to attend.'

'But what did you expect me to do?'

'Well, Tsugi particularly asked us to have you come, since she thinks you're much more clever than she. And she's convinced that even if she couldn't form an opinion of him, you'd certainly be able to make various comments later.'

'Well, if you'd told me that from the beginning, I'd have gone with that in mind.'

'But she also said she didn't want us to do that. She said we definitely had to keep quiet about the real purpose of the evening.'

'I wonder why.'

O-Nobu turned for a moment towards her aunt. Her uncle tried to prevent his wife from answering that the reason was that Tsugiko was embarrassed.

'It's not only because she was embarrassed. She was worried that if O-Nobu knew all about it she wouldn't be able to make a good judgment. In other words, she said she wanted to hear O-Nobu's first impression given fairly without prejudice.'

O-Nobu finally understood why her uncle had tried to force her to speak.

66

In O-Nobu's eyes Tsugiko occupied a special position. In concern for O-Nobu's welfare Tsugiko did not equal her aunt. And in compatibility with her she was very far removed from her uncle. But, as if in compensation for these, instead of the intimacy of blood aunt and niece or the attraction based on the difference in sex, Tsugiko did possess a good point of contact with her in their similarity in age.

As they faced the various problems that stir the hearts of young women, and as they pondered them with eyes filled with interest, quite naturally O-Nobu became more intimate with Tsugiko than with either her uncle or her aunt. And in such situations, perhaps because of her natural endowments, she was always Tsugiko's superior. Of course, in the matter of experience, she was undoubtedly Tsugiko's elder. At least she knew very well that from Tsugiko's point of view she existed on a higher plane.

This young admirer had the habit of considering everything O-Nobu said to be true. O-Nobu now realized that by living together in the same house for so long she had almost unwittingly created this extremely passive cousin by the excessive wilfulness and positiveness of her own actions and statements.

'A woman should be able to judge a man at a glance.'

She had previously spoken in this way and had astonished the innocent Tsugiko. She had confronted Tsugiko as someone who possessed the actual perceptiveness necessary to carry out such a policy. And just when Tsugiko's amazement had changed from envy into admiration, and had finally approached the quality of worship, quite accidentally the love affair between O-Nobu and Tsuda, which could not but confirm O-Nobu's self-confidence, took place, flaring in front of Tsugiko very much like a mysterious flame. Thus her words had finally become for Tsugiko eternal truth itself. She who was triumphant before the world had become particularly so for Tsugiko.

The image of Tsuda, as viewed by O-Nobu, was immediately transmitted to Tsugiko. Since Tsugiko did not herself have the opportunity for daily contact with him, those unknown areas extending beyond the realm of her senses were all filled in by the indirect knowledge provided by O-Nobu, and she easily constructed an ideal whole around the name of Tsuda.

O-Nobu's opinion of Tsuda at that time, after more than half a year of marriage, had changed. But Tsugiko's opinion of him had not changed in the least. She believed O-Nobu implicitly. O-Nobu too was not one to retract her previous words after so long a time. In front of Tsugiko she professed herself to be one of those few fortunate persons who have been able to receive happiness from God by having had complete clarity of foresight.

O-Nobu, forced to face this present situation while inevitably remembering the past relationship between them, was sad rather than distressed. For she thought that everyone had conspired to condemn her indirectly and have her speedily confess the weak points she had glossed over until then. It seemed as if in addition to the torments inflicted by herself all the others were tormenting her.

'If I suffer for my own mistakes, that should be enough.'

She had always secretly maintained such justification for herself. But she could not use it to retaliate against her uncle, her aunt, and Tsugiko, who knew nothing at all about it. For if she were to use it, it would be tantamount to stirring up the three of them unnecessarily, and of charging God with having rebuked her.

Her uncle, who, having had his tray cleared away, had begun to gulp down the tea his wife had just drawn, could not know that such involved vexations were surging through O-Nobu's mind. As he looked out at the newly-constructed single-level garden, he cheerfully exchanged a few words with his wife about the disposition of certain trees and stones according to his plan.

'I think I'll plant a maple beside that pine next year. Somehow, when I look at it from here, that's the only place that seems to have a gap, and it looks odd.'

O-Nobu looked without any real interest in the direction he was painting. He had purposely banked the earth up high near the wall adjoining the land of the neighbouring house, and the area near the small but dense bamboo grove which he had planted there was, as he said, sparse and open. O-Nobu, who for some time had wanted very much to change the subject and who had been secretly waiting for an opportunity to do so, quickly showed her presence of mind.

'That's true, isn't it? If you don't block that place, it will seem rather strange that you planted that grove, won't it?'

As she had anticipated, the conversation then flowed in another direction. But when it returned again to its previous course, she had to pass down an even steeper incline than before.

67

This happened when her uncle was called by the family gardener, who had earlier been hoeing in front of the house; after leaving his place for a while, her uncle returned to the living-room again from the garden.

The conversation between O-Nobu and her aunt, which began by touching upon Yuriko and Hajime, who had not yet returned from school, then turned again by chance towards Tsugiko.

'That culture-greedy daughter of mine should have returned already. I wonder what's happened to her.'

O-Nobu's aunt purposely used the epithet for Tsugiko which Yuriko had given her. O-Nobu immediately recalled Tsugiko's avidity for cultural attainments. While Tsugiko was utterly unrestrained within the small world allowed her, when she stepped one pace outside it she would quickly withdraw and seem the very model of propriety; in her home and under her parents' supervision, she was exactly like a small bird, which chirps seemingly very happily within its cage, but which, once the doors have been opened and it is allowed outside, does not know where to fly and forgets how to sing.

'What did she go to practise today?'

After her aunt had asked her to guess, she swiftly satisfied the curiosity which O-Nobu had had from the time she had met Tsugiko on the hill. When O-Nobu heard, however, that the subject of her cousin's study was a foreign language which she had earnestly begun recently, she was again astonished at Tsugiko's many interests. She even wondered what in the world Tsugiko intended to do by trying her hand at so many different things.

'In the case of languages, however, her study actually has a special purpose.'

O-Nobu's aunt said this, explaining to O-Nobu Tsugiko's purpose by way of an attempt at justification. Since this was related, although indirectly, to the current problem of Tsugiko's forthcoming marriage, O-Nobu had to assume a serious expression in front of her aunt, and nod in approval.

There was no doubt that a woman's efforts to anticipate what her future husband will like, or to anticipate those things which it will be convenient for her to know in connection with his profession, and to learn them before marriage, constituted kindness towards him. It also was undoubtedly merely a useful means of causing a man to like her. But for Tsugiko there still remained many other important accomplishments, in addition to these, as a human being and as a wife. These interests, as they were sketched in O-Nobu's mind, were unfortunately not of a kind to make her a better woman. But they would make her a shrewder one. They would doubtless chafe her cruelly. But they would hone her to keenness. O-Nobu had learned her first step in these areas from her aunt. And thanks to her uncle she had been able to continue to develop her talents until that day. The two of them, who in this sense had reared her, seemed to look at her with eyes of satisfaction.

'But I wonder why those same eyes can be satisfied with Tsugiko.'

On this one point she could not understand her uncle and aunt, who had never shown the slightest sign of being discontented with either of her cousins. If she had been forced to give an explanation, it would have been simply that they distinguished between niece and daughters. When she was assailed by this idea, O-Nobu suddenly became annoyed. Moreover such an idea occasionally seized her mind like a paroxysm. And yet before it could flare up it was always extinguished by her uncle's open and considerate attitude and by her aunt's impartial kindness. O-Nobu would often bring her sleeve to her face to conceal her blushing, and would observe their moods with astonishment, as if they were insoluble riddles.

'But Tsugiko's fortunate, isn't she? She's not a worrier like me.'

'Actually that girl's much more of a worrier than you are. It's just that when she's at home there's nothing to worry about, no matter how much she may wish to, so that she's able to be quite carefree.'

'Even so, I think that from the time I lived with you I was much more inclined to worry.'

'Well, you and Tsugi. . . .'

Her aunt stopped in the middle and did not seem to know what she was going to say. Before O-Nobu could pursue her words, which could be interpreted as meaning that their temperaments differed, or that their status differed, or even that their circumstances differed, she was taken aback. For she felt she had suddenly encountered something she had never noticed before.

'I wonder whether I may not have been asked to be present at yesterday's gathering to be the less attractive and thereby, by contrast, to enhance Tsugiko's good looks.'

When this suggestion flashed like a spark through her mind, her will too exerted its pressure on her with a much greater force than usual. She finally was able to subdue her emotions, and she did not show any heightened colour in her face.

'Tsugiko's a lucky one. She's liked by everyone.'

'Not necessarily. But people's tastes differ. Even a foolish girl like Tsugi. . . .'

Her uncle came back on the veranda and her aunt began to speak this way almost simultaneously. As he asked in a loud voice about what had happened to Tsugiko, he entered the living-room again.

68

Then an emotion of the kind O-Nobu had until then been suppressing welled up in her breast. The extremely good-natured, extremely healthy, and extremely optimistic, rotund face of her uncle momentarily stimulated her.

'Uncle, you're quite crafty, aren't you?'

She suddenly felt she had to say that. O-Nobu's voice, in using these everyday words they had exchanged hundreds of times before, was quite different from the usual. In her expression as well there were special features. But her uncle, who had not noticed at all what kind of ebb and flow of emotion had been taking place for some time in O-Nobu's heart, was wholly innocent, and this innocence was at variance with his customary discernment.

'Am I really that bad?'

In his usual tone he purposely feigned ignorance, and composedly stuffed cut tobacco in the bowl of his pipe.

'While I was out your aunt said something to you, didn't she?'

O-Nobu still did not speak. But her aunt swiftly joined in : 'She knows perfectly well how nasty you are without having me tell her.'

'Of course. O-Nobu has a keen intuition, as we well know. Perhaps that's it. You can't be off your guard with her because she's the sort of woman who can tell just by looking at a man how much money he has in his pocket and just exactly where it's placed.'

Her uncle's bantering certainly did not produce the result he antici-pated. O-Nobu looked down, moving her eyebrows and eyelashes at the same time. At the tips of her eyelashes tears had gathered before she was aware of it. Her uncle's comments, which had missed their mark, stopped suddenly. A strange pall instantly settled over the three of them.

'What's happened to O-Nobu?'

Her uncle expressed his concern, and to fill the vacuum which fol-lowed, struck the ash-pot with his pipe. Her aunt too felt she had to say something to put a good face on the matter.

'You're being very childish, O-Nobu. How in the world can you cry over such a thing? Isn't it just one of your uncle's usual jokes?'

Her aunt's reprimand did not sound merely like a formal remark made out of consideration for her uncle. Since she recognized her position in the relationship between uncle and niece, her attitude was entirely impartial. O-Nobu knew this very well. But the more she realized that her aunt's reproof was justified, the more she wanted to cry. Her lips trembled. The tears she was unable to repress poured forth. At the same time the barrier which until then had restrained her words also broke. Still weeping, she finally cried out : 'Why did you have to tease me so much?'

Her uncle looked perplexed.

'I didn't tease you—I praised you. Before you married Yoshio you made your evaluation of him, didn't you? Well, we all secretly admired that. That's why. . . .'

'That's quite enough. I don't want to hear that. Anyway it was wrong of me to have gone to the theatre.'

A brief silence followed.

'Well, somehow everything seems to have gone wrong. Is it that my way of joking with you was wrong?'

'No, it was all my fault.'

'You mustn't say that. I'm asking because I don't know what went wrong.'

'That's why I'm telling you it was all my fault.'

'But you don't give any reason.'

'There isn't any reason.'

'Do you mean there isn't any because you're just sad?'

O-Nobu began to cry even more. Her aunt looked displeased.

'I don't understand this girl. And she's no longer a fretful child, either. And what's more, when she was with us, no matter how much you teased her, she never cried this way. It's too bad if young girls nowadays, just as soon as they're married and cared for a bit by their husbands, behave this way.'

O-Nobu bit her lip and remained silent. Her uncle, who was convinced that all the causes of her behaviour lay with him, on the contrary looked at her pityingly.

'It won't do to scold her that way. I was wrong in teasing you a bit too much. . . . That's it, isn't it, O-Nobu? I'm sure of it. All right, all right, now instead of making you cry, I'm going to give you something nice.'

As her crying gradually subsided, O-Nobu wondered how she should behave, now that she was being treated as a child by her uncle in this way, so as to provide an easy transition from the awkward situation.

69

At that point Tsugiko, who knew nothing whatever of what had happened, returned from her foreign language practice and unexpectedly put in an appearance.

'I'm back.'

The three, embarrassed at having lost the mainstay of polite conversation, were delighted to use Tsugiko as a way out of their difficulty. And they returned her greeting almost simultaneously.

'We're glad you are.'

'You're late, aren't you? We've been waiting for you for quite some time.'

'Yes indeed, we've been waiting for you impatiently, wondering what you've been up to all this time.'

Since in Okamoto's nervous attitude there was clearly a sense of his trying to redeem the previous failure, he was much livelier than usual.

'It seems we all have something we want very much to speak to you about.'

He went so far as to say that, and even though to O-Nobu he seemed to be doing something which would bring about precisely the opposite of what he was attempting to achieve, he himself seemed wholly oblivious of this.

When the maid came and knelt beyond the open sliding-door to announce that the bath was ready, however, he quickly stood up as if something had suddenly occurred to him.

'I can't take a bath yet. I still have a few things to do in the garden. . . . It's all right if you all take it first.'

He went out into the garden again to use the remainder of the autumn day for pottering about with the gardener, of whom he was very fond. But after turning his back to the living-room he again turned around to say :

'O-Nobu, please take a bath, and have dinner here too, won't you?'

After saying this, he walked about five or six yards, and then turned around yet again. O-Nobu admiringly observed this restless manner of his, whereby he seemed to be thinking of many things at once, and felt it was most characteristic of him.

'Since you're here, O-Nobu, shall I invite Fujii too for dinner?'

Even though Fujii's occupation differed from that of her uncle, he had been an old acquaintance of his since they had both gone to the same school, and now through the relationship with Tsuda he had become much closer to him than before. Although O-Nobu realized that her uncle was doing this out of kindness to her, she could not be particularly happy about it. She was far less intimate with the Fujii family than Tsuda was.

When her uncle said, 'But I wonder whether he'll come,' his expression indeed indicated what she was secretly thinking.

'Lately everybody's been saying I've retired from active life, but compared to Fujii's way of retirement, which has been going on for the longest time, I'm the most active person in the world. How about it, O-Nobu? Do you think your Uncle Fujii will come to dinner if I ask him?'

'I'm afraid I wouldn't know about that.'

Then her aunt expressed her own opinion in a roundabout way : 'He probably won't come.'

'Yes, I suppose he isn't very likely to come at a moment's notice. All right then, I'll give it up. . . . But it might be good to give him a ring just in case.'

O-Nobu laughed.

'How can you possibly do that? I'm certain he doesn't have a phone.'

'Well then, that's out. I'll send a servant.'

Whether it was too bothersome to write a note or whether he begrudged the time to do it, he spoke as he did, and swiftly walked out into the garden. O-Nobu's aunt stood up as she said, 'Well then, forgive me but I'll take my bath first.'*

Knowing her uncle's meticulousness, O-Nobu viewed with envy her aunt's behaviour as she alone proceeded, without the slightest hesitation, to put into effect her husband's words, while the rest of them held back. And yet while O-Nobu was envious she also felt that her aunt's action was offensive. For even though it was laudable as a self-asserting, individualistic act, it was also unpleasantly unwomanly. The feeling that it would be fine if she could behave that way and the feeling that no matter how old she got she never wanted to behave that way were, as always, entangled in her mind.

As O-Nobu looked dully at the retreating figure of her aunt, Tsugiko, who remained alone with her, suddenly asked her : 'Won't you come to my room?'

The two left the brazier and the tea things scattered as they were in the living-room, and went out.

70

Tsugiko's private room had in fact been O-Nobu's as well before she married Tsuda. The feeling from the past, when the two of them had had their desks lined up together there, seemed to remain on the walls and ceiling. The wood-carved doll too, placed carefully on top of the small bookcase with glass doors, was as it had been. The pin-cushion also, inserted in a basket with an embroidered rose design, was the same. The blue-and-white porcelain single-stalk flower vase with the arabesque design, which they had bought together at Mitsukoshi's, was also there.

As O-Nobu looked about, she sensed everywhere the scent of her girl-hood when she had lived there with her cousin. When her goal, namely her marriage to Tsuda, had finally been realized, she had been ecstatic, as this scent, filled with sweet sentiment, had suddenly been transformed into a bright flame. She had thought it had burst instantly into flame because there had been a highly inflammable element present to ignite it, even though it had not been visible to the eye. She had concluded that there was no need to place any distinction between fantasy and reality. As she reflected, she realized that already more than half a year had elapsed since then. She had at some point begun to feel that fantasy would still remain fantasy, and that it would never be realized no matter how long she lived. Or rather it had begun to seem extremely difficult to realize. She even wished to heave a faint sigh of resignation.

* Japanese custom decrees that the head of the family take his bath first, then the adult male children; the women and younger children follow.

'Isn't the past, like some transitory dream, gradually receding from my present reality?'

With this thought she looked at her cousin sitting in front of her. Tsugiko would probably have to walk the same road she had walked; or she might even have to face a future deviating even more from her expectations than O-Nobu's had from hers. Indeed this young girl's destiny would be decided eternally in a few days, as soon as the dice of approval or disapproval, which her father held in his hand, were thrown on the floor.

O-Nobu smiled as she said :

'Tsugiko, should I choose a fortune for you today?'

'Why?'

'For no particular reason. Just because I want to.'

'But that's no fun. You should decide on something.'

'All right then, I shall. I wonder what it should be.'

'Well, I certainly don't know. That's up to you to decide.'

Tsugiko could not bring herself to mention the problem of her marriage very easily. But for the subject to be mentioned first by O-Nobu also seemed awkward. And yet it seemed clear to O-Nobu that Tsugiko wanted her to touch on the matter indirectly. O-Nobu wanted to please her cousin, but she disliked having a responsibility which later might prove burdensome to her.

'All right, I'll draw one, but you should choose the question you want answered by yourself. Do you agree? Of all the questions you have in your mind now, there's one you want the answer to most, isn't there? Decide on that, all by yourself. All right?'

O-Nobu tried to pick up the gift she and Tsuda had given Tsugiko, which as usual was on her desk, but Tsugiko quickly pushed her hand away.

'No, I don't want to.'

O-Nobu did not withdraw her hand.

'Why not? It's all right, I tell you. Just lend it to me for a minute. I'll draw an answer that will make you happy.'

Although O-Nobu did not really have any very great interest in the written oracles, she suddenly wanted to tease Tsugiko in this way. It was a good way of making her recall her own feelings as a young girl before her marriage. The strength of her arm, as she used it to probe the weak points of her adversary, made her rather actively aggressive. When she thrust back her hand which had been repelled she had already forgotten her first objective. She now merely wanted to seize the fortune-box from the top of Tsugiko's desk. Or rather, with that as an excuse, she merely wanted to tussle with Tsugiko. And they did indeed fight, letting loose, without compunction, strange little girlish shrieks which added interest to their playful contest. They finally knocked over the valuable single-stem flower vase which had been set up in front of the inkstone-box. As the flower vase tumbled from its red sandalwood stand, the water in it naturally spilled out all over the *tatami*. At last they stopped fighting. They looked, without speaking, in much the same way, at the attractive vase which had suddenly fallen from its natural position. Then, just as soon as they looked at each other again, they burst into laughter as if from an irresistible impulse.

71

This unexpected event made O-Nobu even more like a little girl. A freedom such as she had never felt in Tsuda's presence was for a moment reborn. She completely forgot her present circumstances.

'Tsugiko, quick, get a rag and let's wipe it up.'

'No, I won't. You were the one who knocked it over. You go and get it.'

Each stubbornly urged the other to do it. They purposely bandied words.

O-Nobu said, 'All right then, let's decide by playing "paper-rock-scissors",'* as she clenched her slender hand, and thrust it forth forcefully at Tsugiko. Tsugiko immediately responded in kind. Fingers sparkling with jewels flashed between them. Then they both laughed.

'You're a sly one!'

'What do you mean! You're the one who is.'

Finally, when O-Nobu lost, the spilled water had already completely soaked into the cloth desk-cover and into the cracks between the *tatami*. She very calmly pressed down the wet places with a handkerchief which she took out of the sleeve-pocket of her kimono.

'We don't need a rag after all. If I do this it will be all right. The water's already disappeared.'

She put the fallen flower-vase back in its original place, and neatly inserted in it the flowers which had been disarranged. And then, completely forgetting her madcap attitude until then, she recovered her composure. But this only seemed unendurably funny to Tsugiko, who continued laughing by herself for a long time.

When the paroxysms had subsided, Tsugiko took out the oracle box from its case, which she had hidden in her obi, and put it back in the drawer of the bookcase near by. She also turned the lock firmly on it, and purposely turned towards O-Nobu.

* A game whereby an issue is decided between two people. Paper (open hand) wraps rock (clenched fist), which breaks scissors (two fingers), which, in turn, cuts paper.

But this meaningless playful emotion, which, as far as Tsugiko was concerned, could have continued indefinitely, could not control O-Nobu for very long. Although she had for a time forgotten herself, she sobered up more quickly than her cousin.

'It's wonderful you're always so carefree, isn't it, Tsugiko?'

As she said this she returned Tsugiko's glance. But Tsugiko did not in any way understand her inoffensive words.

'Do you mean to say then that you're not?'

In her tone of voice, which all but declared her carefree manner, was also mingled her long-standing dissatisfaction with being treated by everyone as a well-bred young lady who knows nothing of the hard facts of life.

'How in the world do you and I actually differ?'

The ages of the two differed. Their temperaments also differed. And yet where and in what way the two of them differed on the point of constraint and sheer difficulty of life were problems about which Tsugiko had not yet even thought.

'All right then, what sort of worries do you have, Nobuko? Please tell me about them, won't you?'

'I don't have any.'

'You see, I told you so. Aren't you too quite carefree, after all?'

'Well, I may be. But it's just that my way of being carefree is slightly different from yours.'

'Why is that?'

O-Nobu was unable to explain. And she also did not wish to do so.

'You'll soon understand.'

'But there's only three years' difference in our ages—that's all.'

Tsugiko in no way took into consideration the difference of the fact that O-Nobu was married but she was not.

'But it's not only a matter of age, you know. It's a change in circumstances. For instance, a girl becomes a wife, and a wife, when she loses her husband, becomes a widow.'

Tsugiko looked at O-Nobu with a slightly dubious expression.

'When have you been more relaxed, Nobuko, when you were at home here, or since you've married Yoshio?'

'Well, uh. . . .'

O-Nobu was at a loss for words. But Tsugiko did not give her the chance to construct an answer.

'You're more carefree now, aren't you? There, you see?'

O-Nobu was forced to answer :

'Not necessarily.'

'But isn't Yoshio the man you yourself wanted?'

'Yes, and that's why I'm happy.'

'I'm sure you're happy, but aren't you also carefree?'

'Yes, I suppose there are times when I am.'

'Well, do you mean that sometimes you're carefree but that you still have worries?'

'You're too much for me, Tsugiko, when you press me in this way.'

'I certainly don't mean to. It's just that I don't understand, and it may seem as if I am.'

72

The conversation, which had gradually come to a rather delicate point, slipped into the problem of Tsugiko's marriage almost before they were aware of it. Yet O-Nobu, who wanted very much to avoid the subject, also felt, because of the circumstances until then, the duty which made her unable to avoid it. Apart from her making any prediction such as a young girl lacking in experience might expect, it was not that O-Nobu, as an older woman who had greater knowledge of the relation between men and women, did not want to show her the kindness of giving her a certain amount of advice. She crossed over the dangerous area in a roundabout way so as not to give offence.

'What you say simply won't do. In the case of Yoshio, I understood things very well because it was my concern, but in the case of others I'm completely out of my element, and I don't understand a thing.'

'Oh, please don't be so afraid to tell me what you think.'

'I'm not afraid to tell you.'

'All right then, you're indifferent.'

O-Nobu waited a moment before answering.

'Tsugiko, you know perfectly well what I mean. A woman's eyes are very keen only when she's in a situation which concerns her deeply. That's the only time when they can accomplish more in one second than in ten years. And furthermore I can assure you there aren't many such incidents in anyone's life. Some may even spend a lifetime without its happening even once. That's why I say my eyes are like a blind man's. Or at least most of the time.'

'But don't you have those very eyes you mentioned, Nobuko? If so, why didn't you use them for me in my case?'

'It isn't that I *didn't* use them; it's that I *couldn't* use them.'

'But don't we often say that onlookers see more than the players? Since you're on the sidelines, you should be able to look at the matter more objectively than I.'

'Do you mean you want to have your entire life decided by an outsider?'

'No, that's not it, but your comments would be useful as reference. Particularly since I trust you so completely.'

O-Nobu was silent again for a while. She then began to speak with a somewhat different approach.

'Tsugiko, I said something to you before, didn't I? I said I was happy, didn't I?'

'Yes.'

O-Nobu paused at that point. Then she quickly went on before Tsugiko could say anything: 'The reason I'm happy is simply this: it's just that I was able to choose my husband myself. It's because I didn't marry on the advice of others. Do you understand?'

Tsugiko looked rather forlorn.

'Then a person like me doesn't have any hope at all of being happy, does she?'

O-Nobu had to say something. But she could not speak immediately. Finally words began to pour forth from her involuntarily in an excited and urgent tone: 'Oh, but you do, you do! By just loving someone and making him love you. If only you do that, you have untold possibilities of being happy.'

In O-Nobu's mind, as she said this, only Tsuda was clearly present. As she was speaking to Tsugiko hardly a trace of an idea of Miyoshi occurred to her. Fortunately Tsugiko, who interpreted O-Nobu's words as being meant only for her, was not so aroused as she might have been if she had received the force of O-Nobu's tone directly.

Slightly surprised, she looked at O-Nobu as she said, 'Who is it I have to love? Do you mean the man I saw last night?'

'It doesn't matter who. If only you love a man you yourself have chosen. And above all if you make him love you.'

An aspect of O-Nobu's character which was usually concealed gradually began to disclose itself. The docile Tsugiko fell back little by little as it did so. Finally she even heaved a faint sigh as she realized the distance separating them and making it difficult for them to come together. Suddenly O-Nobu raised the pitch of her voice again.

'Do you doubt what I'm saying? It's true, I tell you. I'm not lying. It's true. I'm really very happy. You understand, don't you?'

After she had tried in this way to force Tsugiko to agree with her, she added, as if to herself:

'It's the same with any woman. Even if she isn't happy now, she can become so in the future only through her own decision. I'm certain of it. I'm certain she can find happiness herself. Don't you agree, Tsugiko?'

Since Tsugiko did not know what was happening in O-Nobu's heart, she was forced to try to apply this prediction rather abstractly to her own case. And yet no matter how hard she tried she hardly understood what it meant.

73

At that point they heard hurried footsteps in the hallway, and the person responsible for them opened the door to the room with a clatter. Yuriko, having returned from school, came in unceremoniously. She took off the bag which hung rather heavily from her shoulder, and placing it on her desk, greeted her sister and cousin merely with, 'Well, I'm back.'

Her desk had been placed in the right-hand corner of the area O-Nobu had used. Since Yuriko had been able to take it over as soon as O-Nobu had married, she had been delighted at her good fortune upon her cousin's departure. And since O-Nobu knew this very well, she purposely said to her : 'I've come to bother you again, Yuriko. I hope you don't mind.'

Yuriko did not even give the usual polite answer. She placed her right leg on a corner of the desk, rubbed with her hand the tip of the toe of her black sock, which seemed about to develop a small hole, and then as she placed her leg back on the *tatami*, answered : 'It's all right if you come to visit. After all, it isn't as if I chased you out.'

O-Nobu laughingly said, 'My, you're certainly blunt,' and after waiting a moment, again spoke to her.

'Yuriko, if Yoshio puts me out, you'll feel a bit sorry for me, won't you?'

'Yes, I think I would.'

'If so, you'd put me up again in this room, wouldn't you?'

'Yes, I suppose so.'

Yuriko thought about the matter a while.

'All right, I'd put you up. That's if it's after Tsugiko's married.'

'No, I mean *before* Tsugiko gets married.'

'You mean Yoshio may put you out before that? Hm, couldn't you stand it a bit longer so that he wouldn't? After all, what about me?'

After saying this she joined in the laughter with the two young women. Then, without taking off her *hakama*, she approached the brazier, sat down, picked up the wooden dish the maid had brought, and quickly started eating the rice cake that was on it.

'So you're having a snack now, are you? When I see that dish I can't help remembering old times.'

O-Nobu recalled the time when she was about Yuriko's age. The scene after returning from school, as she stretched out her hand to the wooden dishes placed in front of them, came vividly to her mind. Tsugiko too, as she smiled at her sister who was enjoying what she was eating, seemed to be remembering the same event.

'Nobuko, do you still have snacks even now that you're married?'

'Oh, every now and then. But it's bothersome to keep things on hand just for that, and somehow even when I do, nothing seems to taste as good as what we used to have.'

'Maybe because you don't exercise enough to work up a good appetite.'

While the other two were talking, Yuriko ate up everything on the wooden dish. Then, quite abruptly, she jumped into their conversation.

'It's true, you know. Tsugiko's getting married very soon.'

'Really? And who is it she's marrying?'

'I don't really know, but she *is* getting married.'

'Yes, but what's his name?'

'I don't know his name, but she's still getting married.'

O-Nobu doggedly asked her the third question.

'Well, what sort of person is he?'

Yuriko answered casually :

'He's probably someone very much like Yoshio. Because Tsugiko likes Yoshio a lot. She keeps saying he's a fine husband, and does everything you want him to.'

Tsugiko, blushing slightly, swiftly turned towards her sister. Yuriko instantly dashed away, shrieking : 'Oh, now I've really done it!'

She stopped for a moment at the doorway, and, leaving O-Nobu and Tsugiko behind, fled from the room.

74

Shortly thereafter O-Nobu again got up from her seat with Tsugiko, having been urged by the maid to come to dinner.

Everyone in the family had gathered in the bright living-room with equally bright faces. Even Hajime, who, having pouted over something, had earlier crawled underneath the veranda and had had to be coaxed to come out, was there, talking cheerfully with her uncle.

When Yuriko came purposely to tell her, 'Hajime acted just like a dog,' O-Nobu heard from this young cousin how he had opened his mouth wide and had been able to bite a rice cake that had been dangled to the tip of his nose.

O-Nobu smiled as she listened to the talk of this so-called dog-like boy.

'Dad, when there's a comet, something bad happens, doesn't it?'

'Well, in olden times people believed that. But now that science has advanced nobody believes that sort of thing any more.'

'What about in foreign countries?'

O-Nobu's uncle did not seem to know whether the same superstition had existed in the West in ancient times.

'Foreign countries? Oh, people there never did.'

'But didn't they say there was a comet just before Caesar died?'

Okamoto said, 'You mean before Caesar was killed, don't you?' and then there seemed to be nothing for him to do but try to deceive his son by adding : 'That's because it was the time of the Roman Empire. That's quite different from what we mean by Europe.'

Hajime accepted this, and fell silent. But he soon asked a second question, much more original than the previous one, and brilliantly presented in the form of a syllogism. Since, in digging a well, one hits water, there must be water underground, and since there is water under the ground, the ground should cave in. Why then does it not? This was the essence of his question. Since his father's answer to it was extremely confused, everyone was amused.

'You're right, it doesn't cave in.'

'But if it's water underneath, why shouldn't it?'

'Well, it just doesn't happen that way.'

When the group of women burst into laughter, Hajime quickly jumped to the third question.

'Dad, wouldn't it be fine if our house were a warship? What do you think?'

'I think I still prefer a simple house to a warship.'

'But if it's a house, and there's an earthquake, it will fall down, won't it?'

'I see, you mean if it's a warship it won't fall down no matter how strong the earthquake is. Of course, I hadn't thought of that. You're quite right.'

O-Nobu smiled as she observed her uncle, who seemed genuinely impressed by his son's comment. Although her uncle had previously said he was going to invite Fujii for dinner, he did not appear to be thinking about that any more. Her aunt too was sitting unconcerned, apparently having forgotten about it. O-Nobu suddenly wanted to ask Hajime something : 'Hajime, you're in the same class with the Fujii boy, Makoto, aren't you?'

He said he was, and quickly satisfied O-Nobu's curiosity concerning Makoto. What he said was rich in observation, criticism, and fact, as only a child's appraisal of a person can be. For a time everyone at the table was amused by the skill of his account.

Among the anecdotes about Makoto which made them all laugh, one was as follows :

On the way home from school one day Makoto and Hajime found and peered into a large, deep hole. Across the hole, which had been dug deep in the middle of the street for some public works project, had been placed a single cedar pole. Hajime told Makoto he would give him a hundred yen if he crossed over on the pole. The daredevil Makoto, with his rucksack on his back, and wearing the aforementioned shoes that he contended were made out of dog-skin, then asked whether he really meant it, and began to cross over on the smooth, slippery pole that had hardly any flat surface. Hajime, who at first watched, thinking Makoto would fall any moment, suddenly became frightened as he saw him slowly approaching, step by step, despite the danger. Leaving his friend behind, right over the middle of the deep hole, he ran away as fast as he could. Since Makoto was still entirely taken up with the problem of where to put his feet, he did not even know Hajime had run off somewhere until he had finished crossing. Finally finishing his adventurous feat, he looked up, thinking he would get the hundred yen that had been promised him, but Hajime had run off without a trace.

O-Nobu's uncle commented on the incident by saying, 'You're a pretty smart fellow, Hajime.'

Her aunt said, without much connection to what had preceded, 'Fujii doesn't seem to come over to visit very much any more, does he?'

75

In addition to the fact that their children were in the same class at school, because they were both now related to O-Nobu there had recently developed special aspects to the relationship between Okamoto and Fujii. Since, whether they liked it or not, there would be many occasions in the future, both happy and unhappy, when they would have to see each other, they both were forced to recognize the convenience of becoming as intimate as circumstances allowed. This was especially true of Okamoto since he represented O-Nobu's interests. Furthermore, O-Nobu's uncle had the kind of social adroitness that successful men often have. He also was innately friendly and outgoing. And his nervous temperament made him fearful of being misunderstood. He particularly feared being called haughty, as well-to-do people often are, by those who are relatively poor. Since he had recently retired for a while to recover his health, impaired by many years of work and study, he also had more than enough leisure. In filling the empty stretches of his time every day in the mosaic-like manner that appealed to him, he wanted to get to know gradually things and people he had formerly passed by casually as utterly unrelated to him.

For all of these various reasons Okamoto would from time to time visit the Fujii home on his own initiative. Fujii, who seemed rather misanthropic, did not even attempt to return these visits faithfully, but also did not in any way seem to dislike them. They would chat quite pleasantly. Even though they would not have any very intimate conversations, they felt a certain interest in merely exchanging news of their respective worlds. Moreover their worlds strangely interlocked. Certain things which, seen from one point of view, were extremely stupid, were, when viewed from the other, extremely edifying, and things which on the one side had to be considered vulgar, were, on the other, thought to be definitely practical; therefore, they both were often able to make unexpected discoveries.

'I suppose you'd call what Fujii does the work of a critic. But it hardly amounts to a real occupation,' her uncle observed.

O-Nobu did not understand very well what a critic was. She was convinced that since he could not be of any real use, he tried to fool people by mouthing many grand-sounding phrases. 'I wonder of what use to the world such people are who can't do any real work and merely play games with their minds. Isn't it perfectly natural they don't make much money and are always in need?' Since she could not advance beyond this point, she smiled, and asked her uncle :

'Have you been to Fujii's place recently?'

'Yes, I stopped in the other day for a while on my way back from a walk. His house is at just the right spot for resting when I'm tired.'

'Did you have another interesting conversation?'

'Oh, as usual he's mulling over some strange subject or other. He's that kind of person. The other day he talked to me for a long time about how men chase after women, and women after men.'

'How disgusting!'

'How stupid! And at his age!'

While O-Nobu and her aunt, in succession, expressed amazement and disapproval, Tsugiko turned away.

'No, actually it's a rather strange thing. I was quite impressed at the way the old fellow investigated the matter. According to him, it's this way : He said it's natural that in every family the boys love their mother and, conversely, the girls love their father. And of course after he said it, I realized he was right.'

Since O-Nobu preferred her uncle by marriage to her blood aunt, she became slightly more serious.

'And what did he conclude from that?'

'Well, this is what he said : If men and women aren't eternally chasing after each other, they can't become complete human beings. In other words, there's something lacking in each of them and they can't possibly get it by themselves.'

O-Nobu's interest quickly abated. What he was saying she already knew perfectly well.

'Isn't he just speaking about the old yin-yang* harmony?'

'But isn't it interesting that, while yin-yang harmony is necessary, its opposite, yin-yang discord, is also necessary?'

'Why?'

'All right, listen. Men and women attract each other because they have different qualities, just as I said.'

'Yes, but what then?'

'Well, these different qualities are of course not parts of themselves. They're something quite different.'

'Yes, I see that.'

'Well, look here. If they're something different from themselves, isn't it clear they can't possibly merge with them? They're forced to remain separated forever, aren't they?'

76

Okamoto went on saying various things, half-jokingly.

Just as a man attains a certain fulfilment when he loves a woman so too does a woman when she loves a man. But this is a truth limited to men and women before marriage. Just as soon as the husband-wife relationship is established this truth is reversed, and precisely the opposite becomes apparent. In other words, if a man is not separated from a woman he cannot attain peace. And if a woman too is not separated from a man, the same thing is true. What until then was tractive power is quickly transformed into repellent power. And we come to recognize what has been said from ancient times, that men and women should, after all, stay with their own sex. In effect, man has created the idea of yin-yang harmony merely to understand the principle of yin-yang discord that shortly must follow.

O-Nobu could not determine very well to what extent her uncle's words were borrowed from Fujii and to what extent they were his own, or how much was serious and how much was jest. Although her uncle was not a skilful writer, he was an exceptionally skilful speaker. On the flimsiest foundation he could build the most original and most complicated structure. All sorts of witticisms and pithy remarks would pour forth from him. The more O-Nobu opposed him the more he warmed to his subject and the more eagerly he spoke. Finally she decided to bring the discussion to an end.

'You're quite a talker, aren't you, Uncle?'

'You can't possibly keep up with him, O-Nobu, so you'd better quit. The more you say, the more obstinate he becomes.'

* The male (*yang*) and female (*yin*) principles from ancient Chinese lore.

'Yes, it's as if he's acting purposely to create the very yin-yang discord he's been talking about.'

While O-Nobu and her aunt were exchanging this criticism of him, O-Nobu's uncle watched them, smilingly, but, after waiting briefly for a break in the conversation, he quietly made a pronouncement:

'So you've finally surrendered, have you? If so, I'll let it go at that. I certainly don't want to press someone who's been defeated. . . . Because, on that point, men, no matter how unfeeling they may seem, have the virtue of pitying those who are weak.'

He stood up with a most victorious expression. After he had opened the sliding-door and left the room, his self-important-sounding footsteps moved towards his study, gradually fading away. But after a while he returned, carrying in one hand four or five small thin books.

'I've brought something interesting for you, O-Nobu. If you're going to the hospital tomorrow, would you please take these to Yoshio?'

'What are they?'

O-Nobu quickly took the books and looked at the covers. The English titles perplexed her somewhat since she was not proficient in any foreign language. She read the titles bit by bit, skipping here and there.

'Book . . . of . . . Jokes. English . . . Wit . . . and . . . Humour. . . . What's all this?'

'They're all intended for amusement. They're collections of jokes and riddles, and that sort of thing. They're just the sort of thing for reading in bed. They won't tax his brain in any way.'

'Of course, they're just what you'd suggest.'

'Even so, I think they'll suit Yoshio too. No matter how serious he may be, I can't imagine he'll become angry if I send him these.'

'Of course he won't become angry. . . .'

'All right then, they're for yin-yang harmony. Take them to him and see what happens.'

As she thanked him and placed the books in her lap, her uncle held in front of her the small piece of paper he had in his other hand.

'This is a reparation for having made you cry earlier. Promise me you'll accept it.'

O-Nobu knew what it was even before she took it from him. He purposely waved it in front of her.

'O-Nobu, when there's yin-yang discord, this is the most effective medicine. In most cases, if you just take one dose, it quickly restores you to health.'

As she looked up at her uncle, who was standing, she resisted weakly:
'But we're not a case of yin-yang discord. We're really in complete harmony, I tell you.'

'If so, that's even better. If you take this medicine when you're in harmony, you'll become happier and even stronger physically. In fact, no matter how things go, this is an infallible remedy.'

As O-Nobu took the cheque from his hand and looked at it fixedly, her eyes filled with tears.

77

O-Nobu declined the rickshaw her uncle wished to order to send her home in. But she could not reject his kind offer of seeing her off at the streetcar stop himself. Finally the two of them went up the long hill towards the riverbank together.

'I think exercise is best for my kind of illness, don't you? . . . I'm the one who wants to walk, so don't worry.'

Since, being stout, he was short of breath, it was amusing to O-Nobu to see how he had to huff and puff his way up the hill. And yet he went on speaking as if he had completely forgotten about going back home himself.

On the way they spoke about how they had spent the previous evening. O-Nobu mentioned how O-Toki had thrown herself down for a nap while waiting for her. Since O-Toki had formerly worked for him, he could not help feeling a certain responsibility towards this maid who was now employed by the newly married couple.

'Your aunt knew that habit of hers very well, but still she thinks O-Toki's a fine, honest girl. She even recommended her as quite suitable for looking after the house while you're out. But even so, it's annoying to have her fall asleep when she's all alone. It's quite unsafe. Of course you have to recognize she's still actually very young. And when you're sleepy, you're sleepy, I suppose.'

O-Nobu, knowing perfectly well that no matter how young she might have been she would never have fallen sound asleep if she had been in a similar situation, merely smiled as she listened to her uncle's comments. For the very reason she was returning so early that evening was that she definitely did not want a repetition of the unfortunate result of her very late return the previous day.

She hurriedly boarded the streetcar as it arrived at the streetcar stop. Then, from within, she turned towards him to say goodbye. He, in turn, said, 'Goodbye. Regards to Yoshio.' The two barely had time to exchange their farewells before the characteristic sound and motion of the streetcar began to dominate her mind.

Within the streetcar she did not think about anything in a very organized manner. The faces and forms of the people she had met the previous day merely passed in front of her as rapidly as the streetcar moved along on its rails. And yet she felt that there was a certain factor common to all of these bewildering mental images. Indeed this was the basic theme and those fragmentary images merely flitted before her. She felt she had to identify that certain factor, but her efforts were not easily rewarded with success. She got off the streetcar, still having recognized only the individual pieces of meat but finally not having been able to identify the skewer piercing them.

As soon as O-Toki heard O-Nobu opening the lattice door of the entrance, she dashed out from the kitchen, and greeting O-Nobu as O-Nobu had anticipated, she bowed politely, with her head touching the *tatami*. O-Nobu felt almost as if this attentive attitude of her maid, differing so from that of the previous day, was somehow a merit of her own.

'I'm rather early today, don't you think?'

Actually O-Toki did not seem to think she had returned so very early. But since, looking at O-Nobu's self-complacent expression, she felt compelled to utter a half-hearted 'Yes, you are,' O-Nobu became conciliatory.

'I did intend to come back even earlier, you know. But the days have become so very short it was dark before I realized it.'

While she was having O-Toki fold the kimono she had taken off hurriedly, O-Nobu asked her:

'Did anything special happen while I was out?'

O-Toki answered in the negative, but, just to make sure, O-Nobu asked her again:

'Didn't anyone at all come?'

O-Toki then answered rather excitedly, as if she had suddenly remembered something she had forgotten:

'Oh yes, someone did. That gentleman by the name of Kobayashi.'

This was not the first time O-Nobu had heard the name of her husband's acquaintance. She remembered having spoken to him two or three times. But she did not like him very much. And she also knew very well that he was not regarded at all highly by Tsuda.

'I wonder what in the world he came for.'

As she was about to let this rather rude remark slip out, she rephrased her comment in a more normal tone.

'Did he have some business he wished to speak to me about?'

'Yes, he came to get that overcoat.'

This statement was utterly incomprehensible to O-Nobu, since she had not been told anything about the matter by Tsuda.

'That overcoat? *Whose* overcoat?'

The canny O-Nobu asked O-Toki several questions in rapid succession in an attempt to find out what Kobayashi had wanted. But this was wholly wasted effort. The more O-Nobu asked her, and the more O-Toki answered her, the further the two of them entered a labyrinth.

When they finally realized that it was Kobayashi who was strange rather than themselves, they burst out laughing. The English word 'nonsense', which Tsuda occasionally used, came to O-Nobu's mind. When she linked Kobayashi with this foreign word, O-Nobu found the entire situation unbearably comical. She gave herself over unreservedly to a feeling of humour, which seized her like a paroxysm, and for a while forgot the weighty problem she had brought back with her from her ride on the streetcar.

78

That evening O-Nobu wrote a letter to her parents in Kyoto. She decided she then absolutely had to finish the letter she had begun two days earlier and had continued but had not finished on the previous day. And yet this certainly did not mean that concern for her parents was uppermost in her mind.

She could not settle down. In an attempt to escape from her uneasiness she felt she had to focus her attention on one thing. She also wanted very much to resolve her previous doubt. Thus she came to think that if she wrote a letter to her parents she might be able to calm her own turbulent feelings.

She took up her writing-brush, and began with the customary seasonal greetings, but after she had mechanically got as far as apologizing for her long silence, she paused awhile. Whenever she had to write to her parents, she always had to place the main emphasis of the letter on her relationship with Tsuda. Of course that was what all parents wished to hear from their newly married daughters. It was also something about which every daughter had to inform her parents. And since O-Nobu even felt that if she did not mention her relationship with Tsuda there was hardly any need of writing a letter home at all, as she held her brush she was forced to consider just exactly how she and Tsuda had been getting along recently. It was not that she was compelled to inform her parents of everything precisely as it had happened. But she did feel quite keenly the necessity of assessing the relationship as a certain wife married to a certain man. She thought about the matter intently. Her brush stayed at the same place, without moving. She had to think about the problem, even forgetting the brush that had ceased to move. But the more she tried to ascertain the truth, the less she was able to grasp anything firmly.

Before writing the letter she had been irked by a restless anxiety. Now that she had begun to write it, her mind gradually became calmer, but then she began to be troubled by another matter. The various images in her mind's eye when she had been on the streetcar earlier were now all focused at one point, and she finally discovered, from various comparisons, the basic source of the uneasiness troubling her, but she could not in any way understand the true nature of it. She therefore had to postpone the solution of her problem.

'If I can't solve it today, I'll simply have to solve it tomorrow. If I can't solve it tomorrow, I'll have to do it the day after that. And if I can't solve it then. . . .'

This was her method of reasoning. It was also her hope. And it was her final decision. For she had already publicly declared herself in front of her cousin Tsugiko.

'It doesn't matter who. But by loving with all my might the man I myself have chosen I must make him love me.'

As she recalled her ringing resolution, she vowed it all over again. She also commanded her emotions to acknowledge the vow and be calm.

Her mood became somewhat lighter. She again moved her brush. She continued to write unhesitatingly of her present relationship with Tsuda so as to please her parents. Their happy life together was described in detail. She was delighted to see the tip of her brush run smoothly and pleasantly over the surface of the paper as if, independent of her, it were filled with emotion. The long letter was completed at one stroke. But she in no way realized how much time had been required for her to be able to write it so swiftly.

When she finally lifted her brush, she re-read, from the beginning, what she had written. Since the same mood that had controlled her hand controlled her eye, she felt no need to make any corrections or additions. She did not even worry about the Chinese characters which she only faintly remembered. Normally, when she felt she had to use them, she would look them up in the *Genkai* dictionary. Thus, she merely changed two or three places where the wrong postpositions would make the sense unclear, and folded the letter. She then made the following declaration to her parents who were to receive it :

'Everything I've written in this letter is true. There's not one word of falsehood, evasion, or exaggeration. If someone doubts me, I loathe him, I despise him, I spit on him, because I know the truth better than he. What I've written here is the true state of things—not merely the outside appearance. Maybe I'm the only one who knows this truth now, but in the future everyone will. I'm certainly not deceiving you. If someone says I've written a false letter just to put you at ease, he's blind. In fact, he's a liar. Please believe me—because God already does.'

She placed the sealed letter near her pillow, and went to bed.

79

She recalled the time she had first met Tsuda in Kyoto. She had returned home to see her parents after a long absence, and two or three days after her arrival her father had asked her to do an errand for him. She had to take a letter and case-enclosed Chinese volumes to Tsuda's home, five or six blocks away. She had then first learned from her father that since he had been suffering from a slight case of neuralgia and had been idling about the house he had occasionally borrowed some books from Tsuda's father to relieve the boredom of his illness. Her errand thus had been to return the old ones and borrow new ones. She had stood at the entrance and had asked to be admitted. In the entrance hall was a large single-leaf screen. As she had gazed, astonished, at the strange characters that seemed to dance on its white surface, the person who had appeared from behind the screen had not been a maid or a houseboy but Yoshio, who, like her, had returned to his home in Kyoto.

Of course neither of them had set eyes on the other before. On her part she had merely heard his name mentioned. But it had been little more than what she had heard from her father that morning, to the effect that he had recently returned home or was returning soon. But that too was nothing more than a result of her father's wanting to borrow some more books and of having written the letter she carried.

Yoshio had then taken the Chinese books from her, and for some reason or other had stared for quite a while at the title, *Special Collection of Ming Poetry*, written in imposing characters. She, in turn, had had to look at him for a long time as he was staring at it. But since he had suddenly lifted his face, he had immediately noticed that she had been looking at him intently. But for her, who had had to wait for his answer, such behaviour had certainly been unavoidable. He had then said, 'My Father's unfortunately out just now.' She had immediately tried to leave, but he had called her back, and had opened in front of her, without any apology at all, the letter addressed to his father. This carefree act of his had also served to arouse her interest. His manner had certainly been somewhat brusque. But it also had definitely been quick and decisive. She had in no way wished to criticize him as being either unrefined or rude.

Having read the letter at a glance, he had left her waiting in the entrance hall, and had gone to the rear of the house to look for the desired Chinese books. But unfortunately he had not been able to find the ones her father wished to borrow. He had come back after about ten minutes and had apologized for having kept her waiting for nothing.

He had said that since he simply could not find the books that had been indicated he would deliver them to her home as soon as his father returned to show him where they were. She had refused, saying that that would be an imposition. Instead she had promised to come and get them herself on the following day, and had returned home.

That very afternoon, however, Yoshio had come, purposely bringing the books from his home. Coincidentally, she had answered the door when he came. The two once again had looked at each other. And this time each had instantly recognized the other. He was carrying about three times as many books as she had taken back that morning. They were wrapped in a printed cotton cloth wrapper, and while swinging them along very much as if he were carrying a bird-cage, he had showed them to her.

He had gone into the living-room, as he had been invited to do, and had talked with her father. He had exchanged with her father, who was of a completely different temperament from his, comments which, as far as she could make out, were of a kind old people would make and should have been unbearably tedious to a young man, but he had not seemed particularly annoyed. He had known nothing at all about the books he had brought, and he had known even less about those she had returned. He had apologized by saying that he simply could not read such books filled with square, many-stroke characters. Even so, with the four-character title of *Wu Mei-ts'un's Poetry*, which she had gone to borrow, as a guide, he had searched everywhere on the bookshelves for the work. Her father had thanked him warmly for his kindness. . . .

The Tsuda of that first meeting stood out clearly in her mind. He was not a different person now from what he had been then. And yet he also was not the same person. To put it plainly, the same person had changed. He had at first seemed indifferent to her, but had gradually been attracted to her. But after having once been drawn to her, was he not now gradually withdrawing from her again? Her doubt was almost a reality for her. To eliminate the doubt she had to overturn the reality.

80

A strong determination filled O-Nobu's entire body. When she awoke the following morning there was nothing further removed from her than timidity. She jumped up instantly as if she had forgotten how on the previous morning she had been so loath to leave the bed. When, throwing aside the bedclothes, she got up from the bed, she could feel the strength in her arms. Together with the stimulus from the morning coolness, her firm muscles made her tense.

She opened the rain shutters by herself. Outside it seemed still much earlier than usual. The fact that on that day, unlike the previous day, she had wanted to get up even earlier than when Tsuda was at home somehow made her happy. It also gave her satisfaction as a compensation for having been lazy and having overslept the day before.

After she had herself put away the Japanese-type quilted bedding and had swept the room, she sat down and faced her dressing-table. She then undid her hair which had been set three days earlier. Since, after passing her comb several times through the oily areas, she discovered that her hair had become quite unmanageable, she was forced to pull it up in a low pompadour. She awakened the maid only after doing that.

She worked together with O-Toki until breakfast was ready, and when she sat down to her tray, O-Toki said to her, 'You got up very early today, didn't you, ma'am?' O-Toki, who knew nothing of what was going on in O-Nobu's mind, seemed to be surprised at her early rising. She also seemed to be thinking she was at fault for getting up later than her mistress.

'Well, today I have to go to visit my husband at the hospital.'

'Do you intend to go this early?'

'Yes. I didn't go yesterday, so I'd like to leave a bit early today.'

O-Nobu's manner of speaking was more polite and more formal than usual. She seemed to express a certain calm in this way. But there was also a certain element in her speech which belied that calm. There was distantly perceptible a decisiveness accompanying that element. Her mood spontaneously appeared in her attitude.

Nevertheless she did not try to go out immediately. She spoke for a while about her visit to the Okamotos to O-Toki, who still held a tray and who had let down her kimono sleeves to wait on O-Nobu. Since, for O-Toki as well, having been employed by them in the past, the Okamoto family was a most interesting topic, the two women often chatted about them until they realized they were repeating themselves. This was especially true of the times when Tsuda was absent. For, if he was there, their conversation would occasionally have the strange effect of appearing to exclude him. O-Nobu had begun to notice this after once or twice having felt rather awkward because of this mere trifle. Also, since she had to avoid the unpleasant possibility of having him consider her a woman who proudly likes to flaunt her wealthy connections, she had previously told O-Toki that they should not talk too much about the Okamotos in front of him.

'Hasn't the young lady become engaged yet?'

'Well, there seemed to be some talk about it, but I don't know exactly how it's going to turn out yet.'

'It would be splendid, wouldn't it, if she were soon to become engaged to some fine young gentleman?'

'It will probably happen quite soon, I think. My uncle's very impatient, you know. And also Tsugiko, unlike me, is so very attractive, isn't she?'

O-Toki was about to say something. But since it would have been embarrassing to be flattered by her maid, O-Nobu immediately added:

'It's quite difficult for a woman if she's not attractive, isn't it? No matter how clever or how sensible she is, if she's homely no man will look at her.'

'That's not necessarily the case.'

Since O-Toki reacted strongly in this way, as if to defend herself, O-Nobu wanted to emphasize her point even more.

'No, it's true. Men are like that, I tell you.'

'But it's only temporary. They're not that way when they're a bit older.'

O-Nobu did not answer. But she was still quite confident of the correctness of her position.

'Really, if someone as ugly as I am isn't reborn with a lovely face, there's no hope at all.'

O-Toki looked at her, quite in amazement.

'If you're ugly, ma'am, what word could possibly describe someone like me?'

O-Toki's words contained both flattery and truth. O-Nobu, who knew perfectly well the extent of each, was satisfied with O-Toki's comment, and rose.

While she was changing her clothes to go out, she heard the footsteps of someone coming to visit. The bell in the entrance hall then sounded, whereupon she heard someone asking O-Toki, who had answered the bell, 'Might I speak for a moment to Mrs Tsuda?' O-Nobu inclined her head in an attempt to determine the identity of the speaker.

81

O-Toki, laughing with her sleeve to her mouth, ran into the parlour, but could not tell O-Nobu the guest's name easily. She could only writhe in front of her as she tried to suppress her laughter. It took her quite some time even to utter the simple name 'Mr Kobayashi.'

O-Nobu did not know how to treat this unforeseen guest. Since she had begun to tie a thick formal obi, she could not go out into the entrance hall right away. But it also would be rude of her to keep him standing there forever, waiting, as if he were a bill-collector. She cowered in front of the full-length mirror, frowning in perplexity. After she had had O-Toki tell him, since it could not be helped, that she could not speak to him for very long as she was just then on her way out, she had him come into the living-room. But upon actually meeting him she realized she could not simply listen to what he wanted and have him leave immediately afterwards. In addition, as to ignorance of the meaning of politeness and consideration for others, Kobayashi was second to none, endowed by God with a special talent in such matters. Although he knew perfectly well that O-Nobu was pressed for time, he seemed somehow to have arrived at the conclusion that if only she did not show her annoyance there was nothing whatever wrong with his sitting there forever.

He knew all about Tsuda's illness. He also spoke to her about having acquired a position and of soon going to Korea. According to him, his new job was an important one with good prospects. He also told her how he was being followed by a detective. As he said that this had happened on the evening of his return from Fujii's place with Tsuda, he watched her startled expression with amusement. He seemed proud of being followed by a detective, and even went so far as to explain to her that he was probably considered a socialist.

There were certain things he said which could shock a timid woman. Since O-Nobu had heard nothing whatever from Tsuda, she was finally drawn into his story, and spent a great deal of her valuable time listening to him rather nervously. And yet even though she nodded meekly in agreement to what he said, there seemed to be no end to it. Finally she could do nothing but urge him to disclose quickly the business he had come on. He appeared somewhat nettled but finally stated his business anyway. It was nothing other than the matter of the overcoat which had made O-Nobu and O-Toki laugh uproariously the previous evening.

'Tsuda's already promised to give it to me, you know.'

He said he was primarily concerned about trying on the overcoat once before leaving for Korea so that if it did not fit him too well he could then have it altered.

O-Nobu immediately thought she would take out the article he wanted from the bottom of a chest of drawers. But she had not yet heard anything about it from Tsuda.

She hesitated and said, 'Of course I don't think he'll be wearing it any more anyway,' but she knew quite well her husband's temperament and how he could be unexpectedly meticulous about such things. She thought it would be unfortunate if, because of one worn-out overcoat, she might on some future occasion be said to have been neglectful as a wife.

'It's all right, I tell you. He most certainly said he'd give it to me. I'm not lying to you.'

It was clear that if she did not take it out and give it to him it would be the equivalent of considering him a liar.

'No matter how drunk I may have been, I was still in my right mind, you know. And furthermore I'm not one to forget about something that's going to be given to me, no matter what the circumstances.'

O-Nobu finally made up her mind.

'All right then, please wait a moment. I'll have the maid call the hospital and check with him.'

'You do everything correctly, don't you, Mrs Tsuda?' said Kobayashi, laughing. But the unhappy expression which O-Nobu secretly feared was nowhere discernible in his face.

'It's just to make sure. If he said something to me afterwards it would be embarrassing.'

Even so she felt she had to add these words of explanation so as not to hurt Kobayashi's feelings.

While O-Toki was running to the public telephone and coming back with Tsuda's answer the two of them still had to confront each other. And they filled this time of waiting for her return with conversation. A sudden comment in that conversation, however, made O-Nobu's heart leap, since it was something she in no way anticipated.

82

'Tsuda seems to have become quite mature recently, doesn't he? I suppose it's entirely your doing, isn't it?'

No sooner had O-Toki left than Kobayashi began all of a sudden to speak in this way. Since he was after all a guest, O-Nobu thought she was forced to give a harmless and inoffensive answer.

'Is that so? And here I've always thought I haven't had the slightest influence on him.'

'Why's that, I wonder? He's a completely changed man, I tell you.'

Since Kobayashi's manner of speaking was much too exaggerated, O-Nobu felt she wanted to ridicule him in return. But since her pride did not allow her, she purposely kept quiet. And Kobayashi was not one to give a second thought to what he said. His conversation, on topics which he selected without caring about order or sequence, meandered erratically here and there, but at times it advanced in a straight line to the extent of making him seem rude.

'But after all there isn't a man alive who can stand up to his wife, is there? . . . Of course a bachelor like me can hardly imagine such things, but I'm sure I have something there.'

At last O-Nobu could not contain herself. She began to laugh.

'Yes, I think you do. There are lots of mysterious things that take place between husband and wife which people like you can't possibly understand.'

'If so, please tell me a few, won't you?'

'But it wouldn't do the least good, would it, to tell such things to a bachelor?'

'Well, just for my information.'

A gleam flashed in her narrow eyes.

'Isn't it better if you get married yourself?'

Kobayashi scratched his head.

'Even if I want to, I can't.'

'Why?'

'No woman will have me, so how can I possibly get married?'

'Oh come now, Japan's a country with too many women. All sorts of them are just waiting to be asked.'

After O-Nobu had spoken in this way, she felt she had gone a bit too far. But Kobayashi did not seem to mind in the least. Long thoroughly accustomed to much stronger and more severe words, he was totally insensitive.

'No matter how large the surplus of women is, I'm just on the point of running off to Korea, and no woman would elope with me.'

Kobayashi's mention of eloping immediately reminded O-Nobu of the lovers' elopement in the play she had just seen. This fascinating Kabuki scene, representing an undying love, came clearly to her mind, and she smiled as she looked at Kobayashi, who, in complete contrast to its romantic mood, was seated in front of her, having come to get someone's worn-out overcoat.

'Well, if you're running off, then it would surely be better if two of you went.'

'Two of us?'

'I mean your wife and you, of course. You'll certainly find someone to run off with you, I'm sure.'

'Do you really mean that?'

Kobayashi said this seriously, sitting erect on the cushion. Since his attitude was certainly not what she had expected, she was somewhat surprised. But she also found the situation more amusing than she had anticipated. Yet Kobayashi was indeed serious. After a slight pause he began to say strange things, as if to himself.

'If there really were a woman who'd go off with me to a new life in far-off Korea, maybe I'd never have become the weird person I am today. Actually it's not just that I don't have a wife. I don't have anything—parents or friends or anything. In fact there's no place for me in this world. You might even say there's not one person who cares for me anywhere.'

O-Nobu felt she had never met anyone like Kobayashi in her entire life. Never having heard words like these from anyone, she even found it difficult to grasp their surface meaning. And when it came to the problem of how best to handle him, she was quite at a loss. Yet he became even more emotional.

'Mrs Tsuda, I have only one sister. I have no one else, so she seems extremely precious to me. You have no idea how much more precious she is to me than she'd be to anyone in a normal situation. But even so I'm forced to leave her behind. She wants to follow me wherever I go. But I can't possibly take her with me yet. It's still safer for her if we separate than if we stay together. There's less danger of her being killed by somebody that way.'

O-Nobu began to feel slightly uncomfortable. O-Toki, who she fervently wished would come back quickly, had not yet returned. She felt compelled to try to change the subject and escape from this pressure. She quickly succeeded, but by doing so she fell into another extraordinary situation.

83

This part of the conversation, which took a special course, was begun by O-Nobu : 'But is what you're saying really true, I wonder?'

Kobayashi quickly changed his rather doleful attitude. And, as O-Nobu expected, he asked her a question in return.

'What are you referring to? What I was saying just now?'

'No, not that.'

O-Nobu skilfully guided him on to a side-path.

'What you were saying earlier. That Yoshio's changed a great deal recently.'

Kobayashi had to return to his former topic.

'Yes, I did say that. I said it because it's perfectly true.'

'But has he really changed that much?'

'Yes, I think he has.'

O-Nobu looked at him as if she did not understand very clearly what he meant. Kobayashi, in turn, looked at her as if he had some proof for what he was saying. While they were observing each other briefly in this way, Kobayashi showed the trace of a faint smile. But it was forced to disappear, not having had the opportunity to become a genuine one.

For O-Nobu showed by her attitude that she did not want to banter with Kobayashi or anyone.

'You've probably noticed it yourself, haven't you, Mrs Tsuda?'

This time it was O-Nobu who was being drawn out by Kobayashi. She had certainly been aware of a change in her husband, but the change she had noticed had been of an entirely different kind. It indeed had thoroughly different aspects from the change about which Kobayashi was thinking, or at least from the one about which he was talking. Since her marriage to Tsuda, that change, which, while still faint, she felt had gradually been becoming clearer, was a subtle thing, moving slowly through different tones of colour which were extremely difficult to distinguish. It was of a kind which an outside observer, no matter how shrewd he was, could not possibly understand. And this change was her secret. How could a man like Kobayashi know of the slight transformation by which the man she loved was withdrawing himself from her, or of the change of heart as he slowly began to recognize the sad truth that he had really been separated from her emotionally from the beginning?

'I haven't noticed it at all. You mean to say there are some ways in which he's changed?'

Kobayashi gave a hearty laugh.

'Mrs Tsuda, you're wonderfully clever in pretending ignorance. I can't possibly compete with you.'

'Aren't you the one who's doing precisely that?'

'All right then, I'll let it go at that. . . . But you really do have skill, Mrs Tsuda. Now I've finally understood—just exactly how Tsuda's come to change that much. I'd really thought it was strange.'

She purposely did not take him up on that remark. But she did not seem particularly annoyed. She even took an attitude of charming casualness. Kobayashi advanced yet a step further.

'Even the Fujiis are all surprised.'

'At what?'

When she heard the name Fujii, O-Nobu's narrow eyes instantly fell on her guest. Knowing she was being lured by him, she still had to ask him that question.

'At your skill, of course. At your brilliant way of getting around Tsuda and of controlling him completely.'

Kobayashi's words were too crude. But even so he seemed able to express them to O-Nobu half-charmingly. She answered tartly:

'Is that so? Do I really have that much power? I'm sure I don't know a thing about it, but if the Fujiis say so, I suppose it must be true.'

'Of course it's true. It's clear to me, and it's clear to anyone, so you'll simply have to accept it.'

'Thank you.'

She thanked him in a rather disparaging tone. The bitter note included in her thanks seemed wholly unanticipated by Kobayashi. He immediately spoke to her in a mollifying tone.

'Since you didn't know Tsuda before your marriage to him, Mrs Tsuda, you probably aren't aware of how much you've influenced him, but. . . .'

'I most certainly did know Yoshio before our marriage.'

'But you didn't know him before you met him.'

'Obviously not.'

'But I've known him very well since long before you met him.'

In this way their conversation finally went back to Tsuda's past.

84

It was certainly of great interest to O-Nobu to enter into those areas of her husband's life as yet unknown to her. She was about to listen delightedly to Kobayashi's stories. But when she actually did, she found that Kobayashi certainly did not say anything very pertinent. Or if he did, he always purposely abbreviated the important sections. For example, he touched briefly on the occasion when the two of them had been caught in a police cordon in the middle of the night, but he purposely glossed over where they had been immediately prior to that incident, and seemed not to want to talk to her about it at all. When she asked him about it, he merely grinned significantly. She even felt he was doing this especially to annoy her.

O-Nobu had always looked down upon Kobayashi. Behind this disdain, half based on her husband's evaluation and half on confidence in her own intuitive powers, there was still a large factor she could not state openly to anyone. It was simply that Kobayashi was poor. It was simply that he did not have status. She could not be expected to consider the editing of a magazine that could not sell to be a definite occupation. Kobayashi, as viewed by O-Nobu, was a man who was always loitering about, looking like a vagrant. He merely roamed about unpleasantly, complaining that he did not have a roof over his head.

Mingled with this scorn there was always a certain degree of unpleasantness. This was particularly true for a woman not accustomed to people of Kobayashi's class, and for one who was so young and inexperienced. At least O-Nobu, as she sat facing Kobayashi, felt that way. She could not say that until then she had never met anyone as poor as he. But those poor people who had occasionally come to the Okamoto home had all been clearly identified as such. They had known very well that there were differences in rank, and they all had dared have relations with her only within the limits carefully prescribed for them. She had never yet come in contact with a person as insolent as Kobayashi. She had certainly never met anyone like him who approached her so unreservedly, or anyone like him who, though without money or position, spoke on important subjects, and who constantly criticized the upper classes.

O-Nobu suddenly observed to herself : 'But isn't the man I'm speaking to now the fool and unmanageable wretch I've always thought he was?'

When the unpleasant aspect latent in her disdain came to the fore abruptly, her attitude instantly changed. Then, as evidence that Kobayashi had perceived this, or whether he was wholly indifferent to it, he began to laugh.

'There are still various other things, Mrs Tsuda. Things you want to know, I mean.'

'Really? I think that's about enough for today, though. If I hear too much all at once, it will spoil my pleasure for the next time.'

'I see. All right then, that's all I'll say for today. Since if I hurt your feelings, and you become too upset, Tsuda will only hate me for it, and say it was all my fault.'

O-Nobu turned around. Behind her was a wall. Even so, since she was near enough to the sitting-room adjoining the kitchen, she showed that she was trying to learn whether O-Toki had returned or not. But the kitchen door was as quiet as ever. Clearly, O-Toki, whom she expected back at any moment, had not yet returned.

'I wonder what has happened to her.'

'Oh, she'll be back any minute. After all, she couldn't possibly have got lost, so you don't have to worry.'

Kobayashi showed no signs of leaving. Since there was nothing else for her to do, on the pretext of making some fresh tea she tried to get up from her seat. Kobayashi prevented her.

'If you can listen, Mrs Tsuda, I'll tell you a lot more stories of the type I've just been telling, just to pass the time. After all, to a good-for-nothing like me, it's all the same whether I spend my time talking or keeping quiet, and you don't have to be the least bit reserved with me. How about it? I suppose there are still lots of things Tsuda hasn't been frank about or hasn't even told you about yet, aren't there?'

'Perhaps there are.'

'No matter how he seems to be, he's really not at all frank, is he?'

O-Nobu gave a start. Although inwardly she was forced to agree with Kobayashi's criticism, her feelings were hurt that much more precisely because he was so accurate. She looked at Kobayashi, and considered him an unspeakably rude person who paid not the slightest attention to his inferior social position. Kobayashi, utterly indifferent, emphasized his point.

'I assure you, Mrs Tsuda, there are still lots of things you don't know.'

'Nevertheless, that's perfectly all right with me.'

'But actually there are still lots of things you'd want to know.'

'I still don't care.'

'Well then, what if I say there are still lots of things you *ought* to know? Do you mean to say you still don't care?'

'Yes, even so, I still don't care.'

85

Waves of sarcasm flowed over Kobayashi's face. An expression of victory clearly appeared, announcing that no matter which way she moved he had her trapped. He seemed to want to extend his moment of triumph eternally, and even acted as if he wanted to spend the rest of his life just looking at her that way.

'What a despicable man!'

Thus O-Nobu secretly assessed him. And for a brief moment she stared right back at him. But then it was Kobayashi who began speaking again.

'There are things I absolutely must tell you as evidence that Tsuda's changed, Mrs Tsuda, but since you seem to be so frightened of them, I'll leave that for later, and first tell you a bit, for your future reference, about how, on the contrary, Tsuda hasn't changed at all. Even if it's unpleasant for you, I must have you listen to me. . . . How about it? You will listen, won't you?'

O-Nobu answered coldly, 'Just as you wish.' Kobayashi laughingly expressed his thanks.

'Tsuda's despised me for a very long time. Even now he despises me. As I've been saying, Tsuda's changed a great deal. But as far as his despising me is concerned, that's the same as ever. It hasn't changed a bit. It seems that on that point alone there's nothing at all to be done, no matter how strong the influence of his clever wife. Of course I'm sure that from your point of view his attitude towards me is perfectly natural.'

Kobayashi paused for a moment at that point, and looked at O-Nobu, who was smiling rather painfully. Then he continued :

'But it isn't that I want him to change. On that score I don't in any way hope for your help, Mrs Tsuda, so please put your mind at ease. To tell the truth, Tsuda's not the only one who despises me. Everybody despises me—even the lowest streetwalker. Actually, the entire world's conspired to despise me.'

Kobayashi's eyes were steady. O-Nobu could not say anything.

'That's the truth. Actually you too recognize it secretly, don't you?'

'Don't be ridiculous.'

'I know very well you feel you have to say that.'

'My, but you're certainly suspicious, aren't you?'

'Yes, maybe I am. But whether I am or not, a fact's a fact. But it really doesn't matter. Since I seem to have been born a good-for-nothing, I suppose it's not strange that I should be so despised. It isn't that I hate anyone for it. But can you possibly understand the feelings of a man who's constantly treated by the world the way I am?'

Kobayashi looked at O-Nobu for a long time, waiting for an answer. But O-Nobu had nothing to say. She wondered how his feelings, which aroused in her not the slightest sympathy, could possibly have any relation to her. For she had problems to think about herself. She did not even wish to exert her imagination on his behalf. As Kobayashi saw this attitude of hers, he began again :

'Mrs Tsuda, I live to be disliked. I purposely say and do things people don't like. If I don't, it's so painful I can't stand it. I can't live any other way. I can't make people recognize my existence. I'm worthless. And no matter how much people despise me I can't carry out any revenge. Since there's nothing else I can do, I've actually tried to be disliked. That's what I really want.'

The psychological state of a man born to an utterly different world was revealed to her. Her own desire was to be loved by everybody, and to behave so as to be loved by everyone. Particularly with regard to Tsuda did she have to behave that way. Furthermore she had always firmly believed that her feelings could be applied, without the slightest variation, to everyone else in the world.

'You seem greatly surprised, don't you, Mrs Tsuda? You've never met such a man before, have you? But there are lots of different people in the world, you know.'

Kobayashi had a rather satisfied expression.

'You've disliked me from the beginning, Mrs Tsuda. You've been wishing with all your might that I'd leave soon. But for some reason or other the maid hasn't come back, and you've been forced to talk to me. I'm perfectly aware of that. But you only think I'm an unpleasant fellow, Mrs Tsuda, and you don't know the reasons why I've become this way. That's why I've explained them to you slightly. I can hardly think I've been this sort of hateful fellow since birth. Of course I'm not too sure about that either, though.'

He again gave a loud laugh.

86

O-Nobu became completely confused in the presence of this strange man. First of all, she did not really understand him. Secondly, she felt no sympathy whatever for him. And thirdly, she doubted his sincerity. Hostility, fear, disdain, distrust, ridicule, hatred, curiosity—she was certainly unable to bring together these various feelings, which mingled confusedly in her brain. Consequently they merely made her uneasy. She finally asked him :

'Do you mean to say then that you admit you came here purposely to annoy me?'

'Oh no, that wasn't my purpose. I came here to get the overcoat.'

'But are you saying that while you came to get the overcoat you also came to annoy me?'

'No, that's not it either. I came without the slightest ulterior motive. I think I'm much less calculating than you are, Mrs Tsuda.'

'Be that as it may, won't you please answer my question directly?'

'All right, that's why I said I came here perfectly naturally, without any ulterior motive. It's merely that as a natural result I seem to have been able to annoy you.'

'In other words, that was your objective, wasn't it?'

'No, it wasn't. But it may have been my basic desire.'

'What's the difference between your objective and your basic desire?'

'You mean you don't think there is any?'

Hatred flashed from O-Nobu's narrow eyes. They clearly warned him that he had better not try to make a fool of her just because she was a woman.

'You mustn't get angry,' Kobayashi said. 'I've merely tried to explain to you that I haven't been trying to get revenge on you from some petty motive. I said that purposely because I wanted you to understand I can't help it if God has made me the kind of person I am and has ordered me to go and annoy people. I'd like you to realize I don't have any bad intentions at all. I'd like you to know that from the outset I've been completely without purpose. But God may perhaps have one. And for His purpose He may be using me. And maybe my basic desire is to be used by Him.'

Kobayashi's statement was a trifle too confused. But O-Nobu did not have the necessary intellect to probe the holes in his logic. Nor did she have mental faculties sufficiently organized to determine whether she should accept his statement unconditionally or not. And yet she certainly was clever enough to grasp the main point of his argument. She quickly summed up Kobayashi's aim in a few words.

'Well then, you mean that as far as annoying people is concerned, you can annoy them as much as you like but that you don't in any way accept the responsibility for your actions.'

'Yes, that's precisely it. That's my main point.'

'Such a cowardly—'

'It's not cowardly. I'm not cowardly for not having a sense of responsibility.'

'You most certainly are! First of all, I don't remember ever having done you the slightest harm. Or if I have, please tell me, I'll be glad to listen.'

'Mrs Tsuda, I'm a man everybody treats as a vagabond.'

'What possible connection does that have with Yoshio or me?'

Kobayashi began to laugh, almost as if to say he had been waiting for her to say that.

'From your point of view there probably isn't any. But from mine there's more than enough.'

'Why is that?'

Kobayashi did not answer immediately. Instead he had an expression which seemed to say that he would like her to try to mull over the answer herself as a kind of homework, and he silently began to smoke a cigarette. She felt even greater annoyance. She almost wanted to tell him to leave. But at the same time she wanted to find out what he meant. His attitude of seeing that she wanted to find out more and of not paying the slightest attention to her also annoyed her. But since O-Toki, whom she had been awaiting with great impatience for quite some time, finally came back just at that point, O-Nobu's vexations had to give way again before she could find the opportunity to express them in a fixed form.

87

O-Toki knelt on the veranda and opened the sliding-door from outside.

'Forgive me, I know I'm terribly late. I had to go by streetcar all the way to the hospital.'

O-Nobu looked at her somewhat angrily.

'Do you mean then that you didn't phone?'

'Oh no, I did phone.'

'You mean you tried to phone but you couldn't get through?'

By several of these exchanges O-Nobu was finally able to understand why O-Toki had gone to the hospital. . . . At first O-Toki had found it impossible to get through by telephone, and finally when she had succeeded she had not been able to state her business. She had asked for the nurse and had tried to have her take the message, but even that had not gone as O-Toki had thought it would. She had always been forced to speak merely to a young man who was the doctor's houseboy or the pharmacist who worked there, and although he had said something or other, she had been utterly unable to make it out. First of all his words had been very unclear. And even the parts she could understand clearly were quite ambiguous. Since, in effect, he had not taken O-Toki's message to Tsuda, she had finally given up, and had left the telephone booth. And yet since she had not accomplished her mission and disliked returning home without having done so, she quickly boarded a streetcar going towards the hospital.

'I did think I might first come back and ask you before going, but then it would just have taken longer and I also thought it wasn't right to keep your guest waiting any longer than necessary.'

What O-Toki said was perfectly understandable. O-Nobu had to thank her. But when she thought that because of O-Toki's delay she had had to endure a most unpleasant experience with Kobayashi, she could not but consider O-Toki hateful even though she had tried to be helpful.

O-Nobu got up and went into the sitting-room. She quickly opened the lowest drawer of the double bureau, with its gleaming copper metalwork. She then took out from the bottom of the drawer the overcoat in question, and placed it in front of Kobayashi.

'It's this, isn't it?'

Kobayashi said it was, and quickly took the coat in his hands. With the eye of an old-clothes dealer examining one of his items, he turned it over.

'It's much dirtier than I thought.'

O-Nobu wanted very much to say, 'That's just about enough out of you,' but without answering she too looked intently at the overcoat. As Kobayashi said, the colour was somewhat changed from what it had first been. This was startlingly obvious if one compared the colour of the main section of the overcoat with that of the unexposed area under the collar.

'But I suppose that since I'm getting it for nothing I can't complain, can I?'

'If it doesn't meet with your approval, by all means don't take it.'

'You mean I should leave it and go, don't you?'

'Yes.'

Nevertheless he did not relinquish it. She looked at him scathingly.

'Do you mind if I just try it on for a moment here, Mrs Tsuda?'

'No, go right ahead.'

She purposely said the opposite of what she felt. And then, still sitting, with a sarcastic glint in her eye she observed him as he squirmed to put his arms through the seemingly narrow sleeves.

'How does it look?'

He asked her this as he turned his back towards her. She could not help seeing the many ugly creases where the coat had been folded. Instead of telling him, as she ought to have, that it badly needed pressing, she said :

'It seems just right to me.'

She was sorry there was no one else there to share her amusement at the comical spectacle he was then presenting.

Kobayashi then turned around swiftly to face her, and still wearing the coat, sat down weightily, crossing his legs in front of her.

'Mrs Tsuda, no matter how odd-looking a man's clothes are, and no matter how much he's laughed at, it's still good to keep on living.'

'Really?'

With that O-Nobu quickly fell silent.

'But I suppose a woman like you who's never known any hardship still doesn't understand that, does she?'

'Maybe not. I think if a person lives only to be laughed at, then it would be much better if he were dead.'

At first Kobayashi did not answer. But then he suddenly spoke :

'Thanks. With your help I can get through this winter too.'

He stood up. O-Nobu did too. As the two were about to file out to the veranda from the living-room, Kobayashi turned around abruptly.

'Mrs Tsuda, if you have that sort of attitude, you'd better be very careful you're not laughed at yourself.'

88

Their faces came to within less than a foot of each other. At the moment O-Nobu had tried to move ahead, Kobayashi had turned around, and the two of them suddenly had to interrupt their movements. They came to an abrupt halt. And then they looked at each other — or rather, they stared at each other.

Kobayashi's thick eyebrows stood out even more clearly and blocked O-Nobu's line of vision. The black pupils under them did not move as he levelled them at her. To learn what they meant she could do nothing but try to make him actually tell her. She finally spoke :

'Your comment's quite unnecessary. I most certainly don't need to listen to any such advice from you.'

'It's surely not that you don't *need* to listen to my advice. I think you mean you don't have any intention of listening to it. Of course there's no doubt that you're a fine, respectable lady. But even so. . . .'

'That's quite enough! Please leave this instant!'

At first Kobayashi did not answer. Then the following exchange took place while they were still within inches of each other:

'But I was talking about Tsuda, not you.'

'Are you saying that Yoshio's done something? Are you saying that I'm a fine, respectable lady but that Yoshio's not a gentleman? Is that it?'

'I have absolutely no idea whether he's a gentleman or what he is. First of all I don't recognize the existence of such class distinctions.'

'Whether you do or not is entirely up to you. But are you saying Yoshio's done something?'

'Do you want to hear about it?'

A streak of lightning flashed directly from her narrow eyes.

'Yoshio's my husband.'

'Yes, that's right, he is. Therefore you want to hear about it, don't you?'

O-Nobu ground her teeth.

'Get out of here!'

'Yes, I'll go. As a matter of fact I'm leaving just now.'

Kobayashi immediately turned around as he said this. He moved about two paces away from O-Nobu on the veranda as he tried to go towards the entrance. O-Nobu, watching him from behind, could not control herself, and called out to stop him.

'Wait a moment!'

'What is it?'

In a hulking manner he turned around and stopped. Wearing the old overcoat, which was much too long for him, he put out both his arms, and after looking around at himself as if to admire his appearance, which was like a figure in a cartoon out of *Punch*, he looked at O-Nobu, as he snickered.

O-Nobu's voice became even sharper.

'Why are you going without saying anything?'

'But I think I did say thank you earlier, didn't I?'

'I'm not talking about the coat.'

Kobayashi purposely put on an innocent look. He even went so far as to feign an expression that indicated he was utterly at a loss as to how to answer her. O-Nobu rebuked him with:

'It's your duty to explain yourself to me.'

'Explain what?'

'What you implied about Yoshio. Yoshio's my husband. To have cast aspersions on a man's character in front of his wife, and especially to have done it in such a roundabout way, is a terrible thing, and it's your duty to explain exactly what you mean.'

'Or else I have only to retract it, I suppose. Since I'm a man who has very little sense of duty or responsibility, it may be rather difficult for me to explain things to your satisfaction, but at the same time, as a man who doesn't know the meaning of shame, it's the easiest thing in the world for me to cancel out what I've said. . . . All right then, I take back my slip of the tongue concerning Tsuda. And I also apologize to you. That makes it all right, doesn't it?'

O-Nobu gave implicit agreement but did not answer. Kobayashi corrected his stance in front of her.

'Once again I'll explain myself here clearly : Tsuda has a splendid character. He's a gentleman—that is, if such a special class exists in society.'

O-Nobu, as before, looked down and did not speak. Kobayashi continued :

'I told you earlier, Mrs Tsuda, that you should be careful not to let yourself be laughed at. And you said there was no need for you to take my advice. Naturally I hesitated to say anything further. Actually I now realize that what I said was a slip of the tongue. I retract it. And if there was anything else that hurt your feelings, I take all that back too. Everything was a result of my impropriety.'

After saying this, he put on his shoes which were lined up at the shoe-removal place in the entrance hall. Finally, as he opened the lattice-door and went out, he turned around and said, 'Goodbye, Mrs Tsuda.'

O-Nobu gave the faintest of polite nods in return, and stood there dully for a long time. Then she quickly dashed up the stairs, and as soon as she had sat down at Tsuda's desk, threw herself over it, and burst out crying.

89

Fortunately O-Toki did not come up from downstairs so that O-Nobu was easily able to achieve her immediate objective. She was able to cry to her heart's content without having anyone see her. And when she had cried herself out to her satisfaction, her tears automatically ceased to flow.

After thrusting her crumpled wet handkerchief in her pocket, she abruptly opened the two drawers of the desk. And yet even after she had investigated them, one after the other, nothing particularly new came to light. That too was as it should be, for two or three days earlier when Tsuda had had to enter the hospital she had already looked there to gather the necessary items for him to take with him. She looked at the remaining envelopes, rulers, receipts of club dues, and the like, and then replaced them carefully one by one. One pamphlet of advertisement, with various Panama and straw hats in lithograph, reminded her of an evening in early summer when the two of them had gone shopping on the Ginza. The pamphlet, which Tsuda had been given when they had stopped at a shop to buy a summer hat for him, was inextricably linked, as a part of a past she was reluctant to leave, with the bright red azaleas that had then been blooming in Hibiya Park, and the tall and luxuriant willows that had cast gentle shadows on a side of the avenue in Kasumigaseki at the end of the vista. O-Nobu remained deep in thought for a while, still holding the open pamphlet. And then, as if she had suddenly come to a decision, she slammed the desk drawer shut.

By the side of the desk there was a bookcase, similarly made in a rectilinear style, with two drawers set within it. Having abandoned the desk, she swiftly turned towards the bookcase. But since, when she put her hand on the metal rings of the drawers and tried to open them, there was not the slightest resistance from either of them, and they came out with the greatest of ease, she was disappointed even before investigating their contents. She could hardly expect that places that could be opened so easily would provide any new discoveries. She looked around vainly among some old notebooks. It would have taken her forever to read them all, but she could not imagine that even if she did she would find out in such jottings the things she wanted so much to know. She knew very well her husband's meticulousness. He was much too careful to put anything of a secret nature in a place that was not under lock and key.

O-Nobu opened the closet, and cast a glance to see whether there was any place that was locked. But there was none. On the upper shelves she found only some uninteresting odds and ends piled up in a disorderly fashion. The bottom of the closet was entirely taken up by an oblong chest.

After she had retraced her steps to the desk, she took out the letters addressed to Tsuda from the letter-rack on the desk, and began to examine them one by one. She thought she would probably find nothing suspicious in such a place. And yet several of the letters which she first glanced at but did not even touch remained where they were for a long time even though they were of a kind that would finally require her to look them over and which aroused her interest. At last she had to pick them up, telling herself that she simply had to make sure.

One after another she turned the envelopes over. She spread out their contents in an orderly way. A fourth, or half, of the remaining letters she read silently. Afterwards she put them back in place in their former order.

Suddenly a dark suspicion seized her. The figure of Tsuda pouring oil on a bundle of old letters and burning them in the yard rose distinctly in her mind. He had fearfully pushed back down, with a bamboo stick, the pieces of paper that had danced upwards, transformed into flames. This had happened on a day in early autumn when the wind had felt cold on one's skin. It had been a Sunday morning. Less than five minutes after they had finished their breakfast together and he had put down his chopsticks, he had brought down from upstairs a bundle wrapped with a thin string. Then, no sooner had he turned and gone out into the yard from the kitchen door than he set fire to the bundle. When O-Nobu had gone out on the veranda, the thick outer wrapping had already been charred, and the letters within had been only partially visible. She had asked him why he was burning the packet. He had answered that papers are hard to deal with if one lets them accumulate. When she had asked him why he did not let her use some of them for setting her hair, he had not said anything. He had simply kept poking, with the bamboo stick, at the letters that appeared from the bottom of the bundle. Each time he had done so, the thick smoke that could not become flame had curled around the tip of the stick. Thus the curling smoke had concealed both the point of the green bamboo stick and the letters he had been pushing down. He had turned his face away from her as he was being suffocated by the smoke. . . .

O-Nobu sat motionless, like a doll, immersed in thought about this past event until O-Toki came up to urge her to come to lunch.

90

It was already past noon. Once again O-Nobu faced her tray alone as O-Toki waited on her. This was in no way different from what the two of them did every day when Tsuda went to his company office. But on that day she was not her usual self. She was extremely tense. And yet her mind was in confusion. Even the kimono she had changed into when she had intended to go out earlier served to increase her sense of its being a special occasion.

If the problem that then concerned her had not been mentioned by O-Toki, O-Nobu might very well have finished her meal without ever saying a word. Actually she had only sat down to her tray, intending to eat in the most perfunctory way, without any real desire to do so, because she disliked having O-Toki wonder why she could not eat.

O-Toki too purposely avoided conversation as if she were somehow rather diffident. But when O-Nobu put down her chopsticks after eating, O-Toki finally asked her, 'Did something happen, ma'am?' And even when O-Nobu merely answered in the negative, she did not immediately take the tray and go into the kitchen.

'I'm very sorry for the trouble I caused.'

O-Toki apologized for having gone to the hospital on her own initiative. O-Nobu, on her part, had something she wished to ask O-Toki.

'I made quite a fuss earlier, didn't I? Did you hear me even in the maid's room?'

'No.'

O-Nobu cast a suspicious eye on her. O-Toki, as if to avoid it, quickly said:

'That guest was certainly—'

But O-Nobu did not take her up on it. Since she merely waited quietly for what O-Toki would add, O-Toki was forced to finish her statement. Their conversation progressed, with that as a beginning.

'Mr Tsuda was quite surprised. He said Mr Kobayashi was certainly a rude man. He said he was just the sort of person who wouldn't wait for you and Mr Tsuda to say he could come and get the overcoat but would come and start speaking to you directly without any apology. And he said Mr Kobayashi knew perfectly well that he was in the hospital.'

O-Nobu gave a faint derisive laugh. But she did not add her own comment.

'Did my husband say anything else to you?'

'He said you should just give him the coat and get rid of him right away. And then when he asked me whether Mr Kobayashi was talking with you and I said he was, he had a very disagreeable expression.'

'Really? Is that all?'

'No. He asked me what you were talking about.'

'And what did you say to that?'

'Since I didn't really know what to say, I said I didn't know.'

'And then what did he do?'

'Then he looked even more displeased. He said it was a mistake to have let him come into the living-room in the first place. . . .'

'Is that the sort of thing he said? But after all, he's his old friend, so what could I possibly have done?'

'That's what I said too. And I also said that since you were just then changing your clothes you couldn't have gone out immediately to the entrance hall and dealt with him there.'

'Yes of course. And what did he say then?'

'Then he admired the fact that since I used to work for the Okamotos I always take your side in everything, and he made fun of me.'

O-Nobu laughed wryly.

'I'm very sorry for you. Is that all?'

'No, there's still more. He asked me whether Mr Kobayashi had been drinking. I hadn't paid much attention, but since it isn't the New Year season I thought it highly unlikely that a man would be drunk so early in the morning and go to visit someone's house. . . .'

'Do you mean you said he wasn't drunk?'

'Yes.'

O-Nobu showed that she thought there was still more to follow. And O-Toki indeed did not stop at that point.

'Mr Tsuda told me, ma'am, that when I came back I was to tell you.'

'Tell me what?'

'That Mr Kobayashi is a man who'll say anything. Especially when he's drunk he's a dangerous person. That's why Mr Tsuda said that no matter what Mr Kobayashi said you weren't to take him up on it. He said you wouldn't be far wrong in considering everything he said to be a lie.'

'Really?'

O-Nobu did not wish to say anything more than that. O-Toki snickered.

'Mrs Hori, who was at his bedside, laughed too.'

That was the first O-Nobu learned that Tsuda's younger sister had gone to visit him at the hospital that morning.

91

Tsuda's sister, who was one year older than O-Nobu, was the mother of two children. Her older boy was already four years old. The simple fact that she was a mother had been enough to awaken her self-consciousness. For the previous four years her entire being had been only that of a mother. Indeed there had not been a single day when she had not been aware of her maternal role.

Her husband led a life of pleasure. And he had the easy-going disposition one often finds in such men. While he indulged freely in all sorts of dissipation he was not in any way difficult towards his wife, but he also did not treat her with any great affection. This then was his attitude towards O-Hide. And indeed he was rather proud of it, for he seemed to think that one could arrive at such a state only after undergoing the long discipline of profligacy. If he had a rule of life to which one could attach the difficult term *Weltanschauung*, it was simply to treat everything casually. It was to pass everything by with a smile. It was to be attached to absolutely nothing. It was to stroll through the world in a carefree way, irresponsibly, indifferently, open-handedly, and affably. This constituted his particular form of so-called connoisseurship. Since he had never been financially inconvenienced he had been able until then to put into practice his views. And also no matter where he went he never felt that anything was lacking. His success in this area made him even more optimistic. Confident he was liked by everybody, he was of course certain that he was liked by O-Hide as well. And he was not in any way mistaken about this, for actually O-Hide did not particularly dislike him.

O-Hide, whom he had selected as a wife because he had found her physically attractive, first learned of her husband's disposition only after marrying him. She gradually came to understand the tastes of this man whose very being seemed to have been washed with the saké of his dissipation. Even the doubt about the need such a carefree man had of marrying her, which she might very well have begun to harbour seriously, was immediately suppressed. Since she was not so firm a woman as O-Nobu, before she understood his reason for marrying her she had already detached herself from him as a wife, and had to cast her eyes, which for the first time shone with a motherly brilliance, on her new-born child.

This was not the only area where O-Hide differed from O-Nobu. Unlike O-Nobu, whose new home was composed only of Tsuda and herself, and where the families of both were in distant Kyoto, O-Hide had her husband's mother living with them. His younger brothers and sisters were also living with them, and there were even other relatives who were hangers-on. Because of these circumstances, therefore, she could not be thinking simply about her husband. Among the various relatives living with them she had to give special care, the extent of which others could not possibly imagine, to her mother-in-law.

As one might expect of a woman who had been married for her beauty, O-Hide seemed to be forever young when viewed superficially. She even seemed younger than O-Nobu, who was actually a year younger than she. She certainly did not appear to be the mother of a four-year-old boy. And yet since she had spent the previous four or five years under quite different conditions from those of O-Nobu she had acquired different skills. For while it was true that she did seem younger than O-Nobu, in a certain sense she certainly appeared more mature. It was not that her speech or external behaviour were more mature, but rather that her entire mentality was. In other words, she seemed to have become more quickly accustomed to family life and its responsibilities.

Since O-Hide had to look at her brother and sister-in-law from her vantage point of greater marital experience, she was always dissatisfied with them. If any incident arose, this dissatisfaction had the tendency of making her the ally of her parents. Nevertheless she tried very hard to avoid any direct clash with her brother. She particularly felt that to make some disparaging comment to her sister-in-law would be even worse than meeting her brother head on, and she had always carefully restrained herself. But her true feelings were rather the reverse of this. She always harboured much more resentment towards O-Nobu, who said nothing, than towards her brother, who would often speak sharply to her. She was forever wishing that her brother had not married such an extravagant woman. Yet she never realized that such a desire was nothing more than partiality towards her blood relative and that it was an unjust criticism of O-Nobu.

O-Hide felt she understood her own attitude towards them very well. She was aware that even if she was not kept at a respectful distance by her brother and his wife she certainly was not thought of highly by them. And yet she in no way felt that she ought to change her attitude. First of all, precisely because the two of them disliked it she was loath to change it. Since their dislike of her attitude was in effect the same thing as their dislike for her, she stubbornly maintained her position at that point. Secondly, she was firmly convinced that she was right. She assured herself that she did not care how much they objected to her position since she was maintaining it for her brother's good. Thirdly, her attitude finally had to be focused on the simple fact that she disliked her extravagant sister-in-law. And yet why was it that on this one point she, who had more leisure than O-Nobu and who could indulge in greater luxury, should be so displeased with her sister-in-law, who was beneath her socially? This question did not arise in O-Hide's mind at all. On the other hand, O-Hide did have a mother-in-law whereas O-Nobu, if one excluded her husband, was wholly her own mistress. O-Hide, however, was not even aware of this difference as a factor in her relations with them.

O-Hide had learned about Tsuda's condition from O-Nobu by telephone, and she had gone to visit him the following day at the hospital just an hour before O-Toki had gone, and at the precise moment that Kobayashi had gone to get the overcoat and had entered the living-room of the Tsuda home.

92

Since Tsuda had not been able to sleep well the previous night he merely touched the contents of the tray the nurse brought him in the morning, and lying down on his back again, he closed his heavy eyelids in an attempt to catch up on his sleep. Since O-Hide came in just as he was beginning to doze off, he woke up immediately at the sound of the sliding-door. He then turned to face his sister, who out of consideration for him had purposely opened the door quietly.

They certainly were not ones to exchange courtesies in such a situation. Nor did they even look at each other happily. For them such acts would have been nothing more than excessively banal social formality and even close to a kind of hypocrisy. They had a tacit understanding such as exists only between brother and sister and which would have been difficult for them to apply to anyone else. This implicit agreement had come to be established over the course of many years, since when they had used up their resources in behaving superficially, like other people who forever try to be thought well of by each other, they were not then going to start all over again; and thus they had decided to dispense with any even more useless efforts to deceive each other and simply to deal with each other as they were, with expressions that did not belie their true feelings. And these expressions were, in effect, totally devoid of affection.

In the first place, like any other brother and sister, they saw a great deal of each other. Therefore, in the sense that they did not need to be reserved, these unamiable exchanges did not disturb them. Secondly, they had specific matters on which they did not see eye to eye. These were a source of controversy, and when Tsuda and O-Hide met they repelled each other.

In Tsuda's eyes, as he raised his head and found O-Hide there, laziness and indifference resulting from these two facets of their relationship were indeed present. As if he had been waiting for something, he turned his head away on the pillow after having raised it briefly. O-Hide, on her part, paid not the slightest attention to his movement, and, without saying a word, entered the room softly.

The first thing she did was to look at the tray near his pillow. The top of the tray was quite untidy. Underneath the milk bottle, turned over on its side, was the shell of one egg, and near it, crushed under the bottle's weight, had been thrown a partially eaten piece of toast with tooth-marks on it. But another slice, placed neatly on a plate, was as yet untouched. And one egg also remained untouched.

'Yoshio, have you finished with this yet? Or are you still eating?'

Actually his manner of finishing his meal was so untidy it could be interpreted either way.

'I've already finished.'

O-Hide raised her eyebrows, and began carrying the tray to the landing at the top of the stairs. The remains of breakfast on the tray, which had been left by her brother's pillow for a long time, perhaps because the nurse was busy, were not a very pleasant sight for her, since she had just left her own home where the cleaning had all been done.

'My, how very untidy !'

She was not scolding anyone, but merely spoke to herself, and then returned to her seat. But Tsuda remained silent, and did not take her up on it.

'How did you know I was here?'

'By phone.'

'You mean O-Nobu phoned?'

'Yes.'

'Even though I told her she didn't have to?'

This time it was O-Hide who did not take him up on it.

'I intended to come right away, but unfortunately yesterday I was somewhat busy and—'

O-Hide did not finish her sentence. After her marriage she had developed, before she was aware of it, this habit of making only half a statement. Depending on the situation, this habit affected Tsuda rather strangely. There were times when he could interpret it as meaning : 'Since I've been married you've become a stranger, Yoshio.' Of course it was not that he did not realize full well that there was considerable justification for such an attitude in view of the fact that both of them now had their respective spouses. Indeed he even went so far as secretly to hope that O-Nobu would behave towards the outside world in a similar manner. And yet he certainly did not derive any pleasure from having O-Hide try to behave towards him with this somewhat distant attitude. But he lacked that margin of self-knowledge to reflect that he himself was forever behaving towards her in precisely the same way.

He spoke as he felt, without asking her to complete her statement.

'You certainly didn't have to make any special effort to come and see me today, especially when you're busy. After all, it isn't such a serious illness.'

'But O-Nobu on the phone particularly said that if I was free I was to come and see you.'

'Did she?'

'And besides, I have a small matter I'd like to speak to you about too.'

He finally turned his head towards her.

93

After the operation a strange feeling had begun to bother him in the area of the incision. It was simply that special sensation which arises when the muscles near the incision, which had been stuffed with gauze, contract for a time, but which, once it has started, continues regularly, very much like respiration or a pulse.

He had felt the first contraction two days earlier, in the afternoon. This sensation, which he had had at the moment when O-Nobu, whom he had allowed to go to the theatre, went downstairs, and left, was not something completely new to him. Having already had the same experience when he had had treatment previously, he could not help exclaiming to himself, 'Oh, it's started again.' And, as if it were purposely evoking the unpleasant memory on his behalf, the throbbing continued regularly. At first the flesh contracted so that he felt it rubbing roughly against the stuffed-in gauze; then the sensation would gradually weaken, and shortly his body would attempt to return to its natural state and become lax; but suddenly, as waves which have withdrawn strike the beach again with great force, the feeling of contraction would return violently. His will would then lose completely its normal power of command over that region of his body. The more impatient he became to have it stop, the more his body refused to respond. . . . These had been the stages through which the pain had passed.

He did not know what kind of connection there was between this strange feeling and O-Nobu. He had been ashamed to treat her like a caged bird, and had thought it was not manly of him to tie her to him forever. Thus he had finally released her to fly forth into the free and open air. But no sooner had she thanked him for his kindness and left his sick-bed than he began to regret that he had been left behind alone. He had strained his ears, hungry for some human sound, and had listened to her footsteps as she had gone down the stairs. When she had opened the entrance door to go out, the ringing of the bell had sounded much too rude to him. The strange feeling in the muscles near the incision had begun again at precisely that time. He reduced it all to a kind of response to a stimulus, and thought it was simply a result of his over-sensitivity. But had O-Nobu's behaviour actually been able to affect him to that extent? Even though he had suddenly begun to feel displeased about her behaviour, he could not carry the argument as far as that. And yet, if he had been forced to speak, he would have had to say it was obviously not a complete coincidence. From his own motives he had constructed a relationship between the two events. He also began to want to tell her about the relationship later. He wanted to do this simply to make her feel sorry that this had been the unfortunate result of her leaving him, lying sick in bed, and of running off for a day's enjoyment at the theatre; but he also wanted to make her repent. Yet he did not know the appropriate words for expressing these desires. For even if he did tell her, he was certain she would not understand. And even if she did, it would be difficult to make her feel precisely as he wished her to feel. Thus he could do nothing but remain silent and feel displeased about the entire episode.

The muscle contraction he began to feel again at the moment he looked up at O-Hide instantly made him recall the previous incident. His face grew pained and bitter.

O-Hide, knowing nothing at all about the episode, could not be expected to know all the involved reasons for his expression at that moment. She interpreted it simply as the usual one he had in talking with her.

'If it's unpleasant for you, let's let it go until after you're out of the hospital, shall we?'

Even though she did not show any special sympathy she still felt she had to show some concern.

'Does it hurt somewhere?'

He merely nodded. O-Hide fell silent for a while, and looked at him. At the same time his muscles near the incision began to throb. The silence between the two continued, and while it did, his pained expression did not change.

'If it hurts that much, it must be quite unpleasant, mustn't it? I wonder why O-Nobu didn't tell me. Yesterday on the phone she said you didn't have any pain or anything.'

'She didn't know about it.'

'You mean it began to hurt after she left?'

Even though he did not say, 'The truth is it began to hurt *because* she left,' he suddenly appeared to himself at that moment as a fretful child. No matter what he was like on the exterior, he was ashamed that inwardly he was not behaving at all like an older brother.

'What in the world is this business you have with me?'

'But I've said it's better not to talk about it when you're in such pain. Let's put it off until next time.'

Tsuda could deceive himself brilliantly. But he did not then wish to do so. He had already forgotten about the uncomfortable feeling. For the contraction had its special characteristic in that if he forgot about it it stopped, and if it stopped he forgot about it.

'It doesn't matter, so go ahead.'

'Well, since I'm the one who's telling it, it won't be a very pleasant story, you know. Are you sure it's all right?'

He had a fairly good idea of what she was going to say.

94

'It's about *that* again, isn't it?'

After a brief pause Tsuda felt he had to speak this way. And yet he had by then already returned to his usual expression of appearing not to want to listen. O-Hide inwardly felt angry at this contradiction.

'But haven't I been saying all along that we should let the matter wait until next time? Yet if you purposely urge me, I begin to want to talk about it.'

'But I keep telling you you can speak as freely as you wish. After all, you came with that intention anyway, didn't you?'

'But it seems so unpleasant for you.'

O-Hide was not one to hold back—at least not with her brother—simply because he appeared annoyed. Consequently he could not be expected to feel sorry for her. On the contrary, he even thought she was her usual self, criticizing him over nothing at all. Without taking her up on it, he jumped ahead of her :

'Have you heard something from Mother and Father again?'

'Yes, well, it actually is about that.'

Since there was almost an unwritten law that the news from Kyoto would largely be transmitted to Tsuda by their father and to O-Hide by their mother, he did not see the need of asking who had been O-Hide's correspondent. And yet, judging from recent circumstances, he did not think it likely that any letter O-Hide received from their mother could be any colder than the one he had already received from their father. Ever since he had sent his parents his second request for funds he had been ceaselessly preoccupied with whether they would send him the money. Even though he tried extremely hard not to mention the subject, which they always referred to between them simply as 'that', he could not help thinking about his great problem of raising the money to cover the end-of-the-month expenses and the hospital bills. Moreover, he knew better than O-Hide the sense in which these two things were inextricably related. He simply had to be the first to make direct reference to the matter.

'And what did she say?'

'You heard something from Father too, didn't you?'

'Yes I did. I think you know quite well what he said without my telling you, don't you?'

O-Hide did not say either that she did know or that she did not. She simply displayed a faint smile around her well-formed mouth. Tsuda was annoyed because it seemed very much to represent a note of pride

171

in her having triumphed over him. O-Hide's beauty, which he usually never noticed at all since he could see her only as his sister, affected him only at times like this, but did so adversely. More than once or twice he had even wondered whether, since she was far better-looking than average, she was not thereby better able to hurt people. Often he even wanted to tell her : I suppose you're going to be proud your entire life of having been married for your looks.

O-Hide shortly looked at him with perfectly composed features.

'And what have you done about it, Yoshio?'

'Well, there's nothing I *can* do, is there?'

'Didn't you say anything at all to Father?'

For a moment Tsuda did not speak. Then he answered her in a tone which showed he was doing so only because he was forced to.

'Yes, I did.'

'And then what happened?'

'There hasn't been any answer yet. Of course something may already have arrived at home, but I won't actually know about that until O-Nobu comes.'

'But you know quite well, Yoshio, the kind of answer Father's going to send you, don't you?'

He did not say anything in return. He probed with his hand the collar of the dressing-gown O-Nobu had made for him, and, with the small toothpick he took out from under its black silk, he began to pick steadily at his front teeth. Since he did not speak for a long time, O-Hide asked him another question with much the same meaning but in different words.

'Do you think Father will send you money willingly?'

'I have no idea.'

His answer was abrupt. Then he added testily :

'Why do you think I've kept asking you what Mother told you?'

O-Hide purposely averted her eyes, and looked at the veranda. She did this simply to avoid having to sigh deeply in front of him.

'It isn't that I won't tell you—because I knew all along it would probably turn out this way.'

95

He finally learned what their mother had written to O-Hide. According to the letter, as relayed by O-Hide, his father's anger was more violent than he had anticipated. It seemed that his father actually believed that if Tsuda made up the end-of-the-month deficiencies by himself that would be fine, but if Tsuda were unable to do even that, then his father might, as a form of punishment, stop any further remittances for a while. When Tsuda thought about it, he realized that what his father had said to him about the repairs of the fences and the arrearage of house-rent had to be lies. Even if the things he had said were not, Tsuda was forced to think they were merely excuses, and he wondered why his father had resorted to such feeble ones. If he were going to punish him, why had he not done so in a more manly way?

He pondered the matter awhile. He thought about his father's face, with its goatee, and how he liked to exaggerate everything, and about his mother, who for no reason at all disliked foreign-style hairdos and put her hair up only in Japanese-style chignons, and realized that such peculiarities provided no key whatever to interpreting the present situation.

O-Hide said, 'After all, Yoshio, you're the one who's at fault since you haven't done as you've promised.' There was nothing, since the incident, which he wanted less to hear than these words, which had been repeated by her endlessly. He knew perfectly well, without having her to tell him, that it had been wrong of him not to do as he had promised. It was just that he did not recognize the necessity of so doing. And he did not want to have his defenceless position pointed out to him by anyone.

O-Hide continued with : 'But that's unreasonable, you know. Even if it's between father and son, a promise is a promise. And if the matter only concerned you and Father, it might be settled any number of ways, but—'

For O-Hide, the fact that her husband was involved was the most important problem.

'My husband's quite distressed, you know—to receive a letter like that from Mother.'

It had been through the efforts of her husband, Hori, that Tsuda had foiled his father's plan whereby, after Tsuda finished school, obtained a good job, and set up a new home, he would somehow or other cease to be dependent on his parents, and would make his own independent livelihood. Having been asked by Tsuda to try to change his father's mind, Hori had readily undertaken the commission, and after easily listing various convenient reasons, such as the rise in prices, the need for keeping up socially, the change in the times, and the difference between Tokyo and other districts, he had finally convinced Tsuda's father, who was the very model of thrift, to continue to help his son financially. In exchange for Tsuda's father's leniency, however, Hori had also made the arrangement whereby he, Hori, would take the greater part of the bonuses which came to Tsuda at mid-summer and the end of the year, and have Tsuda repay his father part of the monthly supplements he had received. Even though, after this plan had been established, Hori had indeed assumed the responsibility for carrying it out, he was an extremely easy-going man. Not only had he not, from the outset, thought very deeply about Tsuda's keeping his promise but also when the time for its fulfilment arrived he had already forgotten about it. Upon receiving from Tsuda's father a letter which was practically a rebuke, he had been amazed, since he had almost put the entire episode out of his mind. Moreover, since he had noticed that Tsuda had not kept his promise only after the bonus had been completely spent, there was nothing much he could do about it. Optimist that he was, he had merely written an apologetic answer, and had thought that that was the end of it. But he had had to be taught by Tsuda's father that the world was not made to conform to his negligence. Tsuda's father considered Hori permanently responsible for the carrying out of the contract.

At about the same time a splendid ring, hardly appropriate to Tsuda's financial resources, had begun to gleam on O-Nobu's hand. And it had been O-Hide who had first noticed it. The curiosity which women have about their own sex had made her eyes even keener. She had praised O-Nobu's ring, but at the same time had tried to find out when and where O-Nobu had bought it. Since O-Nobu had known nothing whatever of the agreement between Tsuda and his father, which had been made with Hori's guarantee, she had been wholly unaware of any appearance of extravagance. The determination to show O-Hide how much she was loved by Tsuda won out over all considerations. She had told O-Hide everything about the ring exactly as it had happened.

O-Hide, who had always disdained O-Nobu as being much too extravagant, immediately reported this event to her parents. Moreover she had written in such a way as to intimate that although O-Nobu knew about the promise regarding the bonuses she had purposely influenced Tsuda and had prevented him from sending the money which had to be remitted. O-Hide had convinced herself that Tsuda's not revealing the true state of his finances to O-Nobu, which he actually had not done out of his own vanity with regard to his wife, was a reflection of O-Nobu's vanity. And she had transmitted her own misunderstanding to Kyoto just as it was; even now she could not rid herself of that initial misconception. Thus, when she spoke about this incident, it was more her sister-in-law than her brother who was her adversary.

'What in the world does O-Nobu intend to do? About this, I mean.'

'This doesn't have a thing to do with her, does it? I haven't spoken to her at all about it.'

'Really? Well then, that's fine for her since she doesn't have to worry, I suppose.'

O-Hide smiled sarcastically. In his mind Tsuda could clearly see the figure of O-Nobu, who on the night before going to the theatre had pointed at the thick obis shining in the lamplight and had asked whether she should pawn them.

96

'Well, I wonder what would be best to do.'

O-Hide's statement could be interpreted as intended both to annoy her imprudent brother and to express her own perplexity, because she also had to consider her husband's role in the matter. And yet further within her mind was anxiety regarding her mother-in-law, towards whom she had to be even more circumspect than towards her husband.

'Of course my husband *was* asked by you, and he *did* have a hand in the matter, but I don't think he ever intended to take his responsibilities that far. On the other hand, he doesn't intend to say he isn't in any way responsible, either. At any rate, if the worst comes to the worst, it isn't that he signed any document saying he has to do anything specific. That's why, when everything's interpreted legally, as it is by Father, I can only feel very sorry for him.'

Tsuda, at least superficially, could not but recognize the validity of his sister's position. And yet, since he could not feel the slightest sympathy for her, his attitude naturally caused an adverse reaction in her. She could not but view him as someone extraordinarily insolent. She felt that he thought of almost nothing but his own convenience. And if he did think of something else, it was only about his wife, whom he had recently married. Moreover, he had come to spoil her, allowing her considerable freedom. To satisfy O-Nobu, he had had to become even more selfish than before in his dealings with the outside world.

Since O-Hide viewed him in this way, she dealt with him with an attitude which he would have said was most lacking in sympathy and wholly unlike that of a younger sister. Expressed quite simply, it was the exceedingly blunt attitude of saying to him in effect : *Your* difficulties, Yoshio, are of your own making, so there's nothing to be done about them, but how are you going to straighten out *my* affairs?

Tsuda did not say what he would do, for he did not intend to do anything. Instead, he told her how difficult it was to determine his father's intentions.

'I wonder what in the world *Father* intends to do about it. Perhaps he thinks if he simply announces he's suddenly going to stop sending money, I'll make arrangements somehow or other. Is that it?'

'Yes, that's precisely it, Yoshio.'

She looked at him significantly, and then added : 'That's why I've said I'm embarrassed in front of my husband.'

A faint suspicion flashed through Tsuda's mind. Like the lightning one sees at the beginning of autumn, it was distant but nonetheless sharp. It concerned his father's character. Rather than saying it was distant in the sense that he had been wholly unaware of it until then, one should have said that, in the matter of whether, upon first entertaining the suspicion, having come to it by considering his father's normal behaviour, he should want to approve of it, it was of a kind to cut most cruelly into Tsuda as his son. Although at the outset he declared to himself that such a suspicion could not be correct, in the next instant he had to change his mind and recognize that it might very well be accurate.

His father's psychological state, as reflected in the mirror of Tsuda's conjecture, was composed of elements which would lead to the following results : First of all, his father would politely refuse to send any money. Tsuda thus would be in difficulty. Because of the previous arrangements he would explain the reasons to Hori. Hori, who would be compelled to feel responsibility towards Tsuda's parents, would for the first time be able to fulfil his duty of guarantor to Tsuda's father by helping Tsuda out of his difficulty. Thus Hori would be forced to pay the monthly allotments. Tsuda's father would merely express his thanks, and remain smug about the whole episode.

When Tsuda actually came to that conclusion, he saw in his father's handling of the affair a kind of cunning. He also saw considerable logic. And of course he could recognize a certain degree of skill. At the same time frankness was utterly lacking. Even if one did not go so far as to say it was mean, it was somewhat devious and crafty. An extraordinary attachment to a small amount of money appeared particularly prominent. In short, everything was being arranged in his father's most characteristic manner.

No matter how much they might clash on other matters, in the matter of not admiring such behaviour in their father, Tsuda and O-Hide were of one accord. Even though, in every sense, she sympathized with her father, when it came to this one matter, even she, like Tsuda, had to raise her eyebrows. Their father's character : that was rather a different problem. But Tsuda was not pleased at the thought of being helped by O-Hide. O-Hide, on her part, was not kindly disposed towards her brother and sister-in-law. Moreover she was forced to remember, with bitterness, her duties towards her husband and mother-in-law. Both O-Hide and Tsuda were primarily bothered by how best to solve the practical problem, and yet neither had the courage to probe verbally to the depth of the matter. Their father's intention, the nature of which had been decided upon by their mutual conjecture, made its appearance in the conversation merely by their tacitly recognizing it.

97

Since they could not unravel the entangled web of emotion and reasoning, their conversation meandered for a long time. Their manner of touching and yet not touching the crucial area made both of them inwardly nervous. And yet they were brother and sister. They both possessed qualities of deviousness, so that although each secretly criticized the other's lack of frankness, neither was willing to take the initiative in displaying the bad manners of being blunt. It was just that finally Tsuda, as the older brother, and as a man, had more skill than O-Hide in bringing the conversation into focus.

'In effect you mean you don't have any sympathy for me, don't you?'

'That's not it at all.'

'If it's not that, then you're saying you don't have any sympathy for O-Nobu. And that—well, no matter how you look at it—that's the same thing, isn't it?'

'Oh my, I haven't said a thing about O-Nobu.'

'Well, what it all boils down to is that I'm the one who's most at fault in the matter, I suppose. I know that perfectly well without having to listen again to any explanation. All right then, let's let the matter drop there. I'll resign myself to accepting my punishment. I'll manage somehow to live through this month without getting any money from Father.'

'Are you so sure you can?'

O-Hide's ridicule immediately brought forth the following response :

'If I can't, there's nothing left to do but die, is there?'

O-Hide finally relaxed the tightly compressed corners of her mouth somewhat, and exposed her white teeth faintly. The figure of O-Nobu fingering the thick obis gleaming in the lamplight again came to Tsuda's mind, and he thought :

'Maybe I'd rather tell O-Nobu everything about my financial situation up until now.'

This was not such an easy method of solution for him. And yet, judging from past experience, he also felt it was not such a difficult confession to make either. He knew quite well O-Nobu's vanity. And for him to try to satisfy it fully was quite simply his own vanity. For him to destroy O-Nobu's confidence in her husband, which for a woman was a most important factor in her life, was tantamount to dealing himself a crushing blow. His great distress lay in the fact that he would have to lower himself in her estimation rather than that it would be unfortunate for her. Even in such a petty situation as this, which would be considered laughable by others, he did not wish to move quickly. For in his family there actually was money—indeed more than enough to maintain his pride in front of O-Nobu. But the actual facts confronting him certainly stood in the way.

In addition, no matter what the situation, he was not a man to lose his temper. Although he thought very little about losing control over one's emotions, he had an innate inability to forget himself in a moment of anger.

After he had retorted, 'If I can't, there's nothing left to do but die, is there?' he continued to observe O-Hide's expression. He felt neither ashamed nor in any way embarrassed that he could think of nothing at all decisive to match his words. Instead, he began to weigh the matter coldly on the scales in his mind. He deliberated between the pain of revealing the situation to O-Nobu and the discomfort of receiving assistance from O-Hide. Then he considered what might arise if he chose the latter course. O-Hide, who was strong enough to accept the challenge, in the first place was most discontented at seeing that he did not repent wholeheartedly. Furthermore she hated the fact that behind him stood the self-satisfied, idolized O-Nobu. She also profoundly resented the fact that her father acted as if her husband were responsible for the whole incident, and kept beating about the bush with regard to his son. Thus, because of these various vexations, even after she had clearly seen through Tsuda's intentions she could not easily, for her part, show him any positive kindness.

At the same time, Tsuda's attitude towards O-Hide as well, who because of her beauty had married into a relatively wealthy family, contained a considerable amount of a kind of pride. He had found in her, after her marriage, a certain odour close to that of a parvenu. Or rather, he thought he had found it. At a certain point he had put on the formidable armour of an older brother and had begun to be controlled by this mentality in his dealings with her. Therefore he could not very easily bow his head in front of her.

At that point neither of them began to speak about money. But both of them were waiting to speak about it. In the very midst of this indecisive, incomplete private conversation the maid O-Toki suddenly entered, abruptly destroying the special mood the two of them had begun to create.

98

And yet before O-Toki's sudden entrance there had already been a telephone call for Tsuda. He had heard the pharmacist calling him from halfway up the stairs in a rather annoyed manner: 'Telephone for Mr Tsuda!' Tsuda had stopped talking with O-Hide for a moment, and had called back: 'Who is it?' As the pharmacist went back down, he answered, 'It's probably from your home.' This brusque exchange irritated Tsuda, who was then involved in a complicated matter with O-Hide. Since he secretly did not look very kindly on O-Nobu's going only to the theatre and not visiting him at the hospital either that day or the previous day, he became even unhappier.

'She's trying to get rid of her obligations by phoning.'

He immediately made this mental observation. He realized that she had telephoned the previous day and now also that morning; he thought that she might very well merely telephone the following morning as well, and that then, having thoroughly drawn people's attention to herself, she might very well suddenly put in an appearance. Judging from O-Nobu's usual attitude towards him, he was convinced there was not any excessive error in this prediction. He could even imagine her smiling face as she abruptly yet gracefully entered to surprise him at a time when he would be completely unprepared for her. But he also realized that her smiling face strangely affected him. By the force of this powerful weapon, which gleamed for but a moment, she always vanquished him instantly. Since the mental attitude which he would have succeeded in maintaining until then would be abruptly over-turned, from his point of view, it would be as if he helplessly fell into her trap.

Even though O-Hide was concerned about the telephone call, Tsuda decided not to pay any attention to it.

'After all, it can't be anything very important. It doesn't matter. Let it go.'

O-Hide was amazed at this comment. First of all it was not in keeping with her brother's dislike of carelessness. Secondly, it went against his usual behaviour of doing everything just as O-Nobu said. But O-Hide interpreted his present action as his having purposely assumed such indifference to conceal from her his usual weakness towards O-Nobu. Even though O-Hide secretly was rather delighted at this, when she heard the loud voice of the pharmacist from below urging someone to take the telephone call she simply had to get up in place of her brother. She took the trouble of going down the stairs, but her action served no purpose whatever, for the pharmacist had arranged everything to suit his convenience, and the receiver was already dead.

She returned to her former place after having at least gone through the motions of fulfilling her duty, but at the time that the two of them again took up their conversation, O-Toki, who was of a rather impatient disposition, was finally despairing of getting anywhere with the public telephone, and was boarding a streetcar. Within less than fifteen minutes Tsuda was amazed to learn from his maid, whom he in no way expected, about another completely unanticipated matter.

After O-Toki had left, his mind did not return to its former state very easily. Since he had been confident that he understood Kobayashi's character very well, and since he had not thought Kobayashi would call suddenly at his house during his absence and carry on a conversation with O-Nobu, with whom he was not on very familiar terms, Tsuda not only was surprised but he also was forced to think about the incident quite carefully. The problem was not whether to give or not to give the overcoat to Kobayashi. It was completely unrelated to that. And yet it concerned precisely Kobayashi's character, which was such as to make him go, in a carefree way, to get someone's overcoat from that man's wife whom he did not know very well. Or rather it concerned his second nature which his circumstances had inevitably created. Tsuda's problem was that if Kobayashi went one step further Tsuda wondered how his character, or personality, would operate with regard to O-Nobu. On this point Tsuda felt complete uncertainty. He even felt desperation. For Kobayashi was forever staring with seeming dissatisfaction at satisfied people, and Tsuda feared that among the satisfied people with whom Kobayashi was able to associate he and O-Nobu, as a newly married couple, had been selected by him as their special representatives. Tsuda was fully aware that by having always been utterly relentless in despising him he had laid the groundwork for Kobayashi's view of him.

'I don't know what he'll say to her.'

Suddenly a kind of fear seized him. But O-Hide instead began to laugh. She hardly understood even why her brother forever wanted to criticize, in various ways, this man called Kobayashi.

'It doesn't matter *what* he says, does it? After all, no one would take seriously what a man like Kobayashi says, would he?'

O-Hide too knew one aspect of Kobayashi's character very well. But that for the most part was limited to the single aspect he displayed in front of her Uncle Fujii, which was a mild one, entirely different from his manner when he had drunk too much saké.

'That's certainly not the case.'

Has he really become that unpleasant recently?'

O-Hide showed by her expression that she could not actually believe what Tsuda implied.

'If you really try to burn down a large house with only one match you can do it, can't you?'

'But then again, if the fire doesn't spread, isn't that all there is to it? . . . no matter how many boxes of matches you bring along with you. O-Nobu isn't the sort of woman to be set on fire by that sort of man. Or maybe. . . .'

99

When Tsuda heard O-Hide's last phrase he purposely did not turn towards her. Still facing away from her, he quietly awaited what would follow. But what he thought he would hear finally did not emerge. O-Hide said only half of what seemed to be weighing on his mind and then swiftly changed the direction of her speech.

'Why is it, Yoshio, that just today you're worrying about such a trifle? Has something special happened?'

Tsuda still was looking away from her. He did this so that she might not in any way suspect what was going on in his mind, and also so that she might not read the expression in his eyes. But he himself was actually affected by this unnatural behaviour, for he somehow felt cowardly. Finally he turned to her.

'I'm not particularly worried, but. . . .'

'You mean you're just a bit nervous, don't you?'

When pressed in this way, he merely seemed to be made a fool of by her. He instantly stopped talking.

At the same time the feeling of contraction he had had earlier recurred in the same area. After he had endured the unpleasantness two or three times he was assailed by the anxiety that it would again be repeated regularly for a fixed period of time.

O-Hide, who did not notice anything, for some reason or other refused to abandon the topic for some time. She immediately presented the problem, which she had not succeeded in doing earlier, to him in another form.

'Just exactly what sort of a person do you think O-Nobu is, Yoshio?'

'Why are you asking me that sort of question again now? It's so ridiculous.'

'All right then, I won't ask it.'

'But why did you? That's what I'd like to know.'

'I asked it because I had to know the answer.'

'Then tell me why you had to know the answer.'

'Actually I had to know for your own sake.'

Tsuda had a strange expression. O-Hide immediately continued.

'Because you were so concerned about Kobayashi, Yoshio. Isn't that rather odd?'

'That's something you know nothing at all about.'

'Yes, I suppose it seems odd because I don't understand. Well then, what sort of thing are you saying Kobayashi might propose to O-Nobu?'

'I didn't say anything about his proposing anything to her, did I?'

'You mean you're afraid he might propose something. That's it, isn't it, if we phrase it in a different way?'

Tsuda did not answer. O-Hide looked at him as if she had found a gap in his defences.

'And yet I can't possibly imagine what he'll say. Can you? If you try thinking about it a bit, no matter how bad Kobayashi's supposed to be, there's nothing for him to say, is there?'

Tsuda still did not answer. But O-Hide tried very hard to press him to reply.

'And even supposing he should say something to her, if O-Nobu doesn't take him up on it, that's all there is to it, isn't there?'

'I hardly need you to tell me that.'

'That's why I'm asking you : What do you think of O-Nobu, Yoshio? Do you trust her or don't you?'

O-Hide instantly followed up with that question. Tsuda did not understand it very well. And yet since he had to remove the sting from her questions, he avoided a clear-cut answer, and forced himself to begin to laugh.

'My, what an angry look! It's exactly as if I were being cross-examined, isn't it?'

'Answer me directly and don't try to avoid the issue.'

'If I do, what do you intend to do about it?'

'I'm your sister.'

'What do you mean by that?'

'Yoshio, the trouble is you're not frank.'

Tsuda tilted his head in a perplexed way.

'This conversation seems somehow to have become terribly complicated, but I think you're somewhat mistaken, aren't you? I certainly never spoke about Kobayashi in such a serious way at all. I merely said he's the sort of unpredictable person who'd meet O-Nobu in my absence and say almost anything.'

'Was that all you meant?'

'Yes, that was all.'

O-Hide immediately looked rather disappointed. But she did not remain silent.

'But Yoshio, just suppose somebody came to my place and spoke to me when my husband was out. Do you think he'd be worried if he knew about it?'

'I have no idea what Hori would do. I suppose you want to claim he wouldn't worry at all.'

'Yes, I do.'

'That's splendid. . . . But what then?'

'That's all I want to say too.'

They were both forced to fall silent.

100

And yet they were both already inextricably involved with each other. They could not really be satisfied unless they extracted, by means of conversation, a certain something from the other's heart. Particularly for Tsuda was this an immediate necessity. For he had in front of him at that moment a financial source which would solve the money problem then troubling him. And if he were to let the opportunity pass, it might never return. He was forced, for that reason alone, into a weaker position than O-Hide. He wondered how he could recover the lost topic of conversation.

'Why don't you eat at the hospital before leaving, O-Hide?'

The time was just right for showing her this courtesy. Since all her in-laws were gone, having taken her mother-in-law and her children to visit relatives in Yokohama, he could conveniently make his offer have a special meaning.

'After all, even if you go home you don't have anything to do, do you?'

She accepted his offer. They easily revived their conversation. And yet it was of a kind that takes place only between brother and sister. Moreover, in this situation such mere brother-and-sister talk did not in any way satisfy them. They each waited for an opportunity to probe more deeply into the other's mind.

'Yoshio, I have something here.'

'Well, what is it?'

'Something you need very much.'

'Really?'

He almost did not take her up on it. His coldness was in direct proportion to his pride. He did not wish to lower himself before her, either actually or formally, but he did want her money. For O-Hide, on the other hand, money was not the main concern, but she did want to make him lower himself in front of her. She was compelled to hold out the money, which he wanted, as bait, to attain her objective. As a result, she succeeded only in annoying him.

'Shall I give it to you?'

'As you wish.'

'Father certainly won't give you any, I'm sure.'

'He probably won't, that's true.'

'Why, Mother particularly said that in her letter to me! I meant to bring the letter to show it to you today, but somehow I seem to have forgotten it.'

'I'm perfectly aware of that. Didn't you just tell me that a few minutes ago?'

'That's why, I tell you. That's why I say I've brought some for you.'

'To tantalize me, or to give it to me?'

O-Hide immediately fell silent as if she had actually been struck physically. In an instant tears welled up in her beautiful eyes. Tsuda could only consider them tears of vexation.

'I wonder why you've become so sarcastic recently, Yoshio. I wonder why you can't accept a person's sincerity as you once did.'

'I haven't changed the least bit from what I once was. You're the one who's changed recently.'

This time O-Hide showed amazement.

'Tell me when and how I've changed! I don't know what you mean.'

'You should be able to work that out for yourself without having to ask anyone.'

'No, I don't understand. So tell me. Please tell me.'

He returned her sharp glance with rather cold eyes. Having come as far as he had, he debated with himself whether it was better to retract the words which had hurt her feelings or to crush her completely all at once. He decided to take a middle course between those two extremes, and began to speak slowly:

'O-Hide, you may not recognize it yourself, but as I see it you've changed a great deal since you've married.'

'But that's to be expected. What woman wouldn't change after marrying and having two children!'

'That's why I said it. Of course it's perfectly natural.'

'But you said I've changed in some way towards you. That's what I want to hear.'

'Well, on that point. . . .'

Tsuda did not answer completely. But he tried to make O-Hide understand from the force of his words that it was not that he was unable to answer. O-Hide paused a moment. Then she quickly retorted:

'I suppose you're always thinking that I've carried tales to Mother and Father, aren't you?'

'That doesn't matter to me at all.'

'That's not so. That's certainly why I'm always being looked at askance.'

'By whom?'

These unhappy words seemed to ignite the name of O-Nobu, which, like a censored term, had not been mentioned by either of them. O-Hide twirled it in front of him like a torch.

'*You're* the one who's different. You're completely different since you married O-Nobu. Anyone can see you're a changed man.'

101

O-Hide, as Tsuda saw her, was deeply prejudiced against him. The last attack in particular was nothing more than the activity of prejudice itself. It was extremely irritating to him to hear her forever mentioning O-Nobu. He felt no little discomfort in front of O-Hide since she interpreted all his behaviour as directed towards satisfying his wife when it was actually directed towards satisfying himself.

'I'm not the hen-pecked husband you think I am, you know.'

'Maybe so. Since even though O-Nobu called you you were able to act coldly and pay no attention to it.'

When it seemed as if these words would pour forth from O-Hide, who was oblivious of the time and place for such remarks, Tsuda was almost forced to forget the advantage which lay in front of him. Once or twice he expressed his annoyance to himself in the following way:

'That's precisely why I was so insistent in telling O-Nobu not to phone her.'

Like a person trying to dispel his nervous excitement, he frequently tugged at his short moustache. Gradually his face hardened into a bitter expression. He spoke less and less.

This attitude of his produced a strange effect on O-Hide. Since she seemed to think only that because his weak points were being revealed one by one to her he finally had come to feel guilty and had fallen silent, she proceeded even more vigorously. Indeed she spoke with a force that seemed to indicate that with one more breath she might even be able to make him repent completely.

'You were more honest, Yoshio, before you married O-Nobu. Or at least you were more frank. Since I don't like you to think I'm speaking without evidence, I'll state things exactly the way they are. That's why I'll ask you too to answer my questions frankly. Do you remember, Yoshio, ever having told Father such lies as you now have before you married O-Nobu?'

At that point Tsuda for the first time felt caught. What O-Hide said was a plain fact, but it had certainly not arisen in the way she thought. He looked upon it as a mere coincidence.

'And I suppose you're saying O-Nobu was the person responsible for that, aren't you?'

O-Hide purposely suppressed the desire to answer that she was.

'No, I'm not saying a thing about O-Nobu. I'm merely emphasizing the fact as evidence that you've changed.'

Tsuda had to acknowledge defeat openly.

'If you want so very much to claim that I've changed, all right then I'll agree. But what's so bad about it even if I have?'

'I'll tell you : You behaved badly towards Mother and Father.'

Tsuda immediately answered with, 'Is that so?' And then added coldly, 'Even if I did, I don't think it matters.'

O-Hide showed how deeply she disapproved of the fact that he still did not repent even though he knew he was in the wrong.

'I have further proof of how you've changed, Yoshio.'

He feigned ignorance. O-Hide went right ahead and presented her evidence : 'Haven't you been worrying, ever since O-Toki came and told you, that Kobayashi's gone to your house while you're not there and maybe has said something to O-Nobu?'

'You're most annoying! Didn't I explain to you before that I'm not worrying?'

'But you certainly are a bit concerned, aren't you?'

'Oh, interpret things any way you want to.'

'I see. But at any rate, isn't that proof you've changed, Yoshio?'

'Don't be ridiculous!'

'But it *is* proof, I tell you. It's real proof. You're so afraid of O-Nobu.'

Tsuda suddenly turned his eyes. While still resting his head on the pillow, he peered up at O-Hide. He then wrinkled his well-shaped nose in a sneer. She had in no way anticipated his complacency. Although she had intended, with a bit more effort, to push him head over heels into the deep valley of repentance, she now began to wonder whether he might still have some level ground behind him. But she had to go as far as she could.

'Yoshio, until recently haven't you been treating Kobayashi with utter disdain? Haven't you been in the habit of paying not the slightest attention to him, no matter what he says? So why is it that just today you're so afraid of him? Isn't the only reason you're so afraid of him now the fact that he's talking to O-Nobu?'

'All right, have it your way. But no matter how afraid I am of him that hardly means that therefore I'm not doing my duty towards Mother and Father.'

'Are you trying to say that therefore it's no business of mine?'

'Well, I suppose that's what I had in mind.'

O-Hide flared up. At the same time a flash of insight raced through her mind.

102

'I see.'

O-Hide spoke very sharply. And yet her changed manner of speaking produced not the slightest external change in Tsuda. He did not seem to respond any longer to her challenges.

'I see everything clearly now, Yoshio.'

O-Hide repeated her words as if she were shaking Tsuda by the shoulders. He was forced to speak :

'What do you see so clearly?'

'Do you mean the reason why you're so careful about O-Nobu?'

Tsuda felt a kind of curiosity about her answer.

'Yes, tell me.'

'I don't have to. It's enough if I make you see that I understand why.'

'If that's the case, you needn't have purposely told me. It would have been better if you'd kept it to yourself.'

'No, it wouldn't have. You don't consider me your sister, Yoshio. You think that unless it has something to do with Mother or Father I have no right to say anything in front of you. That's why I won't tell you. But even though I won't, I assure you I can see everything perfectly clearly. And since it would be a mistake for you to think I'm not speaking because I don't know, I said what little I did.'

Tsuda thought there was nothing to do but cut off the conversation at that point since he felt that the more they became involved the more troublesome the entire matter became. And yet he certainly did not want to lower himself before her. To make a theatrical repentance in front of her was the furthest thing from his mind. If he were ever able to do such a thing it most certainly would never be for his sister, whom he had always scorned and before whom he was exceptionally proud. Moreover his pride appeared externally rather more easily when he was dealing with her than with others. Thus, no matter how conciliatory he might be in his speech, it did not help very much. It only meant that all his disdain of O-Hide was conveyed in a lukewarm fashion. And O-Hide, on her part, showed not the slightest consideration for him, even though he had for some time been looking as if he could not tolerate the discussion any longer. She began again by calling him by name.

He then discovered a change in her which until then he had failed to notice. Previously she had always pointed the tip of her spear at O-Nobu by passing through him. It would not have been wrong to say that she was also attacking him, but even when she neglected him as he stood in the front line, her true intent was above all to bring down her sister-in-law who lurked in the rear. That situation, however, had now suddenly changed. She had arbitrarily changed her target. And she was now advancing in a straight line towards him.

'Does a sister then, Yoshio, have no right to say anything about her brother's character? All right, suppose she hasn't. If she has even the slightest doubt about it, then it's her brother's duty to clear that up for her completely—I'll retract the word "duty" because it may be improper for me to use it. But at least a brother should want to clear it up. As a sister then, I'm deeply saddened to see in front of me now a brother who doesn't want to.'

'How dare you be so insolent! Shut up! You don't know what the hell you're talking about!'

For the first time his annoyance exploded into rage :

'Do you have any idea what the word "character" means? You've only gone to a girls' finishing school and you have the audacity to use such a word in front of me!'

'I wasn't putting any special emphasis on the word. It's the actual problem that concerns me.'

'What's the actual problem? Do you really think a woman with your limited education can actually understand what's going on in *my* brain? You simpleton!'

'If you persist in insulting me that way, I'll simply tell you as a warning. Will you let me?'

'I don't have to answer such a damn fool question! What the hell's the matter with you anyway! Coming to someone when he's sick, with that kind of attitude! And you think you're acting like a sister!'

'It's all because you're not acting like a brother.'

'Just shut up, will you!'

'I will not. I'll say what I have to say : You let O-Nobu do as she pleases. You care more for her than you do for Mother and Father or for me.'

'It's the most natural thing in the world to care more for your wife than for your sister!'

'If that were the only thing it wouldn't matter. But in your case, Yoshio, it isn't. While you're caring so much for O-Nobu there's still someone else you're concerned about.'

'What in the world are you talking about?'

'That's why you fear O-Nobu so. And, what's more, by being so afraid of her—'

As O-Hide began to talk in this way, the sliding-door to the sick-room opened softly. The pale face of O-Nobu suddenly appeared before them.

103

She had arrived at the vestibule of the doctor's office three or four minutes earlier. The doctor's consultation hours were divided into morning and afternoon hours, and since those in the afternoon had been fixed at from four to eight to meet the convenience of office-workers, O-Nobu had been able to enter by opening a relatively noiseless door, for the bell had been silenced.

Actually she did not find, as she had when she had come several days earlier, even a single pair of men's footwear such as laced shoes or matted-clogs on the shoe-removal stone. And of course there were no patients. Since she had in no way realized she was coming between hours, she looked around her in bewilderment as if everything were extremely strange.

She observed only one pair of women's clogs lined up neatly on the shoe-removal stone in the quiet vestibule. Those new clogs, which, judging from the price, she felt certain were hardly of a kind to be worn by such people as the nurse, suddenly made her heart leap. For they were obviously those of a young woman. Since her mind was filled with the doubt implanted by Kobayashi, for a few minutes she could not take her eyes off them, and looked at them intently.

From the small square window on the right the face of the doctor's houseboy emerged. When he recognized her motionless figure, he gave her a look as if to challenge her right to be there. She swiftly found out whether Tsuda had a visitor or not. She even asked whether it was a young woman. Then, purposely rejecting the boy's offer to guide her, she went to the foot of the stairs by herself, and looked up towards the second floor.

She could hear the voices of an unbroken conversation upstairs. But it was quite different from a normal conversation where the words of the speakers flow back and forth with ease. Strong emotions were at work there, and excitement as well. Moreover she could clearly perceive the efforts being made to suppress that emotion and excitement. The conversation, which could only be interpreted as one that was not intended to be heard by an outsider, made her nerves needle-sharp. She became even tenser than when she had observed the clogs, and she listened even more intently.

Tsuda's room was directly above the consultation room. The construction of the building was such that as one climbed the stairs there was a wall directly ahead and to the right there was a small four-and-a-half-mat room; therefore, one had to cross the connecting corridor in front of that small room in order to reach Tsuda's room. Consequently the conversation O-Nobu wanted so much to hear came from a direction which made it awkward for her to do so, namely from behind her.

She climbed the stairs softly. Since she had a slender, graceful body her footsteps were as quiet as a cat's. And, like a cat's, her stealth was rewarded with success.

To one side of the landing was a banister about a yard long to prevent one from falling. O-Nobu leaned against it and listened to what Tsuda was saying. Then suddenly O-Hide's sharp voice struck her ears. Her own name sounded in her ear-drum with special force. As she realized she had been utterly mistaken she again was made to reflect. But before her extraordinary tension had time to diminish, it once again seized her. For she absolutely had to know in what sense her name had been hurled forth by O-Hide at Tsuda. She strained her ears.

The force of the words of the two became even greater as she listened. It was quite clear they were quarrelling. And she herself had been drawn into the very midst of the quarrel without knowing anything about it. Or perhaps she was even its main cause.

And yet since she did not know the circumstances of the dispute, she could not, merely from what she heard, determine her own position. In addition, the words they, or rather O-Hide, used came as swift as hail. O-Nobu hardly had time to pick up the grains one by one and examine them since they fell ceaselessly. Such expressions as 'character', 'care more for', and 'most natural thing in the world' merely bounced off her one after another as she stood there.

She thought she might continue to stand there perfectly still until she had made out the nature of the dispute. But at that moment the sentence 'While you're caring so much for O-Nobu there's still someone else you're concerned about,' burst forth from O-Hide like a final barrage of gunfire and suddenly shook O-Nobu to her very heart. Nothing in the world was more important to her than this one sentence which she had heard exceptionally clearly; but at the same time nothing was more unclear to her. If she did not hear what followed, that one independent sentence would be of no use to her whatsoever. She felt that no matter what the cost she would not be satisfied unless she heard what followed. And yet, on the other hand, she was utterly unable to hear what followed, for she was made to realize that the exchange between the two, which for some time with every word had been heightening in intensity, had then reached its peak. It had arrived at the extreme point where it could not advance one step further. If either did try to push it further, he would have to use physical force. Thus, to prevent such a possibility, she absolutely had to enter the sick-room.

She knew very well how things stood between brother and sister. She also had always known that the cause of their discord lay with her. Thus, to make her appearance there at that time required considerable dexterity. But she was completely confident that she possessed it. She decided on her move in a split second, and then she purposely opened the sliding door to the sick-room quietly.

104

The two had finally fallen silent. And yet the silence, like that of a storm which suddenly stops its progress for a moment, just as it is about to become fiercer, was certainly not an omen of peace. In that wordless moment during which their passions were unnaturally suppressed a certain terrible element was latent.

Because of their respective positions Tsuda was the first to see O-Nobu. Since he was lying with his pillow towards the southern veranda, it was natural that he should have been the first to catch sight of her as she entered from the opposite direction. At that instant two aspects of himself were grasped by O-Nobu. One was his distress. The other was his sense of relief. The feeling that he was distressed by her entry and the feeling that he was relieved by it appeared in his face simultaneously before he had time to conceal them. And these feelings accorded perfectly with the expectations of O-Nobu upon her sudden entry. From one aspect of Tsuda's expression at that time she gathered the evidence that she had been justified in her vague suspicions. But what precisely lay behind these suspicions still remained a mystery. She was forced, upon the moment of her entry, to be concerned only about her response to the other aspect of his expression. With a forced smile creasing her pale cheeks, she looked at him. And since she did so at the precise moment that O-Hide turned around, her smile was interpreted by O-Hide as a silent agreement between them, excluding her. A pink wave spontaneously flushed O-Hide's cheeks.

'Oh my, I had no idea. . . .'

'How are you, O-Hide?'

The two women exchanged simple greetings. But when they were concluded, normal conversation did not follow. Both of them could not help sensing the embarrassment and awkwardness of the situation. O-Nobu, cautious in her speech, opened instead the cloth-wrapped bundle she had at her side, and taking out the English books of humour lent her by her uncle, handed them to Tsuda. On one of her fingers shone the very ring that had so long been troubling O-Hide.

Tsuda took up the small slender volumes one by one, but after merely glancing through the pages briefly, placed them again near his pillow. He did not wish to read even a single line of them, nor did he even have the strength to comment on them. He did not say a word. During the interval O-Nobu again exchanged two or three words with O-Hide. But O-Nobu began all the comments, and it was as if she had to force the necessary answers out of O-Hide's throat.

O-Nobu then took a letter out of her pocket.

'On my way here just now I looked in the mailbox and found this, so I brought it along with me.'

She spoke very carefully and even somewhat formally. Compared to the times when she was alone with Tsuda she was very correct and behaved like a completely different person. She secretly disliked such a formal, distant manner, but in other people's presence, especially O-Hide's, she felt compelled, for some reason or other, to use this unnatural way of speaking.

The letter was the one they had awaited from Tsuda's father in Kyoto. Since, like the previous one, it had not been sent by registered mail, even O-Nobu, who had not yet heard anything from O-Hide, could guess fairly accurately that it contained little to answer their present need.

Tsuda spoke to her before breaking the seal :

'It seems it won't do any good.'

'Really? What do you mean?'

'It seems that no matter how much I ask Father he won't send us any more money.'

Tsuda's way of speaking was strangely filled with sincerity. From being filled with rancour towards O-Hide he had suddenly become direct and straightforward towards O-Nobu. Moreover, he himself was completely unaware of this development. This unaffected manner of his made O-Nobu happy, and she answered in a warm tone as if to console him. Even her manner of speaking showed that she had become her normal self without realizing it.

'Even so, it doesn't matter, dear. We'll manage somehow.'

Without speaking, Tsuda opened the envelope. The letter he took out was not very long. Moreover it was written in such large characters that anyone in the room could read it at a glance. Yet the two women, as in the case of the books of humour, did not say a word about it to each other. They merely turned their attentive glances equally to the old-fashioned letter paper. Therefore, when Tsuda finished reading the letter and, after inserting it back in the envelope, threw it down near his pillow, both of them had already grasped its general meaning. Nevertheless, O-Hide purposely asked :

'What did it say, Yoshio?'

Tsuda, with a dispirited expression, answered with a vague mutter. O-Hide turned away for a moment. Then she again asked :

'It's just as I said, isn't it?'

The letter was, after all, as she had surmised. But he simply could not endure her I-told-you-so manner. Even without that, because of what had happened earlier he was much too angry to give her a simple answer.

105

O-Nobu could read Tsuda's feelings very clearly. She secretly feared a second clash. At the same time she wondered about his true intent. For Tsuda, as she judged him, normally maintained his self-control. And he maintained not only his self-control but also a coldness in the depths of his heart whenever he had contempt for the person with whom he was dealing. Yet she also believed that despite these special characteristics of his a certain element was latent which he could not yet control. Although this was for her as yet an unknown quantity, she was confident that if only she distinctly touched it she would be able to handle him satisfactorily without any difficulty. And yet, as far as his outward appearance alone was concerned, it was not so difficult to characterize by the simple statement : he does not become angry easily. She wondered therefore why this man who, as they say in English, was not of a kind to lose his temper, should have exploded as he had in confrontation with his younger sister. Strictly speaking, she wondered why he had exploded so violently just before she had entered the room. At any rate, she felt she had to come between the two before the turbulent waves which had receded rolled back again. Thus she tried to take on his adversary in the quarrel herself.

'Did you have some news from Father too, Hideko?'

'No, from Mother.'

'Oh did you? Still about this same matter?"

'Yes.'

O-Hide did not say anything further. O-Nobu went on :

'I suppose it's because in Kyoto too they've had a lot of expenses. And also because we've really been the ones at fault from the beginning.'

For O-Hide the gem on O-Nobu's finger never shone more brilliantly than at that moment. Moreover O-Nobu, seemingly rather innocently, stretched forth the gleaming ring in front of O-Hide. O-Hide spoke :

'That's not necessarily the case. Old people behave strangely sometimes and they believe Yoshio can handle the matter. They think he can raise the money to tide him over in any number of ways.'

O-Nobu smiled.

'Well, if the worse comes to the worse, I'm sure we'll manage somehow. Won't we, dear?'

O-Nobu looked at Tsuda as she said this, and her glance meant that she wished him to say quickly that they would manage. But on Tsuda's part, even if he did notice the movement of her eye, its meaning completely escaped him. He repeated the same things he had been saying all along:

'I'm not saying we won't manage somehow, but still what Father says seems extremely strange to me. He said he repaired some fences and the rent hasn't come in, but such things, after all, are mere trifles, aren't they?'

'It's not as easy as that, dear. Just try having your own house and see.'

'What are you talking about? We *do* have our own house, don't we?'

This time O-Nobu showed her own special smile to O-Hide. O-Hide commented, also without begrudging the same degree of charm:

'Yoshio doubts Father's sincerity and thinks there's some underhand scheme at the bottom of it all.'

'That's not very nice, dear—to doubt your own father. There's no reason why he should have some underhand scheme, is there? Isn't that so, Hideko?'

'No, that's not it exactly. He thinks the plot involves somebody else even more than Father or Mother.'

'Somebody else?'

O-Nobu looked surprised.

'Yes, I'm sure he thinks there's somebody else.'

O-Nobu again turned towards her husband.

'But why is that, dear?'

'It was O-Hide who said it, so try asking her.'

O-Nobu gave a strained smile. It was O-Hide's turn to speak.

'Yoshio feels we secretly egged Mother and Father on to act this way.'

'But—'

O-Nobu could say nothing more than that. And what she had said had almost no meaning. O-Hide swiftly filled the vacuum.

'And that's why he was so dreadfully bad-tempered a while ago. Of course I realize that whenever Yoshio and I get together we're bound to have a quarrel—particularly on this subject.'

After O-Nobu responded with a sigh, 'How very troublesome,' she asked him again: 'But is that really true, dear? I'm sure you don't really have such petty ideas, do you?'

'I don't know what this is all about, but it seems that way to O-Hide, I suppose.'

'But if you think O-Hide and her husband are doing such a thing, of what possible benefit do you think it is to them?'

'They're probably doing it to teach me a lesson, I suppose. But I don't know for sure.'

'A lesson about what? What in the world is the crime you've committed, dear?'

'I have no idea.'

Tsuda said this in an annoyed way. O-Nobu looked at O-Hide as if to say she had been thrown upon her own resources. An expression that meant 'Please help me out in some way' appeared between her narrow eyes and her eyebrows.

106

'My, but Yoshio's stubborn!' O-Hide began by saying. Since she had been pushed to the point where she had somehow to explain herself in front of her sister-in-law, she secretly hated O-Nobu even more as she spoke in this way. There was no more false nor more impudent woman than O-Nobu, as O-Hide saw her at that moment.

O-Nobu answered, 'Yes, that's true, he *is* stubborn,' and immediately turned to Tsuda.

'You really *are* stubborn, dear. It's just as Hideko says. You're simply going to have to get rid of that bad habit.'

'How the hell am I being stubborn?'

'Well I don't know how exactly.'

'Is it because I'm trying to get money out of Father in various ways?'

'Yes, I think that's it.'

'But I haven't said anything at all about taking any money, have I?'

'Yes, that's right. You couldn't have said any such thing. And even if you had, it wouldn't have done you any good anyway, would it?'

'Well then, how am I being stubborn?'

'It's no use asking how. Because I don't really know myself. But somehow or other you *are*.'

'Don't be ridiculous.'

Although she had in effect been called a fool, O-Nobu on the contrary smiled pleasantly. O-Hide could endure the situation no longer.

'Yoshio, why don't you accept what I've brought without making a fuss?'

'Fuss or no fuss, and whether I accept it or not is not the problem. You haven't offered it to me yet, have you?'

'I can't offer it to you because you haven't said you'll accept it.'

'As I look at it, I haven't accepted it because you haven't offered it.'

'But if you don't act as though you want to accept it that's most unpleasant for me.'

'Well, what should we do then?'

'You know perfectly well what *you* should do.'

The three did not speak for a while.

Suddenly Tsuda began again:

'How about apologizing to O-Hide, O-Nobu?'

O-Nobu looked at him in amazement.

'About what?'

'If you just apologize I think she'll take out what she's brought. That's O-Hide's plan.'

'It's quite simple for me to apologize. If you say I should, I'll apologize as much as you like. But. . . .'

At this point O-Nobu turned an appealing glance at O-Hide. O-Hide interrupted her.

'What in the world are you saying, Yoshio! When did I ever say I wanted O-Nobu to apologize to me? By fabricating such a story aren't you only trying to embarrass me in front of her?'

Silence again fell over the three of them. Tsuda purposely did not speak. O-Nobu did not need to speak. But O-Hide prepared her next speech.

'Yoshio, in spite of all this I still intend to do my duty towards both of you. I—'

When O-Hide finally began to speak, Tsuda suddenly broke in with a question:

'Wait a minute now. Is it duty or kindness? In what sense are you speaking?'

'For me they're the same thing.'

'Is that so? If that's the case there's nothing to be done. And what then?'

'It's not a matter of "what then?" It's a matter of what follows of necessity. I can't stand to have you think that by going behind your back and stirring up Father and Mother I've tried to cause you and O-Nobu trouble. That's why I say that I've purposely brought this money here with me today with the good intention of somehow giving you the same amount Father would have. Actually when O-Nobu phoned yesterday I thought I'd come right away, but in the morning I had things to do at home and in the afternoon I had to go to the bank on business so I finally couldn't make it. Of course it's a small amount and I don't in the least wish to complain about any hardship in giving it to you, but I do want to say only that I regret very much that my feelings have utterly failed to penetrate to you, Yoshio.'

O-Nobu peered at Tsuda who still was silent.

'Please say something, dear.'

'What do you want me to say?'

'Why to say thank you of course. To say thank you to O-Hide for her kindness.'

'I don't like being burdened with a sense of indebtedness just to receive such a small amount of money.'

O-Hide defended herself in a somewhat annoyed tone with :

'But haven't I said just now that I'm not trying to make you feel indebted to me?'

O-Nobu did not alter her previous calm tone :

'That's why I'm telling you to stop being so stubborn and to say thank you. If you don't like borrowing money it's all right if you don't accept it. But just say thank you.'

O-Hide had an odd expression on her face. Tsuda indicated by his attitude that he wanted O-Nobu to stop saying such ridiculous things.

107

The three had fallen into a strange predicament. Since by force of circumstances they were linked together in a special relationship, it had become increasingly difficult for them to change the subject of the conversation; and of course they could not leave. Thus, while remaining where they were, they had to resolve their problem one way or another.

And yet, seen objectively, it certainly was not an important one. In the eyes of anyone able to view their situation from a distance dispassionately, it could not but appear insignificant. They knew this very well without needing to have it brought to their attention. They were, however, forced to quarrel. Some controlling power extended its hand from an unfathomable, remote past, and manipulated them at will.

Finally there took place the following exchange between Tsuda and O-Hide :

'If I'd remained silent from the beginning, there wouldn't have been any difficulty; but now that I've begun speaking I can't possibly leave without giving you what I've brought, so I beg you to accept it.'

'If you want to leave it here, why then do so.'

'Then please act the way you should in accepting it, won't you?'

'What in the world do I have to do to please you—I'm sure I don't know. Wouldn't it be better if you explained more clearly what condition you attach to my accepting it?'

'I'm not setting up any condition at all. If you just accept it graciously, that's all I ask. In short, if you accept it in a brotherly way, that's all I require. And if you'd only once tell Father you're sincerely sorry, there wouldn't be any problem.'

'I've already told him I was long ago. Surely you know that! And not merely once or twice.'

'But I don't mean that kind of formal apology. I mean a heartfelt repentance.'

Tsuda could only think she was making a great fuss over nothing. He was far from thinking of repentance.

'Are you implying my apology wasn't sincere? I may want money, but I'm still a man. Do you think I'm one to grovel in that way?'

'And yet you really do want money, don't you?'

'I'm not saying I don't.'

'And you say you've already apologized to Father about it.'

'If not for that, what need would there have been of apologizing?'

'That's exactly why he stopped giving you any. You don't see that, do you?'

Tsuda did not speak. O-Hide immediately continued:

'As long as you're in your present frame of mind, Yoshio, Father's not the only one who won't give anything, I won't either.'

'All right then, don't. I'm certainly not going to force you to.'

'But didn't you just say you absolutely have to get some money?'

'When did I say such a thing?'

'You were saying so just now.'

'Don't make accusations like that, idiot!'

'It's not an accusation. Just now weren't you continually saying so to yourself? You're the one who isn't being frank. That's why you haven't said it openly.'

Tsuda looked at O-Hide. In his fierce eyes hatred clearly shone, and there was not a trace of shame in his heart. When he began speaking, even O-Hide was surprised at his intensity. In the coldest, most sarcastic tone he could summon up, he said the exact opposite of what she anticipated.

'O-Hide, it's just as you say. I must once again confess myself: I desperately need the money you've brought. Once again I must state this openly: You're a woman filled with the deepest sisterly love. Your brother thanks you for your kindness. Therefore, please leave the money at my pillow and go.'

O-Hide's hand trembled with rage. Blood rushed to both her cheeks as if it had come all at once from some place in her heart to lodge in her face. Since she normally had a fair complexion, her anger was even more apparent; yet her manner of speaking did not change appreciably. She was even able to smile in the midst of her rage, and suddenly turning from Tsuda, cast her gleaming eyes on O-Nobu.

'What should I do, O-Nobu? Since Yoshio speaks the way he does, should I leave the money and go?'

'I really don't know. That's up to you to decide.'

'I see. And yet he says he absolutely must have this money.'

'Yes, perhaps that's true for Yoshio. But as far as I'm concerned, it's quite the opposite.'

'Do you mean you and he are entirely separate?'

'No, not at all. Since we're husband and wife, we're very much united.'

'But, didn't you just say. . . .'

O-Nobu did not allow her to finish.

'But when it's a question of something my husband positively needs, I'm quite capable of providing it.'

She then drew out from her obi the cheque she had just received from her uncle on the previous day.

108

As she passed the cheque to Tsuda, at the same time pointedly showing it to O-Hide, her manner indicated a kind of command towards her husband. Indeed it was a distinct command emerging both from the course of the conversation and from her natural disposition. She prayed Tsuda would attune himself with her feelings and accept the cheque willingly. Whether he would smile genially, nod, and cast it gently near his pillow, or whether he would say just one word to her expressive of extreme gratitude, and then return it to her—in either event, if by the effect of this cheque O-Hide could only be shown that a strong bond of conjugal affection existed between them, she would be satisfied.

Unfortunately, both O-Nobu's action and the emergence of the cheque were too sudden for Tsuda. Furthermore, the dramatic sense he derived from such a situation differed somewhat from O-Nobu's. He looked at the cheque strangely, and then asked quietly :

'What in the world did you do to get this?'

Already, at the outset, this cold tone and the equally cold question itself sadly dampened her enthusiasm. Her expectations were betrayed.

'I didn't do anything. It's just that you needed it, so I managed to get it.'

Even though she spoke lightly, inwardly she trembled. She was afraid that he would continue to ask prying questions, which would be tantamount to revealing to O-Hide that there did not exist any perfect accord between them.

'You needn't ask for any explanation while you're ill. You'll find out all about it afterwards anyway.'

Even after she had said this she was still extremely uncomfortable, and before Tsuda could say anything in response, she immediately proceeded :

'It certainly doesn't matter if you don't understand now, does it? After all, it isn't such a great amount. When we really need money, I can always get it from somewhere.'

Tsuda finally threw down by his pillow the cheque he had been holding in his hand. He was a man who liked money; yet he was not one who worshipped it. Though he felt more keenly than others its necessity for having things one wants, with regard to despising money itself he was of a disposition that accorded completely with O-Nobu's words. He therefore made no comment, and for the same reason uttered no word of thanks to his wife.

She was dissatisfied, thinking that even if he said nothing to her, he should at least have said something to his sister to satisfy his grudge against her.

On her part, O-Hide, who had been observing the behaviour of the two during their conversation, suddenly addressed her brother. She then took out from her kimono a handsome woman's purse.

'Yoshio, I'm going to leave here what I brought.'

She took something wrapped in white paper out of her purse, and placed it near the cheque.

'It's all right if I leave it here in this way, isn't it?'

Even though O-Hide had addressed Tsuda, it seemed as if she were really waiting for an answer from O-Nobu. The latter swiftly responded.

'Really, Hideko, that's quite unnecessary. Please don't trouble yourself. If we weren't able to manage by ourselves, that would be a different matter, but we've already solved our problem.'

'But I'm the one who'd feel bad if I didn't leave it. Since I purposely wrapped it up in this way and brought it, please accept it without saying anything like that, won't you?'

They both attempted to preserve appearances. They began the same exchange again. Tsuda continued to listen to them patiently, but they finally had to turn to him for his decision.

'Yoshio, please accept it.'

'Do you think we should?' O-Nobu asked her husband.

Tsuda gave a broad grin.

'You're very strange, O-Hide. Before, you were so firm. Now you've become so foolishly weak in trying to make me accept it. Which actually is your true attitude?'

O-Hide gave him a very stern look.

'Both are true.'

Tsuda felt this answer was abrupt, and its stern tone completely upset his attempt to behave dispassionately. O-Nobu was even more disconcerted. She looked at O-Hide, startled. The latter's face was flushed as before. However, in her cool eyes dwelt a light which was not only that of rage. In addition to a bitter and violent hostility, something else which was yet to be determined flickered therein. But exactly what that was, there was no other way of learning than by listening to her directly. The two were strangely fascinated. A change in the attitude they had been maintaining until then was clearly required. Without attempting to stop her, they prepared to listen to her impassioned explanation. While they were anticipating them, O-Hide's words burst forth.

109

'Actually I've been wondering for quite a while whether I should say this or not, but now that I've been ridiculed by you in such a way, Yoshio, I can't possibly remain silent. So I'm going to say what I should right here and now. But first of all let me explain that my tone will be a bit different from the one I've used up to now, and if you listen with the same attitude you've had heretofore, I'm afraid I may become annoyed, not just because I don't like to be misunderstood, but rather because my feelings may not even penetrate to yours.'

O-Hide's explanation began with these words. They further intensified the expectation of the other two, who had already began to change their attitude. They waited silently for what was to follow, but O-Hide had to emphasize her point once again.

"You'll listen quite seriously to what I have to say, won't you? Because on my part I'm in dead earnest.' She then turned her piercing eyes from Tsuda to O-Nobu.

'Of course I don't mean to imply I haven't been in earnest up until now. But in any case, if you'll stay here with us, O-Nobu, everything will be all right, because if it should turn into the usual brother-and-sister quarrel you can intervene and stop it.'

O-Nobu smiled, but O-Hide did not respond.

'I've been thinking of saying this to you for a long time—even before you married O-Nobu. But I've never had the opportunity, and till today I haven't done so. Now I'm going to say it to the two of you together. It's nothing more than this : Are you quite prepared to hear it? It's simply that both of you think of nothing but yourselves. If only you are well off, no matter how much others may suffer or be in need, you just turn your heads away and take not the least notice.'

Tsuda was able to take this criticism with composure because he did not doubt that it was a statement of a general human characteristic rather than specifically of one of his own. To O-Nobu, however, there could have been no more gratuitous criticism. She was utterly amazed, but fortunately or unfortunately, O-Hide continued before she could open her mouth.

'Yoshio, you only love yourself. And you, O-Nobu, seek only to be loved by him. In your eyes, that's all that matters. As for a sister or anyone like that, of course she doesn't exist, but neither do your mother or father.'

From this point O-Hide raced on; she seemed to be afraid that one of them would try to interrupt her.

'I'm merely saying the things as they appear to me; it isn't that I want you to act in a certain way. That time has already passed. To tell the truth, that state of things ended today. Actually, it ended just this minute. It ended, and you weren't even aware of it. There's nothing for me to do but resign myself to it. And yet I absolutely must have you listen to the conclusion I draw from your behaviour.'

O-Hide again turned her eyes from her brother to her sister-in-law. Neither of them had any clear idea of what her conclusion was to be. Consequently they were curious to hear it, and did not speak.

'The conclusion is simple,' O-Hide said. 'So simple it can be said quite briefly. But you probably won't understand. You've probably never noticed that you're thoroughly incapable of accepting kindnesses from anyone. Even though my saying this now still doesn't register with you, I'll repeat it : What I mean is that since you can think of nothing but yourselves you've lost the ability to respond as human beings to the kindness of others. In short, you've fallen to the level of people who can't be grateful for favours. Maybe you think you're self-sufficient. Maybe you think you haven't the slightest need for anything. But as I see it, it's a terrible misfortune for both of you. It's as if you were deprived by God of the ability to be happy. Yoshio, you say you need this money I've brought, don't you? But you also say you don't need the kindness that made me bring it. From my point of view, it's exactly the opposite. As a human being, I repeat, it's exactly the opposite. I consider this a terrible misfortune; and you, Yoshio, aren't in the least aware of it. O-Nobu, you also think it's right for your husband not to accept the money I've brought. Before, you were trying desperately to keep him from accepting it, because by refusing it, at the same time you're also eliminating my kindness. That's your object, isn't it, O-Nobu? Your sense of values, too, is completely reversed. The fact that the good feeling you'd have in compliantly receiving this token of affection from me would make you many, many times happier than your peculiarity in rebuffing the kindness of others—that fact is utterly unknown to you.'

O-Nobu could not remain silent, but O-Hide was even less able to do so. In a heated manner she repressed her sister-in-law, who wanted to interrupt her, and was not satisfied until she had finished saying everything she wished.

110

'O-Nobu, if you have something to say, I'll listen quietly to it afterwards, but for now I beg you to allow me to finish what I have to say, however unpleasant it may be for you. It will soon be over. I won't take that long.'

O-Hide's manner of apology was strangely calm. In contrast with that of a moment earlier when she had clashed with Tsuda, she now adopted a completely different attitude, passing from extreme agitation to complete tranquillity. That this was an extraordinary phenomenon under such circumstances was reflected in the eyes of her two listeners.

'Yoshio,' O-Hide began, 'why do you think I waited so long to take out what I'd wrapped up to bring you? And why did I now give it to you without any ill-will? Ponder that for a while. You too, O-Nobu, think about it.'

Without for a second reflecting on what she had said, the two accepted it merely as O-Hide's casuistry. Particularly did this appear to be true of O-Nobu. Yet O-Hide was perfectly serious.

'With this money I was trying to make you behave in a brotherly fashion. You may very well ridicule my attempt because the amount is so small. But as far as I'm concerned, the amount has nothing to do with it. If an occasion should arise when I might, even in a small matter, make you behave in a more brotherly manner, I think I'd always take advantage of it. Today I tried to do that here as best I could, and I failed spectacularly. Especially after O-Nobu arrived on the scene my failure became increasingly apparent. It was then that I had to cast away forever all the affection I've ever had for you as a sister—O-Nobu, I beg you, please bear with me a bit longer.'

O-Hide, by so speaking, prevented her sister-in-law from interrupting.

'I understand your attitude perfectly. I don't intend to listen for hours to your explanations. Since from what I've seen here just now I think I can understand you much better, I shan't ask you anything further. But I still must explain my own behaviour, and that's what I'd like you to listen to at all costs.'

O-Nobu said nothing even though she thought O-Hide an exceedingly wilful woman. However, since from the beginning of the encounter she was enjoying the leisure of the victor, she could remain silent without too much dissatisfaction.

'Yoshio,' O-Hide again began. 'Please look at this. It's carefully wrapped up in paper. This is proof that your sister prepared it and brought it from her home. Here lies the meaning of what she's trying to say.'

O-Hide purposely took up the paper-wrapped money from the edge of the pillow and showed it to him.

'This is what is called kindness. Since you're quite incapable of comprehending its meaning, I've been forced to explain it to you myself. Furthermore, even though you haven't behaved in a brotherly way at all, I must also explain that I now have no choice but to leave this "kindness" here. Do you consider this my kindness or my duty? You asked me that question earlier, and I said the two were the same— since, if you refuse to accept my kindness, and I'm of a mind to persist in showing it to you, where then does it differ from duty? Haven't you merely succeeded in transforming my kindness into duty?'

'O-Hide, I've already grasped what you mean,' Tsuda began to say. His sister's meaning had indeed clearly entered his mind, but the emotion she had anticipated was not in any way aroused. He had merely endured her irritating manner and listened to her complaints. As he judged his sister, she was neither kind nor sincere. She had neither charm nor nobility : she was merely annoying.

'I get your point. That's quite enough now. That's really more than enough.'

Since O-Hide had already resigned herself to her defeat, she did not appear particularly resentful. She merely said :

'This isn't money my husband has advanced me. Since you broke the arrangement he made with Father, he now feels responsible to Father for your behaviour. And if he had advanced this money, even you couldn't accept it willingly. I too don't wish to bother him on that account. Therefore, I tell you plainly : This money has nothing to do with him. It's mine. Therefore you can accept it without a protest, can't you? Even though you won't accept my kindness, you can accept this money, can't you? Rather than extending any half-hearted thanks to me now, it would make me feel far better if you were to take it in silence. It's ceased to be a problem concerning you; it merely concerns me. Yoshio, for my sake, please take this.'

With that, O-Hide concluded and rose. O-Nobu looked at Tsuda, but she could not discern any indication of what she should do. However, she was forced to go down the stairs to see O-Hide out of the hospital. At the entrance the two exchanged the customary politenesses and parted.

I I I

Merely meeting her sister-in-law at the hospital was in no way startling to O-Nobu. However, the result of that meeting could only be described as startling in the extreme. Even though she was quite aware of O-Hide's attitude towards her, she had not even remotely suspected she would become her opponent in this kind of 'scene'. Even after she had become ranged against her, she could only interpret this as the result of an unfortunate coincidence. She did not even make an effort to trace the past events which had made the encounter inevitable. In simpler terms, her psychological state was one of feeling that she was not in the least responsible for the incident. The entire blame rested on O-Hide's shoulders. Consequently, her heart was remarkably un-ruffled; at least it would not have been easy to discover in her any painful twitchings of conscience.

O-Nobu had gleaned two things from the encounter. One was the unpleasant sensation she had at its conclusion. In that unpleasantness was woven the realization of the strife that would probably continue between them. Of course she felt fully capable of seeing her way through that difficulty, but only under the condition that Tsuda lend her his full support. In her relations with O-Hide, she had felt more calm than uneasy, but it was still intensely important for her to deter-mine the extent to which she had diminished that uneasiness by her behaviour that day. She also felt that she had at least acquired some self-confidence in the sense that she had demonstrated to Tsuda, to the fullest extent of her ability, her faithfulness to him, in an attempt to win his love, or rather to win it back.

While this must be recognized as of the utmost significance to O-Nobu among the various things she had learned from the incident, another advantage accrued to her naturally without her perceiving it. Of course it was only a temporary advantage, namely that she had luckily escaped her husband's suspicious eyes, which should naturally have been turned on her. For the Tsuda of prior to the encounter with O-Hide and the Tsuda of after this encounter, in which he had been made to suffer, were completely different beings both as to temperament and as the object of her attention. O-Nobu, by appearing at the critical moment of this transformation and by broadening its scope in a natural way, had, unknown to herself, received a godsend.

She had been spared the inconvenience of explaining to Tsuda all the details of why her uncle had demanded that she go to the theatre and also why she had had to go to the Okamoto home on the previous day. Furthermore, there had not been time for her to say a word even about what Kobayashi had said, something she almost wanted to tell. For after O-Hide left, the minds of the two were completely occupied by what had just taken place.

They both knew this from the expression on the other's face, and they looked at each other at the very instant that O-Nobu, who had climbed the stairs after saying goodbye to O-Hide, appeared at the entrance to Tsuda's room. O-Nobu smiled, and Tsuda did the same. At that moment they were aware of nothing else but themselves, and the smile of each penetrated to the depth of the other's spirit. At least O-Nobu had the feeling that for the first time in a long while she was perceiving the true Tsuda. She did not quite know what that smile portended; it was just that the form his mouth took as it became that smile constituted a thing of joy for her, and she carefully preserved it in her heart.

Then the smiles of the two swiftly changed. They both opened their mouths, revealing their teeth, and burst into laughter simultaneously.

'Well, I'm simply amazed!' O-Nobu cried.

With that, she came to Tsuda's pillow. He answered quite calmly.

'That's why I told you not to phone her.'

The two naturally had to discuss the quarrel.

'Hideko couldn't be a Christian by any chance, could she?'

'Why do you ask that?'

'For a lot of reasons.'

'Do you mean because she left the money?'

'No, it's not just that.'

'Perhaps you mean because she preached us such a sermon.'

'Well yes, I suppose so. It was the first time I ever heard her argue that way.'

'Oh, she loves to argue. In fact she isn't content unless she gets herself worked up in that way.'

'Well, I merely said that for me it was the first time.'

'It may have been so for you; but as for me, I don't know how many times I've had to listen to her. She has the terrible habit of delivering a lecture over nothing at all. And it's become even worse since she's come under the influence of Fujii.'

'Why is that?'

'Why, by being with him all the time and by watching how he loves to argue, she's finally become as skilful as he in using her tongue.'

Tsuda showed that he thought his sister a fool. O-Nobu merely laughed derisively.

112

O-Nobu was happy to be dealing directly with her husband for the first time in quite a long while. She felt hopeful because the thin curtain that had somehow been drawn between them had suddenly fallen away.

She absolutely had to make him love her by loving him. This had been the determination which had spurred her to very great efforts. But fortunately these efforts had not been in vain. Now she had finally been rewarded, at least to the extent that she could have hope for the future. This rupture with O-Hide, which could only be termed an unforeseen event, was, in effect, the dawn of rebirth for her. She could now see a faint pink glow on the distant horizon, and with this fond hope she forgot all the unpleasantness that might arise from the dispute. The one dark spot, the exact nature of which she did not understand, which Kobayashi had cruelly left behind, still remained with her. The one mysterious phrase which had burst forth from O-Hide also had become a cloud of doubt, casting its pall over her. Nevertheless these unpleasant things had already receded into the far distance. At least they did not now cause her very much pain, and she did not even see the necessity of recalling the excitement they had aroused upon her hearing them.

'Even if something dreadful should happen, I'll manage somehow.'

O-Nobu at that time could even summon up this sort of self-confidence about her future relations with Tsuda. Consequently she felt that she had the resources to meet any emergency. She was also aided by the feeling that if it was only a matter of handling her opponent she could manage that easily enough.

If she had been asked, 'Your opponent? What sort of an opponent?' what would she have answered? That it was someone sketched in light grey ink. That it was a woman. And that it was someone who was stealing Tsuda's love from her. She knew nothing whatever other than that. But she still was certain such an opponent lurked somewhere. If the conflict between O-Hide and the two of them had ended without any danger to her, it surely was now time to search out from afar this adversary who had wormed her way into Tsuda's heart.

As she reflected on this whole problem, which had once disturbed her so much, she was indeed rather happy. She certainly did not think it would be unbearable to continue to be concerned about it. Instead she thought it would be excellent strategy to make as good use as possible of this occasion and to etch in her husband's mind this present image of herself as a kind wife.

No sooner had she decided on this course than she told a lie. It was a very small one. But since in the present circumstances she firmly believed that by bringing the cheque with her she had rescued Tsuda from a predicament which had both material and spiritual dimensions, the lie had considerable significance.

At that moment Tsuda took up the cheque and looked at it again. The amount indicated on it was even larger than he needed. But before commenting on that act, he thanked her as follows :

'Thanks a lot, O-Nobu. Thanks to you I'm out of this mess with O-Hide.'

O-Nobu's lie followed this last word of thanks, and slipped easily out of her mouth.

'I went to the Okamotos' yesterday to get it from my uncle for you.'

Tsuda looked quite startled. Was it this very O-Nobu, who when he had asked her to go and get some money from the Okamotos had refused pointblank, who had now brought him this cheque? As he wondered how, within a week, such goodwill had suddenly welled up within her, he found her behaviour extremely strange. She explained the matter to him :

'Yes, I won't say it wasn't unpleasant—to have to annoy my uncle about a money matter in addition to everything else. But there was nothing else to do, was there, dear? If in an emergency I didn't have at least that much courage I certainly wouldn't be doing my duty as a wife, would I?'

'Did you tell your uncle why we needed it?'

'Yes, but it was quite difficult for me, as you can well imagine.'

They both knew that when she had married Tsuda her uncle had provided the greater part of her dowry and trousseau.

'And besides until yesterday I never once showed I was in the slightest need of money. That's why I felt even worse about it.'

Tsuda could understand quite well, judging from his own character, how O-Nobu might feel under those circumstances.

'You did very well.'

'If I asked him, I knew I'd succeed, dear. After all, it isn't that he doesn't have the money. It's just that it was difficult to ask him, that's all.'

'But that's because there are a lot of difficult people in the world, like Father and O-Hide.'

Tsuda's expression seemed to be one of wounded pride. O-Nobu spoke so as to repair it :

'That's not the only reason my uncle gave me money. You see he'd promised to buy me a ring. And he's been saying for quite some time now that since he didn't buy one for me when I got married he'd buy one for me now. That's probably how he looked at it when he gave me the money. So you needn't worry about it at all.'

Tsuda looked at her finger. The jewel he himself had bought her still gleamed there.

113

The feelings of the two merged as they had rarely done before. Tsuda's heart, which until then had been carefully guarded to preserve his dignity in front of her, softened involuntarily. His caution in trying so very hard to draw a curtain of vagueness over his relations with his parents, both because of his concern that his father might appear to her to be a miser and also because of his fear that she might despise his father's financial resources for being less than she had anticipated, melted away. And he was not aware that this had happened. Without any effort and without exerting his will in any way he had been gently pushed in this direction by a natural force. It was exactly as if the episode had gently lifted the cautious Tsuda up and carried him to that point for her. O-Nobu was very happy about this development. For his attitude had changed naturally, without his deciding to change it.

At the same time in O-Nobu as well, as Tsuda saw her, the very same mood emerged. Setting aside other matters for the moment, one could say that a strange secret struggle concerning money had always been going on between the two since their marriage. This struggle had come about in the following way: Tsuda, who like most well-to-do people liked to pride himself on his wealth, had on this point intimated to O-Nobu that his father's wealth was far greater than it actually was, so as to have her value him as highly as possible. If that had been all he had done it would not have been so bad, but his weakness had swiftly made him go a step further. He had deliberately given her the impression that before his marriage he had been in much easier circumstances than he actually was, that he had been able to ask for any amount of help from his father whenever he needed any, and that even if he had not asked he certainly had never had the slightest worry about monthly expenses. When he had married her it had been exactly as if he had already been burdened with the responsibility for backing up these claims. Clever man that he was, in placing such an emphasis on money he knew perfectly well O-Nobu's character of not lagging behind him and of even outdoing him in this respect. To use extreme terms, since he was even capable of believing that love itself could arise from the gleam of gold, he had the anxiety of somehow making his financial situation look all right to O-Nobu. On this point particularly he deeply feared she would despise him. The reason he had asked Hori to persuade his father to help him each month was also actually that, apart from his real need, he secretly maintained this concern about appearances. And yet even so he had certain areas of diffidence within him. At least there was a considerable distance between his outward behaviour towards O-Nobu and his inner feelings towards her. And the shrewd O-Nobu knew that distance precisely. She could not help being dissatisfied about it, but rather than attacking his falseness she hated his lack of frankness. She looked upon it as merely a kind of unpleasant reserve. She was pained at not knowing why he could not reveal his weak points to her like a man. Finally, she decided that if he was so distant, and did not dare expose himself, then she would simply have to resign herself to this fact. But this attitude of hers produced a reverberation, like an echo, in his mind. Thus, no matter how far they had gone in their relations they had never been able to deal directly with one another. Moreover since they were both reserved, they had both been extremely careful not to touch on that sensitive point. The dissension with O-Hide, however, had accidentally burst open this locked door in O-Nobu's mind. And O-Nobu herself was not in the least aware of this. Without any effort or decision at all to open herself up to him she had quite naturally done precisely that. Thus to Tsuda too she appeared happily as a completely different person.

In this way their minds and hearts merged with one another as they had rarely done. Then, just at that point a strange thing suddenly happened : they freely took up the problem they had been avoiding until then. Together they began to discuss remedial measures concerning their relations with Tsuda's parents in Kyoto.

They both had the same presentiment. They both were worried that the incident with O-Hide would not end there. She would certainly do something further. And if she did, it would doubtless be to deal directly with Tsuda's parents. It was also certain that the natural result of her action would be to their disadvantage. Up to that point the two were in agreement. Beyond that, however, there arose the important matter of finding a remedy. But when they came to that problem their opinions differed, and they could not easily resolve those differences.

First of all, O-Nobu suggested Tsuda's uncle Fujii as mediator. But Tsuda shook his head. He knew very well that both his uncle and aunt were on O-Hide's side. Next, Tsuda was the one to ask how Okamoto would do. But, because Okamoto was not very intimate with Tsuda's father, this time it was O-Nobu who opposed the suggestion. She then put forth the plan that the simplest thing would be for her to visit O-Hide to try to achieve a reconciliation. To this suggestion Tsuda did not show any particular opposition. After all, even if they did not have a reconciliation after the present incident, so long as they did not hope for a complete rupture, relations between the two families were certain to be resumed under some form or other. Nevertheless they tried to discuss at the same time a slightly more effective method than O-Nobu's last suggestion. They thought about the problem for a while.

Finally they mentioned the name of Yoshikawa simultaneously. His social position, his relations with Tsuda's father, his recent acceptance of the special commission from Tsuda's father to look after Tsuda for him—from every conceivable point of view all the advantageous conditions were fulfilled. But there was also one awkward aspect in selecting him. For if they were to have Yoshikawa, who was rather difficult to approach, speak for them on so intimate a matter, they would absolutely have to bring his wife into compliance first. But his wife, for O-Nobu, was a very difficult person with whom to deal. Before agreeing to Tsuda's proposal O-Nobu cocked her head slightly in hesitation, but since Tsuda, who was on such good terms with Mrs Yoshikawa, could see great hopes for success in his plan, he eagerly urged O-Nobu to accept it. Finally she yielded.

After the two had opened their hearts and had had this kind of discussion in the wake of the unpleasant episode with O-Hide, they parted affectionately.

114

Since Tsuda felt the additional weariness of not having slept well the previous night, that night he was able to go to sleep remarkably easily. On the following day, as the bright sunlight struck his eyes and as he watched the clear sky outside the windows, he heard the familiar sound of washing from the neighbouring laundry and inhaled the all-pervading atmosphere of autumn.

'. . . if you go there, go ahead and wear it. Shisshisshi!'

The men at the laundry inserted the meaningless refrain 'Shisshisshi' at intervals as they sang a popular song. This made Tsuda imagine just how busily they were working.

Suddenly they carried the white articles of clothing through a strange hole and came out on the roof. Then they climbed to the clothes-drier and spread out the white things, without a space between them, against the autumn sky. Their activity, which they had repeated every day since he had come there, seemed monotonous to him. But there was no denying they were diligent. And yet after all he could not really feel any affinity with them.

He preferred to think about things much more closely related to his present condition. The image of Mrs Yoshikawa came to his mind. Whenever he would sketch his future it was extremely vague. And whenever he tried to cast it into shape, Mrs Yoshikawa would always appear. This focal point, which normally represented his future for him, had a special significance at that time.

First of all, there were the implications of the visit he had made a short while before. It had been she who had then suddenly touched again upon the particular topic that had been banned between them. He had tried not to ask anything further. But he had also wanted very much to do so. If it was she who had broken the silence on the subject he thought he had the right to investigate it further.

Secondly, his relations with his parents troubled him. If he had to decide which was more important, it was this latter problem which had suddenly become urgent. It seemed the best policy to see Mrs Yoshikawa as soon as possible. It was so important that since it was clear he certainly could not move about for yet another four or five days he had tried, on the previous day, before O-Nobu had left, to persuade her to go to see Mrs Yoshikawa in his place. Since O-Nobu had refused, the plan had not succeeded, but even so he believed this was the appropriate measure to take.

It seemed exceedingly strange to him that O-Nobu disliked to undertake such a commission and call on Mrs Yoshikawa. Especially was this so since he was sure that all women liked to visit such wealthy people's homes even when they did not have any real business to transact. Or at least so he thought at the time. He had even emphasized his proposal so that it had been exactly as if he had deliberately made up the business to enable her to see Mrs Yoshikawa. But since O-Nobu had disliked so much to undertake the request he had not then wished actually to compel her to go. The reason he had not done so may have been the harmonious mood existing between them but it was related also to the way in which O-Nobu had declined. She had said that if she were to go she would surely fail. But instead of stating why she would fail she had maintained that if he went he would most certainly succeed. When he called attention to the fact that even if he were to succeed he could not visit her until after he left the hospital and he was therefore afraid that it would be too late, she had again given him a strange answer. For she had asserted that Mrs Yoshikawa would surely come to visit him at the hospital. She had assured him that if only he were to use that occasion it would be most natural, and the whole thing would be carried out quite simply.

As he looked at the laundry clothes-drier, he reflected in this way on their discussion of the previous day, tracing back their comments one by one. As he did so, it seemed to him that Mrs Yoshikawa might come to visit him. But it also seemed that she might not. And he did not understand why O-Nobu had maintained so strongly that she would come. He tried to imagine the theatre party seated around the dinner table at the theatre restaurant. He even tried to construct, as in a scene in a novel, the kind of conversation that O-Nobu and Mrs Yoshikawa had exchanged. But when it came to the question of how such a prediction had emerged from their conversation he was forced to give it up as something incomprehensible. He had already allowed to O-Nobu a certain intuition, an intuition which God had unfortunately not granted him. Since on that point he had always had to fear her somewhat, he did not have the courage to touch on that area boldly. At the same time, since he could not actually rely on that intuition, he wondered whether there might not be some way of making certain that Mrs Yoshikawa would come to the hospital. He immediately thought of telephoning, but he was at a loss to find a way of doing so and having her come there naturally without his seeming impudent or without his action seeming deliberate. But no matter how much effort he expended in this direction he achieved nothing. When he realized that this was so because he was trying to achieve something basically impossible, he smiled wryly to himself, and again looked out through the front windows.

Outside meanwhile a wind had risen. The branches of the single willow in front of the laundry swayed gently together with the white clothes which were drying. The three electric wires, stretched so as to graze them, also moved slowly as if in rhythm with the other elements in the scene.

115

The doctor, who had climbed the stairs, found that Tsuda seemed extremely bored. After asking him how he was, he immediately added, 'You'll only have to bear up a bit longer,' as if to console him. Then he changed the bandages.

'It's still dangerous to tamper with the incision in any way.'

He warned Tsuda in this way, telling him for his own good that if he tried to loosen a little the sections of the bandages pressing directly on the affected area, the cut would bleed.

The doctor changed only a part of the bandages. Tsuda too realized that he could not possibly return home yet, if he was in such physical condition that the cut would bleed if the main sections of the bandages were removed.

'I suppose, after all, there's nothing to do but stay here, without moving, as many days as originally planned.'

The doctor looked at him pityingly.

'If you let things take their proper course you won't have to take such extraordinary care later.'

Nevertheless the doctor seemed to treat Tsuda as a patient in comfortable circumstances, lacking neither money nor leisure.

'You surely don't have any particular important business to attend to, do you?'

'No, it's all right if I stay here for about a week. But still a slight emergency has come up and. . . .'

'Hm, I see. But everything will soon be over. Just bear up a bit longer.'

Perhaps because the doctor, who could give no other encouragement than this, did not yet have too many out-patients, he sat there and told Tsuda one or two stories. One of them, concerning an incident that had occurred when the doctor was still an intern at a large hospital, made Tsuda laugh despite himself. The story, about a man who, suspecting that a patient had died because a nurse had administered the wrong medicine, had barged into the medical office and had absolutely demanded that the nurse be beaten as punishment, was, from Tsuda's point of view, quite amusing. Since Tsuda had a personality rather different from that of the man in the doctor's story, he could find nothing whatever in it but foolishness. In short, he saw only the other man's weaknesses. And at the same time he congratulated himself on his own self-control. Thus the result was that he completely overlooked his own shortcomings.

After the doctor's examination, Tsuda brooded over his present condition, one in which, because of a nasty illness, he had to be confined to one room for a whole week. Perhaps it was his mood at the moment but the present time seemed precious to him. He even secretly regretted that he had not postponed the medical treatment for a bit longer.

He again began to think about Mrs Yoshikawa. He gradually moved from a consideration of whether there was some way of making her come there to a consideration of how pleasant it would be if she would actually visit him. Despite the fact that he normally disparaged O-Nobu's intuition since he did not like to think she might be able to see through his motives, under these exceptional circumstances he rather tended to wish it would be proved correct.

He picked up a book from among those O-Nobu had left for him. He could see they belonged to Okamoto's library. Unfortunately he could not really understand humour. Even if the meaning of the words penetrated his mind, his heart did not give much response, and there were many words even his mind could not understand. Since he was not actually forced to read the book, he skimmed through the pages rapidly, trying to find something that would suit him, and by accident his eye fell upon the following :

The girl's father faced the young man, and when he asked him whether he loved his daughter the young man answered that it was not a question of loving her, since he would willingly even die for her. If he could be favoured with even one soft glance from her lovely eyes, he would gladly die. He would throw himself from a two-hundred-foot cliff and crush himself on the rocks below, he answered. The girl's father shook his head, and said : 'I'm a bit of a liar myself, but in my small family I'll have to think twice about having two of them.'

The word 'liar' made Tsuda laugh more sardonically than usual. He realized he himself was a 'liar', but at the same time he accepted uncritically the lies of others and was not in the least distressed by them. On the contrary, he believed one had to tell lies to be able to live. He did not know he himself had been living until then according to such a nebulous philosophy of life. He merely went on living. Therefore, even if he had probed his attitude a little more deeply, he would simply not have understood his own position.

'Love and Deception.'

After reading the two words which were the title of the brief anecdote, he was perplexed as to how to explain their relationship. He was at that point in his life burdened with a certain important problem. He absolutely had to solve it because of the demands of his deepest feelings, but as long as he did not have the opportunity to experiment with a solution he could only think about it abstractly. Not being a philosopher, he was incapable of spreading out before his mind's eye in any organized form even the view of life he had himself been maintaining until then.

116

He thought about things in this way in random fashion, one after another. As he did so, it was past noon before he realized it. His mind was tired, and he did not have the energy to continue thinking for long about even one more thing. But even though it was autumn the days were still too long for him to go to sleep so early. He began to feel bored. Then his thoughts turned to O-Nobu. He was sufficiently demanding to expect her to visit him that day as well. Having worn himself out until then in thinking only of things he would have to be careful about mentioning in front of her, he did not sense the irony in his hoping that she might come in at any moment. Even the realization that he could not be responsible for things that came spontaneously into his mind did not then occur to him. Perhaps he distantly realized that it was more significant that he himself kept locked within him facts which O-Nobu did not know than that she withheld certain facts from him; yet even this fact he could not be expected to apprehend in distinct form unless an emergency arose.

O-Nobu still did not come. And of course Mrs Yoshikawa, whom he was awaiting even more eagerly, did not appear either. He was annoyed. The Noh chanting, which he disliked intensely, which someone nearby had been engaged in for quite some time, further irritated him. He suddenly remembered that he had seen a long narrow sign, announcing instruction in Noh chanting, on the two-storey building diagonally opposite the laundry. The second floor seemed to be the place where the practice was going on, and even though it was rather far away the chanting sounded excessively loud. Since he realized full well that he had no right to stop people from doing what they wanted to do, he could do nothing whatever about his discontent. He merely wanted to leave the hospital as soon as possible.

He then looked listlessly, with an eye that only half took in what it was seeing, at a crest which looked like the name of a firm, composed of a single horizontal stroke drawn underneath the outline of a mountain, on the red brick warehouse behind the willow, and at things resembling large hooks, the purpose of which he did not understand, which stuck out from the walls on either side of the crest; as he did so, he suddenly heard bold footsteps, and someone strode rapidly up the stairs. He was taken by surprise. For from the sound of those footsteps he could already guess reasonably accurately whose they were.

His presentiment quickly became reality. At almost the same time that he turned his eyes towards the entrance of the room Kobayashi entered abruptly, still wearing the overcoat he had just borrowed the day before.

'How's it going?'

He immediately sat cross-legged on the *tatami*. Tsuda gave a rather painful laugh in place of a greeting. As soon as he saw him, Tsuda felt annoyed and wondered what in the world he had come for.

'This is it,' Kobayashi said, as he shoved the sleeves of the overcoat at Tsuda to show it to him.

'Thanks. With your help I can get through this winter too.'

Kobayashi repeated to Tsuda the exact words he had used to O-Nobu. But since Tsuda had not heard them from her, he did not consider them especially sarcastic.

'Your wife came, I suppose, didn't she?' Kobayashi asked him.

'Of course she did. That's only natural, isn't it?'

'She said something to you, I suppose, didn't she?'

Tsuda vacillated a bit between answering yes and answering no. He wanted very much to know what sort of things Kobayashi had told her. If only he could now make him repeat what he had said to her it did not matter to him which answer he gave. But he could not decide on the spur of the moment which of them would produce the desired result. And yet his attitude seemed to have a strange significance, and produced a reaction in Kobayashi.

'She was quite angry, wasn't she? I certainly thought she might be.'

Having easily found a clue to his problem, Tsuda swiftly followed it up.

'That's because you annoyed her so.'

'I didn't annoy her. I may just have teased her a bit too much, unfortunately. But she didn't cry, did she?'

Tsuda was a bit surprised.

'Did you say things that would have made her do so?'

'How should I know! After all, you know I can say all sorts of things. It's just that since she was brought up in an upper-class home like the Okamotos' she still doesn't know crude men like me exist in the world. That's why she's bothered by every little thing I say. If you'd only teach her not to pay any attention to a fool like me, everything would be all right.'

'But I *have* been trying to teach her exactly that,' Tsuda retorted, not in the least abashed. Kobayashi gave a loud laugh.

'Well, your discipline as a teacher leaves a bit to be desired, doesn't it?'

Tsuda changed his manner of speaking.

'But what in the world did you say to tease her so much?'

'You've already heard about it from her, haven't you?'

'No, I haven't.'

The two of them looked squarely at each other. They attempted simultaneously to assess each other's thoughts.

117

There was a special significance in Tsuda's trying to make Kobayashi disclose his real intent. He knew very well O-Nobu's character in its extraordinarily differing phases. Utterly unlike O-Hide, she never failed to present to him an extremely docile and ladylike exterior, but at the same time she clearly possessed in the same degree aspects which served to constrain him. Her abilities were essentially of one kind. But their application extended over both of the above areas. For when it came to things she thought she should not tell her husband, or things she decided it would be best to hide from him, in such situations she was thoroughly unmanageable. The more obedient she was, the less he was able to get anything out of her. He could have done nothing about finding out what exchange had taken place between her and Kobayashi on the previous day since because of the uproar with O-Hide he had not even had time to ask for any details. On the other hand, he seriously doubted whether, even if such an obstruction to their conversation had not arisen, and she had been asked by him to give a precise account of the incident, she would have satisfied his request and without holding back details would have done as he hoped. Judging from her normal behaviour, he thought she would surely have deceived him. Particularly if he considered that Kobayashi had spoken unreservedly about things he should not have, did it seem to him likely that she would feign having heard nothing and would remain silent in front of him. At least Tsuda felt there was more than sufficient margin for such behaviour in O-Nobu's personality. Thus, if he already had to resign himself to learning nothing from O-Nobu, he could only turn to Kobayashi as the source of the information he required.

Somehow Kobayashi seemed to be aware of this.

'I didn't really say anything to her, you know. If you think I'm lying, go ahead and ask her again. Of course as I was leaving I did feel maybe I'd done wrong and I apologized to her. But actually I myself don't even know what I had to apologize about.'

He laughed as he said this. Then, stretching out his hand casually, he took up the book Tsuda had begun to look at, which was by Tsuda's pillow, and read it to himself for about a minute.

'So you read this sort of stuff, do you?' he asked Tsuda in a rather disparaging tone. He turned the pages roughly, going from back to front. Then, when he discovered Okamoto's small private seal there, he said:

'Hm, so O-Nobu brought it, did she? No wonder I thought it was strange. By the way, Okamoto's quite rich, isn't he?'

'I have no idea.'

'What do you mean! That's the home O-Nobu came from, isn't it?'

'I didn't get married after first investigating how much money Okamoto had.'

'Oh you didn't, did you?'

This simple comment sounded strange to Tsuda. He could even interpret it as meaning: 'Would you really ever have married without finding out how much money Okamoto had!'

'Okamoto's O-Nobu's uncle. Don't tell me you don't know that! He's not any closer to her than that.'

'Oh he isn't, is he?'

Kobayashi made the same type of comment as before. Tsuda became even more annoyed.

'If you really want to know that badly how much money he has, do you want me to find out for you?'

Kobayashi gave a little laugh.

'When you're poor you just can't help being concerned about other people's wealth.'

Tsuda did not take him up on that. But just when Tsuda thought that Kobayashi had finished with the subject, he returned to it suddenly.

'But I wonder how much he really does have.'

This kind of attitude was indeed a special characteristic of his. And it could always be interpreted in two different ways. Though it was a simple matter to decide that Kobayashi was a fool and let it go at that, if Tsuda once began to think that maybe he was the one who was being made a fool of, then there was no limit to how far such an interpretation could be carried. With regard to the seriousness of Kobayashi's statement, Tsuda actually stood at the precise mid-point between doubt and belief. But in a situation such as that one, in which his own weakness was even partially involved, he could not but lean towards the interpretation that it was actually he who was being made a fool of. But since he could do nothing but be careful that he did not make Kobayashi even more impudent, he merely smiled.

'Shall I borrow some for you?'

'I certainly don't want to borrow any. If he'd *give* me some outright, then I'd take it, though. No, on second thoughts, I wouldn't take it even then. Anyway he'd never want to give me any, so I don't have to worry. If there's nothing else to do, I just might steal it from him.' Kobayashi gave a loud laugh at that point, before continuing : 'Yes, before going off to Korea I might just possibly think up some clever scheme to steal a bit of money from Okamoto.'

Tsuda immediately brought the conversation around to the subject of Korea.

'By the way, when are you leaving?'

'I don't exactly know yet.'

'But you *are* leaving, aren't you?'

'Yes, I'm leaving. I'll leave all right when the day comes, with or without your prodding.'

'I'm not prodding you. I'm only thinking that if there's time I'd like to give you a going-away party.'

Since Tsuda thought that if he could not learn enough from Kobayashi at that time he might use the occasion of a going-away party, he spoke as he did, and secretly prepared to make use of it.

118

Such care may indeed have been necessary since, whether on purpose or accidentally, Kobayashi would simply not move in the direction Tsuda was trying to make him move. For a long time Kobayashi took the position of answering while somehow not really answering Tsuda's questions. And he stubbornly stuck only to his own topics. Since these topics had a close, if indirect, relationship to what Tsuda wanted to hear, however, Tsuda was both irritated and provokingly tantalized. He even felt he was somehow being blackmailed in a roundabout way.

'Are Yoshikawa and Okamoto related by any chance?' Kobayashi began by asking.

Tsuda could not possibly think this question an innocent one.

'No, they're not. They're only friends. You already asked me that once and I told you, didn't I?'

'Oh did you? Since it was about people who are so far removed from me I must have forgotten. But even if they're friends they're not *just* friends, are they?'

'What the hell are you implying?'

Tsuda wanted very much to add 'you damn fool' to his remark.

'Nothing at all. I just meant that they're probably very close friends, that's all. You don't have to get so angry.'

Yoshikawa and Okamoto were undoubtedly connected in the way Kobayashi imagined. The simple fact was precisely that. But at the same time Tsuda was free to view that fact as having two sides, with the reverse side referring to him and O-Nobu.

'You're a lucky man,' Kobayashi said, 'because if you just take good care of O-Nobu you can't go wrong.'

'That's why I *am* taking good care of her. I know that much without your telling me.'

'Oh do you?'

Kobayashi again used the same type of expression. And each time he did, in a mock-serious tone, Tsuda felt as if he were being threatened by him.

'But you're quite different from me. You're very clever about it. Everybody thinks you've capitulated completely to O-Nobu.'

'Whom are you referring to by "everybody"?'

'Oh, such people as Fujii and his wife.'

Tsuda too was quite certain that both his uncle and aunt looked upon his marriage in that way.

'Since I actually *have* capitulated completely to her, it can't be helped if it does look that way.'

'Really? But an honest man like me can't possibly behave the way you do. You certainly are a great fellow, aren't you?'

'So you're honest and I'm false, eh? And my falseness makes me great while you, the honest one, are a fool. Is that the way it is? Since when have you invented that kind of philosophy?'

'I invented the philosophy a long time ago. I'm merely announcing it now—in connection with my going to Korea.'

A strange hint gleamed in Tsuda's mind.

'Do you already have your travel money?'

'I think I can get it in any number of ways.'

'Has it been decided that the company will pay it for you?'

'No. I've already decided to borrow it from Fujii.'

'Really? That's quite convenient for you.'

'It's not in the least convenient for me. I feel bad enough as it is to be helped so much by him.'

Even though Kobayashi spoke as he did, he had quite casually given to Fujii the responsibility for finding a husband for his own younger sister, O-Kin.

'No matter how shameless I may be, I still feel bad to be bothering Fujii about money on top of everything else.'

Tsuda did not say anything in return. Kobayashi then spoke in an innocent tone, as if he were consulting him.

'You wouldn't know of some place where I could squeeze some money out of somebody, would you?'

'I'm afraid not,' Tsuda declared, purposely turning away.

'You don't, eh? Still it seems to me there should be some place.'

'Well there isn't. Times have been bad lately.'

'How about you? No matter how badly off the rest of the world may be, you always seem to do quite well, don't you?'

'Don't be ridiculous!'

Since he had handed over to O-Nobu both the cheque from Okamoto and the paper-wrapped money which O-Hide had left, his purse was as good as empty. And even if he had had the money at hand he certainly did not want to make any financial sacrifice for Kobayashi at that time. So long as he was not absolutely compelled to, he did not see the slightest need of answering Kobayashi's plea.

Strangely enough Kobayashi himself did not press Tsuda further. Instead he suddenly startled Tsuda by opening up another and quite different topic.

That morning he had gone to see Fujii, and after he had had lunch there as usual, as he was spending a great deal of time in going over manuscripts, the lattice door of the entrance had opened, and he had gone out to see who it was. He had been quite surprised to find that it was none other than O-Hide.

When Tsuda had heard only that much of Kobayashi's story he could not help thinking : 'The wretch! So she's beat me to it, has she!' But Kobayashi's story did not end there. He still had other news with which to startle Tsuda.

119

But Kobayashi's way of startling him had an order all its own. He first had to tease him :

'So you had quite a fight with your sister, didn't you? Both Fujii and his wife got quite an earful from her. She went on forever about it.'

'Were you right there listening to it?'

Kobayashi scratched his head as he gave a forced laugh.

'Well, it isn't that I wanted to, you know. It's just that I heard it all naturally. And you know how it is when O-Hide's the one who talks and Fujii's the one who's egging her on.'

O-Hide had a rather stubborn and persistent streak in her. When she received a certain stimulus, utterly unlike Tsuda, she lost her normal calm completely, and an unusual violence suddenly emerged. And Tsuda's uncle was one who was never satisfied unless, without holding back, he probed to the very bottom of everything. Since he did not care if this probing was only a formal matter, he would show the person he was speaking to on such occasions that he wanted to make sure everything was consistent, or more colloquially, that everything fitted neatly into place. His habit of forever writing about intellectual problems had come to dominate him as well in his everyday life, apart from such problems, and it appeared very clearly at this point. He would make the person he was conversing with talk inordinately. And he would also ask him an inordinate number of questions. Very often when this process had reached a certain stage, his manner would cease to have the character of questioning and would become a kind of cross-examination.

Tsuda visualized his uncle and his sister sitting across from each other. He even wondered whether another disturbance might not have taken place there. But to preserve appearances in front of Kobayashi he purposely made light of the episode.

'She probably said all sorts of nasty things about me, didn't she?'

After Kobayashi had given only a cackle in response to this comment, he then spoke :

'But it isn't like you, Tsuda—to fight that way with O-Hide.'

'She's that way only with me, I tell you. If she's dealing with her husband she's much more reserved, I assure you.'

'So that's the way it is, eh? They always say husband and wife fight a lot but actually fights between brother and sister are much more common, I suppose. I haven't had any experience with a wife yet so I can't say a thing on that score, but since I do have a sister I'm quite aware of the other problem. What do you think of this, Tsuda? Even a fellow like me can't remember ever once having fought with his sister.'

'That depends entirely on who the sister is.'

'But I should think it also depends on who the brother is, too.'

'No matter how good a brother he may be there are bound to be times when he gets a bit angry.'

Kobayashi was grinning broadly.

'But I suppose even you don't think it's a good policy to make O-Hide angry, do you?'

'Of course I don't. Who in the world would want to have a fight? And especially with someone like her.'

Kobayashi laughed even harder. And each time he did so he became more relaxed and carefree.

'It probably couldn't be helped, I suppose. But it's just as I've been saying all along. Take me, for instance. I'm the sort of fellow that it doesn't matter who I quarrel with. I'm so down and out already I can't lose a thing no matter who I fight with. In fact if anything comes of the fight at all it certainly won't be any loss to me, because I've never had a thing to lose in the first place. In fact, any change resulting from a fight can only mean some gain for me, so I'm rather of the type who hopes for them. But *you're* different, Tsuda. *Your* quarrels could never possibly be of any benefit to you. And there aren't very many men in the world who know the pros and cons of a situation the way you do. It's not just that you know about them, either. You're the sort who's forever acting on such knowledge, from morning to night, asleep or awake. Or at least you're always thinking you should act on it. That's all right with me, though. But then a man like you. . . .'

Tsuda, quite annoyed, interrupted him.

'That's enough. I see what you mean. I see what you mean, I tell you. In other words, you're warning me not to fight with anyone. Especially if I fight with you it can only mean some loss for me, so you're advising me to settle any differences with you as amicably as possible. That's your main point, I suppose.'

Kobayashi feigned ignorance and became serious again.

'*You* fight with *me*? But I don't have the slightest intention of fighting with you.'

'I've already told you I see what you're driving at.'

'If you do, that's perfectly all right with me. But let me tell you so you don't misunderstand. I was really only talking about O-Hide before, I assure you, Tsuda.'

'I know all about that too.'

'What you mean is you know all about the problem with your parents, I suppose. You mean you'll fall into disfavour with them.'

'Of course.'

'But that's not the only thing, Tsuda. If you're not careful it may affect other things too.'

Kobayashi stopped at that point and looked to Tsuda to test the effect of his words. Tsuda was finally unable to appear unconcerned.

120

Kobayashi seized his opportunity.

When he began by saying, 'Now about O-Hide, Tsuda,' Tsuda was already his captive.

'Now about O-Hide, Tsuda. . . . Before she came to see Fujii, she went round to another place too, you know. Can you imagine where that was?'

He could not. At least concerning this particular episode it seemed there could be no place but the Fujiis' where she might possibly go.

'I can't imagine any such place in Tokyo!'

'Well, I'm afraid there *is* such a place.'

Tsuda was forced to try to think of several possibilities. But no matter how much he tried he simply could not come up with anything. Finally when Kobayashi laughingly told him the name of the place, he could only shout in amazement:

'To the Yoshikawas'? Why the hell did she go there? They don't have a thing to do with it!'

He could not but consider his sister's action extremely strange.

If it was only a matter of linking Yoshikawa and Hori, he too could do that easily enough. Nor did he in any way have to rely on the help of a vivid imagination. It was clear to anyone that at the time of his marriage Mr and Mrs Yoshikawa, who had publicly performed the role of go-betweens, had had social relations with his younger sister O-Hide, and with Hori, her husband. But nowhere could he discover why O-Hide, solely on that basis, should have gone especially to the Yoshikawas with this particular problem.

'She probably went just to visit. Simply to pay her respects, I suppose, didn't she?' Tsuda ventured.

'But it seems she didn't just do that. Not as I heard her story, at least.'

Tsuda instantly wanted to hear what she had said. But instead of satisfying his curiosity Kobayashi warned him.

'A fellow like you, Tsuda, who seems so extremely careful, finally forgot something, didn't he? Probably because you try so very hard not to overlook anything you naturally can't take care of everything. This affair is a case in point, isn't it? In the first place, to make O-Hide angry wasn't at all the thing to do, was it, from your standpoint? And then, by having made her angry, to make her go running to the Yoshikawas was stupid of you, wasn't it? Furthermore, you were convinced she couldn't possibly go to see them and you treated the whole affair lightly from the beginning. Isn't that very unlike your normal behaviour?'

It was easy for Kobayashi, after the event, to find the gap in Tsuda's precautions.

'After all, your father and Yoshikawa are friends, aren't they? And your father asked him to look out for you in everything, didn't he? Isn't it natural therefore that O-Hide should go running to them about this?'

Tsuda recalled what he had heard from Yoshikawa in the director's office before entering the hospital : 'Don't worry your father. We know everything you're doing here in Tokyo, and if something bad happens I'll let him know about it. But be careful.' Even if he tried to interpret those words from his present position they still seemed to be nothing more than half-joking advice. But if someone could at that point change them into something thoroughly serious then that person was O-Hide.

'She's certainly an eccentric one!'

The element of amazement in Tsuda's comment was in direct proportion to the absence of eccentricity in their family history.

'What the hell did she have to say to the Yoshikawas? When it comes to taking the full force of what she has to say, I'm the only one who can handle her. Because when she deals with others everything's sure to go wrong, and I'll be in a real mess.'

In addition to the direct effect of what O-Hide might say, Tsuda could clearly foresee serious effects in more distant areas. He did not know how Yoshikawa's patronage, Yoshikawa's and Okamoto's relationship, Okamoto's and O-Nobu's closeness, and other things, might be undermined through this single action of O-Hide's.

'Women are such stupid creatures, aren't they?'

Kobayashi immediately began to laugh upon hearing this remark. His laughter, louder than on any previous occasion, startled Tsuda. And Tsuda for the first time realized what he was actually saying.

'But be that as it may, what sort of thing did O-Hide chatter about when she went to the Yoshikawas'? If you heard what she was telling my uncle, then tell me, won't you?'

'She did keep telling him something, that's true. But actually it was so tiresome for me I'm afraid I didn't listen very carefully.'

Kobayashi, having come to the important section, pretended not to know anything and dropped the subject. Tsuda was greatly annoyed at learning nothing further. But after he had been forced to endure that annoyance awhile, Kobayashi returned to the subject.

'But just wait a bit longer. For better or worse, you'll soon hear all about it, I assure you.'

Tsuda thought it most unlikely that O-Hide would come again.

'No, I don't mean O-Hide. She won't come again right away. Mrs Yoshikawa's the one who's coming instead. Don't think I'm making this all up. I heard it myself with my own ears, I tell you. O-Hide even stated quite clearly the time that she'd come. She'll probably be here in a little while, I think.'

O-Nobu's prediction had come true. Mrs Yoshikawa, whom he had been trying somehow to have come and see him, would shortly arrive.

121

Two things flashed through Tsuda's mind in quick succession. One was the realization that he had to handle Mrs Yoshikawa, who was coming shortly, skilfully. Undoubtedly her visiting him at the hospital of her own accord was what he most desired, and in accordance with his pre-arranged plan, but since her visit had now acquired a new meaning, his manner of receiving it also had to change. As he tried to sketch in his imagination Mrs Yoshikawa's attitude on this occasion he felt considerable uneasiness. Even as only seen through his eyes, the Mrs Yoshikawa who would just have been filled with biased ideas by O-Hide, and the Mrs Yoshikawa who was not yet incited to antipathy, were quite different. But in this matter his usual self-confidence also played a role. For he was more than convinced that by meeting her only once he could easily overcome whatever prejudice or antipathy Mrs Yoshikawa might bring with her. Yet it was clear that if he did not at least try to do so at that point his own future was in jeopardy. Thus he awaited her visit with about three parts of uneasiness to seven parts of confidence.

The other thing that had flashed through his mind taught him the advantage of again temporarily changing his attitude towards O-Nobu. Until a short while before he had, out of sheer boredom, been hoping she might appear at any moment. But he now felt a special tension, for he was expecting something from an utterly different source. O-Nobu was no longer necessary. In fact, if she came it would instead be awkward. He also had a special problem which he wanted to discuss with Mrs Yoshikawa alone, just the two of them. He therefore decided he absolutely had to prevent O-Nobu and Mrs Yoshikawa from meeting there accidentally.

As a further precaution, he also had to find some means of getting rid of Kobayashi quickly. And yet even while this Kobayashi was saying that Mrs Yoshikawa would appear at any moment he did not show the slightest sign of leaving himself. He was hardly the type of man to worry that his presence might annoy someone. In fact, depending on the time and circumstances, he was even one who, knowing how annoying he was, would purposely annoy others. Moreover he was particularly irritating in that, if he went that far, he would get through the situation nonchalantly without letting the other person know precisely whether he was being a nuisance without actually being aware that he was or whether he knew perfectly well that he was and was annoying him on purpose.

Tsuda gave a yawn. This act, utterly out of keeping with his feelings at the time, showed his ambivalence. For while with one part of himself he was nervous, the special characteristic of his mood which had been interrupted when he had had to talk to Kobayashi persisted despite the changed situation. Even so Kobayashi appeared unconcerned. Tsuda took up the watch at his pillow, and as he placed it down he was forced to ask him :

'Do you have some special business you want to talk to me about?'

'Well, it's not that I don't, but at any rate I don't have to talk about it now.'

Tsuda understood more or less what he meant. But Tsuda was not yet in the mood to surrender to him. Nevertheless he was even more lacking in the courage to send him away immediately. He could do nothing but remain silent. Then Kobayashi began again with :

'I wonder whether I should stay and meet Mrs Yoshikawa myself.'

Tsuda thought to himself that Kobayashi's statement was no joking matter.

'Do you have some business with her?'

'You're forever talking about business, Tsuda, but you don't necessarily have to have any business to meet someone, you know.'

'But you don't even know her, do you?'

'No, I don't, but that's exactly why I'd like to meet her now. I'd like to see what she looks like. I'm the sort who's never even been inside rich people's homes and I've never even had anything to do with such people, so I'd just like to meet her, even for a few minutes, at a time like this.'

'She's not on exhibition, you know.'

'I know that, but it's just simple curiosity on my part. Besides, I don't have anything else to do.'

Tsuda was thoroughly disgusted with him. It would be most distasteful to him to let Mrs Yoshikawa know that he had among his friends such a miserable wretch as Kobayashi. He even feared that if he should ever be looked down upon for associating with such a man his own future might be adversely affected.

'You're certainly carefree, aren't you? You know very well why Mrs Yoshikawa is coming here today, don't you?'

'Yes I do. Do you mean I might be in the way?'

There was nothing left for Tsuda to do but to give him the *coup de grâce*.

'You certainly will be! So please leave right away before she gets here.'

Kobayashi did not become particularly angry at this remark.

'I see. Well, I don't mind going. I don't mind going, but before I do I think I'll tell you what's on my mind. After all, I took the trouble of coming here, you know.'

Tsuda was annoyed, and finally mentioned himself what he thought Kobayashi's business with him was.

'It's about money, isn't it? If you really need some, I'll see what I can do about it. But I don't have a penny here. And I certainly don't want you to go and get it at my home in my absence the way you did the overcoat.'

Kobayashi grinned and by his expression asked the question: 'Well then, what *do* you want me to do?' Since Tsuda still wanted to ask Kobayashi about something, it was to Tsuda's advantage to see him again before his departure. But to do so at the hospital would be inconvenient since he was worried that Kobayashi and O-Nobu might accidentally meet there. After fixing the date, time of day, and place where he and Kobayashi were to meet, under the pretext of a farewell party, Tsuda finally succeeded in getting rid of the nuisance.

122

Tsuda immediately turned to the second preventive measure. No sooner did he remove the small dressing-case placed over his bed and take out from the bottom of it the usual lavender letter paper and envelopes of the same colour than he began to write rapidly with his fountain pen. It took him hardly a minute to dash off a simple note to O-Nobu to ask that she put off coming to visit him since he had some slight matter to attend to that day. He was in such a hurry he did not even bother to read the note over. He quickly sealed it, not paying the slightest attention to the kind of doubts it might raise in O-Nobu's mind by having been so hastily and imperfectly phrased. The circumstance which had robbed him of his usual caution not only made him careless but also made him act with only one thing in mind. Still holding the letter, he swiftly went downstairs and called the nurse.

'It's a matter of some urgency so please give this to the rickshaw-man right away and have him take it to my home.'

The nurse gave a slight exclamation of surprise as she took the note, and with an expression indicating that she wondered how this sudden urgency had arisen, she looked at the address. Tsuda inwardly even calculated the time it would take for the rickshaw-man to go there and back.

'Please ask him to go by streetcar.'

He was afraid the rickshaw-man and O-Nobu might cross each other on the way. If O-Nobu came to the hospital before receiving the note all his efforts would be in vain.

Even after he had gone back upstairs this was the only thing that worried him. As he thought about it he even had the feeling that O-Nobu had in fact already left the house, was on the streetcar, and moving in his direction. And naturally Kobayashi was entangled in this concern. Tsuda thought that if, before his objective were attained, O-Nobu were suddenly to make her appearance at the head of the stairs it would undoubtedly be entirely Kobayashi's fault. When Tsuda, having been forced to spend his precious time in vain, had asked Kobayashi to leave and had watched his retreating figure, he had been on the very point, even so, of using Kobayashi to transact his urgent business. 'It may be a bother but would you stop for a moment at my home on your way back and tell O-Nobu she mustn't come today?' He was surprised that these words had been on the very tip of his tongue, and he had quickly withdrawn them. He actually even thought how convenient it would have been for him on that occasion if it had not been Kobayashi.

Tsuda's nerves were sharp, and as they were controlled by the subtle anticipation that she was coming shortly, he awaited Mrs Yoshikawa from one moment to the next. Meanwhile the note to O-Nobu he had given to the nurse had had a destiny he had in no way anticipated.

The note had been handed over to the rickshaw-man without delay, as he had ordered. The rickshaw-man then, following the nurse's instructions, had immediately boarded a streetcar holding the note in his hand. Then he had alighted at the proper streetcar stop, as he had been instructed to do. After he had gone on beyond the streetcar stop a short distance and had turned off the broad street at the usual narrow road, he had found without any difficulty the surname on the gate name-plate of the attractive two-storey dwelling. He had gone to the main entrance, and there he had handed over to O-Toki, who had come out to meet him, the note he had carried.

Up to that point everything went as Tsuda had thought it would. But thereafter new factors emerged which he had in no way foreseen when he was writing the note, for it did not fall into O-Nobu's hands immediately.

And yet the reason O-Nobu was not at home, as Tsuda feared she might not be, was not, as he also feared, that she had set out for the hospital. She had a completely different destination. Moreover this change was a result of her showing in full measure her dexterity by exploiting brilliantly a rather risky situation.

Since that morning O-Nobu had been her usual self. She arose as usual and performed her tasks in the usual manner. But even though she did everything precisely as when Tsuda was there, she spent a leisurely morning, with more than enough time to spare, as the inevitable result of his absence. After eating lunch she went to the public bath. She thought she wanted to freshen up a bit before appearing at the hospital. After deliberately spending a considerable amount of time there, she returned home feeling pleasantly refreshed and with her skin glowing. It was then that she heard from O-Toki something which she could hardly believe.

'Mrs Hori called while you were out, ma'am.'

O-Nobu was so amazed she simply could not believe what O-Toki said. That the very day following yesterday's dreadful scene O-Hide should purposely come and visit her! It was most unlikely that there could ever be such a strange visit. She asked O-Toki two or three times to make absolutely certain. She was most dissatisfied that O-Toki had not asked O-Hide her reason for coming. And why in the world had she not made her wait for her? But O-Toki knew nothing at all about the entire situation. O-Nobu learned that O-Hide had told O-Toki only that she had merely stopped in for a moment because she was passing the Tsuda home on her way back from the Fujiis'.

In an instant O-Nobu changed her plans. She decided she would have to give up going to the hospital and go instead to O-Hide's house. This decision was simply the fulfilment of the promise she had made to Tsuda, and she also felt that then was the moment to carry out the promise without her action seeming in any way unnatural. Thus she left her home to pursue O-Hide.

123

Since the Hori home was in approximately the same direction as the hospital, she got off the streetcar at just two stops before the hospital, and by turning to the right immediately at the point where she got off and by walking about four or five blocks, she came out directly in front of the gate.

Unlike either the Fujii or Okamoto home, the Hori residence was far from the suburbs and had hardly anything that could be called a garden. Of course it did not have either a rickshaw- or carriage-drive. There was only an area of less than six yards between the gate and the two-storey dwelling so that one could say it was practically built on the street. And since that area was entirely paved with stones, the colour of the earth was nowhere to be seen.

Since as a result of city planning the street had been broadened quite some time before, it was of a width which one could hardly find else-where. Even so there was hardly a shop engaged in trade in the entire block. There was only a line of lawyers' and doctors' offices, and expensive inns, so that the area was always as quiet as it was prosperous-looking.

In addition, on either side of the street a line of willow trees had been planted at regular intervals. Consequently, at the proper season even the city wind, which could hardly be termed poetic, evoked a kind of elegant mood as it blew under the green arch swaying on both sides. Since the largest willow among them extended its long branches from precisely the edge of the Hori wall diagonally over the gate, it was so impressive as to seem to the casual observer to have been purposely moved there to harmonize with the house.

Among the other distinguishing characteristics of the home was a large iron rain tub in front of the entrance. This rather useless object, which made one think of some sort of downtown pawn-shop, also blended quite well with the construction of the entrance-way, imme-diately to one side of it. The relatively large entrance-way was closed off only by a narrow lattice-work with neither the decoration of a frame door nor the usual type of sliding-door.

Even though, if, by looking only at its external appearance, one were to characterize the house in a phrase as that of a wealthy retired mer-chant of elegant tastes, one would thereby have immediately guessed correctly the nature of the occupation of its owners, or at least of its past owners, its present owner did not quite conform to such a charac-terization. Actually he had never yet given a thought to the kind of house in which he was living. Since he was a man who never worried in the least about such things, he was absolutely indifferent to what others might say was his occupation. He was a pleasure-seeker, but unlike wholly uneducated men who have become rich, he was so extremely unconcerned about appearances that for him to be living in such a splendid mansion, of the type an actor might like to own, was perhaps rather inappropriate. To look on the bad side of it, he was a man wholly lacking in any sense of individuality. Since he got by in everything by following the habits of the world he was so carefree as not even to attempt to change the special habits of his own home. In this way he was content to live in this massive, godown-style house, which, according to his parents, had been built by his ancestors and had about it something of the flavour of a public entertainer's dwelling. If one were to consider that his good points were revealed in his unconcern, then one could only praise his attitude of purposely not being proud of his house. And yet it seemed to him that there was no reason for him to be proud of it, for his home appeared to him much too commonplace to inspire such an emotion.

Every time O-Nobu saw the Hori home she felt the lack of harmony that existed between it and herself. Even after entering it she often recalled this sense of alienation from it. As far as she was concerned, the only person who was really suited to the house was Hori's mother. But his mother was the woman O-Nobu disliked most in the entire family. Or, more precisely, O-Nobu found her to be the woman with whom it was most difficult to deal. They were of different generations, or, to speak more cruelly, O-Nobu felt Hori's mother belonged to another age; if this phrase did not apply, there was any number of others to describe her feeling, such as that their dispositions clashed, or that their backgrounds differed, but they all amounted to the same thing.

Next, Hori himself was a problem. As O-Nobu viewed the owner of the house, he seemed both to blend and not to blend with it. Since, if she went a step further, this was tantamount to saying that no matter what sort of house he lived in he was of a kind who would seem both to blend and not to blend with it, there was not much difference from saying that she never really took him seriously from the beginning. This ambiguous aspect expressed precisely O-Nobu's sentiments towards him. For actually she seemed both to like him and dislike him.

When she finally came to O-Hide, she could express in just one phrase the essence of her feeling. As O-Nobu saw her, O-Hide had been reared so as to be the most unsuited for the house. If O-Nobu added a bit more substance to this assertion and translated it into psychological terms, it was that O-Hide could never merge with the mood of that home. Whenever O-Nobu tried to think of O-Hide and O-Hide's mother-in-law together, she could not but feel a kind of contradiction. Yet she could not easily determine whether the result of such a contradiction was a tragedy or a comedy.

As O-Nobu matched in this way the house and its occupants, only one thing struck her as strange.

'While Hori's mother, who blends best with the house, is the one who puts me at my wit's end, O-Hide, who's constituted in the exact opposite way, in a different sense, is the one who's most likely to cause me pain.'

As she opened the lattice door, the loud ringing of the bell caused this sort of idea, which she always had at the back of her mind, to come suddenly alive again.

124

O-Nobu, upon being shown into the living-room, was surprised to learn that Hori's mother, who the previous day had taken her grandchildren and had gone to see relatives in Yokohama, had not yet returned. While this fact, which, depending on the point of view, could be either convenient or awkward, had removed an old woman with whom O-Nobu found it difficult to talk, it also created the disadvantage of her having to confront her adversary O-Hide with no one else present.

This situation, which O-Nobu could not have foreseen, upset her composure from the very beginning of the visit. At the point where, on all other occasions, Hori's mother, with her hair done up in a small chignon, would have left whatever she was doing and would have been the very first to come out to fuss over her in a dutiful manner, only O-Hide appeared, and there was not the slightest sign of the old lady for whom O-Nobu was prepared. O-Nobu therefore had the natural reaction of one whose normal expectations have been betrayed at the outset. In her first glance at O-Hide O-Nobu showed her confusion. But this confusion was in no way intended as a sign of her repentance nor of her regret for what had happened the previous day. It was merely a kind of awkwardness arising from her pride in having won the previous day's battle, it was the faint fear of not knowing what sort of revenge O-Hide might have in store for her, and it was also the mental confusion of worrying how she could best get through the situation.

At the moment O-Nobu gave O-Hide this one glance she sensed that O-Hide already understood her present mood. But this was after the single glance had suddenly flashed from the deep spring of her artifice, which she could in no way control. Since she did not have the power to check this small act, which by chance had sprung from some unfathomable area of her being, she could do nothing but tamely await its effect.

It did indeed have an effect on O-Hide. But her reaction was most unexpected. If any observer had linked O-Hide's normal behaviour with the fact that on the previous day her usual composure had been destroyed and that Tsuda and O-Nobu had joined forces to destroy it, he would certainly not have thought that she would calm down easily. Even O-Nobu, with all her confidence in her own prowess, could not believe that she could settle things without causing a subsequent disturbance, whether great or small.

That was why she was surprised. When O-Hide sat down and greeted her, contrary to O-Nobu's expectations, even more warmly than usual, she was so astonished she almost doubted where she was. And when she saw O-Hide continuing to treat her kindly without any let-up so as to remove completely any doubts O-Nobu might have had about her sincerity, O-Nobu felt rather that the situation was uncanny. But after her amazement at such a transformation, distrust as to what it all meant welled up within her.

And yet O-Hide never tried to explain the motives for this warm reception, which O-Nobu wanted so much to learn. Nor did O-Hide show the slightest sign of mentioning a word about the unfortunate disagreement they had had at the hospital on the previous day.

Since O-Hide seemed to avoid the touchy subject on purpose, it was awkward for O-Nobu to broach it. First of all, there was no need whatever for her to touch on the painful area deliberately. And yet if at some point they did not put an end to their shilly-shallying and become frank with each other, there would be no sense in her having taken the trouble to go there that day. But since they were already enjoying the fruits of a reconciliation without having actually passed through the form of one, it was after all also foolish of her to bring up the unpleasant subject.

The clever O-Nobu was perplexed. The more the conversation proceeded smoothly the more frustrated she became. Finally she decided she would try to break through O-Hide's barriers at some point and peer inside. Even though, when she came to this decision, she showed considerable courage, this did not mean that she did not realize the danger that might arise under these circumstances if she happened to fail in her attempt. But again this realization was tempered by the fact that she also was quite confident of her own social adroitness.

In addition O-Nobu hoped, if the occasion allowed, to sound O-Hide out on a certain important point. To listen carefully to what would emerge naturally once she touched that sensitive area in O-Hide was certainly not the main purpose of her visit, as O-Nobu had planned it with Tsuda, but for O-Nobu herself it was infinitely more important than achieving a reconciliation.

This matter which she had to conceal from Tsuda was very similar to the episode which Tsuda had to keep secret from her. And just as Tsuda was concerned about what Kobayashi had told her during his absence, so too did she want very much to find out what O-Hide had told Tsuda during her absence.

After thinking about where it would be best to begin, she finally decided she would have to refer again to O-Hide's visit to her house on her way back from the Fujiis'. But since she had already, upon sitting down, made the comment, 'I understand you called on me earlier, but unfortunately I'd just gone out to the public bath,' to open the conversation, she then tried to resurrect the topic by asking, 'Did you have something you wanted to talk to me about?' When she did so, however, O-Hide merely answered with a curt 'No,' and neatly rebuffed her.

125

O-Nobu next tried to develop the conversation by talking about Fujii. O-Hide's admission that she had that morning called at her uncle's place provided O-Nobu with a convenient means of guiding the conversation in that direction. But the gate to O-Hide's mind was, as before, tightly shut on that side as well. Only when the necessity arose did she purposely go outside that gate to meet O-Nobu affably. O-Nobu knew very well that O-Hide was deeply indebted to her uncle Fujii for many things. She knew too that O-Hide had been greatly influenced by him in developing her views on life. Therefore O-Nobu felt she had to speak glibly, in a way that would please O-Hide, about her uncle's character and way of life. Since O-Hide, however, considered that O-Nobu's every word was filled with exaggeration and had a false ring, not only did O-Hide not find any point where she could take O-Nobu up seriously on the subject, but she also, as O-Nobu continued on the same topic for quite a while, could not help showing by her expression how naturally displeased she was. As soon as the quick-witted O-Nobu realized she had underestimated O-Hide's perceptiveness in seeing through her flattery, she closed the subject and concluded her comments. Then it was O-Hide's turn to begin to make conversation about Okamoto. Although this uncle, who stood in precisely the same relationship to O-Nobu as Fujii did to O-Hide, was for O-Nobu a most important individual, for O-Hide he was a complete stranger for whom she could not feel the slightest affection. Consequently O-Hide's words had merely a sleek and glossy surface and no real substance whatsoever. Nevertheless, O-Nobu was forced to swallow this return-flattery which O-Hide had devised, as if it gave her considerable pleasure.

But when her turn came around again, O-Nobu was hardly so foolish as to try to outdo O-Hide and force even greater flattery on her in a second round. Instead she looked for an opportunity to end that subject skilfully and then to liven the conversation by talking about Mrs

Yoshikawa. But she feared that if she used the same method as before and merely chanted Mrs Yoshikawa's praises she might meet with the same failure. Therefore she purposely did not make any value judgments, but simply tried to mention Mrs Yoshikawa's name. And she decided to take her next step after seeing what effect that name had.

O-Nobu knew only that while she had been out at the public bath O-Hide had stopped at her house on her way back from the Fujiis'. But she in no way suspected that O-Hide had already called on Mrs Yoshikawa before going to the Fujiis'. Moreover she never dreamed that as a result of the clash at the hospital on the previous day O-Hide would ever actually take the trouble of visiting her. Since on this one point she was as naïve as Tsuda, she could not but be as astonished by O-Hide as Tsuda had been by Kobayashi on the same subject. And yet the ways in which they were astonished were utterly different. Kobayashi had simply made an announcement of the plain fact. But O-Hide's method of astonishing O-Nobu consisted of a meaningful silence and a flush on her face simultaneously.

When O-Nobu first mentioned Mrs Yoshikawa's name she felt that drops of some miraculous balm had fallen from heaven on them. For she saw before her its immediate effect. But unfortunately the effect did her no good whatsoever. At least she did not know how to exploit it. Its unexpectedness merely stunned her. No sooner had she mentioned the name than she even thought she might have to apologize on the spot for her slip of the tongue.

But then another unexpected thing happened. When she saw that O-Hide turned her face away for a moment O-Nobu knew she had to correct her first impression. She now realized that O-Hide's change of colour was certainly not on account of anger. The flush on O-Hide's face, which O-Nobu had always considered so commonplace she had wearied of seeing it and which she had been forced to interpret as simple ill-temper, could not but surprise O-Nobu again. She clearly recognized this different meaning behind O-Hide's blushing. But she could hardly be expected to ascertain how this new meaning had emerged, without waiting for O-Hide's explanation.

While O-Nobu was perplexed as to how to proceed, O-Hide in a very unnatural way suddenly changed the topic. The new topic, having absolutely no relationship with anything up until then, was so strange as to astonish O-Nobu for the third time. But O-Nobu still retained her self-confidence, and immediately proceeded to take O-Hide up on it.

126

In the strange phrase that slipped out from O-Hide, the very first thing that struck O-Nobu's ear was the word 'love'. Undoubtedly the main reason this one trite, over-used word appeared before O-Nobu with the suddenness of troops in ambush was that it stood alone, without any context, but another reason was that such a word had never yet been a topic of conversation between them.

Compared to O-Nobu, O-Hide was quite addicted to argument. But to arrive at such a conclusion on the relative arguing skills of the two women one would have had to provide a great deal of explanation. For O-Nobu was a woman who carried her own theories into the realm of action. Therefore the reason she usually did not engage in arguments was not that she could not but rather that she had no need to do so. But when it came to the kind of knowledge one acquires from reading, she had no very great amount stored up. Lately she rarely took up even the magazines she had been accustomed to reading during her school-days. Nevertheless she had never yet felt any particular weakness in intellectual matters. The reason that, despite her great vanity, her desire in these areas had not been especially stimulated was not that she did not have enough leisure, nor was it that she did not have anyone to talk with and vie with in these matters, but quite simply that she did not see any great lack in herself.

But O-Hide, in the matter of education, was entirely different. Reading was almost the only thing that made her a distinctive person. At least she had been made to think so. Her having been educated largely by her uncle Fujii, who was himself a great reader, had produced a rather strange effect on her, in both the good and the bad sense. For she had come to attach greater importance to books than to herself. And yet no matter how much weight she attached to books, she still had to live and work in her own way, independent of them. Thus, of necessity she and the books she valued only grew farther and farther apart. Or more significantly, she fell into the bad habit of often getting into arguments beyond her depth. Yet her reflective powers were such that she was still a long way from realizing how sterile it was to argue for the sake of arguing. In the matter of will, she had too strong an ego. In plainer terms, one could also say that while her ego constituted her own basic essence, she would purposely drag out from the books she admired a reasoning that did not accord with that essence, and with the force of the words written there she would try to defend herself.

At times a humorous situation would arise as she would employ a large cannon instead of the dagger that was required.

The problem between O-Nobu and O-Hide arose in fact from O-Hide's reference to a certain magazine. The question asked by O-Hide, who had read the views on love of several writers published in that monthly magazine, did not really interest O-Nobu very much. But when she confessed that she had not yet looked at the article her curiosity was suddenly piqued. She was determined to make this abstract problem somehow come alive in her own way.

At first she accepted rather easily the weak points in O-Hide's argument, which had the tendency to become merely empty theory. If O-Nobu intended to jump from this to sensitive practical problems this was not such a disadvantageous position for her to take. But if she was only going to argue for the sake of argument, then it would have been much better for her not to have agreed from the beginning. Thus she felt she absolutely had to bring her opponent down to the level of practical problems and vanquish her there. But unfortunately O-Hide on that occasion never touched ground from the beginning. The love O-Hide spoke of was neither Tsuda's love, nor Hori's love, nor even O-Nobu's nor her own love. It was nothing at all. It was a love which merely floated at random in the atmosphere. Consequently O-Nobu's efforts had first to be directed towards pulling down O-Hide's balloon-like theories.

When O-Nobu discovered that, although O-Hide already had two children and was in everything far more domesticated than she, O-Hide was, on this point of preferring abstractions, far less practical than she, she became inwardly irritated even though outwardly she kept agreeing with everything O-Hide said. She wanted very much to say, 'Stop all this meaningless talk, and come to the point. Then I'll take you on in real terms,' and she tried to find a way to make her argumentative sister-in-law actually come to the point.

O-Nobu shortly came to a decision. It was quite simply that to make the problem meaningful she would have to sacrifice either O-Hide or herself, for if she did neither, the discussion would never amount to anything. It would not be difficult to sacrifice her opponent. If she only broke through somewhere at one of O-Hide's weak points, that would suffice. Whether that weak point was actual or hypothetical was not then O-Nobu's concern. By comparison with the effect she was attempting to obtain merely from O-Hide's natural reaction, the investigation of the truth or falsehood of O-Hide's weakness was an unnecessary consideration. But she still sensed a certain danger in her action. O-Hide would undoubtedly become angry. And to make her angry both was and was not O-Nobu's objective. Therefore O-Nobu was necessarily perplexed as to how to move.

Finally she roused herself to seize a certain opportunity. And as she did so she had already decided on sacrificing herself.

127

'If you speak that way, a person like me doesn't really know what to say. You see, I'm dreadfully concerned about whether Yoshio loves me or not. On that point, Hideko, you're most fortunate, aren't you? From the very beginning you've had every assurance of your husband's love.'

Even before her marriage to Tsuda O-Nobu had known that O-Hide had been married for her beauty. For most women, and particularly for one such as O-Nobu, this was doubtless something for which to envy O-Hide. When O-Nobu had first heard about it from Tsuda, she had felt slightly jealous of O-Hide even without having met her. But when she later learned that the fact that O-Hide had been married for her beauty had precious little real meaning, she had even had the pleasant sensation of revenge, while she had given a faintly sarcastic smile. Thereafter O-Nobu's attitude towards O-Hide, on the issue of love, had always been one of disdain. Thus, while she openly treated the fact as though it were a happy one, and feigned that it was mutually enjoyable, of course her statement was pure flattery. More crudely, it was a kind of ridicule.

Happily, O-Hide did not notice this. And there was a good reason. It was simply that no matter how expert she was verbally, when it came actually to the experience of love, she could not be compared to O-Nobu. Since she could not remember ever having loved passionately or having been loved purely and wholly, she did not yet know how strong and how great this force, at its maximum, could be. Nevertheless, as a wife she was satisfied with her husband. The proverb 'Ignorance is bliss' indeed described O-Hide in this case very well. Since, at the time of her marriage, she intended to retain forever, as the usual guarantee of their link, and as an omen for her future, the promise of love that Hori had made, she was so innocent as to accept O-Nobu's words seriously and earnestly.

O-Hide, as a woman who had never truly understood the actual state of love, not only was seen through by the sharp-witted O-Nobu as she casually used the ambiguous word 'love', but she also was naïve in judging the relationship between Tsuda and O-Nobu on the basis of her own relationship with her husband. That was evident even from O-Hide's expression of genuine surprise upon hearing O-Nobu's words. Her expression in effect asked why at that point O-Nobu should be so concerned whether Tsuda loved her or not. Also, what could it mean to hear such a thing from Tsuda's wife herself? And even more amazing than that, what in the world was the point of O-Nobu's having said that to her husband's sister? Such was the force of O-Hide's expression.

Actually O-Nobu, as viewed by O-Hide, was either a very demanding woman who did not know how to be satisfied with Tsuda's present love or, if not that, simply a false woman, who, while having her husband neatly wrapped around her little finger, purposely pretended not to notice that fact. O-Hide prefaced her comment with an exclamation of surprise.

'My, do you mean you want Yoshio to love you even more than he does already?'

This comment was precisely the one O-Nobu would normally have wanted to hear. But at that time it could hardly give her any satisfaction. She was forced to say something to make her intention clear. Were she to express it clearly she would only make the blunt statement: 'If I feel he still loves someone else, I certainly can't be satisfied with things the way they are, can I?' Since she realized that, if she did come right out and say that, it would be tantamount to destroying her own plan herself, she merely began with the meaningless interjection. 'But really. . . .' and hesitated, unable to proceed, at that point.

'Do you feel something's still lacking?'

As she said this, O-Hide cast the full force of her gaze on O-Nobu's hand. The ring shone there impudently. And yet O-Hide's sharp glance could not affect O-Nobu in any way. With regard to the ring, O-Nobu's naïveté had not changed in the slightest from what it had been the day before. O-Hide became slightly irritated.

'But aren't you happy, Nobuko? You can have Yoshio buy you anything you want, you can have him take you anywhere you want to go. . . .'

'Yes, on those points I *am* happy.'

Since O-Nobu had come to think that if she did not emphasize to others her happiness and contentment it would be embarrassing because it would seem to expose her weakness, she finally used on this occasion as well the usual comment she always had at her disposal. But then she found she had come to an impasse. After she had repeated the very same words she had used when, on the day after she had gone to the theatre, she had spoken to Tsugiko at her uncle's house, she realized that it was O-Hide to whom she was speaking. And O-Hide had an expression tantamount to saying: 'If you're happy on those points, isn't that quite enough?'

O-Nobu did not want to give O-Hide any indication that she doubted Tsuda even for a moment. And yet she disliked even more to pretend that she did not know anything and helplessly to be made a fool of by O-Hide. Thus she had to find just the right way of responding to her. She had to exert a great deal of effort to attain her objective. But she did not realize that she would have to exert such effort without the slightest success. Again she changed her attitude suddenly.

128

She boldly jumped ahead. She decided to break through all the round-about talk entwined with personal considerations and to meet O-Hide directly. Nevertheless her words had to be abstract. Even so, stimulated by the discussion, she thought it was better to ascertain what the real facts were.

'Do you think a man can really love more than one woman at a time?'

When O-Nobu advanced on her with this question as the starting-point, O-Hide did not have a single answer ready. Her knowledge, gained from books and magazines, concerned merely love in general and was of no use whatever in this particular situation. Although she had nothing at all stored up in her mind she made a pretence of thinking. Then she answered honestly :

'I'm afraid I don't know about that.'

O-Nobu actually felt sorry for her. 'Doesn't she already have her husband as a living example on this one point? Doesn't she see his attitude towards women by being with him from morning to night?' As O-Nobu was thinking in this way, O-Hide again spoke :

'You wouldn't expect me to know, would you? After all, I'm a woman.'

O-Nobu thought that that too was a foolish answer. If it represented O-Hide's true mental state, O-Nobu could easily imagine how sluggishly her mind operated. And yet O-Nobu immediately began to liven up this foolish answer of O-Hide's.

'All right then, let's look at it from a woman's point of view. Can a woman imagine her own husband in love with another woman?'

When O-Hide answered, 'Do you mean to say you can't, Nobuko?' O-Nobu was quite taken aback.

'I suppose I'm now in the position where I'm forced to, am I not?'

O-Hide quickly reassured her with : 'You don't have to worry.' O-Nobu instantly echoed her words.

'I don't have to worry?!'

The meaning of this expression, half an exclamation and half an interrogation, was not clear even to O-Nobu herself.

'No, you don't have to worry.'

O-Hide also repeated her comment. At that moment O-Nobu could make out the faint trace of a sneer around O-Hide's lips. But she quickly dispelled it with :

'Of course that's easy enough for you to say, Hideko. Since you know perfectly well why your husband married you.'

'And what about you, Nobuko? Wasn't Yoshio completely infatuated with you when he married you?'

'That's not true. Complete infatuation better describes your husband's attitude towards you, and you know it.'

O-Hide did not respond immediately. O-Nobu too avoided continuing on the same subject which had netted her nothing.

'I wonder what sort of ideas Yoshio has about women?'

'I should think a wife would know more about that than a sister.'

Having been rebuffed in this way, O-Nobu realized that she too, like O-Hide, had asked a foolish question.

'But I think you know more about Yoshio's general attitudes since you see him as a brother.'

'Well, maybe I do, but no matter how much I know I'm sure it won't do you any good, Nobuko.'

'Why of course it would. But actually I've known about that myself for quite some time.'

O-Nobu's trick had touched a sensitive point. O-Hide finally took her up on it.

'But you don't have to worry, I tell you. In your case, Nobuko, you really don't.'

'I don't have to worry, but still it's cause for concern. I'd like very much to hear all about it from you, Hideko.'

'Oh my, I don't know anything, I tell you.'

As O-Hide said this she suddenly blushed. No matter how strained O-Nobu's nerves were she still could not guess what shame had given rise to this. But she had not yet forgotten how the very same thing had happened at the beginning of her visit. O-Nobu could not determine what kind of relationship there was between the blush she had observed when she had mentioned the name of Mrs Yoshikawa, and the blush that was then being shown to her, no matter how skilful she was in detecting subtle shades of feeling. In this case she wanted very much to force a link between the two. But however much she looked for one, she could not for the life of her find any. The most unfortunate thing was that she felt certain some connection existed between these two things which it was beyond her power to discover at that time. And she had a kind of presentiment that such a connection undoubtedly had great significance for her then. Naturally she could do nothing but try to press further on that point.

129

On a sudden impulse, O-Nobu could not refrain from telling a lie.

'I heard something from Mrs Yoshikawa.'

Only after she had said this, did O-Nobu realize her own boldness. She was forced to stop at that point and view the result of her daring. O-Hide then asked her a question in return, her expression having changed completely from the previous blush.

'My, what was it?'

'About that.'

'About what? What sort of thing do you mean?'

O-Nobu could say nothing further. O-Hide went on :

'You're joking of course, aren't you?'

'No I'm not, I tell you. It's about Yoshio.'

Suddenly O-Hide ceased to reply to O-Nobu. Instead she purposely showed the outlines of a sneer at the corners of her well-shaped mouth. As this sneer appeared much more prominently than it had a moment earlier, O-Nobu felt she had lost her footing and plunged into the mire. If her special kind of obstinacy had not been operating strongly within her, she might very well have bowed her head before O-Hide and have asked her for help. O-Hide, however, finally spoke :

'That's strange, isn't it? There's no reason for Mrs Yoshikawa to speak to you about Yoshio. But what actually happened?'

'It's true, I tell you, Hideko.'

O-Hide for the first time laughed out loud.

'I'm sure it *is* true. No one's saying it isn't. But what in the world is it all about?'

'It's about Yoshio.'

'All right, so it's about Yoshio. What then?'

'I can't say. Not until I hear what you have to say.'

'My, but that's an unreasonable request. You say I'm supposed to tell you something, but I haven't the slightest idea what you want me to say.'

O-Hide showed that she was completely calm and quite ready for anything O-Nobu might do. O-Nobu actually began to perspire. Suddenly she flung out the following words :

'Hideko, you're a Christian, aren't you?'

O-Hide looked very much surprised.

'No.'

'If you aren't, I don't think you'd have said what you did yesterday.'

243

Their positions were now completely reversed from what they had been on the previous day. O-Hide maintained in every respect the relaxed attitude of one who has the upper hand.

'Do you really think so? All right then, have it your way. You probably dislike Christianity, don't you, Nobuko?'

'On the contrary, I approve of it. That's why I'm asking you now. That's why I want you to have pity on me now, from that lofty and noble position you showed me yesterday. If I was wrong yesterday, I bow my head and apologize to you in complete sincerity.'

O-Nobu placed her hands with the gleaming jewelled rings on them in front of O-Hide and, just as she said, actually bowed her head.

'Hideko, please be honest with me and don't hold back anything. I beg you to tell me everything. See how *I'm* being honest with *you*. See how I've repented for what I've done.'

As O-Nobu demonstrated her characteristic habit of twitching her eyebrows, tears fell from her narrow eyes to her lap.

'Yoshio's my husband. You're his sister. In the same way he's important to you he's important to me. And it's for his sake I'm asking you. Please tell me all you know for his sake. Yoshio loves me. Just as he loves you as a sister he loves me as a wife. Since he loves me in this way, I simply have to know everything for his sake. And since he loves you too you'll tell me everything you know, won't you? That would be your kindness as a sister. Even if you don't feel any affection for me right now I certainly don't hate you for it. But I think you'll always show kindness to Yoshio because he's your brother. I can tell quite well by your expression that you still have a great deal of affection for him. You certainly aren't a cold or cruel person. You're kind, just as you said yourself yesterday.'

When O-Nobu finished and looked at O-Hide, she noted a particular change in her face. Instead of blushing, O-Hide had become slightly pale. Then, in a most vehement tone, she spoke so as to reject O-Nobu's words as soon as possible.

'I don't recall ever having done you any wrong. I've only had good-will towards both Yoshio and you. I've never had the slightest feeling of malice. Please don't misinterpret anything I've said or done.'

130

O-Hide's self-vindication was both sudden and unexpected. O-Nobu was at a complete loss to know what had prompted such a statement or know why it had been made. She was simply amazed. She wondered whether there might not be something behind this present manner of

O-Hide's which seemed to be one of complete charity. O-Nobu quickly tried to probe its depths. And her third lie slipped easily from her.

'I'm quite aware of that, Hideko. I understand perfectly well what you've done and the spirit in which you've done it. That's why I beg you not to hide anything and tell me all you know. Don't you want to?'

As she said this O-Nobu looked at O-Hide, while expressing as much charm as possible with her narrow eyes. But this act, which could be expected to be most effective when directed towards the opposite sex, missed its mark completely. O-Hide, quite startled, asked abruptly:

'Nobuko, before coming here today did you by any chance go to the hospital?'

'No.'

'Well then, did you first go somewhere else?'

'No. I came directly here from my house.'

O-Hide finally seemed to feel relieved, but she did not make any comment on O-Nobu's answer. O-Nobu clung to the same subject:

'It's all right, isn't it? Please tell me, Hideko.'

This time a cruel gleam flashed in O-Hide's cool eyes.

'You're extremely wilful, aren't you, Nobuko? It seems you won't be satisfied unless you alone are loved utterly and passionately.'

'Of course I won't. Do you mean to say it doesn't matter to you if you're not?'

'Take a look at my husband, and you'll see.'

O-Hide responded swiftly, thrusting O-Nobu aside in this way. O-Nobu purposely removed Hori from the conversation.

'Your husband doesn't enter into it. Let's talk honestly and leave him out of it. Anyway there's no reason why you should like a man who's capricious and runs from one woman to another, is there?'

'But isn't it most unlikely that such a docile man exists who'd act as if there weren't any other women in the world than oneself?'

O-Hide, who looked for her source of knowledge only to magazines and books, suddenly appeared before O-Nobu at that moment as the familiar type of practical woman. But O-Nobu did not even have the time to notice this contradiction.

'But there *is* such a man, I tell you. There has to be, doesn't there? If we're going to call him a husband at all.'

'Do you really think so? Where in the world are you going to find such a paragon?'

O-Hide once again turned her derisive eyes on O-Nobu. O-Nobu definitely did not have the courage to shout out Tsuda's name. She was forced to answer rather perfunctorily.

'At any rate that's my ideal. And I can't be satisfied until Yoshio conforms to it.'

While O-Hide had become practical O-Nobu had suddenly become an idealist. The positions of the two of them until then were now reversed. And without either of them in any way noticing this, they were carried forward wherever their emotions led them. The remaining conversation became a contest to the finish, definable neither as one of theory nor as one of practice.

'No matter how much of an ideal it may be for you, it simply won't do. Because when that ideal's realized all other women than the man's wife have to lose their qualification as women completely.'

'But I think a couple can only experience perfect love at that point. If they don't go as far as that they won't be able to feel true love their entire lives, will they?'

'I don't know anything about that, but if you don't consider other women to be women and you think you're the only woman in the entire world, that can hardly be said to be reasonable, can it?'

O-Hide finally flared up and showed her anger in her specific and direct attack on O-Nobu. But O-Nobu paid no attention at all.

'I don't know what's reasonable or not, but if my husband thinks of me as the only woman in the world then that's all right with me.'

'You say you want him to think only of you as a woman, do you. That much I can understand. But when it comes to saying he shouldn't think of other women as women then that's the same as suicide. If there should be a husband who can somehow live without thinking of other women as women he'll certainly come to think of you too as not a woman either, won't he? It's the same thing as saying only the flowers blooming in your own garden are real and all the others are only dead weeds.'

'As far as I'm concerned it doesn't matter if they *are* just dead weeds.'

'That may be so for *you*. But for a man they aren't so there's nothing you can do about it. Why can't you be satisfied instead that it's you he loves most among the many women in the world he's fond of? That's what it means to be really loved.'

'I want to try in every way possible to be loved absolutely. I've never liked comparisons.'

O-Hide showed her disdain by her expression. Deep within it, could clearly be perceived her assessment of O-Nobu as a woman sadly lacking in understanding. O-Nobu, on her part, spoke with passion :

'Anyway, since I'm a fool, I don't understand such a thing as logic !'

'You have only to show me a concrete example of your "ideal" husband ! That will do very nicely, thank you !'

O-Hide coldly cut off the conversation at that point. O-Nobu was vexed and mortified to the depth of her being. All her efforts had netted her nothing more than this. She left the Hori residence without know-

ing that a note had come from Tsuda during her absence and was
waiting for her at her home.

131

While O-Nobu and O-Hide were in direct confrontation, at the hospital
another encounter, prepared for by Tsuda, was progressing in its own
way.

Mrs Yoshikawa, for whom Tsuda had been waiting, made her
appearance there before the rickshaw-man, who had been asked to
deliver the note Tsuda had written to O-Nobu, had yet returned, and,
in actual time, just about ten minutes after Kobayashi had left.

When Tsuda heard Mrs Yoshikawa's name from the nurse, he first
of all was deeply thankful for the good fortune whereby Mrs Yoshikawa
and Kobayashi, who were almost of different races, had not come face
to face with each other in that narrow room. At that moment he hardly
had the leisure to reflect on the material sacrifice he had been forced to
make to bring about this good fortune.

As soon as he saw the figure of Mrs Yoshikawa he tried to raise
himself from the bed. But, still standing, she stopped him. Then she
turned round for a moment to look at the potted dwarf-tree which she
had asked the nurse, who had shown her to the room, to hold, and
asked, as if consulting her : 'Where do you think we should put it?'
Tsuda thought the red leaves looked beautiful against the nurse's
white uniform. Under the *bonsai*'s three narrow trunks, which had
been arranged harmoniously although they looked rather cramped in
the small pot, well-shaped and appropriate stones had also been placed.
After the *bonsai* had been put in the traditional decorative alcove, Mrs
Yoshikawa finally sat down.

'How are you feeling?'

Tsuda, who had been observing her manner since her entry, for the
first time could then be certain of her attitude towards him. It was
exactly as if half the worry he had been secretly nurturing was elimi-
nated by that one expression of hers. Mrs Yoshikawa was not as cheerful
as usual, but neither was she as flippant as usual. In effect she seemed
to have entered his room in a kind of mood he had never previously
noticed in her. For while on the one hand she was extremely calm, on
the other she still seemed to express her magnanimity to the highest
degree. He was slightly surprised by this, and even though he was surprised in the good sense he also could not help feeling a bit puzzled by
her attitude. For even if this new attitude of hers did not represent any
ill-will towards him, he did not know what there might be behind it,

and even if there were nothing fearful behind it now, he could not predict how her feelings might change as their conversation progressed. He had always been one to allow Mrs Yoshikawa, who was long accustomed to having people curry favour with her, to change her feelings arbitrarily as much as she wished, and he even thought there was nothing wrong in her doing so. In fact in a certain sense he was forced to show respect to her as a kind of female tyrant. To use the old Chinese expression, her 'every frown and every smile' became a matter of concern for him. This was particularly true on that occasion.

'Hideko called on me today, you know.'

She brought up O-Hide's visit as the first item of discussion between them. Of course he had to answer her, and he had already been thinking, before she arrived, about how he should do so. Knowing full well that O-Hide had visited her, he intended to feign ignorance. For if he were asked from whom he had heard it he certainly did not want to mention Kobayashi.

'Hm, is that so? I suppose she felt it was wrong of her to have neglected you for so long and she made just a formal courtesy call.'

'No, that's not it.'

Immediately upon hearing her remark he told his next lie.

'But she couldn't have had any real business with you, I suppose.'

'As a matter of fact she did.'

'How very strange!'

After his exclamation he waited for what would follow.

'Guess what it was she talked to me about.'

He looked blank but then pretended to think.

'Let me see, what could O-Hide have had to say? . . . hm, what could it have been?'

'Don't you know?'

'Well, I'm afraid I don't. First of all, though O-Hide and I are brother and sister, our personalities are very different, you know.'

He here purposely alluded to their rather involved brother-and-sister relationship. He did this so as to defend himself in advance before O-Hide's criticism of him was mentioned. He did it also because he wanted to learn what sort of a reaction Mrs Yoshikawa would have.

'She's a bit argumentative, isn't she?'

As soon as he heard this one adjective he readily took advantage of his opportunity.

'When it comes to that, I can assure you that even though I'm her older brother she's almost too much for me. In fact there's not a soul who's ever been able to endure listening to her quietly for any length of time. That's why, whenever I quarrel with her, I always break off the discussion as soon as possible. And when I do, she always seems pleased and goes around everywhere telling everybody things to suit her convenience as if she won the argument or something.'

Mrs Yoshikawa smiled. He could interpret her smile as meaning that she certainly had sympathy for him. But then she spoke in a way quite contrary to this interpretation.

'Oh come now, I'm sure that's not true. But anyway she certainly has a fine and well-disciplined mind, doesn't she? For my part I really like her.'

He forced a smile.

'Of course I'm sure she's not such a fool as to visit you at your home and senselessly show her true colours.'

'No, you're wrong. She was quite honest. She was much more honest than most people.'

Mrs Yoshikawa did not say precisely who O-Hide was more honest than.

132

Tsuda's curiosity was piqued. His imagination was also stimulated. But to get at the matter in a roundabout way went against his intentions. It was enough for him to probe directly and find out about this new relationship between Mrs Yoshikawa and O-Hide. Of course he was sure that Mrs Yoshikawa would talk to him in a friendly way about it as a part of her visit to his sick-bed. And yet she also had a special way of behaving in such matters. Since she had unlimited leisure, whenever she had the opportunity she delighted in meddling in other people's affairs without even being asked, and in giving advice in various ways to people beneath her socially, particularly if they were social inferiors whom she liked. At the same time she felt perfectly free to show at every turn her basic nature which made her act in such a way only for her own pleasure. At certain times she would be over-eager as she hurriedly and heedlessly tried to settle everything, while at other times she would behave in precisely the opposite manner. As she was purposely toying with someone in an idle fashion she would seem to be smugly deriving considerable enjoyment from the slow process. Her behaviour at such times was like that of a cat playing with a mouse, and yet despite what any observer might have thought of it, she herself seemed to interpret it as the necessary privilege of a superior who should be allowed to add a dash of excitement to her leisurely existence. For the person who at such times was trapped by her, endurance was all-important. The reward for such endurance was sure to come. Moreover she mollified her prey by showing him that it would indeed come, and she considered that this fact revealed her own ethical stature. By complying with this tacit agreement between them, Tsuda had until then incurred only one great loss, and on this point he was quite clever enough not to overlook how much responsibility she must secretly be feeling towards him. Although in everything he was acting with her wishes as the focal point, he was inwardly relying on this one element of strength. And yet this was merely a weapon which he kept in reserve in case of emergency. His usual posture was to content himself with being the mouse to her cat and to allow her to toy with him exactly as she wished. On this occasion as well she took an inordinately long time in coming to the main point.

'I suppose Hideko came yesterday, didn't she? Here, I mean.'

'Yes, she did.'

'And Nobuko came too, I suppose.'

'Yes.'

'And what about today?'

'She hasn't come yet.'

'But she'll come soon, I suppose.'

He did not know exactly. He could not tell Mrs Yoshikawa that he had just sent O-Nobu a note telling her not to come. He also was actually a bit worried since, contrary to his expectations, he had not yet received an answer from her.

'I don't quite know.'

'Do you mean to say you don't know whether she's coming or not?'

'Yes, I'm not quite sure. I think she probably won't come, though.'

'Isn't that being rather nonchalant about everything?'

She gave a rather derisive laugh.

'Do you mean that *I'm* being nonchalant?'

'No, both of you.'

After waiting for Tsuda to finish his forced laugh, she spoke again.

'Nobuko and Hideko met here yesterday, didn't they?'

'Yes.'

'And something happened, didn't it? Something strange, I mean.'

'Not especially. . . .'

'Don't act as if you don't know. If something *did* happen, say so openly like a man.'

Mrs Yoshikawa finally began to display her own special manner of speaking and her own particular temperament. Tsuda was perplexed as to how to answer her, but he thought it would be best for him to remain silent and see how things went for a while.

'Didn't Hideko say you treated her very badly? Both of you, that is?'

'We did nothing of the sort! It was just that she became extremely angry and finally left.'

'Yes, that's so. But you *did* fight, didn't you? When I say "fight" of course I don't mean you came to blows, but. . . .'

'Yes, but it wasn't the sort of exaggerated thing O-Hide said it was.'

'That may very well be, but even though it was a minor one, you *did* have a fight, didn't you?'

'Well, we did have a slight misunderstanding.'

'And I suppose that then you and Nobuko attacked Hideko together.'

'We didn't attack her. She just spouted a lot of that Christian nonsense.'

'But at any rate you don't deny there were two of you and only one of her.'

'Well, that may be, but. . . .'

'See, wasn't that wrong of you?'

Mrs Yoshikawa's conclusion had neither sense nor logic. Consequently he could not possibly understand where he had been wrong. But in such a situation he was already thoroughly conditioned to accepting Mrs Yoshikawa's rather eccentric behaviour as something he could not possibly contradict. He could do nothing but meekly accept her reprimand.

'We didn't actually intend to join forces against her. It was just that somehow or other I suppose it naturally turned out that way.'

'Don't say you "suppose". Say that that's the way it was. It may seem rude of me to say this, but I'm convinced the root of the whole matter is that you take too good care of Nobuko.'

Tsuda turned his head in perplexity.

133

Despite his usual discernment, Tsuda could not understand very clearly the relationship between Mrs Yoshikawa and O-Nobu. Since he had to show consideration to Mrs Yoshikawa at the same time that he had to have regard for O-Nobu's feelings, his mind, which normally would have been able to assess the attitudes of the two women towards each other directly and objectively, was thereby clouded. Although he would usually take women's comments with more than a few grains of salt, in this particular case he did not operate with such detachment. Therefore, he not only accepted as true the evaluation Mrs Yoshikawa would make to him of O-Nobu but he also did not doubt O-Nobu's evaluation of Mrs Yoshikawa, which he would hear from time to time. Moreover both of these opinions had until then been expressed in glowing terms.

Whatever the two women had really felt about each other they had until then taken great pains not to show on the outside. But now was the time that the subtle friction this stifling of emotion had caused would, by a natural force, have to be revealed to him, just as mist very gradually clears.

He spoke to Mrs Yoshikawa directly :

'Since she's not the sort of wife I have to take such very good care of, you really don't have to worry on that score.'

'But I'm afraid that's not true. The whole world thinks you do take too good care of her.'

The exaggeration of the term 'the whole world' startled him. Mrs Yoshikawa was forced to explain.

'By "the whole world" I mean of course everybody who knows you.'

He could not make out clearly even what was meant by 'everybody'. But it certainly was not difficult to guess what Mrs Yoshikawa was trying to emphasize by using such exaggerated terms. She seemed absolutely intent upon pounding her point home. He purposely gave a laugh.

'By "everybody" you mean O-Hide, I suppose.'

'Well of course Hideko's included.'

'You mean, don't you, that she's one of them and also their representative?'

'Perhaps.'

He again gave a loud laugh. But immediately thereafter he realized what he had done. It was of course already too late to retract the laughter, which had had a bad effect on her. But, realizing the convenience of admitting his guilt without grumbling, he swiftly altered his attitude.

'At any rate I'll be more careful from now on.'

Mrs Yoshikawa still was not satisfied.

'You're quite mistaken if you think Hideko's the only one. You should bear in mind the fact that your uncle and aunt think the same way.'

'Oh really?'

It was clear that she had also heard from O-Hide about the Fujiis.

Mrs Yoshikawa further added that there were still others. Tsuda merely gave another exclamation of surprise, and when he looked at her the words he anticipated immediately came forth from her.

'To tell the truth, I too have the same opinion as everybody else.'

Face to face with her, as she finally spoke in this way in an authoritative tone, he of course did not see the need for summoning up his courage to oppose her. And yet at the same time he secretly felt he had made a strange miscalculation. He pondered the problem :

'I wonder why in the world she's suddenly taken this kind of attitude. By attacking me in saying it's wrong for me to be too considerate of O-Nobu isn't she after all also attacking O-Nobu herself?'

This doubt was something completely new to him. Even to envisage the process which would enable him to arrive at Mrs Yoshikawa's real intention was so new a thing as to be difficult. Before he could confront this doubt he still had to ask her one question remaining in his mind.

'I wonder if Mr Okamoto also would make that kind of criticism.'

'Mr Okamoto's different. He doesn't have anything to do with what I'm saying.'

When Mrs Yoshikawa answered abruptly in this way, Tsuda could not help being surprised. He almost asked the next question, 'Well then, you and Mr Okamoto think differently on the subject, don't you?' as a natural consequence of her comment.

Actually he was not taking such good care of O-Nobu as 'the whole world' thought. Even though, if he tried to explain to others how and why this inaccurate idea had arisen, it would require a great deal of complex reasoning, in his own mind he had a clear picture of the situation, and he understood all the ins and outs so as to discern them distinctly.

The first person responsible was O-Nobu herself. It was doubtless she who did not hesitate to employ at every point her skill in making the world know, in a most circuitous way, just how much she was loved by him and just how free she could be with him. The second person responsible was O-Hide. An element of envy was added to her appraisal of him and O-Nobu which was already characterized by a kind of exaggeration of every detail. He did not know how such envy had arisen. He had first realized after his marriage that O-Hide was behaving like an interfering sister-in-law, but since, even though he had come to such a realization, he could not understand its cause, it had been too much for him to handle. And the third group of persons responsible was his uncle and aunt, the Fujiis. Here there existed neither exaggeration nor envy but instead a very strong dislike of extravagance. Therefore the result was much the same as misunderstanding.

134

He had had a special reason for having let this misunderstanding continue, and it was precisely the one that Kobayashi had already seen through. For Tsuda had tried very hard to maintain, for his own convenience, the goodwill of the Okamotos, which he had easily gained by this misunderstanding. By being considerate towards O-Nobu he was in effect currying favour with the Okamoto family, and since Okamoto and Yoshikawa were as intimate as brothers, this naturally meant that the more care he took of O-Nobu the more secure his own future became.

Since he prided himself on his shrewdness and alertness in the cold logic of things pertaining to his own advantage, he was not such a fool as to be pleased merely because of the honour shown him by Mr and Mrs Yoshikawa's involvement in his marriage to O-Nobu as formal go-betweens. He perceived in that fact something far more significant than honour.

Yet this was nothing more than the usual reality that underlies such situations. But if one peeled off yet another layer and probed even deeper, one would have found still something else. For such things to reach the stage that they had, Tsuda and Mrs Yoshikawa had already to be bound by a relationship which others did not perceive. Since they had passed through many internal and external complications known only to themselves, they were forced to view this new relationship of Tsuda to O-Nobu, established half a year earlier, with a somewhat more complex attitude than that of others.

To state the matter bluntly, Tsuda had loved another woman before marrying O-Nobu. And the one who had brought about this love affair had been Mrs Yoshikawa. This officious woman had freely employed various wiles to bring the two young people together and occasionally even to draw them apart, and each time she had enjoyed observing both of them as they alternately showed excitement or bewilderment. But Tsuda had firmly believed, without a moment's doubt, in Mrs Yoshikawa's kindness. And she too had not hesitated to affirm the young couple's joint destiny which she believed would finally have to be fulfilled. Furthermore she had kept looking for the right opportunity as she planned to have the two unite permanently. And yet at the critical moment her confidence had been spectacularly shattered. Nor had Tsuda's pride been in any way able to be salvaged either. At one stroke both had been devastated. For the rare bird had suddenly flown away from her, never to return.

Mrs Yoshikawa blamed Tsuda. Tsuda in turn blamed Mrs Yoshikawa. She however felt responsibility whereas he did not. To that very day he did not know the meaning of the word and was still wandering about in a maze. In the midst of this confusion the problem of his marriage to O-Nobu had arisen. Mrs Yoshikawa had again exerted herself so as to become involved in this second relationship, and, together with her husband, had brought everything to a brilliant conclusion as the official go-betweens.

At the time Tsuda had observed her carefully, and had commented knowingly to himself :

'That's her way of making it up to me, I suppose.'

That was how he had looked upon the matter. And he had tried to chart his future course of action largely on the basis of this feeling. He had been convinced that to live on good terms with O-Nobu was one aspect of his duty towards Mrs Yoshikawa. He had even calculated that if only he did not quarrel with O-Nobu his future was assured.

It was perfectly natural therefore that, since from the outset he had decided that in his dealings with Mrs Yoshikawa there could not possibly be any untoward result from such a calculation, he should now be quite surprised at discovering, even though it was very much veiled, an indication of Mrs Yoshikawa's hostility towards O-Nobu. Before changing his own position so as to please Mrs Yoshikawa, he first had to ascertain hers.

'If, besides saying it's wrong for me to take too good care of O-Nobu, you feel there may be some defect in O-Nobu herself, I want you to advise me with complete frankness.'

'Well, actually, that's the real reason I came today.'

Upon hearing that, he was filled with curiosity at what would follow. She continued :

'I'm going to tell you this because I think there's no one else but me who can tell you it to your face. But I won't like it if you think I'm merely parroting O-Hide. Because if afterwards you make trouble for her I'll be dreadfully embarrassed. You understand, don't you? Of course that's undoubtedly why O-Hide also purposely came to visit you. And yet her main objective was slightly different. She was primarily concerned about your parents. Of course since this problem's a matter relating especially to your father, you certainly can't overlook that aspect of it. Even my husband, when you consider that he was particularly asked by your father to look out for you, can't possibly overlook it and be silent. Nevertheless, since that's merely an outgrowth, and the root of the matter is elsewhere, I think it would be far more effective to start from the latter and cure that first. If not, there will certainly be another misunderstanding like the present one. And if that were all it wouldn't be so bad, but if O-Hide should then call on me again I really don't know what I'd say.'

Tsuda had no doubt whatever that Mrs Yoshikawa meant O-Nobu when she spoke of the root of the trouble. But why did she say she intended to 'cure' that root? He thought that since it was hardly a physical illness, she could not really use such a word unless she was referring to a divorce or some form of separation.

135

He was forced to ask her :

'But what do you seriously think I should do?'

Mrs Yoshikawa appeared quite motherly upon hearing his childish question. But she did not immediately come to the point. She merely smiled, as much as to say that what Tsuda had asked was the real problem.

'Let me ask you what you really think of Nobuko.'

Tsuda recalled what he had said to O-Hide when on the previous day he had been asked the same question in very much the same words. He had not made any special preparations for answering Mrs Yoshikawa. But he was also free to answer any way he wished. In fact he intended to give any answer that might please her. Yet he could not possibly imagine what sort of an answer she wanted. He gave a grin in the midst of his bewilderment. Mrs Yoshikawa had to advance a step further.

'You've always been very affectionate towards Nobuko, I suppose.'

On this point also he was not too well prepared to comment. If it was simply a matter of dealing with Mrs Yoshikawa in a half-joking way, he could manage that easily enough. But when he tried seriously to give a straightforward, responsible answer, in the form that would please her, such an answer certainly did not emerge very easily. His feelings towards O-Nobu were such that he could answer freely either in a way that would be most advantageous or in one that would be most disadvantageous to him. In other words, he could do either because he actually loved O-Nobu to a certain extent and also did not love her so very much.

Mrs Yoshikawa seemed to become increasingly serious. Then she asked her third question in a rather imperative tone.

'Answer me frankly, since it will be in strictest confidence only between you and me. What I want to hear is not really such a big thing. I'll be satisfied if you tell me very simply just what you're thinking.'

Since he had no idea how to answer he became even more embarrassed. Mrs Yoshikawa spoke again:

'You can be most provoking, you know! Why can't you speak up and say what you have to, like a man? After all, no one's asking you such a very difficult question.'

He was finally forced to speak.

'It isn't that I can't answer. It's just that the question's so very vague. . . .'

'All right, since there's nothing else to do shall I tell you myself? Is that all right with you?'

'By all means. Please go right ahead.'

She began to speak but then broke off for a moment before continuing:

'Is it really all right with you? Since I'm of a very frank nature, I very often have to repent for having said things I can't really take back, when I say, as I intend to now, exactly what I think.'

'That doesn't matter at all.'

'But if you get angry everything will end there. Because I certainly don't want to do anything so foolish that it would be too late to mend matters afterwards no matter how much I apologize.'

'But if I don't think anything of it, then it's all right, isn't it?'

'If I could only be sure of that, then of course it is.'

'Don't worry. Whatever you say, whether it's true or not, I certainly won't become angry, so please speak with complete frankness.'

Since Tsuda thought it would be far easier for him to have her take all the responsibility, he looked at Mrs Yoshikawa so as to urge her to speak, after they had agreed in the above way. She then finally began to speak after having several times made sure that he would not have an adverse reaction.

'Please forgive me if I'm mistaken. Isn't it all just as you've been thinking, that is, that you secretly haven't been so very much concerned about Nobuko, after all. Unlike Hideko, I've thought so for quite some time. Well? Isn't my guess quite correct?'

He in no way opposed her.

'Of course it is. Didn't I say so before? That I'm not taking such good care of O-Nobu.'

'But you only said it out of politeness, didn't you?'

'No, I really meant it.'

She stubbornly refused to accept his statement.

'Don't try to fool me! Is it all right then if I go on?'

'Yes, please do.'

'Even though you're not really so concerned about Nobuko, by acting as if you are you're trying so very hard to make others believe you are, aren't you?'

'Has O-Nobu said such a thing?'

'No.' Mrs Yoshikawa vigorously denied it. 'It's just that you're the one who's said it. It's just that your whole attitude clearly indicates it!'

Mrs Yoshikawa paused for a bit at that point. But then she proceeded:

'How about it? I've seen through you, haven't I? And I even know exactly why you've put up such a façade.'

136

Tsuda until that moment had never heard words of this kind from Mrs Yoshikawa. He had now finally been made to realize that he had been rather unconcerned about how she might be secretly observing his relationship with O-Nobu. And yet, while he was thinking that if that was the case it would have been better if she had warned him earlier, he still felt it would be wise to listen meekly to her appraisal and ideas until she finished.

'Please go right ahead and tell me everything quite frankly. It will be very useful to me in the future.'

Since Mrs Yoshikawa was only half-way through, and even if he had not asked her to continue she could not have stopped at that point anyway, she immediately revealed the rest of her ideas.

'You take such good care of Nobuko because you're concerned about what my husband and Mr Okamoto might think, aren't you? If you'd like me to speak even more bluntly, I'm quite capable of it, you know. On the surface you seem to be very affectionate towards Nobuko, don't you? Even if inwardly you really aren't. That's it, isn't it?'

He had never even remotely suspected that her observations would reach such a sarcastic point.

'Do my character and manner really seem that way to you, Mrs Yoshikawa?'

'They do indeed.'

He felt exactly as if he had been pierced by a sword. But, having been pierced, he asked the reason for her cruel remark.

'Why? Why do they seem so to you?'

'Wouldn't it be better if you stopped hiding your real feelings?'

'I haven't particularly tried to hide them but. . . .'

Mrs Yoshikawa firmly believed she had hit the target with ten out of ten of her guesses. Tsuda's remarks, which showed that he inwardly accepted only a little more than half of what she said, naturally somehow left a note of ambiguity in the atmosphere. It was easy for her to see that this might then become the source of misunderstanding. She therefore kept repeating herself and tried to push him in the direction she wanted.

'It won't do to hide them. If you do, it will just make it impossible for me to say anything further.'

He certainly wished to hear what would follow. And since he did, he could do nothing but agree completely with her speculations. After she had forced him to agree and had exclaimed, 'There, you see!' she went on :

'You have a basic misunderstanding of the matter, you know. You think of me as being together with my husband, I suppose. And you also think of my husband and Mr Okamoto as being together in the same way, don't you? That's a great mistake. To think of Mr Okamoto and my husband together may not be so far wrong, but isn't it rather odd that you should think of me in the same way as you do of the two of them? Of course only on this one matter, I mean. Actually, it isn't at all like you, who are so intelligent, to make such a mistake, is it?"

He had finally learned her position. But he still did not understand what connection her position had with him. She continued :

'Isn't it perfectly clear? That I'm the only one who has a special relationship with you.'

Tsuda understood very clearly what she meant by the term 'special relationship'. But this was not his present problem. For he believed that if only he accepted this special relationship he would give to his own activity up to the present a kind of colouring and tone corresponding to it. When he realized that upon making sure of how this special relationship controlled Mrs Yoshikawa's behaviour a new problem would arise, he knew that the matter would not simply end with his recognizing his own misunderstanding.

Mrs Yoshikawa with one word swept away his apprehensions.

'I'm on your side.'

Tsuda replied :

'I've never for a moment doubted that. I believe you completely, Mrs Yoshikawa. And on that point I'm deeply grateful to you. But in what sense are you on my side in this case? What exactly do you mean? I'm a dullard so I can't understand very well. Please speak more clearly.'

'I think there's only one thing I can do for you at a time like this by being on your side. But you probably—'

She broke off there, and looked at him. He thought she would tease him again. But Mrs Yoshikawa's question, which showed she would definitely not tease him, swiftly changed.

'Will you or won't you listen to what I say?'

Tsuda still retained his common sense. He thought about what anyone would think when pushed as far as he was being pushed. But he did not have the courage to declare openly to Mrs Yoshikawa just what he was thinking. His attitude could not but be an indecisive one. He hesitated, unable to say either that he would or would not listen.

'Well, please go ahead and speak.'

'Don't say "well". If you don't have a more clear-cut attitude, I certainly won't say anything.'

'But. . . .'

'Don't say "but" either. Say you'll listen like a man !'

137

Tsuda was secretly afraid, not having any idea what sort of demand there. He tried to imagine how Mrs Yoshikawa would behave under Mrs Yoshikawa might make. If, having agreed, he fell into a predicament from which he would have to withdraw, everything would end there. He tried to imagine how Mrs Yoshikawa would behave under those circumstances. Judging from her social position, her character, and even from her special relationship to him, he thought she was certainly not one to forgive him. And if she never forgave him, his position would be tantamount to one of suspended animation in which he would have been robbed of the means of resuscitation. Cautious man that he was, he did not have the courage to enter a dangerous area from which he could not be certain he would return unharmed.

In addition, he did not know what sort of difficult task Mrs Yoshikawa, unlike ordinary people, might set for him. Having been accustomed for so very long to having too much leisure, she could hardly realize her own unreasonableness. If she said something it was usually acted upon. And if occasionally it was not, she had only to force it through by her will. What was particularly vexing to Tsuda was her complacency in feeling no need of examining clearly her own motives. In fact, more than her complacency it was her thorough arbitrariness that disturbed him. Since she was absolutely convinced that all of her activity in meddling in other people's affairs was an expression of her kindness and goodwill and that there was not a particle of selfishness in it, she could not be expected to have any misgivings about it. She had arrived at this position as the natural result of having almost never turned her critical faculty on herself from the outset and of not listening to others' criticism nor of even trying to listen.

Since, when he was pressed by her in this way, these ideas kept revolving in his mind, he made even less headway in coming to a decision. When Mrs Yoshikawa saw his expression, she finally began to laugh.

'Why are you pondering so much? You probably think I'm going to begin to ask you all sorts of unreasonable things, I suppose. But I assure you I'm not going to ask you anything outrageous. If you really want to do it, it's something you can do quite easily. And what results will only be to your advantage.'

'Can I really do it that simply?'

'Yes, it's really a very small thing. I could almost say it's a harmless little prank. So say you'll definitely do it, won't you?'

Everything was a riddle to him. But he finally felt that if it was actually only a prank it did not really matter so much. At last he made up his mind to comply with her request.

'I haven't the faintest idea what it is but I'll try to do it anyway. Please tell me now, won't you?'

Nevertheless Mrs Yoshikawa did not immediately explain the nature of the prank. After she had obtained Tsuda's assurance she again changed the subject. And what she spoke about was in every sense utterly unrelated to a prank. At least for Tsuda it was of the utmost importance.

She first broached the new topic with :

'Have you met Kiyoko since then?'

'No.'

Tsuda was slightly surprised, not only because the question was abrupt but also because Mrs Yoshikawa had suddenly mentioned the name of the woman who had unexpectedly jilted him and the responsibility for whose action Mrs Yoshikawa had half undertaken. She continued :

'Well then, I suppose you don't know what she's doing now, do you?'

'I haven't the slightest idea.'

'Do you mind not knowing?'

'Even if I do, there's nothing I can do about it, is there? After all, she married somebody else, you know.'

'You attended her wedding reception, didn't you?'

'No, I didn't. If I had, wouldn't it have been a bit awkward?'

'Did you get an invitation?'

'Yes, I did.'

'It seems she didn't come to *your* wedding reception either, did she?'

'No, she didn't.'

'Did you send her an invitation?'

'Yes, I at least did that.'

'Then that's all there was to it, I suppose—on both your parts.'

'Of course that's all there was to it. If not, wouldn't there have been quite a problem?'

'Yes, I suppose so. But there are all sorts of ways of handling problems, I should imagine.'

He did not understand too clearly what she meant. But before she explained herself she again changed her course.

'Does Nobuko know about Kiyoko, I wonder?'

He was at a loss for an answer. Unless he gave Kobayashi a thorough cross-examination he could not say definitely. Mrs Yoshikawa asked her question again in a different way :

'You didn't by any chance speak to her yourself, did you?'

'No, I didn't.'

'Well then, Nobuko doesn't know anything about it, does she?'

'That's right. At least she certainly didn't hear anything from me about it.'

'I see. Well then, she's completely in the dark, isn't she? Or does she perhaps have some slight suspicion?'

'I wonder.'

He could not help thinking about the problem. But even so he was forced to suspend judgment on the answer.

138

As they were speaking Tsuda discovered an unforeseen element in Mrs Yoshikawa's psychology. He then finally realized that it was obvious that by not informing O-Nobu about Kiyoko it had not only suited his own convenience but had also been what Mrs Yoshikawa wished. For no matter how he thought about it, it now seemed that Mrs Yoshikawa wanted to make O-Nobu suspicious.

Mrs Yoshikawa said, 'I should think she probably has a fairly good idea, don't you?' Precisely because Tsuda knew O-Nobu's character he found it that much more difficult to answer.

'Do you have to know whether she knows?'

'Yes.'

Tsuda could not understand why. But he replied :

'If necessary I could speak to her but. . . .'

Mrs Yoshikawa began to laugh.

'If you were to do that now you'd ruin everything. You have to pretend you know nothing until the very end.'

After saying just that and clearly ending one aspect of the discussion, she started again :

'Shall I tell you how I look at it? I think that since Nobuko's so clever she certainly suspects something already. But of course she can't possibly know everything, and also, if she did, that would be most awkward for us. The best thing for us, and the most convenient, is for her to half know and half not know about it. That way, as I see it, she'll undoubtedly be in just the right position to do as I wish.'

Tsuda could only say 'Is that so?' But he secretly thought Mrs Yoshikawa could hardly have the evidence to come to the conclusion she had. And yet she began to say that she actually did have enough.

'If O-Nobu doesn't know something about Kiyoko, she'd hardly be bluffing as much as she is.'

Mrs Yoshikawa was the first person to judge that O-Nobu was bluffing. Although Tsuda had to be dubious about this one word 'bluffing', in another sense he had to agree with Mrs Yoshikawa's bit of sarcasm. Nevertheless he could not give his consent without some hesitation. Mrs Yoshikawa again laughed carelessly.

'But of course it doesn't really matter. Since, if she should just possibly be utterly unsuspecting, then I can think up any number of things at that time to take care of such a situation.'

Tsuda waited in silence for what would follow. But she did not continue on the same subject and suddenly turned the conversation back to Kiyoko.

'I suppose you still have regrets about Kiyoko, don't you?'

'No. I don't.'

'Not in the least?'

'Not in the least.'

'That's what I'd call a man's lie.'

Although he had not intended to lie he also realized that he had not told the whole truth.

'Do I seem to you to have regrets the way I am now?'

'No, I really can't say you do.'

'Well then, why did you say I do?'

'That's exactly why. Because you don't seem to is the very reason I think you do.'

Mrs Yoshikawa's logic was completely different from her usual kind. That is, there was not the slightest confusion in it. She proudly amplified her remark.

'To other people your exterior and interior seem just the same, I suppose. But for me I can only think that since your regret can't appear on the outside it's forced to turn inside.'

'You say that, I suppose, because you decided from the beginning I had regrets, didn't you?'

'Why was I so wrong in deciding that?'

'I don't particularly like it when you freely presume that way.'

'When have I freely presumed anything? It's not my presumption. It's a fact. I say it's a fact known only to you and me. It's a fact, and, no matter how much you're able to deceive others, you don't have any reason to hide it from me, do you? After all, I know it quite well already. If it were only something that concerned you it wouldn't matter, but since it's something that concerns us both equally, we'll remember it as long as we have memory—that is, unless after discussing it together we get rid of it somehow.'

'Well then, how about discussing it here and getting rid of it?'

'Why do you want to? Why do you have to get rid of it? Instead of that, why don't you revive it and make use of it?'

' "Revive it and make use of it"? No matter what situation I'm in now I still don't want to do anything wrong.'

'Who's talking about doing something wrong? When did I ever say you should do such a thing?'

'But didn't you just now. . . .'

'You still haven't listened to everything I have to say, have you?'

Tsuda's eyes shone with curiosity.

139

It was as if Mrs Yoshikawa had already defeated Tsuda by showing him clear-cut evidence that he still was attached to Kiyoko. His attitude, equivalent to one a person might have after a confession, strengthened Mrs Yoshikawa, as she put an end to one phase of the contest between them. But on this one point she was not such a tyrant as Tsuda had first thought. She seemed to be paying much closer attention than he would have thought to his psychological state. Once she had won her point she showed him evidence of the truth of her statement.

'I'm not just making a huge fuss over nothing by simply speaking of your regret over having lost her, I assure you. I'm holding something quite concrete. And with it I intend to explain to others what kind of a thing your regret is.'

Tsuda had no idea what she was talking about.

'Won't you please explain a bit what you mean?'

'If you really want me to, I don't mind doing so. But if I do, that means simply that I'll have to explain your own actions and thoughts.'

'That's all right with me.'

Mrs Yoshikawa began to laugh.

'It won't do for you to pretend you don't understand what other people are saying. Isn't it rather foolish for you to hold back the important facts and at the same time say you don't understand and ask someone else to explain them to you?'

If the situation was as she described it he was indeed behaving foolishly. He inclined his head.

'But I really don't understand, I tell you.'

'But I say you do.'

'Well then, I suppose I'm not aware of it.'

'Oh yes you are!'

'All right then, what am I really doing? Are you saying it all boils down to the fact that I'm hiding something?'

'Yes, that's just about it.'

He gave up. Even he could hardly think it was reasonable to continue to try to hide something after having been pushed as far as he had been.

'If I'm a fool, there's nothing I can do about it. In fact I accept without complaint the criticism that I'm behaving foolishly, so please explain things to me.'

Mrs Yoshikawa heaved a faint sigh.

'My, my, how very discouraging, if that's the case. Despite all the trouble I've gone to for your sake, if the very person I've done it all for behaves like this, then it's exactly as if I've done it all for nothing, I suppose. Perhaps I'd better go back without saying anything at all.'

Tsuda only entered deeper into the maze. But while he knew he was entering deeper, he had to pursue her. His own curiosity was great. His sense of duty and deference towards her were also certainly not minor factors. He repeated the same thing any number of times, urging her to explain.

Mrs Yoshikawa's attitude, when she finally gave in with 'Well then, I'll tell you,' was rather one of triumph. But Tsuda was taken aback when at the beginning of her explanation she still begged off by saying, 'But first I'll ask you a question.'

'Why didn't you marry Kiyoko?'

The question was most unexpected. He was suddenly struck dumb. When she saw he could not speak she rephrased her question.

'All right then, I'll change the question. Why didn't Kiyoko marry you?'

This time he replied, almost echoing her words.

'I don't have the slightest idea why. It's very strange, that's all. No matter how much I think about it I can't come up with anything.'

'She suddenly married Seki, didn't she?'

'Yes, quite suddenly. To tell the truth, "suddenly" isn't a strong enough word! There was barely time to say anything before she was already married.'

'Who had barely time to say anything?'

To him there could be no more meaningless question. To ask who had had barely time to say anything could only seem uncalled-for interference. But Mrs Yoshikawa stuck to her point.

'Was it you who had barely time? Or was it Kiyoko? Or was it both of you?'

'Hm. I'm not quite sure.'

Tsuda was forced to reflect. Mrs Yoshikawa moved ahead of him.

'Wasn't Kiyoko rather unconcerned about it?'

'I'm not sure.'

'Don't say that. How did she seem to you at the time? Didn't she seem unconcerned?'

'Yes, she did somehow.'

Mrs Yoshikawa gave him a disdainful glance.

'You're certainly quite carefree about it yourself, aren't you? If it was Kiyoko who was unconcerned, then it was you who were surprised and had barely time to assess the fact, wasn't it?'

'That may very well be.'

'If that's the case, how do you intend to get over your surprise and over the entire affair?'

'I'm not especially trying to get over it.'

'You're not trying to but actually you'd like to, I suppose.'

'Yes. That's why I've thought of various ways.'

'And by thinking it over did you finally understand everything?'

'No, I didn't. In fact the more I thought about it the less I understood.'

'And is that why you've already given up thinking about it?'

'No, I still can't get over it.'

'Well then, you're still thinking about it, aren't you?'

'Yes, I am.'

'See, didn't I tell you? Isn't that your regret over her having jilted you?'

She had finally pushed him where she wanted him.

140

The preparations were about ready. The main point now had to be shown to him. Mrs Yoshikawa saw her opportunity, and gradually moved in that direction.

The first words she spoke were ambiguous :

'If that's the case, why don't you behave more like a man?'

Tsuda then thought she was merely harping on the same old subject. Each time he had had to listen to such phrases as 'act like a man' or 'not like a man' he had secretly derided her. He wondered if she really knew what 'acting like a man' meant. He could only interpret her constant and arbitrary use of the term as showing not only that she in no way attempted to rid herself of her hypercritical manner but also that she looked at the matter only from her own point of view and tried to drive him into a corner. Forcing a smile, he asked :

'What do you mean by saying I should behave "like a man"? What do I have to do to behave that way?'

'You just have to get rid of your old attachment to Kiyoko. Isn't that perfectly clear?'

'How?'

'How do *you* think the whole matter could be cleared up?'

'I really don't know.'

She suddenly spoke with great vehemence :

'You're a fool! Of what earthly use are you if you can't figure out a simple thing like that! Can't you see that all you have to do is meet her and speak to her?'

Tsuda could not answer. If it was really that necessary for him to meet Kiyoko then it became a question of the method and the place and the manner of doing so. Those problems would have to be solved first.

When Mrs Yoshikawa said, 'Isn't that the reason I purposely came here today?' Tsuda could not help looking at her directly.

'Actually I've been thinking of asking your opinion for quite some time, you know. And since O-Hide came this morning about that other matter, I thought this would be just the right opportunity, and I decided to come and visit you here.'

Tsuda was simply confused because he had made no preparations for this sudden proposal. Mrs Yoshikawa watched him intently before speaking :

'You mustn't misunderstand me. I am myself, and O-Hide is O-Hide. I'm sure you understand there's no need whatever for me to come just because O-Hide asked me, and to take only her side of the argument. As I said before, I'm really still on *your* side, you know.'

'Yes, I'm well aware of that.'

At this point Mrs Yoshikawa put an end to one aspect of their conversation, but without a pause she entered the second stage leading to the important problem.

'Do you know where Kiyoko is now?'

'Since she's married to him, she's at Seki's place, isn't she?'

'Oh, that's her permanent home. I mean "Do you know where she is *now*?" Whether it's in Tokyo or not.'

'No, I don't.'

'Try guessing.'

Tsuda showed that he considered it ridiculous to try, and kept silent. Then she suddenly mentioned a thoroughly unexpected place-name. The memory of that rather famous hot spring, which was a day's journey from Tokyo, was not such an old one for him. As he quickly recalled the scenery in the vicinity, he merely uttered an exclamation of surprise but did not come up with anything further.

She explained everything to him in a kindly manner. From what she said, Kiyoko was spending some time at the hot spring convalescing. Mrs Yoshikawa even knew why such convalescence was necessary. When she told him that Kiyoko had gone there primarily to recover from a miscarriage, she looked at Tsuda and smiled knowingly. He inwardly felt that he could, for the most part, understand what that smile meant. But that sort of thing was no longer the pressing problem, either for Mrs Yoshikawa or for him. Since he did not wish to add even one comment he merely remained her attentive listener. At the same time she jumped to the third stage of the problem.

'Why don't you go there too?'

His mind was already in a turmoil before hearing those words. But even after hearing them he could not decide to go. She pressed him further.

'Go ahead and go there! After all, even if you do you won't be causing anyone any trouble, will you? If you go and pretend ignorance, that's all there is to it, isn't there?'

'Yes, that's true.'

'You've always been independent so you don't have to worry about anything. If you start burdening yourself with all sorts of restraints and scruples everything will just become that much more bothersome. Also it would be good for you if you went for a while to such a place after leaving here. If you ask me, I think there's sufficient reason for you to go just on matters of health. Therefore by all means do go. Go, and act as if you went there perfectly naturally. And then get rid of your attachment to her like a man.'

She further urged him by saying she would even pay his travel expenses.

141

Undoubtedly anyone would have been pleased to receive travel money, to have arrangements made at his place of work for his absence, and to recuperate after an illness at a pleasant hot spring. Especially for Tsuda, who considered his own pleasure his main object in life, this was a rare opportunity made expressly to suit his taste. From his point of view it would have been the height of foolishness to allow it to slip by. And yet in this case the condition that was attached was certainly not an ordinary one. He carefully considered the proposal.

The nature of the psychological factor restraining him was perfectly clear. But he merely was aware of the extraordinary force of that factor, and did not have time to reflect on its meaning. On this point too Mrs Yoshikawa was a much more careful observer of his psychological states than he himself. When she saw that he was somehow vacillating although she thought he had already made his decision between the two answers, she commented:

'Even though you really want to go you're still hesitating to say so, aren't you? As far as I'm concerned that's the worst feature of your inability to act like a man.'

Tsuda, who was not very greatly pained at again being criticized as unmanly, answered:

'That may very well be, but if I don't think about it a bit. . . .'

'Your habit of always thinking about things is a curse.'

He gave an exclamation of surprise. She paid no attention to it.

'A woman doesn't think in such a situation.'

'Well then, if I do, doesn't that mean I'm acting like a man?'

Upon hearing his comment, her tone suddenly became sharp.

'Don't be so impertinent! If you get the better of someone simply by being clever with words, what does it really profit you? How can you be so foolish? Like most men who've been to college and studied a lot you're quite incapable of seeing yourself as you really are, and that's most unfortunate. What's more, that, after all, is why Kiyoko jilted you.'

He again uttered an exclamation of surprise, and again she paid no attention to it.

'If you don't understand, I suppose I'll have to tell you myself. I know perfectly well why you don't want to go. You're a coward, and you can't bear seeing Kiyoko.'

'That's not so. I. . . .'

'Wait a minute. You're going to say you do have courage, I suppose. But you'll also say your pride would be wounded, I suppose. From my point of view, to be so concerned about your dignity is nothing more than cowardice. Now hear me out, will you? I'll tell you why I said that. Isn't that pride simple vanity? Or to be even more blunt, isn't it just concern for appearances? If you take away worry and concern about what the world thinks, what's left? It's exactly the same thing as a new daughter-in-law worrying herself and eating moderately in her new in-laws' home when no one has said anything at all.'

Tsuda was amazed at her vehemence, but her reprimand continued.

'Actually, since you have too much appeal for women, you begin to be concerned about such trifles, I suppose. Then it becomes your conceit and crops up in strange places.'

Tsuda was forced to keep quiet. Mrs Yoshikawa unsparingly continued further dissecting his conceit.

'You'll say that you should go on forever keeping silence politely. You're trying to end everything by keeping still and not making a move. But at the same time inwardly you're forever suffering over what happened. Look a bit more closely at what you're really doing. You're thinking that while you're mulling the whole problem over maybe Kiyoko will be the one who'll soon come and explain things somehow—'

'How can you think I'm thinking such a thing! No matter what sort of a person I may be. . . .'

'No, I'm just saying it's the same thing as if you were thinking that. If there actually isn't any difference, I can't help criticizing you that way, can I?'

Tsuda no longer had the courage to resist. The astute Mrs Yoshikawa took advantage of him at that point.

'Aren't you of a rather impudent nature after all? And you even think that being impudent is an advantage in making one's way in the world.'

'Oh now really.'

'Yes, I mean it. If you think I'm not yet aware of that aspect of your character you're making a great mistake. But isn't it perfectly all right anyway . . . to be impudent, I mean. I like impudence. That's why you should use now this natural gift of yours fully like a man. To that end I've gone to very great pains.'

Tsuda first said, 'So it's a matter of utilizing impudence, is it?' and then changed his tone by adding :

'Did she go there alone?'

'Of course she's alone.'

'What about Seki?'

'Her husband's here in Tokyo. He has business here.'

Tsuda finally decided he would go.

141

But another problem still had to be settled between them. Without turning back to it they could not possibly conclude their conversation. Before Mrs Yoshikawa had a chance to return to it herself Tsuda had already done so.

'Well then, if I do go, what happens? Regarding what you were talking about earlier, I mean.'

'That's precisely the question. That's just what I was going to talk about now. If you ask me, *I* think there couldn't possibly be any better remedy than this. What do *you* think?'

He did not answer. She pressed her point.

'I'm sure you understand what I mean, don't you? Without my saying anything further.'

He could understand quite well what she meant without waiting for her explanation. But when it came to the matter of how she intended to have all of this affect O-Nobu he did not have any very fixed idea. Mrs Yoshikawa began to laugh.

'Everything will be fine if you just pretend you don't know anything. I'll take care of the rest.'

Although Tsuda answered with the commonplace 'Oh really?' he still had his doubts. If he entrusted the remainder of the problem to Mrs Yoshikawa it was the same as handing over O-Nobu's destiny to another person. He was worried because he feared Mrs Yoshikawa's methods somewhat. He was filled with apprehension because he did not know what she might do to her.

'I don't mind letting you take care of the rest of it, but if you know what sort of means you're going to use I think it would be right for me to ask you about them first.'

'You don't have to know anything about that sort of thing, I tell you. Just wait and see. Because I'll certainly manage to turn O-Nobu into a much more wifelike wife for you, I assure you.'

Of course O-Nobu, as he viewed her, was imperfect. But the defects of which he disapproved were not necessarily the ones which Mrs Yoshikawa was intent on correcting. At least Mrs Yoshikawa, who seemed to confuse the two, seemed to think mistakenly that if only she created an O-Nobu to conform to her own ideals she would thereby be creating the most suitable wife for Tsuda himself. But that was not all, for if he looked a bit further into Mrs Yoshikawa's mind, and probed her real intent, he might perhaps come to an outrageous conclusion. He could not be sure that simply because she disliked O-Nobu she might not think up some way of hurting her. He could not be sure that she might not be thinking up some means of punishing her opponent on the mere grounds that she detested her. Fortunately Mrs Yoshikawa herself was quite carefree because she was in a position where neither the world in general nor she herself so forced her to reflect that she had to recognize those aspects of the problem. 'O-Nobu's education'—she boldly used these very words. Since he had never had the opportunity to see through the relationship between Mrs Yoshikawa and O-Nobu at first hand, he was not really qualified to doubt those words. For the most part he firmly believed in Mrs Yoshikawa's benevolence. But when it came to her way of expressing such benevolence, he could not help being fearful.

'How can you possibly have anything to worry about! Haven't I said you should just wait and see how splendidly I've managed everything?'

Since no matter how much he asked her she would not give any details, after she had made light of his fears in this way she spoke to him as if lecturing him :

'O-Nobu's just a little too conceited, you know. And also what she does and what she thinks are still a little too far apart, aren't they? On the surface she's very polite but inside she's so stubborn as to be a trifle too stubborn. Of course she doesn't show everything on the outside because she's so clever, but even so she's much, much too proud. That's why if I don't manage to eliminate all of that. . . .'

At the very point where Mrs Yoshikawa was making this open attack on O-Nobu, they heard the voice of the nurse, who had come halfway up the stairs.

'There's a telephone call for Mrs Yoshikawa from a lady named Mrs Hori.'

Mrs Yoshikawa answered that she was coming, and immediately got up, but at the entrance-way she turned to look back at Tsuda.

'I wonder what she could want.'

Tsuda too had no idea, but after Mrs Yoshikawa had gone downstairs to find out what O-Hide wanted, she swiftly came back up again, and without ceremony exclaimed :

'How dreadful, how dreadful !'

'What is ? Has something happened ?'

Mrs Yoshikawa, while laughing, calmed down, and replied :

'Hideko went to the trouble of warning me.'

'About what ?'

'She said that Nobuko's been at her place up till now talking to her. And she said she just wanted to warn me that Nobuko might stop at the hospital on her way back home. It seems Nobuko's just this minute left her home. My, how lucky I am ! If she'd come in on me just as I'm saying these nasty things about her I'd have been frightfully embarrassed.'

Although she had sat down for a moment she shortly got up again.

'Well, I'd better go now, don't you think ?'

Having made the kind of arrangements with Tsuda which she had she seemed to think it would be awkward to have to meet O-Nobu.

'I think I'll leave right away before she comes. Please give her my best regards.'

With that single parting remark Mrs Yoshikawa finally left the sick-room.

143

At that moment O-Nobu was already on her way towards the hospital.

To go from the Hori home to the doctor's place she had to leave the gate and walk eastward one or two blocks, and there she had to cross over to a street beyond a broad one that formed a large T with another one. When she came to this corner she found that a southbound street-car had stopped at a place diagonally across from her but still in front of her. For no special reason she raised her head and, without really trying to, looked at the window facing her. At that moment, through the windowpane, she saw a particular woman among the passengers. Because of their respective positions O-Nobu saw only half or one-third of the woman's profile, but even with that she was taken aback. For she was suddenly overwhelmed by the impression that the woman had certainly been Mrs Yoshikawa.

The streetcar soon began to move. After O-Nobu had looked for a while at it as it moved away without giving her sufficient time to make absolutely certain who the woman had been, she crossed the street in an easterly direction.

The streets along which she was walking were now only side streets. Since she was very familiar with the geography of the district, she intended to arrive at the hospital quickly by the shortest route, after turning a few times to the right and to the left down several narrow lanes. But after the episode of the streetcar her pace suddenly slackened. When she had come already to within two or three blocks of her objective, she began to think that she would return home for a while without stopping in at the hospital.

She had already been depressed at the time she left the Hori home. Her mind was filled with the unpleasant realization of having rashly irritated O-Hide and of having bungled badly in so doing. There was the chagrin of having purposely been made to catch a hint of the important matter in a roundabout way without grasping it firmly. In fact the uneasiness she felt was only made that much deeper by barely making out the mystery. The thing that stood out above everything was that she suspected that her own weaknesses had been seen through and that the tables had been turned and she had been made a fool of by O-Hide.

But O-Nobu was even more greatly concerned with another problem. She even went so far as to think that a plot had been hatched against her and was secretly progressing somewhere. No matter who the chief architect was, she was certain O-Hide was one of the plotters. She clearly inferred that Mrs Yoshikawa was also involved. As she thought in this way she rapidly became even more despondent. The feeling assailed her from afar that she had become like an isolated unit, which, without its knowing it, has found itself surrounded on all sides. She looked around her, but there was no one on whom to lean apart from her husband. She had first to put everything aside and run to him. For even though she doubted him she still retained some faith in him. As she thought that no matter what happened at least he surely would never become one of the plotters, no sooner had she gone out through the Hori gate than her feet almost spontaneously turned in the direction of the hospital.

Since this psychological action now had to come to a halt, O-Nobu, from the bottom of her heart, cursed the streetcar she had just seen. If the person in the streetcar was Mrs Yoshikawa, if Mrs Yoshikawa had gone to visit Tsuda, and if while she was visiting him— No matter how clever O-Nobu was, she could not easily come up with an idea of what might follow thereafter. Nevertheless only one thing resulted from this new factor : her mind swiftly jumped from O-Hide to Mrs Yoshikawa, and from Mrs Yoshikawa to Tsuda. She could not help but begin to consider the three of them as forming a closely-knit trio.

'Perhaps the three of them communicate with each other by a kind of telepathy that I can't possibly understand.'

She was forced to this idea at the very moment that she was thinking only of running to her husband to find a refuge.

'As things are now, it won't do just to go to the hospital. Because if I do go, how exactly would I behave?'

She then realized that she was walking towards the hospital without any real idea of what she would do once she arrived there. And she also began to realize that it was rather important to decide upon the kind of attitude she should have and upon the most effective way to meet Tsuda at this time. Having never heard the criticism that it would be wrong to visit him in her best clothes since they were simply husband and wife,* she decided that the best policy would be to return home for a while to calm herself and then to set forth again without changing her clothes. Thus, at about the halfway point in the lane down which she would have to walk, to arrive at the hospital within five or six minutes, she turned back. She then walked from the broad street lined with willows to the bustling thoroughfare and immediately boarded a streetcar.

144

O-Nobu returned home at about the time the sun was setting. Having walked for about a block after getting off the streetcar and having been enveloped by the evening mist, which seemed to penetrate her very being, what she desired above all else was to be near a charcoal brazier. As soon as she took off her coat she sat down near the brazier and stretched her hands over it.

But she was given hardly a minute's respite. No sooner had she sat down than she received Tsuda's note from O-Toki. Its content was of course simple. She was able to scan it in about as much time as it took her to open the envelope. But after reading the note she was no longer the same woman. The words in the three short lines moved her more deeply than an entire volume. Her heart leapt in the face of this note, which in an instant set afire the feelings she had brought with her from outside.

* Sōseki here seems to have forgotten Tsuda's criticism of O-Nobu's dress which he makes in Section 39.

'What possible reason could he have for saying I shouldn't go to the hospital today!'

Even without this additional worry she hardly had time to relax since she had intended to go out again almost immediately anyway. She thus startled O-Toki, who had brought in her tray from the kitchen, by swiftly standing up to go.

'I'll take my meal when I come back.'

She again put on her coat which she had just taken off, and went out the gate. But when she had gone as far as the street with the street-car tracks she stopped at the corner of the lane. For some reason or other she felt she could not endure going to the hospital just then. She suddenly began to realize that if she were to go to visit Tsuda in her present frame of mind it would do her no good whatsoever.

'With Yoshio the sort of person he is, I can't even expect him to explain to me frankly why he wrote what he did.'

She became despondent, and watched the streetcars in front of her as they went to the right and to the left. If she took one of those going to the right she would arrive at the hospital and if she took one of those going to the left she would go towards the Okamotos' home. She thought she might better abandon her present plan and go to her uncle's place, but no sooner had she thought of this than she realized that there were difficulties in that direction as well. If she went to the Okamotos and entered into conversation she would be forced to disclose everything. If the very foundations of her relation with Tsuda, which she had been concealing until then, were not exposed, she would not be able to advance one step further. She therefore would have to make a sweeping confession to her uncle and aunt that her intuition concerning Tsuda had failed her. But she thought that events had not yet become so pressing as to make her endure such shame. Although there was hardly sufficient basis for her to expect any resurrection of her former confidence, what she most despised was the honesty that would make her destroy her self-respect on a moment's whim.

Unable to make her decision, she began to sway to the right and left. At the very same time that O-Nobu was perplexed in this way, Tsuda, who obviously was wholly unaware of her problem, was sitting up in his bed and was casually facing the tray which the nurse had brought. Earlier, when there had been the telephone call from O-Hide, he had already been anticipating O-Nobu's visit, and he had secretly been preparing himself mentally for seeing her enter his sick-room immediately upon the departure of Mrs Yoshikawa. But since O-Nobu had turned back halfway, during the period of his slight disappointment, as he was waiting for supper-time to come, perhaps because he was tired of waiting, he began talking to the nurse as soon as he saw her.

'So it's finally mealtime, eh? When you're here all alone like this the day certainly seems long, doesn't it?'

The nurse was a small girl with a rather poor complexion. She had the sort of nondescript face that made it extremely difficult for him to judge her age. The fact that she was always wearing her white uniform separated her even further from the common run of young women. He was forever wondering about her; when she was wearing ordinary clothes did she still have to take a tuck at the shoulders as she always did with her nurse's uniform, or did she let it out? He had at one point actually asked her that question seriously. Since she had then giggled and answered that she was still in training, he had been able to make a fairly good guess as to her age.

After placing his tray near his pillow she did not immediately go downstairs.

'You must be quite bored,' she said with a giggle, and swiftly added : 'Your wife didn't come today, did she?'

'No, that's right, she didn't.'

Tsuda had spoken with his mouth already filled with a large bite of a piece of toast, and he could not say anything further. The nurse, however, was perfectly free to continue the conversation.

'But instead of your wife another visitor came, didn't she?'

'Yes. You mean that older lady, I suppose. She's quite stout, isn't she?'

Since the nurse gave no indication of concurring in his unflattering remark, he had to continue talking alone.

He made the nurse laugh by saying, 'If a lot of much younger and prettier women came to visit me I'd recover much more quickly,' but she swiftly responded in kind.

'What do you mean ! You already have just young women visiting you every day as it is, don't you? You seem to be very lucky on that score.'

She did not seem to know that Kobayashi had come.

'The lady who came yesterday was very lovely, wasn't she?'

'Well, I don't think so. She's my younger sister, you know. She resembles me in some ways, doesn't she?'

Without answering that she did or not, the nurse just kept on giggling.

145

That day represented a stroke of unexpected good fortune for the nurse. Since the doctor himself seemed to have come down with some intestinal upset he had been unable to come that day to his consultation room as usual, and the friend whom he had asked to substitute for him had been able to arrange to come only in the morning; from noon on he had not put in an appearance, and the office was therefore closed.

'It seems he's on duty somewhere today and can't come in the afternoon or evening.'

As she spoke in this way she showed no signs of her usual business, and in a leisurely manner she remained seated in front of Tsuda's tray.

Since Tsuda was pleased to have found a good conversational partner to while away the tedium, he kept on chatting with her. He asked her various questions in a half-joking manner.

'What part of the country are you from?'

'Tochigi Prefecture.'

'Of course. Now that you actually say so, I can tell from your accent. So it's Tochigi, is it? By the way, what did you say your name was?'

'I don't think I'll answer that question.'

She simply would not divulge her name. Tsuda, pleased at the resistance he had discovered in her at that point, purposely kept asking her the same thing several times.

'Well then, I suppose there's nothing for me to do from now on but call you Miss Tochigi Prefecture, is there? Is that all right with you?'

'Yes, perfectly all right.'

She did finally reveal, however, that the first syllable of her given name was 'Tsu'.

'Is it Tsuyu then?'

'No.'

'Hm, I rather thought it wouldn't be. Well then, how about Tsuchi?'

'No.'

'Oh, wait a minute! If it's not Tsuyu and not Tsuchi either. . . . Ah yes, I've got it. It must be Tsuya. Or if not that, then maybe Tsune.'

He came out with any number of girls' names beginning with 'Tsu'. But at each the nurse shook her head and giggled. And each time she did so he again pressed her with another. When he had finally learned that her name was Tsuki,* he went on bantering with her by making fun of this strange name.

* Tsuki means 'moon' and is a rather uncommon woman's name.

'So then I'd have to call you O-Tsuki,* wouldn't I? O-Tsuki's a fine name. Who gave it to you?'

Instead of answering she suddenly countered with :

'By the way, what's your wife's name?'

'Try to guess.'

After purposely mentioning two or three very feminine-sounding women's names she said :

'It's probably O-Nobu.'

She had made an excellent guess. Or, more accurately, she recalled having heard O-Nobu's name at one time or other.

'You're quite a clever one, aren't you, O-Tsuki?'

Just as he was showing considerable interest in his bantering, O-Nobu herself appeared on the scene. The nurse turned around in surprise and immediately stood up while holding the tray.

'Oh my, here she is,' she exclaimed.

O-Nobu, entering the room as the nurse left, sat down near Tsuda's pillow, and suddenly looked at him.

'You probably thought I wasn't coming, didn't you?'

'No, not necessarily. It was just that since it's already late I was wondering about it.'

There was no falsehood in his words. O-Nobu was quite able to perceive that. But if so then the contradictions of the situation only increased.

'But you sent me a note earlier, didn't you?'

'Yes, I did.'

'And you wrote that I wasn't to come today, didn't you?'

'Yes, because it would have been rather awkward.'

'Why would it have been awkward for you if I'd come earlier?'

He finally realized the situation. As he observed her manner he responded :

'Why, it's nothing at all. It's a mere trifle, I tell you.'

'But it was enough to make you purposely send the note by a messenger so there must surely have been more to it than that.'

He tried to deceive her about the entire episode.

'It's really nothing at all, I assure you. Why in the world should you worry about such a thing! It's rather foolish of you, isn't it?'

The words he spoke with the intention of soothing her produced the opposite effect. She twitched her dark eyebrows. Without saying a word she put her hand in her obi and withdrew from it the note in question.

'Please read it once again.'

He took it from her in silence.

* The 'O' is a polite prefix, which, at the time this novel was written, was almost always used with women's given names.

As he said, 'There isn't anything particularly important written in it, is there?' his heart finally denied his words. The note was simple. But it was quite sufficient to arouse O-Nobu's suspicion. Having already a vulnerable point which could very well be suspected by O-Nobu, he now felt that he had blundered.

'I'm asking you to explain what it means precisely because you don't really say anything in it,' O-Nobu retorted. 'Shouldn't you at least tell me about it? After all, that's why I've come.'

'Do you mean to say you came just to ask me that?'

'Yes.'

'On purpose? Just for that?'

'Yes.'

She simply would not budge from the issue. When he finally realized her stubbornness, he accidentally thought of a very convenient lie.

'Actually, Kobayashi came.'

The simple surname Kobayashi certainly excited her. But the matter did not end at that point. To satisfy O-Nobu Tsuda had instead to explain what he meant by his last remark.

146

'I thought you too would surely find it unpleasant to meet anyone like Kobayashi. That's why, when I realized that, I purposely told you not to come.'

Even though he said this, O-Nobu still did not show any signs of being convinced, and therefore he was forced to amplify his statement to mollify her.

'And even if it might not have been unpleasant for you, it would most certainly have been unpleasant for me—to have you meet a man like that. Furthermore, he brought up a nasty piece of business I wouldn't want you to hear about.'

'Something it would be wrong for me to hear? You mean then a secret between the two of you?'

Tsuda said, 'No, I don't mean that at all,' and when he saw her narrow eyes fixed unflinchingly on him he hurriedly added :

'He came to extort money from me again. That's all.'

'Well then, why would it have been wrong for me to hear it?'

'I didn't say it would be *wrong* for you to hear it. I just said I didn't want you to hear it.'

'If that's the case, then you sent me the note just out of kindness, didn't you?'

'Yes, I suppose that's what you'd call it.'

As O-Nobu's narrow eyes, which until then had been looking intently at her husband, became even narrower, a faint laugh escaped her.

'Well, thank you very much.'

Tsuda could not remain composed. He had lost the opportunity to remove the sting from the words he had written quite carelessly.

'But it would have been unpleasant for you to meet such a fellow, wouldn't it?'

'No, not in the least.'

'That's a lie.'

'Why do you say that?'

'Why it seems Kobayashi said something to you, didn't he?'

'Yes.'

'That's why, don't you see? That's why I'm saying I thought it would be unpleasant for you to meet him.'

'Well then, do you know what sort of thing I heard from him?'

'No, I don't. But in any event, since it came from him, I can't imagine it was anything nice. What in the world did he actually say, anyway?'

O-Nobu, stifling the words which were about to emerge from her, then asked a question in return.

'What did he say to you here?'

'He didn't say anything at all.'

'Now that's really a lie. You're hiding it from me.'

'Aren't you the one who's hiding something? You were told some outrageous story by him, and while you accepted it as absolute truth. . . .'

'Perhaps I *am* hiding that. But as long as you persist in keeping things secret from me there's nothing else for me to do.'

Tsuda fell silent. O-Nobu too said nothing. They were both waiting for the other to speak. But O-Nobu's endurance broke earlier than Tsuda's. She suddenly spoke very sharply.

'It's a lie. Everything you say is a lie. Kobayashi never even came here, and there was nothing of the sort, but you thought you'd try to deceive me by purposely making up such a story!'

'If I did, there wouldn't be any particular advantage to me, would there?'

'Yes there would. To conceal the fact that another person came you purposely decided to drag in Kobayashi.'

'Another person? What other person?'

O-Nobu's eye fell up on the maple *bonsai* placed in the raised alcove.

'Who was it who brought *that*?'

Tsuda realized he was defeated. He regretted that he had not admitted right away that Mrs Yoshikawa had come. He had not mentioned the fact at first out of a sense of prudence. It would have been easy enough to talk about her visit, but since the nature of the things he had discussed with Mrs Yoshikawa was such as naturally to make him a coward in front of O-Nobu, his conscience reproached him, and he decided it would be the wiser policy to avoid the subject.

He turned to look at the *bonsai*, but when he stammered slightly as he tried to say Mrs Yoshikawa's name, O-Nobu took the initiative.

'Mrs Yoshikawa came, didn't she?'

He spoke without thinking:

'How do you know?'

'I know, I tell you. At least that much.'

Tsuda, who had been paying attention to O-Nobu's manner, finally recovered his nerve.

'Yes, she did come. In other words your prediction came true.'

'I even know quite well that she came by streetcar.'

Tsuda was again surprised. But he thought only that perhaps the Yoshikawa automobile had been parked on the broad street near their home and that O-Nobu had therefore concluded that Mrs Yoshikawa had come by streetcar, and he paid no further attention to Mrs Yoshikawa's means of transportation.

'Did you meet her somewhere?'

'No.'

'Well then, how do you know?'

Instead of answering, O-Nobu asked him a question in return.

'Why did she come to visit you?'

He answered casually:

'That's what I thought I'd talk to you about now. But I don't want you to misunderstand me. Because that doesn't mean that Kobayashi didn't come. First Kobayashi came, and then Mrs Yoshikawa. In fact, one came as the other left.'

147

O-Nobu realized that she was more flurried than her husband. When she forsook the argument upon realizing that if it went on in this vein he could no longer be defeated, she turned aside adroitly before betraying her own weakness.

'Really? If so that's all right with me. After all I had no way of knowing whether Kobayashi came or not. But instead of talking about that, please tell me why Mrs Yoshikawa came. Of course I know perfectly well it wasn't simply a courtesy sick-call.'

'Just the same, it isn't that she came on any very important business. I'll tell you that in advance because if you're waiting for some startling revelation you may be disappointed on hearing what she said.'

'It doesn't matter if I am. If you just tell me everything exactly the way it happened that will clear things up for me anyway.'

'Well, the main reason was to pay me a sick-call, and whatever else she had to say was secondary. You see what I mean, don't you?'

'Yes. Go ahead.'

Tsuda spoke to her very frankly only about the advice Mrs Yoshikawa had given him of going to a hot spring. Since, just as O-Nobu had a kind of tact peculiar to her so too did Tsuda have his own type of finesse, he skilfully abbreviated the parts it would be awkward for her to hear, and he easily gave her an explanation which would have seemed to anyone to be candid and rational. She could not find the smallest gap where she could insert a word of criticism of his account.

And yet they both were ill at ease. O-Nobu tried to probe beneath this very simple explanation. Tsuda was determined never to let her see what was behind it. This extremely peaceful secret battle had to be enacted as a test of nerve and artifice. It was only natural, however, that since Tsuda had the vulnerable point which he was defending, O-Nobu, who was attacking, should, to that extent, have had the advantage. Therefore, setting aside the natural endowments of the two, and looking only at their relative positions, one would have had to say that O-Nobu was already the superior before the fighting began. Even if one made the clear merits of the case the standard, she was already in a winning position before the contest started. Tsuda was quite aware of these facts. And O-Nobu too realized much the same thing.

It was natural that their war had to attain a certain phase on the basis of whether these internalized facts could be brought to the surface precisely as they were. If only Tsuda were honest, there could hardly be an easier contest than this one for O-Nobu. But if he retained a particular area of dishonesty, he could also become a fortress which would be extremely difficult for her to breach. Unfortunately for O-Nobu she had not yet prepared the weapons with which to expel him from his strong position. Since she then could not consider any other means of dealing with him than to press him to open the gates to his fortress himself, her position was an almost ineffectual one.

Why could she not conclude everything beautifully, having won the contest in her heart? Why could she not be satisfied unless she had the form of victory as well as the substance? The reason was that she did not then have the kind of emotional margin to allow her to be content solely with the latter. She had far more important problems to consider than this contest. Since these second and third objectives were still awaiting fulfilment, she felt that unless she broke through his defences at this point she would not be able to do anything later.

And it was not only this, for actually, as far as O-Nobu was concerned, this contest did not have primary significance. What she really was aiming at was rather the true facts of the case. Her principal objective was to dispel her own suspicions rather than to vanquish her husband. For to dispel these suspicions was absolutely essential for her existence, which had as its object Tsuda's love. This in itself was already a great objective. It loomed before her eyes as a problem, the significance of which was so enormous as almost to blot out all methods of solution.

From the context of the situation she was forced to adhere to that one point with the force of her entire being and to the limit of her powers of thought and judgment. It was her nature to do so. Unfortunately, however, the entirety of nature, which included her own, was greater than she. Extending far above and beyond her, it did not hesitate to cast an impartial light on the young couple and even to attempt to destroy her in her pitiable state.

Each time she tried to pin down one item he retreated from her one step. If she tried to pin him down to two items he retreated two steps. Each time she attempted to get at the true facts the distance between her and Tsuda only increased. The larger scheme of things wantonly thwarted her efforts, which emerged from her own smaller nature. With each step it did not hesitate to destroy her objectives. She was dimly aware of what was happening, but she could not understand its significance. She simply remained convinced that the contest ought not to turn out that way. And finally she lost her temper.

'Even though I devote myself entirely to you, you don't seem to realize that at all.'

He showed that he could not tolerate such a comment.

'But I've never doubted your devotion to me in the slightest!'

'I should hope not! If on top of everything else you should start doubting me, it would be far better for me to be dead!'

'There's no need whatever to exaggerate in that way. In the first place there's no real problem at all between us, is there? At least none that I can see. And if there should be, please tell me what it is, won't you? Then I'd try to defend myself and explain things, but if from the outset you have these wholly groundless complaints, then there isn't really very much I can do, is there?'

'They aren't groundless. The root of it all surely lies in your own feelings.'

'Well then, that poses quite a problem, doesn't it? You were stirred up by Kobayashi about something, weren't you? That's it, I'm sure. Tell me then what he actually said. You don't have to hold anything back.'

148

Judging from Tsuda's words and expression, O-Nobu could guess clearly what was in his mind. He was worried about Koyabashi's having gone to their home in his absence. He was even more concerned about what Kobayashi had told her. But he did not yet grasp clearly what precisely Kobayashi had said. That was why he was then trying to extract the information from her.

There was obviously a secret. Everything that had until then been accumulating in her mind as evidence pointed in that direction without the slightest doubt and without the slightest possibility of contradiction. That there was a secret was certain. It was as clear as the noonday sun in a cloudless sky. But at the same time, like the noonday sun in a cloudless sky, it did not cast a shadow anywhere. She could merely stare at the secret, but she did not know how to put forth her hand to take it and unravel it.

Since O-Nobu, in the midst of her mental confusion, had the cleverness to retain a bit of foresight, without fending off Tsuda's probe she immediately retorted:

'All right then, I'll tell you the truth. I heard everything down to the last detail from Kobayashi. That's why it won't do you any good to hide things any longer. And you're aware that you appear quite horrid from it all, aren't you?'

What she said was close to utter nonsense. But judging from her feeling as she said it, she thought it was not a whit different from a statement of complete sincerity. She had simply been forced to call him 'quite horrid' in an impassioned tone.

His reaction was immediate. He showed signs of retreating in the face of her outburst. O-Nobu had not learned her lesson from her bitter failure with O-Hide, but her courage in trying the same dangerous course again seemed about to be rewarded this time. She leapt even further ahead.

'Why didn't you tell me everything before this happened?'

Her words 'before this happened' were ambiguous. Tsuda had difficulty in grasping their meaning. But O-Nobu herself understood them even less. Therefore, even though he asked her, she did not explain them. Tsuda, perplexed, asked her again in a roundabout way.

'You surely can't be referring to my going to the hot spring, can you? If you say that's awkward for you, I don't mind giving it up, you know.'

O-Nobu looked startled.

'Who would ever say such a thing! If you've made arrangements with your firm and can go somewhere to get well, there couldn't be anything finer than that, could there? Do you think I could possibly say that's wrong and insist on your not going? Don't be ridiculous. I'm hardly one to become hysterical if you go off for a few days.'

'Then it's all right if I go, isn't it?'

As she said, 'Of course it's all right,' she suddenly took a handkerchief out of the sleeve-pocket of her kimono and, putting it to her face, began to sob. The rest of her speech came out in fragments, bit by bit, without making complete sentences, in between her sobs.

'No matter what you think of me—even though you say I'm selfish —to do such a dreadful thing—as to prevent you from getting well— I've always been grateful for all the freedom you've allowed me—and that you should say I'd stop you—from taking a trip to a hot spring—'

Tsuda's mind was finally at ease. But O-Nobu had more to say. As her paroxysms calmed down her words came out relatively smoothly.

'I certainly wasn't thinking about such a minor matter. No matter how much of a woman I am, and no matter how much of a fool I may be, I still have my own sense of honour. Therefore, if I'm a woman it's as a woman, and if I'm a fool it's as a fool, but I still intend to maintain that honour. And if it should be threatened in any way. . . .'

O-Nobu got only as far as that before she began to cry again. What followed again came out in bits and snatches.

'And if—that sort of thing should ever happen—I'd be so ashamed —I could never, never see—either my uncle—or my aunt—again—But even as it is—I've already been made a complete fool of by O-Hide and others—and you've watched them do it to me—but you've acted completely unconcerned—and pretended not to know anything.'

Tsuda immediately retorted with :

'You say O-Hide's made a fool of you? When? When you went to visit her today?'

He had unwittingly said something very foolish. He ought not to have known about O-Nobu's and O-Hide's encounter without O-Nobu's telling him. O-Nobu's eyes finally flared.

'See! What did I tell you! You already know I went to visit O-Hide today, don't you?'

He could not answer immediately that O-Hide had telephoned him. He was perplexed as to whether he should say so. But he was not allowed a moment's respite. The more bewildered he became the worse the situation grew. He was almost at an impasse. But at the most dangerous point, where all was virtually lost, a brilliant excuse came to him as a godsend.

'Because the rickshaw-man said so when he came back. Probably O-Toki told him.'

Fortunately O-Toki also knew that O-Nobu had gone chasing after O-Hide. When his spur-of-the-moment excuse met with unexpected success, Tsuda gave another long sigh of relief.

149

O-Nobu, who had desperately tried to break through Tsuda's defences, stopped abruptly. Since her efforts were checked by the thought that he was not deceiving her as much as she feared, she could not advance, even though she had fully intended to do so without a break. Tsuda took advantage of his opportunity.

'It doesn't matter what O-Hide or anybody said, does it? After all, O-Hide's O-Hide and you're you, aren't you?'

O-Nobu retorted with :

'If that's the case, it doesn't matter either what Kobayashi or anybody else said to me, does it? After all, you're you and Kobayashi's Kobayashi.'

'No, it actually doesn't. That is, if you'd only believe in me. But if you start having suspicions and misunderstandings and they get spread about recklessly that's quite annoying, so I can't just remain silent.'

'It's the same with me. No matter how much O-Hide makes a fool of me, and no matter how coldly your Aunt Fujii acts towards me, if you only believe in me and remain faithful yourself, then there isn't any real problem. But if *you* should begin to. . . .'

O-Nobu was tongue-tied. She did not have any clear facts, and therefore she could hardly come up with a coherent statement. Tsuda again took advantage of her momentary bewilderment.

'You're probably thinking I might do something wrong that would humiliate you as a wife? But instead of thinking about that wouldn't it be better if you trusted me a bit more and put your mind at ease?'

She suddenly cried out :

'I *want* to trust you. I *want* to put my mind at ease. I want to trust you more than you can imagine.'

'Are you saying I can't imagine?'

'No, you can't possibly. Because if you could, you'd have to change. Since you can't imagine, you're as unconcerned as you are.'

'I'm not unconcerned !'

'Well, you certainly aren't sorry for me and you don't have any pity on me.'

'What do you mean by feeling sorry for you or having pity on you?'

After he had in effect rejected her criticism, he was quiet for a while. He then faltered a bit as he attempted to evade the issue.

'You say I'm not concerned about you—no matter how much I actually am. Because you can be sure that if there's reason to be I will be. But if there isn't, what am I supposed to do?'

Her voice trembled with tension.

'Oh, Yoshio, listen to me!'

He said nothing.

'Please tell me I don't have to worry, I beg of you. Put my mind at ease and rescue me, because I have no one else to turn to but you. I'm helpless, and I'll die if you turn me aside. So please say I can put my mind at ease. Just one word will do, but please say I don't have to worry.'

'Everything's all right. Don't worry, I tell you.'

'Do you really mean that?'

'Yes, I do. Please stop worrying.'

She immediately pounced upon these words with startling force.

'All right then, tell me. Please tell me. Tell me everything right here and now without holding anything back. And really put my mind at ease once and for all.'

Tsuda was taken aback. His mind began to waver in uncertainty as he wondered whether he dared reveal to her everything about Kiyoko. But he quickly concluded that he was then only suspected and that it was not that O-Nobu held any actual evidence against him. He also decided that if she really knew the facts of the case she would hardly have pushed him that far without thrusting them at him.

He was in a difficult position. Yet he still had an avenue of escape. His moral sense and self-interest struggled with each other. But on the side of one the weight of the factor of going to the hot spring had suddenly been added. It was his duty to fulfil the promise he had made to Mrs Yoshikawa. It was also his desire which had emerged from necessity. Thus the feeling that it would be the best policy not to disclose anything, at least until after he had fulfilled that promise, won out.

'To speak about such tiresome things will only embarrass us both and there will be no end to it, so why don't we stop it? Instead of that isn't it all right if I give you a guarantee?'

'A guarantee?'

'Yes, give you a guarantee. I'll assure you that you'll never be humiliated.'

'How?'

'Why, by simply swearing that I will, since there's no other way.'

She fell silent.

'In other words, if you'll only say you trust me everything will be fine. And if something *should* happen then it's all right to ask me to be responsible. If you do, then on my part I'll say I've already accepted the responsibility. How about it? Can't we reach a compromise at that point?'

150

However inappropriate the word 'compromise' might seem in this case, it was extremely appropriate to describe the state of Tsuda's mind at that time. For it was quite true that he actually had feelings corresponding very closely to this word. When the discerning O-Nobu realized this, her excitement gradually subsided. Tsuda, who had secretly been worrying lest her emotions flare up even higher, was relieved. He then had enough time to devise a means of diverting the force of her emotions, which he had checked, in the opposite direction. He began to console her, using many of the expressions most calculated to please her. Although he normally presented a cool exterior, he also was adroit enough to adapt himself to the feelings of others in an emergency. His efforts were not in vain. O-Nobu saw, for the first time in a long while, a Tsuda such as he had been before their marriage. Memories of their engagement were revived within her.

'He hasn't really changed. He's the same person he used to be, after all.'

O-Nobu's satisfaction, as she viewed him in this way, was enough to rescue him from his predicament. Their conflict, which had seemed about to develop into a fully-fledged storm, finally subsided. But they were not the same couple they had been before the incident. They had at some point altered their relationship without being aware of it.

As their conflict died down, Tsuda had the following realization:

'Women are, after all, very easy to pacify.'

He was secretly pleased at the self-confidence which this one episode of discord had netted him. Until then, whenever he had quarrelled with O-Nobu, he had always felt somehow that she was a most difficult person with whom to deal. Every day some incident had taken place in which he had been forced to endure the unpleasantness of having been bested by her, at the same time that he looked down upon her for being a woman. He had not yet been able to make a clear analysis of the reasons for this, and could not determine whether it was her intuition, or her resourcefulness, which could also be considered the practical application of her intuition, or whether it was something else which was responsible, but in any event, his losing to her was an unmistakable fact. Moreover he had undoubtedly hidden this fact in his own mind and had not yet disclosed it to anyone. Thus, even though it was true, it was actually also a secret. Why then had he purposely made this obvious fact into a secret? Quite simply he had done so because he wished to think of himself as highly as possible. Even though he viewed his married life with O-Nobu as a battle over love and even though he had always been the loser, he also had considerable pride. And since he had been subjugated by O-Nobu against his will, he had obviously not given himself up to her from the heart. It was not that he splendidly became a prisoner of love but rather that he was always being duped by her. Just as O-Nobu, without realizing that she was undermining his pride, felt the satisfaction of love only in vanquishing him, so too did Tsuda, who disliked losing, surrender each time that his strength was not equal to hers and he was pinned down, although he still regretted so doing. When this one night's lovers' quarrel, then, upset this special relationship, it was perfectly natural that his idea of O-Nobu should change. He had never before seen O-Nobu, who seemed to have so violently and directly obtained the upper hand, actually and unmistakably emerge as the loser. While still retaining his vulnerable point and trying to dodge her thrusts, he had for the first time been able to beat her. The result was quite clear : he could finally despise her. But at the same time he could show her much more sympathy than he had ever shown before.

O-Nobu also, in her own way, was beginning to feel the changes wrought by the quarrel. She had never until then shown herself to him in such a way, and indeed she profoundly regretted that because she had been so taken up with piercing his weakness at a stroke she had instead ended by showing him her own weakness, which she had never exposed before. She wished only to be loved by him, but she had always relied on her own strength to attain that objective. She had been determined to maintain her own self-respect to the end. Of course this pride could not be said to be complex. It was simply the determination never to humiliate herself by bowing her head and asking for mercy, no matter how necessary his love was in her existence. It was the firm determination to show freely how much strength she really had, if he did not love her as she wished. That she had ceaselessly carried out this determination meant in effect that she was forever tense. Such an extreme degree of tension simply had to break at some point, and it was obvious that if it did the result would be tantamount to her having destroyed her own pride herself. Unfortunately she pushed on without realizing this contradiction. Finally the tension did break, and as it did she repented of what she had done. But happily the outcome was not as cruel as she thought it would be. For at the same time that she exposed her own weakness she received a kind of reward. The attitude of her husband, with whom she had never been satisfied until then no matter how many victories she had won over him, changed slightly, and began to approximate one that would satisfy her. He clearly used the word 'compromise', indirectly confessing that the secret she was trying desperately to extract from him was latent behind that word. A confession? She tried repeating this word to herself. And when she realized that it was doubtless a confession which was close to a tacit admission, she was pleased although at the same time she was vexed at not knowing more. She did not press him further. Just as Tsuda had begun to feel sorry for her, so too could she feel sorry for him.

151

The objective situation, however, was more difficult than they thought. They could not part at that point. The storm, which by a strange circumstance had for a time calmed down, seemed shortly about to rage again.

This happened after O-Nobu's excitement had subsided somewhat. She already began to show, by her mood, the effects of the disturbance she had just been through. With the attitude of someone who feels himself drunk and tries to exploit that drunkenness, she turned to him.

'Well then, about when are you going to the hot spring?'

'I'll go as soon as I leave here. That would seem best for my health.'

'Yes of course. The sooner the better. Now that you've decided to go.'

He was relieved at that remark. But suddenly she added :

'It's all right if I go too, isn't it?'

Having just relaxed a bit, he instantly became tense again. He had first of all to think before answering. From the very outset he had not even considered taking her along with him. And yet it was even more difficult to refuse to do so. He did not know how O-Nobu might change depending on the way he refused. While he was wondering what sort of an answer he should make, his chance to speak passed. She pressed him.

'It's all right, isn't it? . . . if I go with you?'

'Well, ye-es, but. . . .'

'I shouldn't?'

'No, it's not that. . . .'

His unwillingness to take her along gradually became obvious in his speech. Since he realized full well that once a glimmer of suspicion appeared in O-Nobu's eyes everything would be lost, he was actually controlled by the same psychological state as O-Nobu. The effect of the previous quarrel was already working in him. There was nothing for him to do but use it in his own way. He immediately thought of the word 'pacify'. 'I'll have to pacify her. If only a woman is pacified everything works out somehow.' He turned to her with this newly acquired plan.

'It's all right if you come. In fact, I'd actually like to have you with me. First of all, it will be rather inconvenient for me to go alone. So just on the matter of your helping me it's clear it would be better if you went.'

'Oh, that's splendid. I'll go then.'

'On the other hand, though. . . .'

O-Nobu showed her displeasure.

'On the other hand, what?'

'Well, I was thinking—what would we do about the house?'

'Toki would stay there, so everything would be fine.'

' "Fine"! I don't like it when you say such childish, irresponsible things.'

'Why? Where am I being so irresponsible? If it's not safe with just Toki we could ask somebody to stay with her.'

O-Nobu mentioned, one after another, the names of two or three people who would be appropriate to look after their house in their absence. But he rejected them all.

'A young man won't do at all! After all, we can hardly leave him alone with Toki, can we?'

O-Nobu began to laugh.

'Oh now really! Nothing can possibly happen, I tell you. It's only for a short while, you know.'

'I can't agree with you. No, I certainly can't.'

While Tsuda showed a firm attitude he also seemed to be thinking.

'I wonder where we can find just the right person. If only there were some old woman that would be just fine, but. . . .'

There was not a single such woman who was unoccupied at the Fujiis', the Okamotos', or anywhere else.

'Well, I'll try to think about it carefully.'

Tsuda failed in trying to end the subject at that point. For O-Nobu would simply not let it drop.

'Suppose you don't think it over so carefully, what happens then? If we can't find some old woman do you mean I shouldn't go under any circumstances?'

'No, I haven't said that.'

'But there isn't any old woman available, is there? That's quite obvious without thinking. If you feel it's wrong for me to go, why don't you come right out and say so instead of beating around the bush?'

Although Tsuda was for the moment caught he was strangely able to come up with another convenient excuse.

'Well, actually, in case of an emergency it wouldn't really matter about not having an older woman look after the house. But in addition to leaving Toki alone, there's still another difficulty. I'm getting the travel money from Mrs Yoshikawa, you know. And it wouldn't be very good to have people think I was using her money simply for us to take a trip together, would it?'

'If that's the case, it wouldn't matter if you didn't accept the money from her, would it? After all, we have that cheque, don't we?'

'If so, we'll be a bit short in paying this month's expenses.'

'But we also have what Hideko left, you know.'

Tsuda was again trapped. But again he found a way out, though a rather dangerous one.

'But I have to lend a bit to Kobayashi.'

'To *that* fellow!'

'You may very well say that, but even he this time is going off to Korea, you know. I can't help feeling sorry for him. And I've already promised him, so there's nothing I can do about it now.'

Of course O-Nobu could not be expected to be pleased. But Tsuda had been able somehow or other to escape from his predicament.

152

Since afterwards their conversation proceeded unexpectedly smoothly, they shortly achieved their second compromise. To promote his friendly relations with Kobayashi and to fulfil the promise he had once made to him, Tsuda had decided to take a certain amount from the cheque he had received from O-Nobu and give it to Kobayashi as a farewell gift before the latter's departure for Korea. Nominally he was of course lending the money, but since, if Kobayashi did not intend to return it, he could not possibly count on it in planning his future budget, he was in effect giving it to him. Of course, when it came to that point, O-Nobu showed considerable disapproval. To give money to such an offensive boor she considered the height of foolishness, and in no corner of her heart could be found even the willingness to help Kobayashi out of a temporary difficulty and have him give an official guarantee of repayment. Moreover, since she seemed disposed to look at the reasons behind Tsuda's trying to behave as he did, Tsuda became quite fearful of her.

'Why in the world you have to go out of your way to show such kindness to *that* sort of fellow I'm sure I don't know!'

She repeated exclamations of this kind two or three times. When Tsuda persisted in his attitude of generosity and did not show any signs of taking her up on what she said, she advanced a step further:

'But can't you at least tell me why? If I can only understand why you somehow won't be fulfilling your obligations if you don't do this, then it doesn't matter if you give him the entire amount of the cheque.'

Since this was precisely the most difficult point for him to understand himself, he could not very well expect O-Nobu to understand it. Instead of defending Kobayashi, he mentioned how close they had been in the past and various pleasant memories from that past association. When she criticized him for using the word 'pleasant' about his relationship with Kobayashi, he was forced to expand his explanation by telling her how different Kobayashi now was from what he had been in the past. Nevertheless, when he saw that she did not seem to understand what he was saying, he swiftly raised the tone of his argument and went so far as to speak grandly of humanitarianism, altruism, and the like. He did not realize, however, that since the humanitarianism of which he was speaking could finally be reduced to a kind of utilitarianism, he was unwittingly advancing toward a trap of his own making, and a situation developed in which O-Nobu made him stumble and he was about to be pushed into that trap. A very simple paraphrase of the type of appeal he made is as follows :

'At any rate, he's in real difficulty, you know. He says that he simply can't stay in Japan and that he's going off to Korea, so isn't it all right if I show him a little sympathy? Furthermore, you're forever attacking his character, but I think it's a bit unfair. I admit he's an incorrigible wretch. He's an incorrigible wretch, all right, but if you just try to think why he became that way, it's easy to understand. It's simply because of his sense of injustice. And if you want to know why he feels that way, it's just that he can't make any money. And yet he's neither lazy nor stupid. As a matter of fact, he has quite a good head on his shoulders. But unfortunately he didn't receive a proper education, and when I realize that's why he became the way he did, I can't help feeling sorry for him. In other words, if you can only realize that it isn't that *he's* bad but that his *circumstances* are bad, then you'll understand. In short, he's a most unfortunate fellow.'

If he had said only that, everything would have been fine, albeit insincere, but he simply could not stop at that point.

'Also, we still have to think about another aspect of the matter; if we ever get in bad with such a reckless fellow, we have no idea what he'll do. He likes to fight with everybody, you know. He actually came here and boasted openly that no matter whom he fights with it can only be to his advantage. He's really unmanageable, I tell you. That's why if I turn down his request now, he'll be furious. And if he'd only become furious that wouldn't be so bad, but he'll surely do something. It's certain he'll get his revenge. But since while I have to maintain my reputation he's not the least bit concerned about his, when it comes to a test I'm no match for him. You understand what I'm driving at, don't you?'

When he arrived at that stage, the earlier façade of humanitarianism had already largely crumbled. And yet even so, if he had only stopped then, O-Nobu would have had to give her tacit approval. However, he continued :

'Also if he only attacked the upper classes and made nasty remarks about rich people in general as a kind of abstract doctrine, then there wouldn't be any problem. But he's not that way. He's much more practical. He says he'll start with what's to hand and then gradually work his way towards his objective. That's why I'm precisely the one who's most in danger. No matter how I look at it, the best policy for me is to show him what kindness I can, to make him feel good, and to have him leave for Korea as soon as possible. If I don't, I don't know what kind of trouble he may make for me some day.'

When he expressed himself in that way, O-Nobu had to say something further.

'No matter how crude Kobayashi may be, if you don't have any weak point, there's no reason to be so afraid, is there?'

With this kind of exchange it took them all of ten minutes to settle the matter of the cheque. But as soon as they had decided on the amount for Kobayashi the disposition of the remainder was swiftly settled. O-Nobu's request that she be allowed to have it as her own spending money to use as she wished was soon accepted. In exchange it was decided that she would not go to the hot spring with him. Furthermore he made her agree that they would accept Mrs Yoshikawa's generosity in paying the expenses for his trip.

Finally all of the differences that had arisen between the young couple on that chilly evening were resolved. They then said goodbye to each other, and O-Nobu left.

153

The post-operative stage which Tsuda had to endure went smoothly. Or rather it went normally. When the fifth day came, after the doctor changed all of the bandages for him, as scheduled, he confirmed this.

'Everything's coming along splendidly. The bleeding's only on the outside. There's none whatever internally.'

On the sixth day the same treatment was repeated. But the incision was closer to being healed.

'How's the bleeding? Has it stopped yet?'

'Yes, it's almost completely stopped now.'

Since Tsuda could not understand the significance of the bleeding he also could not understand this answer. But by arbitrarily making the interpretation that he was now completely recovered he was very much pleased. Yet the actual facts were not as he thought. The exchange between him and the doctor made this very clear.

'What would happen if it doesn't heal properly?'

'I'd have to operate again. And it would leave a somewhat larger scar than before.'

'That's not very pleasant to contemplate.'

'Yes, but it's eighty or ninety per cent certain it will heal.'

'Even so, for complete healing in the true sense it still will take quite some time, won't it?'

'At the earliest, three weeks, and at the latest, four.'

'Do you mean before I can leave here?'

'Oh no, you'll be able to leave about the day after tomorrow.'

Naturally Tsuda was pleased. And he decided that when he did leave he would go directly to the hot spring. He purposely did not mention this to the doctor for he thought that if he did consult him and if the doctor forbade his taking a trip then he would simply get upset. This was somewhat rash of him and did not at all accord with his normal behaviour. Even while he was determined to carry out this imprudence he was already aware of the contradiction, and thus he felt rather uneasy. To conceal this feeling he asked the doctor a wholly unnecessary question.

'You say you didn't cut the sphincterial muscles, but why then has gauze been packed in from the bottom?'

'Those muscles aren't near the outside. They're about half an inch up. And the place where I scraped at them is diagonally about a third of an inch from the bottom.'

That evening Tsuda began eating gruel. Having subsisted for so long on bread alone, the taste of the watery rice was quite new for him. Even though he normally could not appreciate the pleasure of such gruel on a cold night, he then was able to sip and relish, even more than the ordinary haiku poet would have, the warmth of thin gruel which contrasted with the chill of the autumn evening.

He had to take a mild laxative again to move his bowels which for so long had been stopped as a necessary part of the healing process. As his stomach and intestines felt lighter, although they had not been causing him too much distress, his whole mood became lighter too before he was aware of it. As his body became more comfortable, he turned over in his bed and simply awaited the day when he could leave the hospital.

That day came very quickly after only one more night had passed. As soon as he saw O-Nobu, who had come for him with a rickshaw, he said to her :

'Well, I'm finally able to go home. What a good feeling !'

'You're probably not *that* happy.'

'Oh, but I am.'

'You mean that home is still better than a hospital.'

'Yes, I suppose that's it.'

After he had said this in his normal tone of voice, he quickly added, as if he had just thought of it :

'The dressing-gown you made for me was really a great help. Maybe it was because the cotton was new, but anyway it felt good when I wore it.'

O-Nobu laughingly bantered with him.

'What's happened to you? You've suddenly become quite a flatterer. But you're wrong about the dressing-gown.'

As she folded the dressing-gown in question, she confessed to him that she had not padded it solely with new cotton. But at that moment Tsuda was changing into his kimono. Since the act of wrapping around him his dappled crepe obi was rather more important to him than any consideration of the material of the dressing-gown, he paid no attention to her honest answer. He merely murmured, 'Oh, is that so?'

'If you like it that much, please take it with you to the hot spring.'

'And from time to time I'd remember your kindness, wouldn't I ?'

'Yes, but if the dressing-gown they lend you at the inn is much better than this one, I'd be shown up, wouldn't I ?'

'That certainly won't happen.'

'Oh, but it might. When something's of poor quality, there's no way of covering it up. And such a thing as kindness is soon forgotten.'

Her sincere statement did not convey to him the simple meaning she intended. He sensed a certain irony was at work in it, and he considered the dressing-gown as a symbol of something. Thus, somewhat irritated, he turned his back on her, and proceeded to tie the ends of his obi into a broad knot.

When, shortly thereafter, the two of them were seen off by the nurse and went out the entrance, they immediately climbed into the rickshaws that they had waiting there for them.

'Goodbye.'

Tsuda's eventful week's stay in the hospital finally was concluded with this one word.

154

As the first item of business in his schedule before setting out for the hot spring area he planned to go to, Tsuda had to meet Kobayashi. When the appointed day came, upon receiving from O-Nobu the necessary money, he turned back to her and said laughingly :

'It seems a shame, doesn't it? To have this much money taken by such a fellow.'

'Well then, why are you giving it to him?'

'I'd certainly prefer not to.'

'If you'd prefer not to, why do it? Do you want me to go in your place and say no for you?'

'Hm, I might ask you.'

'Where are you meeting him? If you just tell me the place, I'll go for you.'

He did not know whether she was serious or not. But if in such a situation he took everything lightly and concluded that it was merely a joke on her part, it was not at all difficult for him to imagine that by having done so he might find himself at his wit's end. For she was a woman who might, when the occasion demanded it, actually carry out precisely what she was saying. Whether he broke his promise to Kobayashi or not, it was not at all impossible that she might willingly undertake to represent him if it was a matter of repelling Kobayashi thereby. Taking care not to enter a dangerous area, he purposely turned the conversation in another direction by making a rather flippant remark :

'You're quite courageous underneath that womanly exterior of yours, aren't you?'

'Yes indeed, I think I am. But I haven't really shown my courage yet so actually I don't know how much I have myself.'

'Well, if *you* don't know, *I* know quite well, and that's more than enough, I assure you. When a wife starts showing as much spunk as you have this can only mean her husband will soon be in trouble.'

'Why should he be in the least trouble? If his wife shows her courage for his sake, there's no need for him to be, is there?'

'I agree there may be some instances where it works to his advantage.' He of course had no intention of answering seriously, and added : 'But up to now I don't remember having seen any particularly praiseworthy display of it.'

'You're quite right. I haven't shown the least bit so far. But just look inside me for a minute. I'm not at all the placid and meek person you think I am.'

He did not answer. And yet she did not leave off.

'Do I seem *that* easy-going to you?'

'Yes, you do. You seem very easy-going indeed.'

In the face of this arbitrary comment she gave a faint sigh, and said :

'How tiresome it is to be a woman ! I wonder why I had to be born as one.'

'It certainly won't do any good to ask *me* that. Express your regrets to your father and mother.'

She forced a smile but still did not give up.

'That's all right. But you just watch one of these days.'

He was slightly surprised as he retorted, '*What* do you want me to watch?'

'It doesn't matter, but just watch one of these days.'

'All right, I will, but what in the world are you going to do?'

'Well, I can't say until the problem actually arises.'

'Doesn't the fact you can't say really mean that you don't know yourself?'

'Yes, I suppose so.'

'Somehow it all seems ridiculous. It's the vaguest kind of prediction imaginable.'

'Nevertheless I'm saying this prediction will soon come true so you just watch.'

He gave a disapproving sniff. Conversely her attitude gradually became more serious.

'I mean it. I don't know why but lately I've always been thinking about it. I'm certain the time will some day come when I'll for once have to show all the courage I have inside me.'

' "Some day"? "For once"? That's why I say it's a kind of fantasy.'

'No, I don't mean some day years from now or once in my lifetime. I mean soon. I mean once some day in the near future.'

'You're just making it worse. I assure you I won't be too happy on that day in the near future when you show me this reckless courage of yours.'

'No, it's *for* you, I tell you. Haven't I been saying that all along? I'd show the courage *for* you.'

As he looked at her serious expression, he gradually was drawn into her mood. He did not have as much poetry in his nature as she did. Instead, he felt that a rather unpleasant event threatened him from afar. O-Nobu's poetry—what he had termed her fantasy—gradually began to be active. When it seemed that the wings of the bird which was fumbling about and which until then he had only thought was dead began suddenly to move, he had a strange feeling, and swiftly cut off the conversation.

He took his watch out from his obi and looked at it.

'It's late. I'd better be on my way.'

As he said this he stood up and started out. O-Nobu followed him into the entrance hall, took his brown felt hat from the hat-rack, and handed it to him.

'Now don't forget to tell Kobayashi I send him my regards.'

Without turning back Tsuda went out into the cold evening air.

155

The meeting place with Kobayashi was on a side street, just a short distance from about the halfway point of the busiest avenue in Tokyo. To avoid the unpleasantness of having Kobayashi come to call for him at his home, and also to eliminate the bother of his calling on Kobayashi at his boarding-house, Tsuda had decided on the time, and had arranged to meet him there.

The appointed time had already passed while he was riding on the streetcar. But this tardiness, which had come about because he had changed his clothes, received the money from O-Nobu, and for a short while had talked with her, was not sufficient to cause him the slightest distress. In plainer terms, he did not wish to show Kobayashi that he was concerned about strictly observing rules of courtesy. On the contrary, by being slightly late he wanted to unnerve the too free and presumptuous Kobayashi. In name it may have been a farewell party but since it actually was a meeting wherein one was to give money and the other was to receive it, Tsuda was certainly in the superior position. Therefore it was advisable for him to demonstrate the privileges of the superior person as much as possible, and to create beforehand the positions of host and guest, as a means of preventing a display of Kobayashi's pride. He felt this was appropriate even as a simple act of spite divorced from any consideration of advantage.

As he looked at his watch on the clanging streetcar he thought that even as it was it was perhaps still a bit too early for the cheeky Kobayashi. He went so far as to calculate that if he arrived too early he would go to have a look at the night stalls and increase Kobayashi's expectations, which were already aroused by desire, a bit further.

When he got off at the streetcar stop, the numerous lights gleaming on all sides of him sufficed to tell him brilliantly of the activity of the metropolis at night. He stood among them, and before turning down the side street which was his objective, for about ten minutes he was perplexed as to whether he should walk along the well-lit main street or not. However, upon folding up the evening newspaper and looking around him, he could not help being surprised.

For Kobayashi, whom he had certainly supposed was already quite tired of waiting, was most unexpectedly standing on the other side of the street. Since he was on a corner of an intersection separated by the pavement and the streetcar track from where Tsuda had alighted, as long as their lines of sight did not actually meet, the night, the crowds, and the flickering lights were helpful in preventing their mutual recognition. Furthermore, Kobayashi was not facing him directly. He was talking to a young man whom Tsuda had never met. Since from Tsuda's position only about two-thirds of the young man's face and about one-third of Kobayashi's were visible, with hardly any fear of being seen himself he could carefully observe the appearance of the two from where he stood at that moment. They certainly were not looking around them. While Tsuda could clearly make them out as they faced each other and maintained the same stance for a long time, he could also clearly perceive that they were engaged in some serious conversation.

Behind them was a wall. Unfortunately since there was no window on the side, there was no strong light cast on them from anywhere. However, an automobile coming from the south screeched as it was about to turn the corner. At that moment the two were caught in the full glare of its large headlights. Tsuda for the first time could clearly make out the features of the young man. His pale complexion, together with an unkempt mass of hair that had not been cut for several months, which hung down on both sides from under his hat, assailed Tsuda's sight. As the car passed, Tsuda turned swiftly around. And he purposely began walking in the opposite direction so as to avoid the sidewalk where the two men stood.

He had no particular objective. His purpose in looking into each of the brilliantly illuminated shops was simply to note the urban beauty of the scene. Apart from the fact that the articles exhibited differed according to the nature of the shops he could not feel any particular interest in them. Nevertheless he sensed satisfaction with everything he saw. Finally, when he saw some stylish neckties displayed in the window of a certain shop selling foreign goods, he entered the shop, took up the one he thought he wanted, and fingered it awhile.

When he thought that it would now be safe for him, he retraced his steps. The two, who had been standing on the sidewalk, had indeed gone off somewhere. He quickened his pace a bit. Cheerful light streamed into the street from the windows of the brick building where they were supposed to meet. The windows were high, and since the light was obstructed by the patterned ivory tablecloths, it was reflected indirectly into the night. The interior scene, as he looked up at it from the street, was one of a pleasant and fashionable, gas-heated restaurant.

The restaurant, which was on the corner of a long block, and which was of rather austere construction, was not so very large. Tsuda had learned of it only recently. A friend had told him that the food was good since it had been opened by the cook of a man who had for a long time been a minister to France and other European countries, and thus simply because Tsuda had eaten there four or five times he had invited Kobayashi to meet him there.

He pushed the door open brusquely and went in. As expected, he found Kobayashi, with what appeared to be an evening paper in front of his serious face, and with an air of being rather ill at ease.

156

Kobayashi raised his eyes and looked towards the entrance for a moment but quickly cast them down again at the newspaper. Tsuda could do nothing but go over, without speaking, near the table where he was sitting and speak to him there.

'I'm sorry I'm a bit late. I suppose I kept you waiting quite a while, didn't I?'

Kobayashi finally folded up the newspaper.

'You do have a watch, don't you?'

Tsuda purposely did not take his watch out. Kobayashi turned around and looked at the large clock hanging on the front wall. The hands showed that it was about forty minutes later than the appointed hour.

'Actually I just got here now myself.'

They took seats facing each other. Since there were only two groups of customers around them, each consisting of a man and a well-dressed woman, the room was unusually quiet. The colour of the fire in the gas stove placed about two yards to one side of them gave considerable warmth to the atmosphere of the clean room, which was painted almost completely white.

A strange contrast came to Tsuda's mind. He could clearly visualize the rather questionable bar he had been dragged to by Kobayashi on that evening a short time before. In a certain sense he was proud of the fact that this time it was he who had invited the same Kobayashi to a place like this.

'Well, what do you think of this place, eh? It's quite attractive and pleasant, isn't it?'

Kobayashi looked around him as if he had just noticed the place.

'Hm, it's all right. There don't seem to be any detectives here at least.'

'And instead there are beautiful women, aren't there?'

Kobayashi suddenly spoke very loud.

'They're geishas, aren't they?'

Tsuda, rather embarrassed, rebuked him with :

'Don't be ridiculous!'

'Why, it's not impossible, is it? It's a world where anything can happen, even geishas being here.'

Tsuda lowered his voice even further.

'But geishas don't dress that way, I tell you!'

'Oh don't they? Well, if you say so, it must be so. A country bumpkin like me can't help it if he doesn't know the difference. I think any woman's a geisha if she just wears pretty clothes.'

'You're the same as ever. Forever making sarcastic remarks, aren't you?'

Tsuda showed he was a trifle annoyed. Kobayashi did not seem to care.

'No, I wasn't being sarcastic at all. By being poor I really can't tell about such things, you know. I honestly thought they actually were geishas, that's all.'

'If so, that's all right.'

'Even if it isn't, there's nothing much you can do about it. But tell me, what's the real difference, Tsuda?'

'What "real difference" are you talking about?'

'I mean is there really that much difference between so-called ladies and geishas?'

Tsuda felt he had to show that he was above the childishness of giving a serious answer to this fellow who delighted so in pretending ignorance. At the same time he also wanted somehow to make some remark in return that would send him reeling. But he held back. Or, more accurately, he could not find the remark capable of doing that.

'Stop joking, will you.'

As Kobayashi said, 'But I wasn't joking, I tell you,' he suddenly looked up at Tsuda. Tsuda then noticed the look in his eyes, and even though he realized Kobayashi was up to something again, he was a bit too clever in his attempt to escape from him. He did not have the courage to get through the situation by paying no attention to him. But he had enough skill to try to turn the conversation to a harmless topic. And yet he still fell into Kobayashi's trap, as he began with :

'What do you think of the food here?'

'The food here or anywhere else—it's all the same to me. A fellow like me doesn't have any well-developed sense of taste, you know.'

'You mean it's all tasteless?'

'No, it's not. It all tastes fine.'

'Well, that's splendid. The owner here happens to be a chef and does the cooking himself, so the food should be quite a bit better than the food in other places.'

'No matter how good the chef is, it's no use trying to please someone like me. He'll just put himself out for nothing.'

'But if the food's good, that's all that matters, isn't it?'

'Sure, if it's good, that's fine. But if I tell him that some ten-sen-a-dish food at some sleazy restaurant's just as good, he won't be very happy about it, will he?'

Tsuda could do nothing but give a painful smirk. Kobayashi went on talking, as if to himself.

'After all, in the condition I'm in now, I can hardly waste my time, showing off my fancy knowledge by saying if it's French cooking it's good or if it's English cooking it's bad, or any nonsense like that. All I can say is if it gets in my mouth it's good.'

'But that certainly doesn't mean you've forgotten why some food is good, does it?'

'It certainly doesn't! It's good because I'm hungry, that's why! What other reason can there be!'

Tsuda again was forced to remain silent. But when the silence between them began to weigh heavily on him, he felt he had to try to say something further. But as he was about to do so, Kobayashi beat him to it.

157

'Maybe from the point of view of a man with your sensitivity, Tsuda, a dull clod like me is worth despising on all points. I recognize that myself. I know it can't be helped if I'm despised. But I've got a few things of my own to say, you know. My dullness isn't necessarily a result of any innate disability. Just give me a little free time. Just give me a little money. And then you'll see what kind of person you'll have to deal with!'

Kobayashi at that time was already feeling the effects of saké somewhat. His bombast, which could not be characterized as either joking or seriousness, began to develop into a kind of diversion in which he purposely tried to exploit the force of his drunkenness. Since Tsuda felt compelled to agree openly with the truth of what Kobayashi was saying, he found it necessary to attune himself somewhat to Kobayashi's manner.

'You're quite right. That's why I sympathize with you. Even you know that, I'm sure. If I didn't, there wouldn't be any reason for me to do what I'm doing, to go to the trouble of having dinner with you and of giving you a send-off to Korea, would there?'

'Thanks.'

'No, I really mean it. Actually the other day I even told O-Nobu all about it.'

A suspicious glance gleamed from under Kobayashi's eyebrows.

'You don't say! Do you really mean it? If you actually defended me in front of your wife, it seems you still have a little bit of your old kindness left, doesn't it? But on that score. . . . Well, what did she say?'

Tsuda, without speaking, put his hand in his pocket. As Kobayashi watched this action, he purposely added, so as to stop it : 'Ah-ha. So that's why you had to defend me! I thought it was a bit odd.'

Tsuda took out the hand he had put in his pocket. As he said, 'Here's O-Nobu's answer,' he hesitated a moment although he intended to hand over to him the money he had purposely brought. Instead he forced the conversation back to its old topic.

'After all, men do differ according to their circumstances, don't they?'

'But I think I said they differ according to the amount of leisure they have.'

Tsuda did not deny this.

'All right, you can also say they differ according to their leisure.'

'From the time I was born right up until today I've lived a life on the lowest possible level. I've lived without even knowing the meaning of the word leisure, so how do you think I differ from people who've been brought up in the lap of luxury and who've lived in utter selfishness?'

Tsuda smiled faintly. But Kobayashi was in earnest.

'You don't *have* to think about it. The two of us are here, aren't we? You and I, I mean. If you just compare the two of us, you'll see right away—the effects of lives lived in leisure or under economic pressure.'

Tsuda inwardly agreed with some of what Kobayashi was saying. But more followed just at the point where he felt there was nothing to do but listen to his complaints.

'So what happens as a result? I'm forever despised by you, and not only by you, by your wife too, and by everybody. No, wait a minute, I have more to say. That's a fact, a fact both you and I know very well. Everything's just as I said before. But there's one thing in this matter neither you nor your wife understands yet. Of course even if I tell you about it now there's no reason at all for our respective positions to change, so it may seem as though there's no point in telling you, but since if I go to Korea I may never live to see you again. . . .'

When Kobayashi got to that point he appeared to be rather excited, but since immediately thereafter he added the honest remark, 'No, it just may be my tough luck to go to Korea and find it's even worse than I thought and not be able to stand it, so there's no saying I won't come back right away,' Tsuda could not help laughing. Kobayashi started all over again, having realized himself that he had come to an impasse.

'Anyway, there's no telling that what I have to say now won't be of some use to you in the future, so listen to me. Actually, in the same way you despise me I despise you too.'

'I'm quite aware of that.'

'No, you're not. You may know the effect of my contempt for you but neither you nor your wife has yet really understood the meaning of it. That's why I say I'll explain it to you now as my farewell to you and in return for your kindness this evening. All right?'

'Go right ahead.'

'Even if you say I shouldn't, there's nothing else for a penniless fellow like me to leave with you anyway.'

'That's why I say go right ahead.'

'You'll listen without saying a word, will you? If you really listen, I'll tell you. I'm a fellow with such undeveloped tastes I think both the French food you eat with so much relish here and the saké in that dirty-looking bar you took me to task for treating you at the other night are equally good. You despise me for that, don't you? But on the contrary I'm proud of it, and in turn I despise you for despising me. You see what I'm driving at, don't you? Just think about it for a minute. On this point which of us, you or I, feels confined, and which of us feels free? Which of us is happy and which of us feels the more restraint? Which of us is at peace and which of us is disturbed? As I see it, you're forever squirming. You're forever nervous. You're always trying to avoid anything that's the least bit unpleasant and always trying to chase after the things you like. And why is that? The answer's quite simple. It's because you've got so much freedom you don't know what to do with it. It's because you've got the margin to be extravagant. It's because you haven't like me been driven to the low point where you can accept everything and let everybody do just as he damn well pleases.'

Tsuda indeed despised Kobayashi. Yet he had to recognize the facts : Kobayashi was certainly made of sterner stuff than he.

158

But Kobayashi was not yet finished with his lecture. As he looked unconcernedly at Tsuda he suddenly reverted to an unexpected topic. It was nothing other than the matter that had come up for a moment between them at the very beginning of their get-together but which had quickly been dispelled by the force of what followed.

'I think you already understand what I mean. And yet you still don't seem to want to say that of course I'm right. That's a contradiction, isn't it? But I know the reason. First of all, it's the fact that the person who's annoying the all-wise Tsuda by telling him these things is someone like me who hasn't any social position, or rank, or money, or even a steady job. If this were coming from Mrs Yoshikawa or somebody like that, then even if what she were saying were a lot less worthwhile than this, I've no doubt you'd sit right up straight and listen very carefully. No, this isn't just my bias or anything like that. It's an unchallengeable fact. But you'll have to think about it, you know. I mean about the fact that since it's me I'm able to say these things. And you'd better also remember that even Fujii or his wife, when it comes to that, can't say anything. And why is that? Well, it's very simple. It's because, no matter how poor Fujii is, he hasn't had the experience I've had. To say nothing of that crowd that lives much more comfortably than Fujii.'

Tsuda did not know very well who was meant by 'that crowd'. He merely thought that Kobayashi probably meant such people as Mrs Yoshikawa and Okamoto. Actually Kobayashi raced on without giving him a chance to ask a question about it.

'Now in the second place—your present circumstances make you feel you don't have to pay attention to the advice I'm now giving you, or maybe you consider it a warning, or simply providing you with knowledge, or you can call it anything you wish, but you still won't pay any attention to it. You understand it with your mind but your heart won't accept it. But this is only you right now. Of course if you reject this simply by saying that since you and I are separated by so much there's nothing that can be done about it, then the matter ends there, but actually what I want to do is make you pay attention to a certain factor. Are you still with me? The distance separating people's circumstances and social positions is not really that great. If one speaks of fundamentals, then ten people, though they're ten different people, repeat approximately the same experience in different forms. Let me state the matter more clearly. I am myself, and I look at things with

306

my keenest eye; you're you, and you look at things with an eye that is most appropriate to you. Well, I suppose it's that degree of difference, isn't it? That's why, don't you see? When those who are prosperous have a setback, or are in difficulty, or fail, their point of view immediately changes. But no matter how it changes, they can't change their ingrained habits immediately, can they? In short, I'm only saying that if you should ever be in need you'll certainly have to remember this advice of mine.'

'Well then, I'll try not to forget it.'

'Yes, try not to. Something will surely bring it to mind.'

'All right, I've got your point.'

'But the funny thing is that no matter how much you get my point it won't do you any good.'

As Kobayashi said this he suddenly began to laugh. Tsuda did not understand what he meant. But Kobayashi explained before he could ask him.

'When the time comes you may possibly become aware of what I'm saying. I'll allow that. But if so, will you be able to change suddenly as you let loose a yelp of pain? Can you change suddenly and become me?'

'Naturally I have no way of knowing.'

'That's not it at all. You know perfectly well. It's absolutely certain you can't become me. May I take the liberty of saying that to come as far as I have requires a great deal of discipline. No matter how much of a fool I may be, I've had to pay in blood to become what I am today.'

Tsuda was annoyed by Kobayashi's pride. What, after all, had the wretch achieved by so much effort? Since Tsuda felt this way, he purposely showed his contempt as he asked him :

'Why in the world are you telling me these things? Even if I should remember what you're saying it wouldn't do me any good in an emergency, would it?'

'No, it probably wouldn't. But it's still better than not having listened at all, isn't it?'

'No, it almost seems better not to have listened.'

Kobayashi, leaning back happily in his chair, began to laugh again.

'That's just it. That's just what I was aiming at.'

'What do you mean?'

'I don't mean anything. I'm just stating the facts. But I'll explain them to you. When you shortly find yourself in real trouble and you can't do anything about it, you'll remember what I've said. You'll remember but you won't be able to act on it at all. And then you'll feel that it would have been better not to have listened to me.'

Tsuda looked displeased.

'Stop being such a fool! So what if that does happen?'

'Oh, nothing particular. It's just that I'd finally have my revenge for your contempt of me.'

Tsuda changed his tone.

'Do you have that much malice towards me?'

'Why in the world do you call it malice? Say rather that I'm filled with goodwill towards you. But it *is* a fact that you're forever despising me. And even though I've seen behind your attitude and pointed out to you the contemptible areas in yourself as well, you've remained loftily unconcerned, haven't you? In other words, just talking to you does no good. And so I'm merely saying that since you'll only learn from actual experience I'm forced to fight it out at that point.'

'Is that it? Now I understand. Is that all you want to say?'

'No, why should it be? Now we're finally getting to the most important part.'

Tsuda watched with some surprise as Kobayashi, at a stroke, brought his glass to his lips and drained it of its beer.

159

Before Kobayashi continued, he first put his glass down, and looked around the room. The woman at one table was wiping her hands with a beautiful handkerchief she had taken out of her pocket after having eaten her portion of fruit, and having dipped her fingers in her finger-bowl. The other woman, about twenty-five or twenty-six, who had taken a seat opposite Kobayashi and had for some time been trying to steal an occasional glance at him and Tsuda, was holding a coffee cup as she watched the smoke from her male partner's cigarette and was talking intently about the theatre. When it became clear to Kobayashi that the meal was progressing in an orderly fashion, and he perceived that both groups of customers, which had arrived before they had, would therefore leave before they would, he spoke out:

'Well, everything's just fine. They're still here.'

Tsuda was again taken aback. Kobayashi was undoubtedly going to say something which he wanted them to hear and which would certainly offend them.

'Come on now, stop it, will you.'

'I haven't said a thing yet, have I?'

'That's why I'm warning you. I'll put up with any attack you want to make against *me*, but be a bit careful about making nasty remarks about complete strangers now that you're in this sort of a place.'

'You certainly are timid, aren't you? You probably mean that I shouldn't confuse this place with some cheap bar, don't you?'

'Well, yes I do.'

'Well, if that's the case, you were wrong in inviting a good-for-nothing like me to such a place.'

'All right, do as you like.'

'You may say that, but inwardly you're quite nervous, aren't you?'

Tsuda said nothing. Kobayashi chuckled.

'I've put one over on you, haven't I? How about it? You've capitulated, haven't you?'

'Well, if you think you've won, go right ahead and think so if you want to.'

'What you really mean is that you'll despise me even more. But I don't give a damn about what you think of me.'

'If you don't, that's all right with me. My, but you're exasperating!'

While Kobayashi stared at Tsuda as if to make out his expression of indignation, he spoke to him:

'Hey, how about it? Have you finally understood? This is what I'd call putting things into practice. And no matter how much leisure you have, no matter how many rich people you know, no matter how high an opinion you have of yourself, if you're defeated in actual practice that's all there is to it. That's why I've been saying this all along: A man who's not trained in the area of actual practice is nothing more than a dunce.'

'All right, have it your way. There's not a man in the world who can stand up to any ruffian or drunken roustabout.'

Instead of saying anything in response immediately, as he might have been expected to, Kobayashi looked around again at the two couples, and then spoke:

'Well, we're finally at point number three: I won't be satisfied unless I say everything I want to say before those women leave. Are you with me? It's a continuation of what I was saying earlier.'

Tsuda was silent and looked to one side. Kobayashi did not pay any attention to this.

'So under point three, or, in other words, if I now enter the main point of the argument, let me say this: You were annoyed with me a while ago, weren't you, when I pointed out those women over there and asked you whether they were geishas? You were annoyed, I suppose, because you considered me a boor who doesn't know the courtesies due to ladies. All right, I *am* a boor. And because I'm a boor I don't know the difference between geishas and ladies. Therefore I asked you, didn't I? I asked you to tell me how in the world geishas and ladies are different.'

As Kobayashi spoke, for the third time he looked over at the couples. The woman who had been wiping her hands with a handkerchief rose as if that were a sort of signal. Her companion called the waiter and paid the bill.

'They've finally got up. If they'd waited a bit longer they'd have come to an interesting section. Too bad for them!'

Kobayashi looked after the couple as they went out.

'Oh my, is the other woman going to get up too? Well, it can't be helped. You'll be the only one left to listen.'

He turned back to look again at Tsuda.

'That's the problem, you see. Since I can't distinguish between French and English cooking, and I'm proud that I confuse slop with some rare delicacy, you won't have anything to do with me. I place no importance on such things and consider it all to be just a problem of filling one's stomach. And yet in essence it's the same as the other, whether it's a matter of my taste being undeveloped or of confusing geishas and ladies.'

Tsuda turned his eyes and looked at Kobayashi with an expression which as much as asked him what conclusion he drew from his remarks.

'Therefore my conclusion must be reduced to one point too. I don't hesitate to assert that just as in the matter of taste, where, while I'm despised by you I'm happier than you, so too in the matter of distinguishing among women, while I'm despised by you I'm in a freer position than you. In other words, I'm saying that the more a man discriminates among women, and says this one's a geisha and that one's a lady, the more trouble he has. See why this is true. Finally neither one will please him. Or else he'll say that it has to be this one or that one. He'll be burdened with a million concerns, won't he?'

'But if he likes to be burdened with those million concerns, there's nothing much you can do about it, is there?'

'All right, you've finally scored a point. Well, I won't argue with you on the matter of food, but when it comes to women then it seems I can't keep quiet. And on *that* point, as concerns an actual problem, I'd now like to argue with you.'

'That's quite enough already.'

'No, it seems that it isn't.'

They looked at each other and smiled wryly.

160

Kobayashi had skilfully ensnared him. Tsuda knew this, but since he had his own plan he deliberately allowed himself to be ensnared. The two finally had to enter the dangerous area.

'Let's take an example,' Kobayashi began by saying. 'You were madly in love with that girl Kiyoko, weren't you? For a time you were saying she absolutely had to be the one, weren't you? And that's not all. You were confident that as far as she was concerned too there was no other man in the entire world. But what actually happened?'

'Just what you see today.'

'You're taking it all very well, aren't you?'

'There's nothing else to be done, is there?'

'Oh, but there is. You could smugly pretend nothing happened. Or else you could even now be doing something actively about it, unknown to me.'

'Don't be ridiculous. You're making a great mistake if you go on spouting such wild nonsense. You'd better be more careful.'

'Well, actually. . . .' Kobayashi began, and then looked at Tsuda as if to ask him if he knew what was going to follow. Tsuda immediately wanted him to continue.

'Well, actually, what is it you're going to say?'

'Well, actually I told your wife everything a few days ago.'

Tsuda's expression changed instantly.

'Everything about *what*?'

Kobayashi was silent for a while as if to savour thoroughly Tsuda's tone and expression. But when he gave his answer his attitude had already changed entirely :

'It isn't true what I said. I lied. There's nothing to worry about.'

'I'm not worrying—even if you did tell her that sort of thing at this late date.'

'You're *not* worrying? Really? Well then, I *was* telling the truth after all. I really was. I *did* tell her everything.'

'You idiot!'

Tsuda's voice was unexpectedly loud. Since the waitress, who was sitting attentively in a chair nearby, raised her head for a moment and looked towards Tsuda, Kobayashi swiftly exploited this.

'Please keep your voice down—you're frightening the ladies. My reputation will be ruined if I go out drinking with a ruffian like you.'

He looked at the waitress and smiled. She too smiled. Tsuda could not be the only one who was angry. Kobayashi again immediately jumped at the opportunity.

'What in the world was the upshot of that whole business? I never asked you the details and you never told them to me. Or is it perhaps that I've forgotten them? Of course it doesn't really matter to me, but was she the one who broke the engagement or was it you?'

'That certainly shouldn't matter now, should it?'

'Naturally it shouldn't matter to *me*, and it actually doesn't. But surely that's not so with you. It must matter a great deal, I should think.'

'Well, of course it does.'

'That's why I've been saying what I have. You have too much leisure. And that leisure makes you too particular. If you want to know what that means, well, it means that as soon as you get one thing you like you immediately want the next thing. And when something that you want escapes you then you're highly indignant and mortified.'

'When did I ever behave that way.'

'You most certainly did! And you're actually still behaving that way. It's all because you're being cursed for having too much leisure. It's something I feel most keenly. It's the law of retribution whereby the poor and lowly get revenge on the rich and noble.'

'If you want to judge others according to standards you yourself have cooked up, go right ahead. Only there's no need for me to defend myself.'

'I'm not cooking up any standards at all. I just want to point out how you actually are. If you don't understand, do you want me to tell you how the facts really are?'

Tsuda, who did not say either that he did or did not want to be told, finally had to endure being told anyway.

'You married O-Nobu of your own free will, didn't you? But now you certainly aren't satisfied with her, are you?'

'Maybe so, but as long as there isn't perfection to be found in this world, that can't be helped, can it?'

'And with that as an excuse, you intend to look around for someone better, I suppose.'

'Stop making such nasty remarks about people! Why do you have to be so rude? You're really just as you say, a complete scoundrel, aren't you? Judging from your vulgar and sarcastic observations and from your impertinent and coarse conduct as well.'

'And that's reason enough for you to despise me, I suppose.'

'Of course.'

'Well, if it comes to that, talking to you is of no use at all. You won't understand unless you actually experience it. I predict that, so let's wait and see. Soon the real battle will begin. And then you'll finally understand that you're not a match for me.'

'That doesn't matter to me. It would be an honour for me to be defeated by someone like you who's lost to all sense of shame.'

'You're quite obstinate, aren't you? But I didn't mean you'd fight with *me*.'

'Well, with whom then?'

'You're already fighting right now with yourself. And in a little while it will actually express itself in action. Your leisure's egging you on to fight a vain, losing battle.'

Tsuda abruptly took his wallet out of his pocket, and, as he and

O-Nobu had agreed, pushed in front of Kobayashi the money he had brought as a farewell present.

'I'm giving it to you now, so take it. Because as I keep talking to you it becomes more and more unpleasant for me to carry out my promise.'

Kobayashi spread out the new ten-yen notes, which were folded in two, and carefully checked the number of them.

'So there are three, eh.'

161

Kobayashi readily shoved the money, just as he had received it, into his suit pocket. And just as his manner was abrupt so too was his way of expressing his thanks impudent.

'Thanks,' he said, using the English expression. 'I may seem to be just borrowing this but you probably intended to give it to me outright, didn't you? Because you've realized from the outset, and with contempt for me, that I have neither the means nor the will to return it.'

Tsuda answered :

'Of course I gave it to you. But now that you've actually received it even you can't help realizing your own contradiction, can you?'

'No, I don't realize anything of the kind. What sort of contradiction? Do you mean it's a contradiction for me to receive money from you?'

'Not exactly.' Tsuda took a condescending attitude. 'But just think about it for a moment. That money was in my wallet up until a minute ago, wasn't it? And in a flash it was transferred to your pocket, wasn't it? If you don't like me to use such fancy language, I'll speak more clearly. Who was it who changed the ownership of that money so suddenly from me to you? Try answering that.'

'It was you. *You* gave it to me.'

'No. No, it wasn't me.'

'What in the world are you talking about? You sound like a Zen priest muttering in his sleep. All right then, who was it?'

'It was no one. It was "leisure"! The leisure you've been attacking all along gave it to you. That's why, by accepting the money without a protest you'll actually be bowing before the very leisure you've been criticizing so severely. And isn't that a contradiction?'

As his eyes twinkled Kobayashi answered with :

'Of course. If that's the way you speak maybe it is. But somehow or other it's funny. Because actually I don't have the slightest feeling of having bowed to that leisure.'

'All right then, give me back the money.'

Tsuda stuck his hand in front of Kobayashi's nose. Kobayashi looked at Tsuda's palm which seemed as soft as a woman's.

'No, I won't. "Leisure" isn't ordering me to give it back to you.'

Tsuda laughed as he withdrew his hand.

'There, I told you so.'

'What do you mean by saying that? It seems you don't understand what I mean when I say that leisure didn't order me to return it to you. You're still just a poor little rich boy.'

As he said this, he turned aside to look towards the door, and then added :

'He should be coming soon now.'

Tsuda, who had been watching Kobayashi's expression carefully, was a trifle startled.

'*Who's* coming?'

'Nobody in particular. Someone who has even less leisure than I.'

Kobayashi studiedly gave a light tap to his pocket into which he had shoved the yen bills.

'The leisure which transmitted this from you to me doesn't say I should give it back to you again. But it does order me to send it in turn to one who has less leisure than I. Leisure's like water, you know. It flows from the high to the low but never goes back from the bottom to the top.'

Tsuda roughly understood what Kobayashi's words themselves meant. But he did not understand their specific application. Consequently he fell into an uneasy state between alertness and bewilderment. Kobayashi then came at him abruptly with the following outburst :

'I bow my head before leisure. I recognize my inconsistency. I assent to your sophistry. It doesn't matter any more what I say. I express my thanks to you. I'm deeply grateful to you.'

He suddenly began to shed large tears. This dramatic transformation made the somewhat startled Tsuda even more uneasy. Since he could not help recalling the scene of that evening a few days earlier at the bar where he had been at his wit's end how to deal with Kobayashi, he frowned while at the same time he noticed that now was a good time to take advantage of him.

'I most certainly am not expecting any gratitude from you. You're the one who's forgetting about the past, you know. While I've been acting just the way I always have in the past, you've been misinterpreting everything. Isn't that why our relations have become more and more strained? For example, even in that matter of your going to my home the other day in my absence and saying something to O-Nobu—'

Tsuda stopped at that point and looked darkly at Kobayashi. But since Kobayashi was looking down just then, Tsuda could not discover any change in his feelings.

'Wouldn't it be better if you stopped your little pranks of sowing dissension between your married friends?'

'I don't remember having said anything about you.'

'But didn't you just say—'

'Oh, that was just a joke. You were making fun of me so I made fun of you in return.'

'Well, I don't know who it was who began making fun of the other, but that's not the problem anyway. At any rate, I think it would be better if you were to tell me the whole truth.'

'But I *am* telling you. I don't know how many times I've repeated that I don't remember having said anything about you. If you try asking your wife, you'll find out.'

'O-Nobu. . . .'

'What did she say?'

'She didn't say anything at all, and that's why I'm upset. If she's dwelling on it secretly without saying anything, then I can't defend myself or explain myself, and I'm the one who's in trouble.'

'I tell you I didn't say a thing! The problem is whether you're going to behave like a good husband from now on or not.'

'I. . . .'

As Tsuda began, someone who had just entered approached and stood near their table.

162

When Tsuda noticed that it was the long-haired youth with whom Kobayashi had earlier been standing and talking on the corner of the avenue, he was again surprised. But mingled with that surprise was the feeling that he had somehow been obscurely waiting for this fellow. Thus Tsuda had the contradictory feelings of being convinced that such a person could not possibly come there and of expecting that, if someone were to come, then it could be no one other than he.

Actually this fellow had seemed very strange to him when Tsuda had seen his figure illuminated by the headlights of the automobile. When Tsuda looked in turn from himself to Kobayashi, and then from Kobayashi to the young fellow, he sensed a tremendous chasm separating them on the various points of class, outlook, profession, and dress. He could not help viewing this newcomer coldly and distantly. Yet the more he did so, the more this fellow's presence was imprinted on his mind.

'So Kobayashi associates with that sort of person, does he.'

As Tsuda made this mental observation, he reflected on his own position wherein he was *not* associating with such a person, and considered how fortunate he was. Thus the attitude he assumed towards the newcomer was an obvious one. He behaved as if he had suddenly been addressed by some very suspicious-looking person.

The youth, who sat down next to Kobayashi while still holding in his hand the soft hat with the turned-up brim which he had taken off, had a strange glint in his eyes and he seemed quite uneasy in Tsuda's presence. It appeared to be a nervous glint arising from a mixture of the resentment, fear, and pride of someone who has grown up wild and is not accustomed to society. Tsuda felt even more uncomfortable. Kobayashi turned to the young man and said:

'Hey, take off your cape.'

The youth got up again without speaking. He swiftly took off his long bell-shaped cape and threw it over the back of his chair.

'He's my friend.'

Kobayashi finally introduced him to Tsuda in this way. Tsuda learned that his name was Hara and that he was an artist.

'How did you make out? Everything went all right, I suppose.'

Kobayashi asked this of Hara. But he did not allow enough time for an answer before he added:

'No, it probably didn't work out. With that sort of fellow there was no hope from the very start. How could someone like that possibly understand your art? But don't worry. Just relax now and eat something.'

Kobayashi quickly turned the point of his knife upward and thumped on the table with the handle of it.

'Hey, bring this fellow something to eat.'

Soon the glass in front of Hara was filled to the brim with beer.

Tsuda, who was silently observing this scene, finally realized that the business he had had there was now concluded. He thought it would be most unfortunate for him if he allowed this kind of encounter to drag on, and he tried to find the right moment to make his withdrawal. But Kobayashi suddenly turned to him:

'Hara paints some fine pictures, you know. Why don't you buy one? The poor fellow's short of money right now.'

'Is that so?'

'How about it? Suppose he went to your house to show you some pictures this coming Sunday or thereabouts.'

Tsuda was amazed by Kobayashi's effrontery.

'I don't understand a thing about painting.'

'Oh, that's impossible. Isn't it, Hara? At any rate, take some and go show them to him.'

'Yes of course, if it wouldn't be an imposition.'

The imposition on Tsuda was obvious.

'Please don't. I'm a man who has no taste whatsoever when it comes to painting or sculpture.'

Hara looked offended. Kobayashi quickly took Tsuda up on his statement :

'How can you say such a thing ! In fact very few men in the world have as highly developed a sense of art appreciation as you have.'

Tsuda could not but give a sarcastic laugh.

'There you go again, spouting nonsense. Stop making a fool of me, will you.'

'No, it's the truth, I tell you. How could you think I'm making a fool of you ! A person like you with such well-developed taste in women can't possibly be insensitive to art. Isn't that so, Hara? When a man likes women he's bound to like art too. No matter how much you try to hide it, it won't do.'

Tsuda could endure the situation no longer.

'It seems this discussion could go on indefinitely, so I'll take my leave now, if you don't mind. Oh waitress, check please."

Just as the waitress was about to get up and come to their table Kobayashi shouted to stop her, and then turned to Tsuda again.

'He's just finished painting a fine one now. He's stopped here on his way back from a prospective buyer's place where he went to consult about the price. It's a splendid opportunity for you, don't you think? Buy it by all means. I told him he shouldn't sell it to some boor who's trying to take advantage of an artist and is forever haggling with him about the price. To tell the truth, I promised him that instead I'd certainly recommend a buyer to him and that therefore he should stop by here on his way back. That's why I'm asking you to buy one from him. It's a simple thing for you.'

'What the devil's the matter with you ! Making such a promise about another person when he hasn't even seen the painting !'

'Oh we'll show you the painting. Didn't you bring it back with you today, Hara?'

'He asked me to wait a little longer so I left it with him.'

'What a fool you were ! He'll end up swindling you out of it completely.'

Upon hearing this exchange, Tsuda heaved a sigh of relief.

163

The two of them, ignoring Tsuda, then carried on a lively conversation about painting. Apart from such strange nouns as Cubism and Futurism which he caught from time to time, he also heard several other Western terms which seemed completely unfamiliar to him. Since he had no interest in such talk at all, he excluded himself from it without having to be excluded by them. But in addition to his excessive boredom at their conversation there was also one positive factor which annoyed him. From the beginning he had been treating the two of them, particularly Kobayashi, as mere dilettantes who delighted in making a display of their knowledge of new art forms. To this initial prejudice he now added the view that their attitude was one of cleverly pretending to be connoisseurs. When, in this connection, it began to seem to him almost as if their goal lay in making him envious of their knowledge, he tried to leave after having been forced to sit down for a while. But again Kobayashi prevented him.

'We'll be finished in a second. I'll go with you. Just wait a bit.'

'No, it's getting rather late. . . .'

'Why do you have to insult people like that! Or maybe you're implying that it impairs a gentleman's dignity to wait until Hara here has finished eating.'

Hara placed the chopped salad on the ham, and halted his hand which had speared it with a fork.

'Oh please, don't let me bother you.'

When Tsuda, bowing slightly in return, again tried to get up, Kobayashi spoke, almost as if in a monologue :

'What the hell do you think this meeting is supposed to be? You say it's a farewell party and you invite a person to come, and then you want to leave the main guest and go home first. It's disgusting to see someone as insulting as you.'

'I didn't intend to insult anyone.'

'If not, then stay awhile.'

'I have something I have to do.'

'So do I.'

'If it's about the painting, no thank you.'

'I'm not going to force you to buy a picture. Don't be such a tight-wad !'

'Well then, please finish quickly whatever business it is.'

'Not if you stay standing. You have to sit down like a gentleman.'

Tsuda, forced to sit down again, took a cigarette out of his pocket, and lit it. As he noticed that the ashtray was already full of the butts of the Shikishima cigarettes, it occurred to him that nothing could be more appropriate as a memento of the evening. Then, when he further realized that the one cigarette he was about to smoke would also, within about three minutes, be transformed into mere ash, smoke, and butt, leaving on the ashtray its useless coldness, he could not help feeling annoyed.

'Well, what is it then? . . . this business of yours. It couldn't be another request for money, could it?'

'No, and haven't I been saying you shouldn't be so concerned about parting with some of your precious money?'

Kobayashi grasped the right front part of his jacket with his right hand and thrust his left hand into the inside pocket. He searched for a while inside his jacket as if he were groping for something in the dark, and during the entire time he kept his eyes fixed on Tsuda. Suddenly Tsuda visualized an extraordinary scene, as a strange fantasy swept over his mind as lightly as the smoke from the cigarette he was then smoking.

'This fellow just might pull a pistol out of his pocket and poke it at my nose.'

As this dramatic scene gently stirred his imagination, his nerve ends too were stirred as is a slender branch when the wind plays with it. At the same time his intellect, which viewed this fantasy he himself had arbitrarily created as though it concerned someone else, and which mocked its absurdity, already was operating.

'What the devil are you looking for?'

'All sorts of things are in here. If I don't feel for it carefully with my fingertips I won't be able to draw it out to show it to you.'

'Yes, it would be awkward if you mistakenly pull out the yen notes you shoved in there earlier.'

'Don't worry about the money. It's quite different from other pieces of paper. I'll soon find what I'm looking for by feeling for it in this way. But it's jumping around in my pocket.'

While Kobayashi answered obstinately, he purposely withdrew an empty hand.

'My, it isn't there! That's strange.'

He then plunged his right hand into his left breast pocket. But he withdrew only a slightly soiled and wrinkled handkerchief.

'Are you thinking maybe of performing sleight of hand with that?'

Kobayashi paid no attention to what Tsuda said. With a serious expression he got up, and after striking both his hips with his hands simultaneously, he announced abruptly:

'Yes, it was *here*.'

What he pulled out of one of his trouser pockets was a letter.

'Actually I want you to read this. And it has to be tonight since I won't be seeing you for quite a while. Please look it over while Hara and I are talking. That's a simple request, isn't it? It's a bit long, though.'

Tsuda's hand which took the letter from him moved almost mechanically.

164

Of course the letter, which had been dashed off in pen on copy paper, was more than twice as long as an average one. Furthermore, although it was clearly addressed to Kobayashi, the sender was someone Tsuda had neither seen nor heard of in his entire life. After Tsuda had glanced at the front and back of the envelope he wondered what possible connection the letter could have with him. Yet a kind of curiosity arose alongside his cold indifference and soon forced his hand to withdraw the letter from the envelope. He looked down at the enclosed lined sheets, with ten twenty-character lines per sheet, and read the letter at one stroke.

I'm forced to regret ever having come to this place. You must surely think I'm capricious. But that difference comes from our difference in character and nothing can be done about it. Please don't heave a sigh and say, 'Oh, not again!' but instead listen to my complaints. 'Please come and stay with us as a caretaker until matters are settled with the bank because in a household of women it's unsafe at night. If you want to write stories you're free to do so. If you want to go to the library, why, take your lunch and go. It's all right too if you go and learn painting in the afternoon. Soon I'll be moving the bank to Tokyo so I'll send you to the Foreign Languages School. Don't worry about the handling of your house. I'll send you money for the move.' I was tempted by these favourable conditions. Of course this doesn't mean I counted on all of them being fulfilled, but I certainly believed some of them would be. Yet when I actually arrived I found that not one of the things he said was true. Absolutely everything was a bold-faced lie. My uncle is in Tokyo much of the time and I'm made to run errands from morning to night just like a house-boy. In fact he calls me his house-boy—and in front of guests, in front of me, too. That's why everything's become my chore, from going to get a bottle of saké to dusting and cleaning the veranda. I haven't yet received one sen from him. When I broke the one-yen pair of clogs I was wearing, he bought a twelve-sen pair and made me wear them. He told us he'd give us money on the following day and made my family move to my sister's place, but after they'd moved he never breathed a word about money so I didn't even have a home to return to.

My uncle's work consists simply of speculation. He has absolutely no money. And he and his wife are extremely cold and extremely stingy people. That's why, after I got here, I couldn't stand being so hungry, and every three days or so I'd go back to my sister's house and have her feed me. There were even times when the rice-bucket was empty and I'd have to make do with baked sweet potatoes or plain white potatoes. Of course this applies only to me. My aunt is a most unpleasant woman. She's calculating in everything, is concerned only with appearances, and is forever finding fault with me and needling me. Even though my uncle doesn't have any money he's always drinking saké. And if he goes to the country he struts around saying he's a lord or some such thing. Yet if you try looking behind this pose everything's in shocking contrast. He's even done lots of things he should be taken to court for. Before coming here I didn't have the money for my train fare, so I had to go running off to a pawn-shop and to my sister's place to raise the money, but my uncle's paid no attention to this and acts as if the money he spends for my food balances this out.

My aunt from the beginning has even seemed to think I should do some writing to pay for my board, and when I have a pen in my hand she makes insinuating remarks by asking me what's happened to the things I write. She also makes cryptic remarks as she shoves the Clerks Wanted advertisements from the Help Wanted columns of the newspapers at me.

When I see this sort of thing keeps going on I wonder why in the world I ever came here. And it makes me think of strange things. The weird life in this fantastic place gives me the feeling of being in a frightful nightmare from morning to night and is bringing a curse down on my head. I realize that if I tell all this to someone he can't possibly understand, and I become even more miserable since I'm forced to think I'm the only one in the world who's surrounded by demons. And sometimes it seems as if I'm going out of my mind. In fact I begin to wonder whether I haven't already gone crazy, and it's unbearably frightening. I seem to be suffering in some sort of underground prison, and I feel not only as if there's no sunlight but as if I have no hands or feet. Because even if I raise my hands or move my feet it's pitch-black everywhere. No matter how much I cry out, the cold, thick walls block out my voice and prevent it from reaching the world. I'm the only person in the world now. I have no friends. Even if I do, it's the same as if I don't. I can hardly expect someone to enter into my ghost-like mental state. I've written this letter out of my deep suffering, not to ask for help. I know your circumstances. I don't have the slightest intention of receiving material assistance, or anything of the kind, from you. I'll be satisfied with simply communicating to you a portion of my pain and arousing in you even a little bit of sympathy. Because in that way I can obtain clear proof that I still exist as a member of society. I wonder if a ray of light from this demon-besieged place can reach the broad human world outside. I even doubt that now. I'll resolve that doubt according to whether an answer comes from you or not.

The letter ended at this point.

165

The ash from the cigarette that Tsuda had lit and begun to smoke earlier had already attained the length of almost one inch before he was aware of it and it fell upon the lined page. His sight was stimulated by this ash as it scattered over the dark blue grid* on the page, and he suddenly realized that until then he had not moved his hand holding the cigarette. Or rather, his mouth and his hand had for a time forgotten the existence of the cigarette. In addition, he had to recognize an interval of absent-mindedness between the two actions, since his finishing reading the letter and the dropping of the cigarette ash were not simultaneous.

Why had such an interval arisen? Basically speaking, nothing could be more unrelated to him than this letter. First of all, he did not know who had written it. Secondly, he had no idea of the relationship between the writer and Kobayashi. As for the things set forth in the letter, they were so far removed from his social position and circumstances as to seem to him to belong to another world.

But this did not mean that his impressions ended at that point. For he was actually quite startled by the letter. Until then he had simply looked directly ahead of him and had been convinced that the world lay within the range of his glance, but now he had suddenly been made to look around him. And he was taken aback to discover an existence utterly different from his own. Then, while he was scrutinizing this phantom-like figure such as he had never encountered before, he began to feel that this person too was after all a human being. The fact that an experience which is extremely far removed from one's own may, paradoxically, be very close became apparent to him.

He stopped at that point, and hesitated. He did not move a step further. In his own way he understood the unpleasant letter.

When Tsuda shook the cigarette ash from the letter paper, Kobayashi, who had been saying something to Hara, turned to him immediately. Tsuda had heard only a few phrases, which seemed to conclude the matter.

'That's all right. Things will work out somehow or other. Don't worry about it,' Kobayashi had assured Hara.

Tsuda, without a word, then held out the letter to Kobayashi, who, before taking it, asked him :

* Japanese copy paper has a grid printed on it to provide a square for each character.

'Did you read it?'

'Yes.'

'What did you think of it?'

He did not answer. But he felt the need of at least finding out Kobayashi's purpose in giving him the letter.

'Why in the world did you make me read it?'

Kobayashi countered with another question :

'Why in the world do you think I made you read it?'

'He's no one I know, is he? . . . the fellow who wrote the letter.'

'Of course not.'

'Setting aside that fact, does this have any connection with me?'

'Do you mean the man or the letter?'

'It doesn't matter which.'

'What do you think?'

Tsuda hesitated. Actually his hesitation was proof that he had understood the significance of the letter. Or, more accurately, the realization that he had been able to understand the letter in his own way blunted his response. After a slight pause he said :

'In your sense of the word, it's utterly unrelated to me.'

'What do you mean by my sense of the word?'

'Don't you know?'

'No. Tell me.'

'That's all right. Forget about it.'

Tsuda wondered whether Kobayashi had foisted the letter on him for the same reason that he had tried to make him buy the picture. For Kobayashi to force him to make material sacrifices and then to put him in the position where he could say to him, 'See, you've finally capitulated, haven't you?' would be an unendurable insult. His pride in not wanting to fall in with this scheme of Kobayashi's no matter how many poor wretches he was threatened with, naturally came into play.

'Wouldn't it be better if you came right out and explained to me like a man what you mean by all this?'

Kobayashi at first merely echoed Tsuda with 'Like a man?' but then he added :

'All right, I'll explain everything to you. This fellow, this letter, and the contents of the letter as well, are all unrelated to you. But that's only from a worldly point of view, you understand. Since you shouldn't misunderstand what I mean when I say "a worldly point of view", I'll explain that to you too. With regard to the contents of this letter, you don't have any so-called social responsibility.'

'That's perfectly obvious, isn't it?'

'That's why I too say that from a worldly point of view they're unrelated to you. But what happens if we enlarge your moral perspective somewhat?'

'No matter how much you enlarge it I'll never feel it's my duty to give any money.'

'Maybe so, if that's the way you look at it. But at least you feel a bit of sympathy, don't you?'

'Naturally I do.'

'That's enough, as far as I'm concerned. If you feel sympathy, that means in effect you want to give him money. At the same time since you actually don't want to give any money you're feeling the uneasiness that comes from a conflict of conscience. My goal has been more than attained at that point.'

After saying this, Kobayashi shoved the letter back in his pocket, and, withdrawing from the same place the three bills he had received earlier, lined them up on the table.

'Go ahead and take a few. Take as many as you need.'

He looked at Hara as he said this.

166

Tsuda was wholly unprepared for Kobayashi's action. Suddenly taken aback and made to feel the full force of Kobayashi's sarcasm, he turned sharply towards him. What can only be described as a swift current of hatred passed through his body in an instant.

At the same time a suspicion flashed in his clever mind :

'I wonder if these two haven't been plotting to make a fool of me all the while.'

Various scenes whirled through his brain in connection with this idea, with the rapidity of set pieces of fireworks going off : the figures of Kobayashi and Hara standing and talking on a corner of the avenue, Kobayashi's behaviour after arriving at the restaurant, the appearance of Hara, who arrived halfway through their meal, and the exchange of conversation among the three of them. Tsuda could not determine which was cause and which was effect. But he could not help thinking as he looked at the three new ten-yen bills lined up carefully on the white tablecloth :

'So this is the grand finale of the farce these scoundrels have cooked up! The fools! I'm certainly not going to fall in with their scheme!'

For the sake of his wounded pride as well, he decided he would leave the two of them after giving a sharp twist to this outrageous ending. But when it came to the question of how, at that late hour, to reverse skilfully this predicament into which he had finally been driven, he felt himself completely powerless, having made no preparations whatever for such an eventuality.

Behind the external calm which he maintained rather easily, his unavailing intelligence operated furiously. But since this intellectual activity led to nothing and provided him with no plan of action, his mental state afterwards was simply one of needless agitation. Unfortunately he even sensed that his agitation was swiftly being transformed into panic.

At this critical moment he encountered another surprising phenomenon : the effect on the young artist of the ten-yen notes which Kobayashi had lined up. Hara had a strange glint in his eyes as he stared at the notes. In this glint were amazement and pleasure. There was also a kind of hunger as well as the force of the desire to pounce upon them. And this amazement, pleasure, hunger, and desire were all the expression of truth itself. No one could possibly interpret them as sham, artifice, or a conspiratorial trick. At least Tsuda could only think they were genuine.

Moreover something soon happened which amply justified this judgment. Hara did not put forth his hand to the notes he desired so eagerly. However, neither did he have the courage to reject decisively Kobayashi's kindness. The quality of the pain he was enduring in restraining his hand from reaching for the notes could be clearly read in his expression. If this pale youth finally did not reach for them, this would mean that Kobayashi's carefully prepared farce would be half ruined. And if Kobayashi returned to his pocket the notes he had withdrawn for a while, without handing over to Hara even a part of them, as he had announced he would do, then the effect would be even more that of a comedy. Since, no matter what happened, the situation appeared to be developing favourably towards repairing his dignity, and he clung to a shred of hope on this account, Tsuda decided to remain silent a bit longer and watch how things went.

Shortly there took place an exchange between Kobayashi and Hara :

'Why don't you take some, Hara?'

'Well, I feel too sorry for you.'

'But I'm the one who feels sorry for *you*.'

'Yes, I understand. Thank you very much.'

'That fellow sitting in front of you feels sorry for me in turn.'

'I see.'

Hara looked at Tsuda with an utterly uncomprehending expression. Kobayashi quickly explained.

'All three of these notes I've just received from him. They're fresh from his pocket.'

'Well then, all the more reason. . . .'

'No, that's not all the more reason to refuse. In fact, that's all the more reason to accept. That's why I can give them to you so easily.

In fact since I can give them to you so easily you can accept them easily too.'

'Is that a special kind of logic, I wonder?'

'Of course it is. If this were money I'd earned by staying up all night doing some hack journalism at thirty-five sen a page, even I couldn't part with it, could I? It wouldn't be fair to the sweat that would have poured from my brow. But this way it's nothing at all for me to give it to you. The money's simply alms which leisure has scattered about in space. The more people who pick up its charity, the happier leisure is. Isn't that right, Tsuda?'

It was as if Tsuda, who had already passed through the difficult part, had been consulted at a rather easy point. His generous consent would be sufficient to provide at least a formally correct conclusion to the unharmonious gathering of the three of them there that evening. He quickly seized the opportunity to prevent his departure from seeming undignified.

'Why yes, that would be fine.'

Kobayashi, after repeated argument, finally handed over one of the notes to Hara. As he replaced the remaining two in his pocket, he spoke to Tsuda.

'This way leisure rather strangely has flowed from the bottom upwards. But from here it won't go back up any farther. So I have to say thanks to you, after all!'

The three of them came out of the restaurant to the edge of the moat, and looked up at the vast expanse of the bright starry sky as they waited for the streetcar.

167

Shortly thereafter the three went their separate ways.

'Well, I'll say goodbye here. I won't go to see you off at the station.'

'You won't? It seems to me it would be proper if you did. After all, your old friend's going off to Korea, you know.'

'Whether it's to Korea or Formosa, I still can't make it.'

'You certainly are one for making cold and unfriendly remarks. Well, if that's the case, *I'll* call on *you* once again to say goodbye before leaving. All right?'

'No, I've had enough. You don't have to come.'

'No, I *will* come. If I don't, I won't feel right somehow.'

'Do as you like. But I won't be there, even if you do. I'm starting on a trip tomorrow.'

'A trip? Where to?'

'I need to rest a bit after my operation.'

'A change of air? My, how elegant!'

'As far as I'm concerned, that's also a gift of leisure. Unlike you, I have to be very grateful to it.'

'You feel you have to show that my advice is utterly meaningless, don't you?'

'To tell the truth, I suppose that's about it.'

'That's fine. Let's see who wins. It will probably be far more effective and appropriate for you to be disciplined by events themselves than to be enlightened by me.'

This was the conversation which took place between them as they parted. However, it was simply the expression of the ill-will which was a carry-over from the earlier part of the evening and of the ill-will which Tsuda had harboured towards Kobayashi from the beginning of that evening's events. For Tsuda, who felt that thereby he had satisfied his grudge somewhat, there was no time to think about the parting words of Kobayashi. Without regard to the merits of the case, Tsuda, for his own self-respect, had to reject the ideas and arguments of a person such as Kobayashi. Once he was by himself on the streetcar, he soon began to imagine what it would be like at the hot spring resort.

The following morning a strong wind was blowing, carrying stray lines of rain to the ground diagonally.

'How annoying!'

Having arisen on schedule, he frowned as he looked out from the veranda. There were clouds in the sky, moving ceaselessly like a wind that could be seen.

'Maybe it will clear by about noon.'

O-Nobu spoke as if to indicate that she approved of his carrying out his plan.

'After all, if you postpone your trip one day that will just mean one day lost. I think it's best if you go right away and return as soon as possible.'

'That's what I intend to do.'

The couple's agreement, which had not been disturbed by the cold rain, was first ruffled somewhat at the moment of departure. O-Nobu took out her own clothing from the bureau drawer and placed it on the tan paper alongside Tsuda's suit. Tsuda noticed this.

'You don't have to go to the station too.'

'Why can't I?'

'For no particular reason, but with this rain it would be rather inconvenient, wouldn't it?'

'Not in the least.'

Her answer was so direct he could not help laughing.

'I'm not asking you not to come because it would be annoying to *me*, but because I'd feel sorry for *you*. To take the trouble of seeing me off to a place that it doesn't even take one day to go to is a bit ridiculous, isn't it? I even told Kobayashi last night I wouldn't go to see him off even though he's leaving for Korea.'

'Really? But if I stay at home I don't have anything to do anyway.'

'Just take it easy. Do anything you want.'

O-Nobu finally laughed mirthlessly and gave up the argument so that Tsuda was able to leave the house alone in a rickshaw.

As he stood in the dismal station, which presented a contrast to the surrounding confusion, looking vaguely at the second-class ticket he had just bought, a servant boy suddenly came up to him and addressed him as if he were an old acquaintance.

'It's bad weather, isn't it?'

It was the Yoshikawas' houseboy, whom he had met for the first time a few days earlier. In contrast to the boy's stand-offish attitude at the Yoshikawa entrance upon answering the door, Tsuda felt he was now quite polite, judging from the way he took off his cap to him. But Tsuda still did not understand what all of this meant.

'Is someone from the Yoshikawas' going somewhere?'

'No, I've just come to say goodbye.'

'But to whom?'

The boy looked perplexed.

'Actually Mrs Yoshikawa was a bit busy today and so she told me to bring this to you in her place.'

The boy showed him the basket of fruit he held in his hand.

'Oh, thank you very much.'

Tsuda was about to take the basket immediately, but the boy did not hand it over.

'No, I'll take it on the train for you.'

As the train left, Tsuda said, 'Regards to Mr and Mrs Yoshikawa,' to the boy, who bowed politely without saying anything in return. As he leisurely took his seat in a corner of a carriage that was relatively uncrowded, Tsuda thought: 'I'm glad O-Nobu didn't come to see me off, after all.'

168

As Tsuda took out from his overcoat pocket the newspaper which O-Nobu had thoughtfully put there for him, and was reading it more attentively than usual, the look of the sky outside the window was gradually worsening. The lines of rain, which until a short while before had been sparse, suddenly increased in number and at once filled the sky as far as the eye could see. As Tsuda looked from the train window, which was quite convenient for surveying the scene, he felt the weather to be all the more menacing.

Above the rain were thick clouds. There were clouds on both sides of the rain too which were visible as long as the view was not obstructed. When the broad area where rain and clouds continued without interval impinged on Tsuda's sight, he could not help comparing the wild scene outside the window with the cheerfulness of the comfortably appointed interior of the train. Tsuda, who considered it the special privilege of civilized man to be able to place himself in a comfortable position, hunched his shoulders as he imagined how it would feel to have to go outside and fight his way through that rainstorm. At the same time a man of about forty, who was looking dully at the lines of rain which formed as the raindrops struck the window glass and trickled down its surface, leaned forward a bit and began speaking to his companion, who was sitting cross-legged opposite him. Since the sound of the rain and that of the train coincided, however, he was not understood the first time he spoke.

'It's begun to rain fiercely, hasn't it? If it keeps up, I'm afraid the roadbed of that rickety train will be washed out again.'

He was forced to speak in a loud voice so that Tsuda also heard him.

'There's no need to worry. Just because we always call it "that rickety train" that doesn't mean it's going to break down every time. If it did, that would be terrible for the passengers.'

This was his companion's answer. The latter was an old man of about sixty, wearing a woollen cloth, Japanese-style overcoat. On his head he had a strange type of brimless hat of the kind that even if one searched a foreign goods store, one would not find. In fact unless one went to a specialty shop which carefully displayed such things as tobacco pouches, pieces of taffeta, and antique print cotton, and especially ordered it, one would certainly not be able to wear it. The owner of this strange hat gave ample proof, from his speech, that he was born in Tokyo. While Tsuda was surprised at this affable old man's vitality, so out of keeping with his dress, he was also surprised at his manner of speaking, which almost bordered on the vulgar.

The term 'rickety train', which had been casually used by the two men in their exchange, was quite significant to Tsuda. For he was one of the travellers who was to be shaken up by that train for several hours that afternoon. Since he thought the two men might be travelling in the same direction as he, he suddenly became most attentive to their conversation. He could hear everything they said as they were forced to endure awkward postures and to speak in exceptionally loud voices because they could not change their seats.

'I never thought we'd have *this* kind of weather, did you? If I'd known, it would have been better to postpone things for a day.'

When the younger, somewhat placid man, wearing the camel's hair coat and soft felt hat, spoke in this way, the old man quickly responded :

'Why, it's just a little rain. What difference does it make if you get a bit wet !'

'But it's annoying with the luggage. I'm somewhat concerned when I think it's going to be simply exposed to the rain on that rickety old train.'

'If that's the case, why don't *we* sit in the exposed section and get wet and have only the luggage put in the car.'

The two men gave a loud laugh. Then the old man spoke again :

'Of course there was all that confusion the time before. You have a right to be concerned because then the boiler developed a leak half-way and the train came to a halt. What a mess that was !'

'How did you finally get where you were going?'

'Why, the train coming from the opposite direction met us in the mountains and we had its locomotive pull us. Don't you remember my telling you?'

'Of course. But what happened to the train whose locomotive you took?'

'That's right. If we took its locomotive then it was the one in a fix.'

'That's why I'm asking you. What happened to the train left behind? It would hardly have come to the rescue and then left itself stranded, would it?'

'Now that I think about it, you're quite right, but at the time we were hardly worrying about the other train. After all, it was getting towards evening, the cold was cutting through us, and we were all shivering.'

Tsuda's conjecture gradually became certain. He even felt sure that the two were going to one of the three hot springs along the route traversed by that 'rickety train'. Nevertheless, if that train, which he would soon have to ride on for two or three hours, was as ramshackle as they said it was, he had no assurance that he would not meet with considerable unpleasantness in all that rain. But the men's speech contained that exaggeration so characteristic of Tokyo people. Tsuda, who had been about to ask them whether that train were really as unreliable as they indicated, realized this fact, and, laughing inwardly, spared himself the trouble of asking that question. Then, as he mentally linked Kiyoko with the rickety train, and considered that his destination was one to which even a woman alone could go easily and safely, he gave up listening to the light conversation which the men were making half in jest.

169

When, slightly before the train arrived at its destination, the weather, which had been troubling the three men, gradually began to improve, Tsuda looked at the sky, on the verge of clearing after the rain, and saw clouds busily moving about. They moved swiftly in the opposite direction from that in which the train was moving, and piled up one after the other, as if intent on chasing the ones in front of them. Shortly, in the midst of this activity a fairly bright patch emerged. Places that seemed clearer than the rest of the sky gradually increased in number. One place in particular gave indication that it would soon be blown away by the wind and allow the bright blue sky to peep through.

When Tsuda, grateful for the weather, which had been kinder to him than he had expected, descended from the train and immediately transferred to the electric car, he saw once again the two men he had met before. Realizing that they were, after all, going in the same direction as he and using the same means of transportation, as he had thought, he paid special attention to their hand luggage. But nowhere did he see anything bulky enough to cause them to worry that it would be placed outside the car to be exposed to the elements. Moreover the old man appeared even to have forgotten already what he had said earlier.

'This is fine. We're really lucky! That's why I say that a person should always set out on a trip on the day he's planned to. Just suppose we'd been wasting time in Tokyo now. We'd only be regretting it and saying, "Confound it! If we'd known it was going to turn out this way it would have been better to have decided to leave this morning." Don't you agree?'

'Yes, I do. But I wonder if the weather's this fine in Tokyo too.'

'Of course we can't possibly know unless we go there and see. Or else find out by phoning. But usually the weather's the same. After all, the sky's the same all over Japan.'

Tsuda was rather amused by this. Then the old man suddenly began speaking to him.

'You're going to a hot spring too, I suppose. I thought you probably were all along.'

'Why is that?'

'Why, because you can tell right away just by looking at someone that he's taking a trip to that kind of place. Isn't that so?'

As he said this, he turned to look at his companion, who was near him. The man with the felt hat was forced to agree with him.

When Tsuda, unable to withhold a wry smile at this clairvoyant, tried to break off the conversation at that point, the affable old fellow would not let him go.

'But travel's become quite convenient these days, hasn't it? No matter where you want to go the only thing you have to move is yourself. It's really wonderful. Particularly for impulsive fellows like us, it's just the thing. This time we didn't bring any luggage with us at all. Apart from this holdall of mine and that fellow's suitcase, the only thing left is our skins. Isn't that so, old codger?'

The man who, despite the fact that he was younger, had been addressed as 'old codger' merely assented with a grunt. If they could not bring inside the car even that small amount of hand luggage, then their so-called 'rickety train' had to be either extremely cramped or else so flimsy as to defy all common sense. Tsuda was about to check on this matter but quickly realized that, even if he did, there was nothing he could do about it, and so remained silent.

When he got off the electric car he lost sight of the two men. While looking at some elaborately designed photographic plates and lithographs advertising the hot spring resorts, he took his lunch at a tea-shop in front of the station. Since he was eating more than an hour later than usual, he practically devoured his food. Even so the 'rickety train' was leaving at any moment, so that as soon as he threw down his chopsticks he had to board it.

The station which was the starting-point for the train was also directly in front of the tea-shop where he had had lunch. While keeping his eye on the train, which was smaller than the electric car, he received the change from his lunch bill from the serving-girl, and quickly went out the front way. There was hardly any distance between the place where he had his ticket punched and the platform. With five or six steps he quickly reached the short stairs leading into the train. In the railway car he met the same two travelling companions.

'Hello there. Please sit over here.'

The old man moved over a bit and made a place for Tsuda, spreading his own wrapper which he had slung over his arm.

'It's good that it's empty today.'

After telling Tsuda, in his usual sprightly manner, how the hot spring visitors thronged that route twice a year, first to flee the cold and then to flee the heat, from the end of the year to the beginning of January and during the two months of July and August, he turned to his companion.

'It's really a crime to bring along women at a time like that. First of all they can't all get on because they have such big buttocks. Then they get train-sick right away and it's a mess. When we're all packed in like sardines they're forever getting nauseous and vomiting. I tell you it's really dreadful.'

He spoke as if completely oblivious of the existence of the young woman seated next to him.

170

Even inside the 'rickety train' Tsuda's serenity was somewhat disturbed by this aged optimist. At times when in the midst of scenes of the inn, the mountains, and the mountain streams, which Tsuda drew in his imagination, images of such things as his reception upon his arrival at his destination, and the attitude he should assume in conformity to it, were ceaselessly revolving, the old man would suddenly startle him out of his reveries.

'They're still making do with a temporary bridge. How easy-going they are! Just look at how those workers are working!'

After the old man had deplored the fact that the regular bridge had been washed away by the flood of the previous year and had not yet been replaced, as if this were all due to the railway company's negligence, he pointed to a newly built house near where the river emptied into the sea, and tried to gain Tsuda's attention again.

'That house too was washed away by the waves last year. But the owners rebuilt it right away, so they're doing quite a bit better than this ramshackle railway.'

'They probably rebuilt it so as not to lose any visitors this summer.'

'If you spend a summer here it will certainly have an effect on you, you know. After all, if you don't have any desires, no work will get done quickly. This train's that way. Since it manages to get along with a temporary bridge, the railway company forever shirks its duty and doesn't rebuild it.'

While Tsuda was forced to assent readily to the old man's point of view, at breaks in the conversation he would pretend to be dozing, and think about things that pertained only to himself.

His mind was a jumble of disorganized, fragmentary images. Among them was O-Nobu's expression as he had seen it that morning. The figure of the Yoshikawas' houseboy who had come to the station to see him off also came to his mind. There appeared as well the basket of fruit which the boy had brought inside the car. He also thought he might open the basket and share Mrs Yoshikawa's gift with his two companions, but he clearly foresaw the trouble and annoyance it would cause as they accepted his kindness and made the inevitable exaggerated expressions of thanks. Then both the old man and the other with the felt hat suddenly vanished from his thoughts, and in their place the silhouette of the stout Mrs Yoshikawa crossed the threshold of his mind and entered directly into his day-dreaming. Then, by mental association he quickly jumped to Kiyoko, who was for him the focal point of the hot spring resort at which he would soon arrive. Thus his mind swayed back and forth together with the motion of the train.

No sooner had this vehicle, which was not worthy of being called a train, rattled its way precariously into the steep mountains bordering directly on the sea than it began threading its way through them, going uphill and downhill any number of times. Most of those mountains were dotted all over with tangerine trees, planted very close together, and gave the effect of a warm southern autumn under a beautiful sky.

'They look delicious, don't they?'

'What do you mean? They're certainly not. They're far better when you look at them from here.'

As the train was twisting its way up a relatively steep hill it suddenly came to a halt. There was nothing resembling a station there, only a few miscellaneous trees tinged by the frost.

'What happened?'

As the old man asked this and stuck his head out of the window, the conductor and the engineer jumped off the train and said something to each other intently.

'The train's derailed.'

When he heard this, the old man quickly looked at Tsuda and the man with the felt hat who was in front of him.

'Didn't I tell you? I was sure something was wrong.'

Suddenly talking as if he had been a prophet, he began jumping about, almost as if to say that the time had finally come for him to give forth with his windy eloquence.

'Well, when I left home I said my final farewells so I've been prepared for the worst all along. But now that it's happened I certainly don't want to have to take my last stand at this sort of place. On the other hand, no matter how long we wait here they'll surely never get the train back on the track for us. What's more, the days are short now, and besides we're all rather short-tempered, so we just can't sit idly by. What do you say? Why don't we all get off and give her a push?'

After the old man spoke this way, he was the very first to jump off the train nimbly. The rest, forcing a smile, stood up and prepared to get off. Since Tsuda could hardly be the only one remaining seated in the train, he got off together with everybody else. Then, with the woman standing vacantly behind them on the yellowish grass, they pushed the train vigorously.

'It's no use. It's gone too far.'

They pulled the train back, then pushed it forward again. By doing this several times, they finally got it back on the track.

'We're late again, aren't we, old codger?'

'We surely are.'

'Thanks to this "rickety train" of course. But if this hadn't happened I'd have been terribly sleepy.'

'With all this bother there was hardly any point in our taking this trip to relax.'

'That's certainly true.'

Tsuda, concerned about the late hour, parted from the sprightly old man at the appointed station, and went out into the evening air alone.

171

The town, sketched dully in tones which could not be defined either as haze or simply the cloak of night, appeared to be the scene of some desolate dream. When Tsuda compared the feeble light from the electric lights flickering on all sides of him, with the vast expanse of darkness extending beyond where that light reached, he certainly had the feeling of being in a dream.

'I'm now about to have the next episode of this dreamlike state. Before I left Tokyo, or, strictly speaking, before I was urged to come here by Mrs Yoshikawa—no, if I go back further, even before I married O-Nobu—but even that's not going back far enough, actually from the moment Kiyoko turned her back on me, I was already cursed by this feeling of being in a dream. And now I'm right in the midst of it. I wonder if, as soon as I reach the inn, I'll wake up all of a sudden from all of this, which, as I look back on it, is a carry-over from what's happened before. That's what Mrs Yoshikawa thinks. So I have to say that by falling in with her idea it's also become my idea as I try to put it into practice. But I wonder if she's right, after all. I wonder if I'll really be able to wake up from this dream entirely, after all. I wonder if I really have that much faith and if I'm really standing here in the middle of this blurred and dreamlike little out-of-the-way village. I wonder whether these low eaves in front of me, this narrow road which seems to have been covered only recently with gravel, the shadows cast by these miserable lamps, these slanted thatched roofs, these one-horse horse-carts with their yellow hoods pulled down—this chill on the skin, this night cold, and this darkness, which make all these elements that I can't classify as either old or new appear even more dreamlike—I wonder whether the feeling I get from all of these indistinct images isn't a symbol of the destiny I've brought with me to this point. Everything up to now has been a dream, what's happening now is a dream, what will happen from now on will be a dream, and I'll return to Tokyo again with the same feeling of being in a dream. There's no telling that that might not be the up-shot of this episode. In fact that's probably what will happen. If so, why then did I leave rainy Tokyo and come to this sort of a place? Because I'm really a fool? If only I could finally decide that everything's foolishness, then I could even turn back at this point.'

These impressions came all at once. In less than half a minute he furnished himself with this much order, reasoning, logic, and imagination, and they all passed through his mind linked to each other. But shortly thereafter he was no longer his own master. A young man suddenly appeared from somewhere and took his luggage. Without a moment's delay he brought Tsuda over to the tea-stall directly in front of them, and in addition to asking him the name of the inn he was going to and finding out whether he wished to ride in a horse-cart or a rickshaw, he freely displayed even a certain charm, which Tsuda was hardly expecting, during the brief busy period he was with Tsuda, and then left.

Tsuda soon was made to board a horse-cart with the canvas hood pulled down. He was surprised to find the same young fellow sitting in front of him while asking Tsuda's pardon for doing so.

'Are you going with me too?'

'Yes, I hope I won't be a bother.'

The young man was a general handyman and workman at the inn to which Tsuda was going.

'There's the pennant of our inn flying here.'

Tsuda turned his head and looked at the small red flag stuck in a corner of the driver's seat. Since it was dark he could not see the characters dyed into it, as it fluttered violently towards his seat in the wind which the speed of the horse-cart was creating. He hunched his shoulders and raised his overcoat collar.

'It's already become quite cold at night now.'

Since the young man, who had the driver's seat at his back, could not feel the wind at all because of his position, this comment sounded to Tsuda somehow a bit gratuitous.

There seemed to be ricefields on both sides of the road. Also Tsuda seemed to hear the murmuring of brooks between the ricefields and the road. He also felt that the ricefields on both sides were hemmed in closely by mountains.

Tsuda, exposing to the wind only the one part of his face he could not cover with his hat and overcoat collar, presented to the young fellow an attitude of meditation as if he were fighting against the cold.

The handyman in turn, behaving as if Tsuda's attitude was agreeable to him, did not try to speak to him.

Then suddenly Tsuda's mood changed.

'Are there many guests?'

'Yes, there are. Thank you for asking.'

'About how many?'

The young man did not say precisely but instead answered in a somewhat apologetic manner.

'Right now, the season being what it is, we really don't have that many. We're busiest during the cold weather, from the end of the year till after New Year's Day, and then again in summer, during the two months of July and August. Then we even have to refuse guests without reservations practically every day.'

'Well, does that mean that right now is your slack season?'

'You might say so. This way you should really relax.'

'Thank you, I'll try to.'

'You've come particularly for your health, haven't you, sir?'

'Yes, you might say so.'

Tsuda, who had begun talking with the purpose of asking about Kiyoko, stopped abruptly at that point. He was perturbed, for he simply could not endure mentioning her name. He also feared some awkwardness might arise by his doing so. Turning his face away from the young workman, and leaning back again against the back of the horse-cart seat, he resumed his attitude of silence.

172

As the horse-cart seemed about to run directly into a large black rock, it veered quickly around the base of it. When Tsuda looked, he saw that on the opposite side as well something which could only be a large broken off section of the same rock was awkwardly blocking the path. The driver jumped down from his seat and quickly took the horse by the bit.

On one side a tall tree soared to the sky. This tree, which, judging from the weird shadow cast by the light of the bright starry night, appeared to be an old pine, and the sound of a rushing stream which he suddenly began to hear on one side, caused in Tsuda, who had not been away from the city for a long time, an unexpected change of mood. He began recalling forgotten experiences.

'Ah, I wonder why I've forgotten until now that such things as this still exist in the world.'

Unfortunately this kind of recollection could not develop in isolation. His mind swiftly sketched the figure of Kiyoko, whom he was to meet shortly. He had never once forgotten her in the almost one year that had elapsed since they had parted. Indeed even as he was being jolted in a horse-cart along a night road in that way he was undoubtedly pursuing her image intently. Earlier, the driver, apparently fearing that it was getting late, had wantonly and frequently cracked his whip against the buttocks of the gaunt horse, even though Tsuda had wished that he would stop doing so. Was not Tsuda, in pursuing the image of that lost woman, if his true intent be frankly described, very like this gaunt horse? But if the pathetic animal in front of him, breathing heavily through its nostrils, was actually Tsuda himself, who then was the one who was applying the cruel whip? Mrs Yoshikawa? No, he could not boldly assert that she was the one. Well then, was it he himself? Since to that problem he did not wish to give an accurate solution, he abandoned it, and could not help thinking, as before, of what would happen thereafter.

'Why am I going to see her? To remember her forever? But isn't it true that even without seeing her I already can't forget her? Well then, is it to forget her? Perhaps. But will I really be able to do so if I see her again? Perhaps. But then again, perhaps not. The colour of the pine and the sound of the water made me remember the existence of mountains and valleys I had completely forgotten until then. What effect then will this woman whom I haven't in the least forgotten, this woman who sparkles in my mind's eye, this woman whom I have purposely pursued all the way from Tokyo, have on me?'

As the cold air of the mountain gorges, the hues of the night, which mysteriously and darkly obscured those mountains, and Tsuda, whose very existence was being swallowed up in those hues, all fused for a moment, he was seized with fright. He trembled with fear.

The driver, leading the horse by the bit, slowly crossed a bridge built over a torrent which gushed noisily and scattered white foam at the edges of the rocks. Since at that point Tsuda caught sight of several electric lights, he thought they had already arrived. He even thought that perhaps one of those lights was then illuminating Kiyoko's figure.

'They're the lights of destiny. I can do nothing but go on my way, with them as my guide.'

Of course, being deficient in poetic sense, he could not express himself in these words. But he was in a mood which might be described in such a way. He leaned forward towards the young man.

'We've arrived, haven't we? Which is your inn?'

'Yes. Mine is a few yards further on.'

The main street of the hot spring resort was just wide enough to allow the horse-cart to pass. Moreover, since it described several irregular and seemingly deliberate curves, it did not allow the driver to crack his whip from the driver's seat again. Even so it took only five or six minutes to reach the inn. The main street of the town was quite narrow considering the breadth of the valley.

As the young fellow had said, the inn was quiet. As Tsuda was being guided to his room in the midst of this hushed atmosphere, which he could think existed not because it was night or the inn was large but simply because there were so few guests, he was grateful for the coincidence of his coming there at the right time. It was convenient for him, even though by nature he would normally have preferred to be one of a crowd. He asked the maid, seated across the low serving-table from him :

'Is is like this even during the day?'

'Yes.'

'Somehow there don't seem to be any guests anywhere.'

She dispelled his doubt by referring to the new building, the annex, and the main building.

'Is the inn really that large? A person who doesn't know his way could get lost, couldn't he?'

He had to find out where Kiyoko was staying. But just as he had been unable to ask the young handyman bluntly so too could he not ask the maid directly.

'I suppose few people would come to this sort of place alone, would they?'

'Not necessarily.'

'If so, they'd be men, I suppose. I don't suppose a woman would ever stay here alone, would she?'

'As a matter of fact, there's one right now.'

'Really? I suppose she's probably been sick.'

'Maybe she has.'

'What's her name?'

Since someone else was in charge of her room, the maid did not know.

'Is she young?'

'Yes, she's a beautiful young lady.'

'Is that so? Well, I'd like you to show her to me.'

'When she goes to take her bath, she passes on the side of this room, so if you want to see her, any time—'

'You mean I'll be able to? Oh, that's fine.'

Having learned only the direction of Kiyoko's room, he had his tray removed.

173

When, intending to take a bath before going to bed, he asked directions of the maid, Tsuda for the first time realized how very large the inn was, just as the maid had told him it was earlier. When he finally found, directly in front of him, the bathroom he was seeking, having turned into unexpected corridors, and gone down unanticipated flights of stairs, he really wondered whether he would be able to return to his room by himself.

There were several private compartments in the bathroom closed off by wood panelling and glass doors. In addition to these six small sunken bathtubs, lined up three on either side, facing each other, there was a large separate one, more than twice the size of a regular public bath.

The maid said, 'This one's the largest and probably the most comfortable,' as she opened for him the frosted glass door with a clatter. No one was inside. Perhaps to prevent the steam from accumulating, the windows, like small sliding glass doors, near the ceiling, serving as transoms would in a regular room, were half open, and through them a cold gust of night air assailed Tsuda like some icy mountain blast as he began taking off his padded dressing-gown.

'My, but it's cold.'

He jumped into the bath with a splash.

'Please take your time and have a pleasant bath.'

As the maid was about to shut the door and leave, she made this comment, but then she turned back and spoke again :

'There's still another bathroom beneath this one, and so if you'd prefer to go there some time, why then please do so.'

Since in getting to the bathroom where he then was he had already gone down one or two staircases, he could hardly imagine yet another floor beneath that one.

'Just how many floors *are* there in this building?'

The maid laughed but did not answer. But she did not forget to conclude her advice on the various baths.

'This one is newer and cleaner but the water in the one below is said to be better for your health. That's why those guests who've really come for a cure all go to the one below. Also, in the one below the water gushes out in a waterfall and you can let it cascade on your shoulders and back.'

Tsuda, with just his head sticking out of the bathtub, answered :

'Thank you. Next time, then, I'll go in that one, so please show me the way.'

'Gladly. But do you have some illness, sir?'

'Yes, I do have some slight trouble.'

After the maid left, Tsuda for some time could not forget her words: 'those guests who've really come for a cure.'

'I wonder whether I actually belong to that category.'

He wanted to think both that he did and that he did not. He knew quite well what the main purpose of his coming was. Yet although he had endured the rain to come as far as he had, there was still a gap in his plans. He hesitated as he sensed that a certain margin for manoeuvring remained. And that margin advised him as follows:

'For the present you can still do as you wish. If you want to become a guest who has truly come for a cure, you can. Whether you want to or not, you're free to choose now. Freedom always means happiness. But on the other hand it can never settle anything, and that's why it's unsatisfactory. Does that mean then that you should throw it away? After you've lost your freedom will you be able, in its place, to grasp something firmly? Are you sure of that? Your future isn't yet decided, you know. You may still have many more riddles than the single one you had in the past. If in solving a riddle of the past you cast away your present freedom and try to ask of the future that things turn out as you wish, will you be acting foolishly or cleverly?'

He could not judge which he would be. It was natural that if he began to doubt that he would succeed at the very moment that he had to act, then he would be completely paralysed.

From the very beginning he had three paths he could follow; there were no others. First, while vacillating forever, he could maintain his present freedom; second, he could move ahead, not caring whether he made a fool of himself; and third, namely what he was aiming at, he could achieve a solution to his satisfaction without behaving foolishly.

Among the three, he had set out from Tokyo with only the third as his goal. However, after being jolted by the train, shaken by the horse-cart, chilled by the mountain air, and boiled in the steamy bath, and now finally at the point where he learned that the person he was seeking was before him and that he could start putting into practice, the following day already, his main aim, suddenly the first possibility opened to him. Moreover, the second also, before he was aware of it, stood smiling by his side. Their arrival was sudden, but not noisy. From the point where the mist which had blocked his view had suddenly lifted, without making even the sound of the wind, he could now see steadily in front of him.

Tsuda, who as one might not have expected, had a romantic streak in him, also was, rather unexpectedly, steady-going. Moreover, he was unaware of the contrast of these two aspects of his personality. Therefore there was no need for him to suffer from this contradiction within himself. Everything would be all right if only he could decide. But, until he did so, a war raged within his heart. It doesn't matter if I make a fool of myself. No, I don't want to be called a fool. Oh, but of course I won't be behaving like a fool. Only when this war had finally been settled would he be able to spring to his feet.

All alone in the large bath, half washing and half rubbing himself, he continued to splash the clear hot water over himself.

174

Then, wholly immersed in his own thoughts, and having completely forgotten his surroundings, he was suddenly startled by the clatter of the glass door being opened. He automatically raised his head and looked towards the entrance. As he noticed there in the midst of the steam part of a woman's figure, his heart beat wildly like an alarm bell. But his apprehension which had arisen in an instant also vanished in an instant. For she was not the one who could really startle him.

This woman, whom he had never in his life seen before, apparently about to go to bed, showed him an aspect of herself which, if it had been daytime, she would have been lacking in modesty to reveal and which she therefore would never have shown anyone. The garish colour of her long undergarment, which under normal circumstances would never have been allowed to extend even beyond the hem of a wadded silk garment, was displayed wantonly and brilliantly before his eyes.

As soon as the woman noticed the naked figure of Tsuda, squatting like a beggar in the midst of the steam, she quickly withdrew from the bathroom.

'Oh, please excuse me.'

Tsuda felt that she had taken away from him the words with which *he* should have apologized. But at that moment he heard the sound of slippers descending the stairs. As soon as they had stopped in front of the glass doors he heard a conversation between a man and woman.

'What happened?'

'Somebody's in there.'

'It's taken, is it? Well, that doesn't matter, does it? So long as it's not crowded.'

'But. . . .'

'All right, let's go in a small one then. If we take a small one, they're probably all vacant.'

'Katsu isn't around by any chance, is he?'

Tsuda wanted to get out quickly for them. But at the same time he did not particularly like the woman's tone which seemed somehow to imply that she would not be satisfied until she could use the bath he was then using. Gathering up his courage as if to say to her, 'If you want to come in here, why come right ahead; there's no need to hold back,' he plunged into the bath again.

He was a tall man. Extending his long legs comfortably, and moving them up and down in the hot water, he looked on with interest as they floated up and down in the transparent liquid.

At that moment he suddenly heard the voice of a man who sounded as if he might be the Katsu about whom the woman had inquired.

'Good evening. You're taking your evening bath very early, aren't you?'

A man's voice answered this greeting of Katsu's.

'Yes, it was too boring so we thought we'd go to bed early today.'

'Really? So you've finished your lesson already?'

'Well, we haven't exactly finished it but. . . .'

Tsuda then heard the woman speaking.

'Katsu, that one's occupied, isn't it?'

'Oh, is it?'

'Isn't there another bath somewhere that's ready?'

'Yes, there is. But it may be a bit hot.'

The sound of the opening of the door of the bath to which Katsu appeared to have guided them came from the opposite direction. A moment later the entrance door to Tsuda's bath rattled open :

'Good evening, sir.'

A square-faced man of slight build entered as he said this.

'Shall I pour water on you, sir?'

The man quickly stepped down to the faucet area and filled an oval wooden tub with hot water. Tsuda then turned his back towards him to have it washed.

'So you're Katsu, I suppose.'

'Yes, that's quite right, sir.'

'I heard your name just now.'

'I see. As a matter of fact I saw you too just now.'

'Yes, I've just arrived.'

Katsu gave a laugh.

'Did you come from Tokyo, sir?'

'Yes.'

Katsu made him answer various questions about which train he had taken coming from Tokyo and which one he planned to take going back. He then asked him other questions, such as whether he had come alone, and why he had not brought along his wife, at the same time that he himself supplied various bits of information such as that the couple who had just been there were silk merchants from Yokohama, that the husband was taking *gidayū** lessons every night from his wife, and that Katsu's own wife was skilful in the *nagauta*.† It seemed to Tsuda, who had to listen even to things which he would have preferred not to hear, as if there were only one subject which Katsu did not touch upon, namely that of Kiyoko. This curious omission caused Tsuda a certain amount of dissatisfaction. Of course Tsuda, on his part as well, was unprepared to discuss that subject. In a rather short period of time Katsu chatted as much as he wished and finished washing Tsuda's back.

'Please take your time finishing your bath, sir.'

As Tsuda watched Katsu's retreating figure after the latter had made that comment and was leaving the bathroom, he felt there was no need to dally any longer. He quickly dried himself, dressed, and went out through the glass doors. But after climbing the stairs of the bathroom, while swinging his wet towel, and passing by the sinks and the mirror, and then making one turn down a corridor, he finally realized he did not know how to return to his room.

175

At first he walked almost without realizing where he was going. Even the doubt whether that was the way he had come when he had been guided by the maid earlier merely stirred his memory like a faint daydream. But when, judging from the length of the corridor he had traversed, he saw that he still did not come out in front of anything resembling his room, he stopped abruptly.

'Let me see—was it farther back, or a bit farther on?'

The corridor was brightly illuminated by electric lights. He could easily go in whatever direction he wished. But he did not hear the footsteps of anyone anywhere. Nor did he see any maid going about her business. Putting his towel and soap down at that point, he tried clapping his hands as he did in calling O-Nobu from his study. There was no answer whatever. Not knowing where he was, he naturally did not know in what direction the maids' quarters lay. Since he had come in by an entrance which was at the end of a shrub-planted walk, hardly different from that of a private dwelling, the whereabouts of the back entrance, the kitchen, and the office were a complete mystery to him.

When, after clapping several times he realized that no one would answer, he forced a smile and picked up his soap and towel again. He

---

* A type of ballad chanting.
† A kind of epic song.

also began to feel that this was rather an amusing experience. His curiosity in wanting to find out whether by roaming around he would end up in front of his room at some time or other also helped him to accept the situation. He began walking again with the attitude of a person who is deliberately enjoying the experience of being in an inn for the first time in his life.

The corridor soon came to an end. If he went up two or three steps around a corner from that point he would be at another lavatory. Since into that row of four sparkling white basins clear mountain water flowed from the nickel faucets in an endless stream, he could clearly see that not only were all four basins full but the crystal water overflowed the edges of the basins and fell away attractively to the sink as a thin curtain of water. Because it was being pushed from the rear as well as being struck from above, the water in the basins vibrated slightly.

The sight of this made Tsuda, accustomed to using only water from the tap, quickly forget where he was. He could only think such an arrangement quite wasteful. But just as he thought of turning off the faucets to save water he finally realized his foolishness. At the same time he was strangely attracted by the indefinite whirlpools, which alternately became large and small, in the white enamelled basins.

The surroundings were quiet. It was just as the maid had told him when he was having supper. In fact it was far quieter than he had imagined as he had listened and had nodded in approval to everything she had said. It was not a matter of wondering where all the guests were but of wondering where anyone was. In that quiet atmosphere the lights lit up every corner. But they only shone, they neither made a sound nor moved. Only the water in front of him moved, forming a whirlpool pattern, which alternately expanded and shrank.

He soon turned away from the water. Then, since with the same glance he suddenly encountered a man's form, he gave a start, and stared at it. But it was only the image of himself reflected in the large mirror hung by the side of the wash basins. The mirror was almost as tall as an average man. And, like one in a barber's shop, it was hung upright. Consequently, not only the reflection of his face but that of his shoulders, waist, and hips as well, were on the same plane as he was, and faced him directly. Even after he realized that it was himself he was looking at, he still did not remove his eyes from the mirror. He noticed that he was rather pale, even though he had just come from the bath, but he was at a loss to know why. Since he had neglected to have a haircut for some time, his hair was bushy and unkempt. It shone like lacquer because it was freshly wet from the bath, and for some reason he thought it looked like a garden after it has been devastated by a windstorm.

He was quite a handsome man, with regular features and a complexion that was so smooth as to seem almost wasted on a man. Having always been rather self-assured of his good looks, he could remember only having his assurance confirmed by every encounter with a mirror. Therefore he was somewhat surprised when the mirror unexpectedly presented him with an unsatisfactory image. Before acknowledging that it was a reflection of himself he was struck with the idea that it was the ghost of himself. Realizing that he looked frightful, he quickly decided to do something about it. He opened his eyes wide, stared at himself even more intently, and swiftly moved two steps forward to pick up the comb in front of the mirror. Then he purposely calmed down and combed his hair, parting it neatly.

But this attitude ended as soon as he threw down the comb. Coming to himself again, he realized his old problem of having to find his room. He looked up the staircase facing the lavatory. He then noticed certain special features of those stairs. First, they were about one-third broader than the usual kind. Secondly, they were built so sturdily that it seemed as if they would not creak even if an elephant walked on them. And thirdly, unlike ordinary stairs, they were entirely covered with a varnish, in imitation of those in a Western-style building.

Even though he was confused about where he was, at least he clearly remembered that he had never come down those stairs before. Realizing that even if he climbed them he could not return to his room, he turned back again, away from the mirror, with the intention of retracing his steps.

176

He then heard a sliding-door of a room on that second floor being opened and then closed again. Even though, judging from the structure of the stairs, he thought the building large enough to have more than one or two rooms on the second floor, since the sound that he then heard was exceptionally clear he could quickly determine, from its clarity, the distance to the room.

The top of the stairs which he looked at from below was in no way different from what one often sees in a restaurant of ordinary construction. There was a broad board-floored landing. Without considering the width, which he could not determine, when he estimated the length of the open space from the position of the wall he was facing, which limited it, he thought it seemed only about six feet. Without climbing the stairs, he could only guess whether the corridor divided in three directions, or twisted in two, from that point, but he did not doubt that the sound of the sliding-door which he had just heard had come from the room nearest the stairs, or the one immediately behind the wall he could see from below.

When, in the silence, he suddenly heard this sound, he first realized there were guests on the floor above too. Or rather, he finally became aware of the existence of other people. He was startled since until then he had been wholly occupied with having gone in the wrong direction. Of course his surprise was slight, but qualitatively it was like the surprise one feels when something one has thought of as dead suddenly comes to life again. He immediately tried to escape, since he disliked showing anyone how stupid he was in groping to find the way back to his room, but more than that he was ashamed to reveal, by his surprise, how he was slightly less attractive than usual.

The natural outcome, however, was somewhat more complex. Just as he was about to turn back he realized that perhaps it was only the maid. As soon as he had reconsidered the matter, he recovered his equilibrium. And once he had overcome his surprise, he felt it would not matter even if it was a guest. 'Whoever he is, if he comes, I'll ask him to show me the way.' With this new attitude, he looked up the stairs, while standing near the almost full-length mirror. He then began to hear light footsteps from behind the wall, as he expected. They were indeed light, so light in fact that if there had not been the slight sound as the backs of the slippers met the heel, he would not have been able to hear them. Then a suspicion seized him : 'It's a woman. But it's not the maid. Perhaps. . . .'

Suddenly realizing this, his own footsteps instantly stopped, as the very person of whom he had been thinking relentlessly appeared in front of him and he was overcome by a surprise many times more intense than the one he had just experienced. His eyes did not move.

It seemed as if the same paralysis bound Kiyoko to the spot even more firmly. When she had come as far as the landing at the head of the stairs and had stopped stock still there, she seemed to him like a figure in a painting. This image of her remained in his mind for a very long time thereafter as an unforgettable impression.

Her act of looking down from above unsuspectingly, and that of recognizing him there, seemed simultaneous, but actually were not. At least so he thought. She needed some time to assimilate the fact of his presence. After a period of surprise, one of wonder, and one of doubt had all elapsed, she finally became completely rigid. Indeed she stood so still and stiff it seemed that if someone had pushed her lightly with one finger she would have toppled more easily than a clay doll.

Like the usual hot spring guest, she seemed about to warm herself by a bedtime bath, and was carrying a small towel. And like Tsuda she also held an unwrapped nickel soap container. Whenever he re-traced the course of that moment afterwards, he would always be amazed at why, since she had been standing there as rigid as a stick, she had not fallen to the floor.

Her appearance was not so casual as that of the woman he had met earlier in the bathroom. But since at that kind of place the guests were already familiar enough with each other to exchange silent greetings, she was not wearing a formal broad obi. Instead she simply wore a bright undersash in a pretty red, blue, and yellow striped pattern wound loosely around her waist. The coloured length of the slip she wore underneath her nightclothes came down to cover the top of her bare feet, which were pushed into light woollen-cloth slippers.

As Kiyoko's body became rigid so too did the muscles of her face. And her forehead and both her cheeks rapidly paled. As Tsuda clearly perceived this change, he regained possession of himself, and realized that something had to be done, or she might actually faint.

He was going to call out to her, but at that moment she moved. She turned around swiftly and fled. Leaving him at the foot of the stairs, she went back along the corridor she had come from, and almost simul-taneously the light at the head of the stairs, which had been illumi-nating her brightly, suddenly went out. He again heard the sound as of a sliding-door being opened in the darkness. At the same time in the small room very near where he was standing, which he had not noticed until then, the maid's bell of response to her having been called sounded shrilly.

He shortly heard hurried footsteps from far back along the corridor. He stopped, midway on her errand to Kiyoko, the maid whose footsteps they were, and learned from her where his room was.

177

That night he could not sleep well. A rustling outside the rain-shutters ceaselessly struck his ear. Unable to ignore it, he wondered what was causing it. Had it begun to rain? Was a mountain torrent flowing under the eaves? While he reasoned that if it was rain it was not sounding on the roof and if it was a torrent it was flowing too slowly, his mind was troubled by a far greater problem.

Since, upon returning to his room, he had found in the middle of it the warm-looking bedding laid out for him by the maid, who had cleverly utilized his absence for the task, he quickly burrowed himself under the quilts and fell to thinking about the adventure he had just had quite accidentally.

As he looked back on himself that evening he felt that he had been almost a somnambulist. He had behaved precisely as if he had wandered about the building without any goal whatsoever. Particularly at the time when, at the base of the stairs, he had been looking at the water slowly revolving in a whirlpool, and when he had suddenly encountered his unattractive face in the mirror, he seemed, judging from the near vantage-point of less than an hour after the event, to have been controlled by an extraordinary psychological state. Since he had had very few experiences of having been abandoned by common sense, this strange mood was undoubtedly one to be ashamed of, as he looked back on it now that he was resting peacefully in bed. But, apart from the fact that it was a rather shameful state to have been in, as he thought about the cause he could not explain why he had had such a feeling.

Be that as it may, when he shifted to the problem of why at that time he had forgotten Kiyoko's existence, he could not but be amazed.

'Is it possible I could be that indifferent to her?'

Of course he did not believe he really was. At dinner he had even had the maid tell him in what part of the inn Kiyoko was staying.

'But you didn't keep that fact in mind, did you?'

While he had been wandering around the corridors, he had actually forgotten where Kiyoko was. But a person who does not know where he himself is can hardly be expected to know where someone else might be.

'But if only I'd kept in mind that she was in that general direction, I'd never have been taken by surprise that way.'

As he thought about this, he realized that he had already missed his first opportunity. When he pieced together and examined such facts as her appearance when she turned back, her behaviour in turning off the light and thereby blocking the way to the landing, and the sound of the bell as she quickly rang to call the maid, he sensed that they were all a warning. They all meant caution. And they all meant a severing of relations.

However, she had been surprised—far more so than he. This could have been simply because she was a woman or because for him there had been an element of expectation behind the surprise but for her it had been a surprise pure and simple. And yet could her reaction be explained entirely in this way? Had she not instantly felt the force of a much more complex past?

She had turned pale. She had become rigid. He found some cause for hope in these facts, trying to interpret them in a way that would make them appear advantageous to himself at that time. Then he overturned that interpretation and tried to look at these same facts from the opposite side. After looking at them carefully from both sides, he had to judge which interpretation was the more rational. Because of an insufficient basis for that judgment he could not arrive at it easily. Even when he did, it collapsed immediately. When he leaned to one interpretation his self-confidence came to destroy it. When he leaned to the other the alarm-bell of disillusionment began to sound in his ear. Strangely enough, he sensed that his self-confidence, or to use the word which he himself disparagingly used, his conceit, lay within him. Yet he felt that the alarm-bell of disillusionment, which came to attack it, always came from outside himself. While he thought he was treating both of them impartially, he always made a distinction on the basis of the degree of intimacy he had with them. Or rather, it seemed as if the two had been provided with the degree of distance between them as natural attributes from the beginning. The result was clear : while reproving it, he coddled his conceit; while he lent an ear to it, he abhorred the sound of the alarm-bell.

Intending to light a cigarette, he took a match from the box at his bedside. He then noticed the padded dressing-gown which the maid had roughly folded and placed on the clothes-rack. Now that he thought about it, he realized that that was the one which O-Nobu had placed in his suitcase for him but which he had not used, and that he had worn one which the inn had provided, and was at that moment wearing it in bed. He suddenly remembered the compliment he had paid O-Nobu on the new dressing-gown upon his leaving the hospital. At the same time her answer was also called up on the stage of his memory.

'Compare them and see which is better.'

On the matter of dressing-gowns, as one might have thought, the inn's was far better. Even to his eye, the distinction between a *meisen** fabric and *itoori*† silk cloth was obvious at a glance. As he was comparing the dressing-gowns, he was naturally thinking about O-Nobu, and at the same time the person whom he was then concerned about deep within his mind also appeared within the realm of his consciousness.

'O-Nobu and Kiyoko.'

As he said their names to himself, he quickly threw his cigarette butt in the spittoon, and after hearing the sizzle at the bottom of it, immediately pulled the covers up around his head.

Only when the determination and effort to go to sleep finally vanished somewhere after having exhausted themselves, was he rewarded. Finally, in spite of himself, he fell into a dream-filled sleep.

---

* A simple, relatively cheap silk fabric.
† A thicker, more expensive fabric.

178

His dreams, interrupted once by the man who came early in the morning to draw open the rain shutters, continued with difficulty while he was in a half-waking state. When he finally arose, after the four corners of the room had become so bright he could sleep no longer and the shadows cast by the morning sun were spreading outside, his eyelids were still heavy. While cleaning his teeth with a toothpick, he opened the sliding-doors to the veranda. Like a man who has now finally awakened from the demon realm of the night before, he looked out and surveyed the scene outside.

The garden in front of his room was quite unlike one in a mountain village. The conventionally disposed scene of the artificially constructed, irregularly shaped pond, surrounded by such shrubs as young pines and azaleas, would have been termed tasteless rather than commonplace. In addition to the stream which flowed from among the rocks of the miniature artificial hill near his room and which fell into the pond in a small waterfall, there was even a fountain, which, though not very high, spouted five or six columns of water, like fireworks, at one time. When, with a wry smile, he discovered the artificial source of the sound of the water which had disturbed his sleep the previous night, his mind quickly turned to consider the matter of Kiyoko, which had caused him much more distress than that sound of the water. He thought that if he went to the root of the matter, it might turn out to be as dreary a thing as the fountain, and if, even worse, it turned out to be as meaningless as the fountain, he felt it would be unendurable.

As he was standing blankly, with the toothpick still in his mouth and with folded arms, at the edge of the veranda, the young man who had for a time been sweeping the fallen leaves in the garden with a bamboo broom approached him and greeted him cordially.

'Good morning, sir. You must have been tired last night.'

'Oh, it was you, was it, who rode with me here in the horse-cart last night.'

'Yes it was, sir. I hope I didn't trouble you.'

'Well, it's certainly as quiet as you said it would be. And the building's terribly large, isn't it?'

'Not really. As you can see, there's very little flat land, so we've had to level it in places and build the inn on several different levels. That's why the connecting hallways are actually the only places that may give the impression that, as you say, the building's extremely large.'

'It's no wonder, then, that last night I actually got lost and confused in coming back from the bath.'

'Oh, I'm sorry about that, sir.'

As the two men were exchanging this sort of idle conversation, a man and a woman descended together the small hill beyond the garden. Since they were following a path among autumn foliage and dried branches which had been cut through the forest in a zigzag fashion so as to make the relatively steep slope easy to climb, it took quite some time for them to reach the garden even though they seemed to be just a few steps away. Nevertheless the inn workman did not stay where he was to wait for them. Eager to promote his own interest by ingratiating himself with them, he suddenly abandoned Tsuda, and, running quickly to the base of the hill, called up to greet them.

Tsuda then saw their faces clearly for the first time. The woman was undoubtedly the one who had opened the door to his bath the night before and had presented such a captivating figure. But since the large, elaborate, Japanese-style hair-do with which she had surprised him at the bath had vanished and her hair had been redone in ordinary Western style, he did not at first notice that she was the same person. He then turned from her to look, in the manner of a casual first meeting, at the man accompanying her, whose voice he had heard but whose face he had not seen. This man, who had a trim modern moustache, somehow had the air of a merchant, just as the bath attendant had said he was. As soon as Tsuda saw his face, he was reminded of O-Hide's husband. He wondered if, just as the name Hori Shōtarō, or, more briefly, Hori no Shō-san, or even more simply, as he often called himself, Hori Shō, designated his brother-in-law very well, that man's name too might not so smack of a merchant as to obliterate his un-merchant-like moustache. Tsuda's impressions, consolidated at a glance, did not stop there but moved yet one step closer to cynicism as he even wondered whether the couple actually were man and wife. Thus while they were saying that they had arisen early and had gone out for a pre-breakfast walk after their morning bath, they seemed to him to be simply an unconventional pair of lovers. He was still standing in his original position, rubbing his teeth with a toothpick. Even though he was looking from a certain distance, he clearly heard the conversation the two of them were having with the young workman.

The woman asked him :

'Do you know what happened to the lady in the annex today?'

The workman answered :

'No, I know nothing at all about it. What do you mean?'

'Well, it's not really very important, but we always see her at the bath in the morning, and today she wasn't there, that's all.'

'Oh really? Perhaps she's still sleeping.'

'Perhaps so. But our times have always been fixed—for going to the bath in the morning.'

'Oh, I see.'

'And also we promised her we'd take a walk with her this morning to the hill and back.'

'Well then, shall I go and have a look?'

'No, that's all right. We've already finished our walk now. I just asked you because I wondered if she might not be feeling very well today.'

'I think the lady's probably just sleeping, or else—'

'Or else what? You don't have to look so serious. I just thought I'd ask you.'

With that the two passed on. With his mouth full of tooth powder, Tsuda went out into the corridor to search again for the bathroom he had used the night before.

179

But the word 'search' did not really apply to his activity that morning. When, despite the difficulty of several turns on the way, he succeeded in going down easily, without a wasted step, to the bath he had gone to the previous evening, he could not help thinking again how foolish he had been the night before.

The autumn morning sunshine streamed through the high windows under the eaves of the bathroom. When, soaking his entire body in the hot water, he looked up through those windows right over his head and caught glimpses of rocks and embankments, he discovered how far beneath the ground level of the main area the bath had been built. And he realized that there was considerable difference in height between the top of the cliff and the place where he was. After he had estimated the distance with his eye as between nine and twelve feet, he realized that if the old bathroom was still further below that one there must indeed be several levels in the one building.

There was a silver leaf bush on top of the cliff, but unfortunately, because the morning sun was not shining there, the colour of its leaves, which shone dully from time to time as they were shaken by the wind, gave him a sense of the cold. From his bath he could also see sasanqua flowers falling. But the scene was a fragmentary one, for apart from the two-foot wide strip which those small windows allowed him to see, he could see absolutely nothing either above or below. Of course that unknowable world was undoubtedly a commonplace one, but for some reason it aroused his curiosity. Even the fact that a brown-eared bulbul apparently began to cry suddenly as it flew very near the cliff and that he could hear its cry but not see its form frustrated him.

But that was merely a secondary dissatisfaction. For actually, since he had been mulling over in his mind an incident which worried him far more, from the time he had descended to the bath he had already secretly been feeling a certain frustration. He had not seen a trace of another human being in that bright bathroom as he had stood in the midst of that extremely desolate building which seemed to tell him that he had free rein over everything, but just to make sure he was alone he had tried to open each of the doors to the small bath compartments in the rows on both sides of the hall. Of course the reason may have been that since the pair of slippers that had been left at the entrance to one of the compartments had caused him a certain concern, he had merely taken the opportunity to investigate all the compartments. Therefore, after having opened each of the doors and finally having come to the one with the slippers in front, which was closed, he had suddenly hesitated. Of course his hesitation had not been involuntary, for he had had a sense of somehow being rude in opening it abruptly. Thus he had listened carefully from outside, but since it had been completely quiet inside and his hand had applied more pressure, he had opened the door with a clatter. Upon having found simply another empty compartment, he had had the mixed feelings of relief and disappointment.

Now after he had undressed and was soaking himself in the bath, a certain anticipation caused by this succession of events was steadily working within him. With a wry smile, he thought about the change in his attitude between the night before and that morning. The previous night he had been so unsuspecting as to have been surprised by the woman with her hair in a chignon. That morning, before anyone had yet come, he had been tense with a kind of expectation.

Perhaps this was a state induced by the sight of the ownerless slippers. But when he considered why those slippers had so perturbed him, he realized the reason was that he had earlier that morning overheard what the woman from Yokohama and the young workman had been saying about Kiyoko. She had not yet arisen. At least she had not yet taken her bath. Thus if she was going to take it at all, she obviously would either have to take it then or else come to take it later.

His alert ear suddenly caught the sound of someone's footsteps coming down the stairs. He instantly stopped his splashing. Then he could no longer hear the footsteps. It may have been his imagination but it seemed as if the footsteps that had stopped for a moment were now going back up the stairs. He could understand why this had happened, and wondered whether it had been wrong for him to leave his own slippers outside the door, as others had done. He even regretted that he had not worn them into the bathroom.

After a short while he unexpectedly heard footsteps again but this time they were outside the building near the bath. This happened after he had looked at the silver leaf flowers and before he heard the cry of the bulbul. He immediately linked the sound of these footsteps with the previous footsteps, easily arriving at the conclusion that the person he had heard leaving the bathroom had purposely gone outside. Then he suddenly heard a woman's voice, but it came from a direction completely different from that of the footsteps. Judging from the appearance of the outside as he looked up at it from below, he estimated that the top of the cliff was a level area of several square yards, and it seemed that the single building in that area had been constructed facing the bathroom. At any rate, the voice came from that direction, and it was certainly that of the woman who had earlier been talking about Kiyoko with the workman upon returning from her walk.

Since the windows under the eaves which had been open the night before to let out the steam were then closed, he could not make out her words clearly. But, judging from the force of her voice and other factors, he thought one thing was certain : she was speaking from the top of the cliff to someone at the bottom of it. Therefore, in the natural order of things, some words of acknowledgement should certainly have come from the bottom of the cliff. But, strangely enough, not a sound came from that direction, and he could not hear any normal exchange of conversation at all. The only one who spoke was the woman on top of the cliff.

On the other hand, the footsteps had not stopped as they had previously. Unmistakably a woman was climbing the cliff, walking up the irregular stone steps in garden clogs. Just as he thought she had probably finished climbing, a portion of her skirt appeared in the upper part of those high windows. Then it quickly vanished. The momentary impression that remained with him was simply one of the fluttering of a beautiful pattern. But he felt that he had recognized, in that pattern as it moved by, the same colours he had seen from the base of the stairs the night before.

181

After returning to his room and sitting down to his breakfast tray, he spoke with the maid who waited on him.

'I wonder if the place where those Yokohama people are is on top of the cliff you can see from the new bathroom?"

'Yes. Did you go over there and see?'

'No, I just thought that's where it probably is.'

'You're quite right. Why don't you go over there and visit awhile. Both the gentleman and his wife are interesting people. They keep saying they're so bored they don't know what to do with themselves all day.'

'Have they been here a long time?'

'Yes, I suppose it's already about ten days.'

'The husband's the one, isn't he? Who does *gidayū* chanting, I mean.'

'Yes. You know all about that, do you. Have you heard him yet?'

'Not yet. I just learned about it from Katsu, that's all.'

Although she shared with him ungrudgingly the knowledge about the couple that he had himself already heard, she nevertheless knew her place. When it came to a delicate point she purposely avoided his question.

'By the way, what actually is that woman?'

'Why, she's the gentleman's wife, of course.'

'I wonder if she's his real wife.'

As the maid said, 'Of course she is,' she began to laugh. 'There certainly isn't any such thing as a false one, is there? Why do you ask?'

'Well, for just a plain wife isn't she a bit on the flamboyant side?'

Instead of answering, she suddenly turned to the topic of Kiyoko.

'The other lady who's farther towards the back is very refined.'

According to the arrangement of the rooms, Kiyoko's was at the back of Tsuda's, and that of the couple mentioned was in front of his. Having discovered that he was between the two, he nodded and commented:

'That means that here I'm just about in the centre, doesn't it?'

Even though he was in the middle, since the rooms were at odd angles with each other, his was not on any connecting corridor.

'Is the other lady by any chance a friend of the couple?'

'Yes, they're on friendly terms with each other.'

'Since before they came here?'

'I'm afraid I don't know anything about that. I suppose they probably got to know each other after they came here. They're forever visiting back and forth. After all, the three of them have all the free time in the world. Yesterday too they went out together to the park.'

He did not try to avoid the basic issue.

'But why is that lady alone, I wonder?'

'I think she's in rather bad health.'

'But what about her husband?'

'When she came, her husband was with her but he went back right away.'

'You mean he left her here all alone? Why, that's dreadful! And hasn't he come back at all?'

'I think he was supposed to return quite soon, but I don't know what's happened.'

'She must be rather bored with herself, I should think.'

'Why don't you go and talk to her for a while?'

'Yes, I wouldn't mind doing that at all. Would you ask her for me whether it's all right?'

The maid merely giggled as she answered, 'You surely don't mean that!' and did not take him seriously.

'I wonder what she does with herself. Do you have any idea?' he then asked.

'Well, she takes hot baths, she goes for walks, she has to listen to the *gidayū* recitation—occasionally she even does some flower-arranging. And in the evenings she often practises calligraphy.'

'Really? And what about books?'

She answered rather half-heartedly, 'I suppose she reads a bit too,' and then began to laugh because his questions were so very commonplace. Tsuda, at last realizing what he was doing, rather nervously changed the subject.

'There was somebody who forgot his slippers outside the bathroom this morning, wasn't there? At first I thought it was occupied and I hesitated to enter, but, when I finally tried opening the door, there was nobody there.'

'Oh really? Well, it must have been that teacher again, I suppose.'

The person she referred to was a calligraphy specialist. Tsuda, who remembered having seen his seal on framed tablets and signs hung here and there, merely indicated mild interest.

'I suppose he's quite old, isn't he.'

'Oh yes, he's a very old man. He has a white beard that's *this* long.'

She put her hand to her breast to show just how long the beard, so appropriate to a calligrapher, actually was.

'I see. Does he still write characters even now?'

'Yes, it seems they're going to be inscribed on a gravestone, and so every day he practises a bit writing very large ones.'

When he heard from her that the calligrapher had come there for the express purpose of writing the gravestone inscription, he was both surprised and overcome with admiration.

'To think he'd go to all that trouble to write such a thing! An amateur thinks he could do it easily in about half a day.'

This comment of his brought forth no response at all from the maid. But in his mind there was a certain element which he did not put into words. He secretly compared the business of this old teacher with his own. He further tried to compare, to himself and the teacher, the couple from Yokohama, who, out of boredom, were taking lessons in the *gidayū*. And then he also placed Kiyoko, who seemed for no particular reason to be doing flower arrangement and practising calligraphy, in the same group and thought about her. When finally he heard the maid's observation on the remaining guest, who neither spoke nor did any exercise but simply sat dully in his room looking at the mountain, he could not help commenting:

'There surely are a lot of different people in the world, aren't there? If it's like this when just five or six get together, it must be terrible in summer or at the New Year.'

'When the inn's full, there are easily a hundred and thirty or forty people.'

Since she did not seem to understand what he was trying to say, she merely mentioned the number of guests there would be in the inn at the busiest season.

181

When he had eaten, Tsuda sat down at the small desk by the side of his bed. After jotting a few words each on the picture postcards he had asked the maid to get for him, he wrote the addresses for them. Even though by sending one to O-Nobu, one to his Uncle Fujii, and one to Mrs Yoshikawa, he thereby completed his essential correspondence, a few of the postcards were left over.

Holding the fountain pen idly in one hand, he glanced blankly at the local scenes with strange names, quite inappropriate for a mountain village, such as the God of Fire Waterfall and Luna Park. Then he made the ink from his pen flow again. This time he completed the cards to O-Hide's husband and to his parents in Kyoto in a few seconds. When he actually began to write in this way, he thought it would be wrong of him not to use all of the picture postcards while he was at it. From the Okamotos, about whom he had not been thinking at first, and the Okamotos' son Hajime, by association he shifted to Hajime's school friend, his own young cousin Makoto, and thereby returned again to his own relatives, listing many more names. Aware of it from the first, the one name he did not list was Kobayashi. Apart from other factors, Tsuda certainly did not want to inform him of the destination of his trip simply out of fear that he would search him out in his refuge. Kobayashi was soon to go off to Korea, and since he was one to act on impulse, he might already actually be jolting along on a train to a port, intent on crossing the sea to the mainland. At the same time, since he led such an irregular life, there was no assurance that even though the day of his announced departure arrived he would move. Tsuda could certainly not assert positively that upon Kobayashi's seeing the postcard (assuming he sent him one), he would not immediately come running to find him.

He automatically tensed his shoulders as he thought about this exasperating friend—or, more accurately, enemy—with whom he had to contend as with changeable weather. But his imagination, once it began to work, did not stop there. Carrying him off, it moved ahead rapidly : he could clearly see, in his mind's eye, the figure of Kobayashi suddenly pulling up to the entrance of the inn in a horse-cart, and storming into his room.

'What the devil did you come here for?'

'For nothing in particular. Just to annoy you.'

'But for what reason?'

'Why in the world do I have to have a reason ! As long as you dislike me, I'll simply hound you forever no matter where you go.'

'Damn you !'

He would suddenly feel compelled to clench his first and punch Kobayashi in the face. Instead of defending himself, Kobayashi would immediately fall flat on his back in the centre of the room with his arms and legs outstretched.

'You hit me, you wretch ! All right, have it your way !'

A riotous scene such as could only take place on a stage would be enacted. It would attract the attention of the entire inn, and Kiyoko would certainly become involved. Everything would be ruined forever.

As Tsuda sketched, without particularly wanting to, this scene, with an imagination more vivid than reality, he suddenly shuddered and came to himself. He wondered what he would do if such an absurd fight actually took place in real life. He had a vague sense of shame and disgrace. To symbolize these emotions he even felt his cheeks begin to burn.

And yet his assessment of such a hypothetical scene could not go beyond that point. If ever he should lose face in front of others, it would be dreadful. This was all there was at the root of all his ethical views. If one tried to express this more simply, one could reduce it to the simple fact that he feared scandal. Therefore the only person in the wrong would be Kobayashi. As if everything had actually happened he even said to himself :

'I'd be blameless, if only that scoundrel hadn't come.'

He thus condemned the Kobayashi who had appeared on the stage of his imagination, making him bear all the responsibility for Tsuda's bringing disgrace upon himself.

After passing sentence on this imaginary criminal, he quickly changed his mood, and took out a visiting card from his wallet. On the reverse side of it he wrote in pen : 'I arrived here last night for a rest.' He cocked his head a moment before adding : 'I heard this morning that you were here,' and again he reflected a bit.

'That's too transparent, it won't do. I have to write something too about meeting her last night.'

But it was rather difficult to touch on that point in a non-committal way. Moreover, the more complex the message the more he would have to write, and the back of a visiting card would not be large enough. He wanted to send as terse a note as possible to avoid writing a troublesome letter.

As if he had just thought of it, he looked up at the side-alcove shelves, and immediately upon noticing that the gift from Mrs Yoshikawa was still lying there untouched since the night before, he took it down. After writing, 'How are you feeling? This is a gift from Mrs Yoshi-kawa,' on the back of a visiting card, he inserted it under the lid of the fruit basket, and called the maid.

'Is there a Mrs Seki staying at the inn?'

The maid, who was the one who had waited on him that morning, began to laugh.

'Mrs Seki is the lady I was telling you about earlier, sir.'

'Indeed? Well, she's the one then. Please take this to her. And tell her I'd like to see her for a while if it's all right with her.'

'Certainly !'

The maid immediately went into the corridor carrying the fruit basket.

182

While waiting for the answer, Tsuda was as ill at ease as some container that does not fit properly. And he was even more nervous because the maid, who was supposed to come back right away, did not do so.

'She couldn't possibly have said no, could she.'

The reason he had used Mrs Yoshikawa's name was that he had already considered such a possibility. The two facts of Mrs Yoshikawa's name and her gift were doubtless a good way of removing Kiyoko's restraint towards him particularly since it was he who had delivered the gift. Even assuming that her real feeling was to try to avoid the annoyance of meeting him, or the accusations that might arise there-from, it would be proper for her, with regard to the basket of fruit, to meet the person who brought it to her, and express her thanks through him. In proportion to his belief that he had thought up an excellent scheme, which no one would think unnatural, he was disturbed by the delay in the maid's return, and, throwing away the cigarette he had begun to smoke, he went out on to the veranda, and for no particular reason silently gazed at the red carp swimming in the pond; then, squatting down there, he stretched forth his hand to the muzzle of the dog lying under the eaves. When, at long last, he heard the maid's footsteps at the turn in the corridor, he was so nervous that he purposely wanted to smooth things over and appear relaxed.

'What happened?'

'I'm sorry I kept you waiting. I suppose I'm very late.'

'No, not really.'

'I had to help the lady a bit.'

'At what?'

'Oh, at tidying up the room, and then I put up her hair for her. When you consider that, I suppose I finished rather quickly.'

Tsuda thought that to put up a woman's hair could not be so very difficult.

'Was it a butterfly coiffure, or a round chignon?'

Taking no notice of him at first, the maid simply began to laugh.

'Why don't you go and see?'

'Gladly, but is it all right for me to go? Haven't I been here waiting for the answer in this way for quite some time?'

'Oh my, I *am* sorry. I completely forgot the important thing. Yes, she said please do go.'

Although finally relieved, while getting up he purposely made doubly sure, half in jest.

'Really? It won't be any bother, will it? I certainly don't want to go there and be made to regret having done so afterwards.'

'You're very suspicious, aren't you, sir? Or maybe both of you are. . . .'

'Who's the other person you're referring to? Mrs Seki? Or my wife?'

'Don't you know which?'

'No, I don't.'

'Are you sure you don't?'

The maid went around the back of Tsuda, who was retying his obi, and put on his *haori* for him as he was about to leave the room.

'Is this the way?'

'I'll show you the way now.'

She went in front of him. When they passed by the aforementioned mirror, the memory of the night before when he had wandered like a sleepwalker suddenly flashed through his mind.

'Oh yes, it was here.'

He spoke without thinking. The maid, who knew nothing about it, asked him innocently:

'*What* was here?'

He immediately started bantering with her.

'I mean it was here that I met a ghost last night!'

The maid had a peculiar expression as she said :

'What foolishness! How could there possibly be a ghost in this building? If you say such things—'

Tsuda, realizing that his bantering was in poor taste at an inn which was in the business of attracting guests, looked up to the second floor, and changed the subject.

'It's up there, isn't it? Mrs Seki's room, I mean.'

'Yes, you're quite right.'

'I know I am.'

'You have a kind of second sight, I suppose.'

'No, not second *sight*. You might say I have second smell, because I can sniff out everything with my nose.'

'Exactly like a dog, eh?'

This conversation, begun on the stairs, was carried on close enough to Kiyoko's room, which was the nearest to the landing, so as to be heard there. He was secretly conscious of this fact.

'By the way, watch me as I sniff out Mrs Seki's room for you.'

As he came to Kiyoko's room, the sound of his slippers came to a dead stop.

'Here it is.'

The maid, looking hard at him from the corner of her eye, burst out laughing.

'Well, how about it? I guessed it, didn't I?' Tsuda boasted.

'Yes indeed, your nose is most effective. It's better than a hunting dog's.'

She again laughed good-naturedly, but there was no reaction at all to this liveliness from within the room. Inside it was as quiet as it had been before so that one simply could not tell whether anyone was there or not.

'Your guest has arrived.'

As the maid called to Kiyoko from the outside, she smoothly slid open for Tsuda the well-fitted sliding-door.

'Pardon me.'

Tsuda, upon entering the room with this single greeting, was startled. For he did not find Kiyoko directly before him, as he had been expecting.

183

The room was actually a suite of two adjoining rooms. The one Tsuda entered was the outer room without the decorative alcove. The thick, crosswise-striped pillow in front of a rectangular mirror with a black persimmon-wood frame and stand, and the small rectangular paulownia wood brazier by its side, gave, though on a small scale, the appearance of a sitting-room in an ordinary home. In a corner was a black-painted clothes-rack. Brilliant, striped silk garments, smooth to the touch, such as women are fond of, were thrown upon it one over another.

The connecting doors were wide open. Tsuda saw some winter chrysanthemums, which seemed to have been newly arranged, in the decorative alcove directly in front of him. In front of the alcove two pillows faced each other. These pillows, with a single round white design of a peony type in the middle of the dark brown, silk crepe fabric, were imposing both as articles of quality and as preparations for a guest's arrival. Before sitting down, he sensed this keenly.

'Everything's so formal. I wonder if this indicates the distance fate has separated us by as we meet today.'

As he suddenly realized this, he also suddenly regretted that he had come there at that time.

But how had this distance arisen? As he thought about it, it seemed only natural that it should have done so. But he had merely forgotten that fact. And why had he forgotten it? Again, as he thought about it, it seemed only natural that he should have done so.

As Tsuda, involved in this kind of reflection, stood in the outer room and gazed heedlessly at the pillows in front of him, without either leaving the room or sitting down, Kiyoko, in her role as hostess, finally appeared from a corner of the veranda. He had no idea whatever what she had been doing out there until then. Nor could he understand why she had purposely gone out there in the first place. Perhaps, after tidying the room, and while waiting for him to come, she had gone to lean against the corner of the railing and had been watching the colours of the autumn leaves spread out on the hillside. Nevertheless, her manner was odd. In describing her behaviour at that time, it would actually have been more appropriate to say that she seemed to be accidentally encountering a guest rather than intentionally greeting one.

And yet, strangely enough, this manner of hers did not disturb him as much as the pillow that was ceremoniously awaiting his sitting down and the rectangular brazier that seemed to have been placed there purposely to thwart the relations between them. In other words, her attitude was not so odd as to be completely irreconcilable with the image of her he had had from the beginning.

The Kiyoko he knew was certainly not a nervous woman. She was always composed. Perhaps a certain slowness would have been the feature he would have singled out to typify her character, or the behaviour which emerged from that character. He had always relied on that special characteristic of hers. And because he had relied too much on it he had, instead, been betrayed. At least he interpreted what had happened in that way. Even while interpreting it in this way, the reliance he had had at that time still remained, though he was unconscious of it. Perhaps her suddenly marrying Seki had been as swift as a swallow's turning in flight but that was one thing and this was another. Only when he tried to link the two and think of them without contradiction did mental confusion occur, but if he looked at them separately, just as the first was a fact so also was the second true.

'Why had such an easy-going person suddenly taken off with the speed of an aeroplane? Why had he had to endure such a turn-about?'

He could properly be expected to harbour doubts on these points. But since, whether he did or not, facts were after all facts, he could certainly not eliminate them in themselves.

Kiyoko the traitress, on that point, was more fortunate than the loyal O-Nobu. If, when he had entered the room, the person who had appeared from a corner of the veranda to surprise him at an off moment had been O-Nobu, and not Kiyoko, what would his reaction have been?

'I wish she'd stop those little tricks!'

He would undoubtedly have reacted this way immediately.

When the same act was performed by Kiyoko, and not O-Nobu, however, the effect was entirely different.

'She's as easy-going as ever, isn't she.'

He could not help judging her in this way, even while, as a result of having been convinced that she was easy-going, he had actually been outdone by her brilliant lightning stroke.

In appearing as she did, Kiyoko not only caught him at an off moment, but she also surprised him by coming from a corner of the veranda carrying with both her hands the large fruit basket which he had earlier given her, saying it was a gift from Mrs Yoshikawa. The mere fact that, for some reason or other, she had burdened herself with it until then made it clear that she bore no malice towards him. Moreover, when he considered that she had had that heavy object in a corner of the veranda until then, and even if he imagined that she had picked it up again after once putting it down, he felt her behaviour was strange. At least it was awkward. It was even somewhat childish. But since he knew her habits so well, he could not help finding in it something so very characteristic of her.

'It's funny. It's funny in a way that's so typical of you. And you aren't in the least aware of it.'

When he saw how she was struggling to carry the heavy basket he almost wanted to say this to her.

184

Then Kiyoko immediately handed the basket over to the maid. Since the maid did not know what to do with it, she merely put forth her hands mechanically and received it from her without speaking. While this simple act was being performed, Tsuda had to stand there as before. But since, instead of the awkward suspense which would normally arise in such circumstances, he was enjoying a kind of relaxation, the moment passed without the slightest uneasiness. He merely observed her action and noted that, as an expression of her easy-going manner, it did not conflict with her habitual behaviour. Therefore his doubts arising from his memory of the previous night doubled in intensity. Why had this unhurried woman turned so pale? Why had she seemed to stiffen so? No matter how he considered it, he simply could not reconcile such amazement with her present composure. He had the feeling of a man who for the first time in his life notices the difference between day and night.

Even before he was invited to do so he sat down by himself in the place prepared for him. Then he watched, as Kiyoko, still standing, instructed the maid to pile the fruit on the plates.

'Thank you very much for the gift.'

This was her first word of greeting. The topic of conversation naturally had to turn from the one who had brought the gift to the kindness of the one who had given it to her. Of course even though Tsuda had lied in using Mrs Yoshikawa's name, he was then no longer even conscious of deceiving her.

'I was just about to give the tangerines away to an old man who was travelling with me, you know.'

'Oh my, why would you do that?'

He felt free to answer any way he wished.

'Because the basket was so heavy it was a bother.'

'Then do you mean you were carrying it in your hands all the way?'

Her question sounded to him so characteristically naïve.

'Don't be ridiculous. Do you think I'm like you, dragging that sort of thing around with me from one end of the veranda to the other?'

Kiyoko merely smiled. There was no defensiveness in that smile. One might even have said that there was a kind of placidity in it. Tsuda, who had started out with lies, felt only that his mood became increasingly carefree.

'It's wonderful that you still don't ever seem to have any worries.'

'Yes, I suppose so.'

'You haven't changed a bit.'

'Well, I'm still the same person, you know.'

Upon hearing this, he suddenly wanted to say something ironical. But at that moment the maid, who was arranging the tangerines on the plates, broke out laughing.

'What are you laughing at?' he asked her.

'Why, what Mrs Seki is saying is so funny.' After defending herself, she noticed Tsuda's serious expression and felt compelled to explain herself more concretely.

'Of course, that's certainly true. While you're alive everybody's the same person, and unless you're born again nobody can become a different one.'

'But that's not necessarily true, you know. There are quite a few people who are born again even though they're still living.'

'Are there really? If so, I'd certainly like to see them.'

'If you want, I don't mind showing them to you.'

'Please do.' After saying this she began giggling again. 'I suppose *this* is working again, isn't it.'

She brought her index finger to the tip of her nose.

'I'm no match for *this*, sir. After all, you were even able to sniff out Mrs Seki's room correctly.'

'Oh, a room's nothing. I can guess everything, from your age, to the place you live, and the place you were born. Just with this one nose of mine.'

'My, you're quite terrifying. I've met my match in you, sir.'

As she said this, she stood up. But upon leaving the room she joked with him again.

'You're probably very good at hunting, aren't you, sir?'

The two of them, left alone in that room with the fine southern exposure, suddenly became silent. Tsuda was seated so as to face the veranda and receive the sun. Kiyoko, with her back to the railing, was seated with her back to the sun. From his seat he could see clearly how the ridges in the mountain, one on top of the other, distinctly showed the difference between sunlight and shadow. The autumn tints which coloured the scene also showed him the distinct gradations of light and shade. But unlike Tsuda, who had this broad vista before him, Kiyoko had nothing at all to see. If she looked she could see only the sliding-doors facing north, and Tsuda's image, which blocked out one section of them. Her line of vision was narrow. But she did not seem to mind very much. She was quite calm by comparison with an O-Nobu, who, in Kiyoko's place, would instantly have had to change her position.

Kiyoko's face, unlike that of the night before, was somewhat more flushed than Tsuda knew it usually to be. But this could be interpreted simply as the physiological effect of the strong autumn sunlight shining on her directly. When, after looking at the hillside, he noticed her ear-lobes, dyed crimson as if she had had an unexpected dizzy spell, he thought this might be the reason. Her ear-lobes were thin, and it seemed as if, because of her position, the sunlight which streamed behind them reached him only after passing through the blood vessels in them.

185

In such a situation, who would be the first to speak? If his partner had been O-Nobu, everything would have been clear without even thinking. For she was a woman who gave him not an inch of leeway. But he also was so constituted as to have little margin for relaxation. She would simply employ all of her devices at will wherever and whenever she wished. He would always be forced to assume a passive role. And he would have to endure the tension and effort of doing battle with her.

But when he had to deal with Kiyoko, an entirely different mood emerged. The line of action was immediately reversed. For she always took her cue from him. Therefore, when he had to deal with her, he could always function positively. And moreover he did so with great ease.

He became aware of this special feature of their relationship only after they were alone together. He suddenly realized that his memories of her had revived effortlessly. The feeling of awkwardness which until then he had been anticipating, strangely enough had vanished, at the precise moment when such awkwardness ought to have arisen. He found himself sitting in front of her feeling thoroughly relaxed. And this was not so very different from the feeling he used to have in her presence before she fled from him. At least he felt certain that it was a feeling of the same quality. Consequently, he was the one who, as in the past, took the initiative of starting the conversation again after it had lapsed. Moreover the very fact that he was able to act as he had in the past gave him unexpected satisfaction.

'How's Seki doing these days? Is he studying as usual? I've neglected to call, so I haven't seen him at all.'

He did not feel there was anything wrong in speaking this way. The question of whether it was proper to mention her husband at the beginning of the conversation, viewed from the concerns of the people involved, or considered from the emotional factors that had arisen between the two of them before then, or even, setting aside these complicated personal considerations, speaking simply from the standpoint of whether it was natural or unnatural, was actually one over which he should have pondered awhile. In bringing up the subject easily, without the slightest misgiving, contrary to his usual caution, he was undoubtedly forgetting the circumspection that he normally used in his daily life with O-Nobu.

But he was no longer speaking to O-Nobu. Proof of the fact that it did not matter that he had forgotten to be careful in his speech could be seen immediately in Kiyoko's manner of answering. She smiled as she did so.

'Thank you for asking. Yes, I suppose you'd say he's about the same. We talk about you from time to time, you know.'

'Do you really? I'm afraid I'm always so busy I've neglected seeing anybody lately. . . .'

'My husband's the same way. Lately there doesn't seem to be anybody who has leisure. That's why we lose touch with one another. But nothing can be done about it. It's just the natural course of things.'

'Yes, that's so.'

Although he answered in that way he felt that he really wanted to ask, 'Is that so?' instead of commenting as he had. 'Is that so? Is that the only reason for our becoming estranged? Is that what you really mean?' These probing questions were already in his mind at that time in unspoken form.

And yet he found before him a Kiyoko who was almost as simple and unpretentious as before, or whose actions at least could be interpreted as nothing other than that. Her manner showed that she certainly was sufficiently composed to make Seki a subject of conversation between them. The ingenuousness to allow her to mention his name without embarrassment was evident. This ingenuousness was something he had been secretly anticipating at the same time that it undoubtedly was something he had scarcely dared hope for. The satisfaction in finding her the same woman as before had to appear together with the dissatisfaction at finding that she was able, with the same open manner as in the past, to talk about her husband freely in front of him.

'I wonder why I'm so displeased by that.'

He did not have the courage to face that question squarely. As long as Seki was actually her husband, he had to accept her attitude and respect it. But this was simply an external reaction. It was the appraisal of anyone who might accidentally pass her on the street. Behind it there was a quite different way of looking at it. At that point there had to be someone who was different from the unconcerned passer-by. And even if he could not say that the usual Tsuda was that person, he did want very much to say that in a certain sense he was qualified to be a 'special person' with regard to Kiyoko. He meant someone who is what a professional is to an amateur, someone who is what an intellectual is to an ignorant man, or what a specialist is to a layman. Therefore he could only think that such a person had the right to say more than the casual observer.

It was natural that his feeling towards Kiyoko, while he outwardly approved of her attitude but inwardly did not, should express itself externally in some form or other.

186

'I'm sorry about last night.'

He said this abruptly, wanting to see how it would affect her.

'I am too.'

Her answer came easily. When he could not detect any uneasiness in it, he wondered :

'Is it possible that this morning she can't relive any of the surprise of last night?'

If she had lost even the ability to recall it, then his mission, for good or for ill, was a vain one.

'Actually, after I frightened you, I was sorry I'd done it.'

'Well then, you shouldn't have done it in the first place.'

'I agree I shouldn't have. But if I didn't know, I couldn't help it, could I? Believe me, I had not the remotest idea you might be here.'

'But didn't you purposely come from Tokyo with the gift for me?'

'That's true. But it's also true that I didn't know exactly where you were staying. Last night I just met you accidentally.'

'Do you really mean that?'

Her agitation, as she seemed to detect a deliberate act in his behaviour the night before, startled him.

'You surely don't think I could have done such a thing on purpose? No matter how eccentric I may be.'

'But you seemed to be standing there for a long time.'

He had undoubtedly been watching the water overflowing the basins. He had also certainly been staring at his image reflected in the mirror. And finally he had certainly picked up the comb that was there and idly combed his hair.

'There wasn't anything I could do, was there, if I was lost and couldn't find my way?'

'Yes, I suppose that's true. But I couldn't look at it that way.'

'Do you mean you think I might have been lying in wait for you? Don't be ridiculous. No matter how effective my nose might be, I could hardly have known the time you take your bath.'

'Yes, of course. That's quite true.'

Since she said these words with a note of trying very hard to convince herself that she meant them, he could not help laughing.

'Why in the world do you doubt me?'

'You certainly know why without my telling you.'

'Can't you see that I don't?'

'Well, it doesn't matter if you don't. It's not something that needs to be explained.'

He was forced to take another tack.

'Well then, why *did* I lie in wait for you? Please tell me that.'

'But I can't tell you.'

'You don't have to hold back so. By all means please do tell me.'

'I'm not holding back. I can't tell you because I can't tell you, that's all.'

'But isn't it something in your own mind? I think if you really want to, you can.'

'There's nothing at all in my mind.'

With this simple phrase she quickly warded off the brunt of his attack. At the same time it increased the emphasis of his own words.

'If so, where did that doubt come from?'

'If it was wrong to doubt you, I apologize. And I won't do it again.'

'But haven't you already done so?'

'Nothing can be done about that. That I doubted you is a fact. And it's also a fact that I confessed to it. No matter how much I apologize I can't possibly eliminate them.'

'That's why I say I'll be satisfied if you just tell me those facts.'

'But haven't I done so already?'

'That's only half, or a third, of it. I want to hear everything.'

'Well, I'm certainly perplexed. I have no idea how to answer.'

'It's quite easy, isn't it? If you only say you had this kind of doubt about me for this kind of reason, everything will be over quite simply.'

Kiyoko, who until then had indeed seemed perplexed, suddenly looked as if she had finally understood.

'Oh, is *that* what you want to hear?'

'Of course. Isn't that why I've been badgering you in this way all this while? And because you were trying to hide it—'

'If that's the case, why didn't you say so earlier? I haven't been trying to hide it, or do anything of the sort. The reason's very simple.

It's just that you're the kind of person who'd do that sort of thing.'

'You mean lie in wait for you?'

'Yes.'

'Don't be ridiculous.'

'But as I see you, that's the sort of person you are, so I can't help it. I'm not lying or saying anything untrue.'

'I see.'

He folded his arms and looked down.

187

A while later he raised his head again.

'Somehow or other our talk seems to have become a formal discussion, hasn't it? But I certainly didn't intend to have any such interview with you.'

Kiyoko answered :

'I certainly didn't intend it to be this way, either. It's just that it naturally went that way—not that I purposely planned it.'

'I agree it wasn't on purpose. It's simply that I pressed you too hard with my questions, I suppose.'

'Yes, I suppose that's it.'

She smiled again. When he noticed the usual placidity in her smile, he could not restrain himself any longer.

'Well, while I'm questioning you, will you please answer one more thing for me?'

'Yes, anything you ask.'

Her manner showed that she was indeed ready to answer every question of his. Thus he was considerably disappointed even before asking the question.

'This woman seems to have forgotten absolutely everything already.'

As he reflected in this way, he also realized that this was one of her basic characteristics. Wanting to make doubly sure, he asked her :

'But you did turn pale last night on the stairs, didn't you?'

'I suppose I did. Of course I couldn't see my own face so I'm not sure, but if you say so, it must be true.'

'Aha, so that means I'm not yet a complete liar in your eyes, doesn't it? Thank you. So you too recognize what I did, don't you?'

'Even if I don't, if I actually turned pale, there's nothing much that can be done about it now, is there.'

'That's true. And you also stiffened, didn't you?'

'Yes, I was aware of that myself. In fact, if I'd stayed that way a bit longer I might actually have fallen down.'

'In other words, you were stunned, weren't you?'

'Yes, I was utterly amazed.'

As he began to say, 'Well then. . . .' he watched Kiyoko's fingers as she looked downwards while carefully peeling an apple. The transformation as the juicy, light green meat of the apple gradually emerged after the moist skin had dampened the knife blade and had peeled off in a spiral reminded him of what had taken place more than one year earlier.

'This woman, in precisely the same posture, peeled exactly this kind of apple for me.'

Her way of holding the knife, her way of moving her fingers, and the way in which her long sleeves opened outward as she kept both her elbows close to her lap—in the midst of everything that was a repetition of that past moment, he noticed only one thing different : the ring with its two beautiful gems gleaming on her finger. If this was the permanent symbol of her marriage, there was nothing that blocked more effectively the relations between them than their tiny glittering light. As he stared at her nimbly moving fingers, he was compelled to recognize this brilliant flash of warning in the midst of his absent-minded reflections on the past.

He quickly turned from her hands to look at her hair. But the hair style into which the maid had arranged it that morning was an ordinary low pompadour. The black sheen, which was not the least bit out of the ordinary, merely showed the vertical traces of a comb having been neatly drawn through it.

He then resolutely resumed the subject he had once been about to abandon.

'Well then, the thing I want to ask you is. . . .'

She did not look up. Paying no attention to this, he continued :

'How can you be so carefree this morning when you were so stunned last night?'

Still looking down, she answered :

'Why do you ask?'

'I ask because I simply can't understand such a psychological reaction.'

She continued to answer without looking at him.

'I don't understand such difficult terms. It's just that last night I was that way, and this morning I'm this way, that's all.'

'And that's your complete explanation?'

'Yes it is.'

If he had felt like being theatrical, that would have been the point for him to heave a sigh. But he did not have the courage to do so. The feeling that, even if he did, it would be of no use somehow prevented him from displaying such artifice.

'But isn't it true that this morning you didn't get up at the usual time?'

Kiyoko looked up immediately.

'Oh my, how do you know such a thing?'

'I just know, that's all.'

She quickly looked down after giving him a glance. Then, while inserting the knife blade in the neatly peeled apple, she answered :

'It's just as you say. You don't have second sight, you have second smell. And actually it's quite effective.'

He retreated in the face of this one comment, which was a mixture of bantering, irony, and seriousness.

She offered him the apple she had finally finished peeling and slicing.

'Why don't you take a piece?'

188

He did not touch the apple she had peeled for him.

'Why don't *you* take one? After all, Mrs Yoshikawa sent the fruit especially for you.'

'That's true, isn't it. And you went to the trouble of bringing it here for me, too. I suppose it would seem as if I didn't appreciate your kindness if I didn't take the first piece.'

As she said this, she took a piece of the apple which was between them. But before bringing it to her mouth she asked him further :

'But it's funny when you think about it. How in the world did it ever happen?'

'How did *what* happen?'

'I had no idea I'd receive a gift from Mrs Yoshikawa. And I had even less of an idea you'd bring it to me.'

He inwardly said, 'Of course—even I had no such idea.' In Kiyoko's eyes, as she looked fixedly at his face, shone the light of anticipation as she awaited an explanation from him. He recalled his own special relation to that light.

'Ah, those were the eyes !'

Past scenes, repeated any number of times between them, came distinctly to his mind. Kiyoko had at that time believed in this one man named Tsuda. Therefore she had looked up to him for all knowledge. She had sought from him the resolution of all doubt. She had seemed to take up the future which she herself did not understand, and had cast it upon him. Thus, even though her eyes had moved they had been at rest. As they had asked him for something they had had the brightness of faith and peace. He had felt that he had been born with the privilege of alone possessing that brightness. He had even thought that precisely because he himself existed did those eyes too exist.

The two had finally separated. And now they had met again. When he sensed that he now was being warned by this new Kiyoko who had left him that those same eyes as in the past still existed, but in a different sense from the way they had existed before, he was profoundly moved.

'They're your most beautiful feature. But are they now merely a beauty to cause me to despair? Please tell me clearly.'

After each had perceived the other's doubt in the meeting of their eyes, Kiyoko was the first to look away. Tsuda watched as she did so. And in that too he detected the difference in ardour between them. She was completely unhurried. She looked away, as if nothing at all mattered, and cast her eyes on the winter chrysanthemums, arranged in the decorative alcove.

Tsuda, from whom she had escaped with her eyes, had to pursue her with words.

'Of course I didn't mean that I'd come only as Mrs Yoshikawa's messenger.'

'Naturally you didn't. That's why it's odd.'

'It's not the least bit odd, I tell you. At a time when I was thinking of coming here on my own, I met Mrs Yoshikawa, and after I learned from her that you were here she simply asked me to bring along her gift.'

'That must be it, of course. If not, no matter how you look at it it's strange.'

'No matter how strange you think it is, there are such things in the world as coincidences, you know. And to continue to think as you seem to. . . .'

'That's why I no longer think it's strange. If only one finds out the reason, everything ends up being quite obvious.'

He almost wanted to say : 'I too have come to ask the reason.' But the question asked by Kiyoko, who did not seem to be concerned with that at all, was a straightforward one.

'Does that mean you've been ill too?'

In a few words he explained the circumstances of his illness. She then commented :

'But that's wonderful for you, isn't it—the fact that your company makes arrangements for you at a time like that. On that score I feel sorry for people like my husband. They seem to be busy from morning to night.'

'But Seki's an eccentric and seems to like it that way, so it can't be helped.'

'How unkind of you ! That's certainly not true.'

'But I mean it in the good sense. In other words, he's so very diligent.'

'My, you *are* clever at turning phrases around.'

Since at that moment they heard the hurried footsteps of someone in *zōri** climbing the stairs from below, Tsuda, who was about to say something, remained silent, and waited to see what would happen. Then a different maid from the previous one looked in.

'The guests from Yokohama said to ask you, Mrs Seki, whether you were going to take a walk with them to the falls this afternoon.'

After the maid heard Kiyoko say, 'Yes, I'll go with them,' she looked at Tsuda as she was about to leave, and said, 'Why don't you go with them, sir?'

'Thank you. By the way, is it noon already?'

'Yes, I'll bring you your lunch soon.'

'Is it really *that* late!'

He finally got up.

Although he intended to say 'Mrs Seki', he forgot and inadvertently called her 'Kiyoko'.

'Kiyoko, about how long will you be staying?'

'I have no fixed schedule at all. If a telegram should come from home, I may even have to leave today.'

This startled him.

'Do you think something like that will come?'

'That I can't say.'

Kiyoko smiled as she said this. Tsuda returned to his own room, while trying to explain to himself the meaning of her smile.

UNFINISHED

---

* Flat clogs, somewhat more formal than wooden *geta*.

Afterword

It is no exaggeration to state that Natsume Sōseki* (Kinnosuke was his given name, but he is always referred to by his sobriquet, Sōseki) is at once the greatest novelist and literary figure of modern Japan. His novels have become modern classics, and a large selection of his work has been written into the textbooks of the Japanese higher and middle schools. Moreover his influence on subsequent Japanese literature was, and continues to be, immense.

Sōseki was born in Tokyo (then named Edo) in January 1867. In 1884 he entered the preparatory department of Tokyo Imperial University and graduated with highest honours in 1893 from the English Literature Department. He taught for a while at the Tokyo Higher Normal School, and in the provincial towns of Matsuyama and Kumamoto. In 1900 he went to England, where he continued his research in English literature. He returned to Japan in 1903 to become a lecturer at Tokyo Imperial University.

In 1907 he took the unprecedented step of abandoning a brilliant academic career to join the staff of the Tokyo *Asahi* newspaper, becoming the chief of its literary section as well as serializing his own novels in its pages. Until about 1904 he had been known among a small group of readers as a *haiku* poet and a writer of short sketches. It was only in 1905 that he began writing fiction. With the publication during that year of his *Tower of London* (*Rondon tō*) and the beginning of the serialization of *I Am a Cat* (*Wagahai wa neko de aru*) he rose to sudden fame. The former is a romantic fantasy suggested by Ainsworth's work of the same name, while the latter is a satirical piece, studded with wit, humour, and irony. It is the record of life in a professor's household, remarkably similar to Sōseki's own, as seen through the eyes of his mischievous cat. This work appeared serially in a popular literary magazine, and it is said that the cat's death in the last instalment actually caused readers to weep. This work, together with *Botchan*, which followed in 1906, are extraordinarily popular even today, and it is a rare Japanese who has not read both of them. *Botchan* is an account of a rather picaresque, young, Tokyo-bred schoolteacher, whose clear sense of justice comes to the fore as he does battle against a hypocritical group of middle school instructors.

* I follow the Japanese practice of writing the surname first.

376

Later in 1906 Sōseki published *The Grass Pillow* (*Kusamakura*),* more a prose-poem than a work of fiction, in which he revealed his views on life and literature. In this work he is exceedingly Oriental in his outlook, and it is proof that while he was undoubtedly influenced by the West he certainly did not reject his Eastern heritage. His first real full-length novel, *The Poppy* (*Gubijinsō*), which was serialized in the *Asahi*, was first published in final form early in 1908.

It is not until the three novels of what is commonly referred to as his 'first trilogy', *Sanshirō* (1908), *And Then* (*Sore kara*, 1909), and *The Gate* (*Mon*, 1910) that we know Sōseki for a superb craftsman. Yet he did not stop there; for if there is anything that can be said about Sōseki, it is the progression in artistic importance and depth that characterizes his novels.

With *The Gate* the mood in Sōseki's created world becomes more sombre, foreshadowing his concerns as revealed in the three novels of his so-called 'second trilogy', *Until After the Equinox* (*Higan sugi made*, 1912), *The Wayfarer* (*Kōjin*, 1913), and *Heart* (*Kokoro*, 1914),† as well as his last two works, *Grass on the Wayside* (*Michikusa*, 1915) and *Light and Darkness* (*Meian*, 1916). After *The Gate* Sōseki's interest in psychological analysis deepened, his style was freed from the ornateness that had previously too often characterized it, and, in his thought, he turned to a consideration of fundamental religious and philosophical problems, dwelling on the nature of man and human destiny. He began to formulate his own philosophy of *sokuten kyoshi* (to model oneself after Heaven and depart from the self), giving it artistic expression in his novels by a ruthless indictment of his main characters, who neither patterned themselves after Heaven nor attempted to overcome their egocentricity. Thus Sōseki expounded his own ideal by depicting the veritable hell that results from egoism : Sunaga of *Until After the Equinox* turns in on himself to contemplate the dreary stretches of his unlovely soul, Ichirō of *The Wayfarer* nearly goes mad from doubting his wife, and Sensei of *Heart* finally commits suicide because of having betrayed his friend.

Grass on the Wayside, his last complete work, is Sōseki's only clearly autobiographical novel, although it is written in the third person and all of the names, together with many of the details, are changed from what they were in actuality. This work can be viewed as providing a

---

* There is a recent English translation by Alan Turney published under the title *The Three Cornered World* (Peter Owen 1965).
† Published in a recent English translation (Peter Owen 1968).

complete catharsis for Sōseki in that he unsparingly dissected his own egoism in the same way that he had dissected that of his other principal characters in his earlier works. It is almost as if he was intent on cleansing his own spirit before embarking on his most ambitious portrayal of egoism, *Light and Darkness*, the very ambitiousness of which may have been responsible for his not living to complete it.

During the first half of 1916, Sōseki's last year of life, he was plagued with illness as indeed he had been for several years. In January he went off to Yugawara Hot Spring* for a twenty-day stay, and returned to Tokyo on 16 February. This information we derive from a letter† to Yamamoto Shōnosuke; in the same letter we find the first mention of Sōseki's intention of writing a serialized novel in the *Asahi* after the conclusion of the one by Tanizaki Jun'ichirō which was currently appearing in that newspaper. Therefore he asked Yamamoto when he thought that Tanizaki's work would be finished.

Sōseki's ailments, however, were by no means ended, for he discovered, through the urinalysis he had to undergo on 19–20 April, that pain in his arm and shoulder were the result of diabetes, not rheumatism, as he had previously thought. In his letter of 2 May to Nomura Kimi he made the statement that he seemed to have been born to be ill since he always had pain somewhere. But he also stated that he was then up out of bed and soon would have to write a *kudaranai mono* (dull thing) for the newspaper. It is interesting for us to note Sōseki's modesty, since the 'dull thing' is *Light and Darkness*, which, though incomplete, is generally considered to be the greatest novel of modern Japan.

Yet it would be wrong to think that Sōseki did not have consolations for his many illnesses. Foremost among them must be counted his friendship with four young men, the budding novelists Akutagawa Ryūnosuke and Kume Masao, and the two Zen acolytes Kimura Genjō and Tomizawa Keidō, the former acting as his literary disciples and turning to him for advice in the artistic realm, and the latter serving as spiritual stimuli and guiding him, despite their youth, to a deeper understanding of Zen truth. It is fascinating to compare these two

* This is undoubtedly the hot spring Sōseki had in mind when writing the last sections of *Light and Darkness*.
† The letters, poetry and excerpts from the novel quoted are translated from a recent definitive edition of Sōseki's complete works, Iwanami Publishing Company, Tokyo, 1956–1958.

correspondences, for in his letters to Akutagawa and Kume he emerges as the literary master who dispenses advice and comments to these two admiring youths, whereas in his letters to Kimura and Tomizawa he is revealed as a humble seeker after religious solace. These two sets of letters, then, can be seen as representing two important facets of Sōseki's personality, dedication to literary artistry and a deep devotion to religious ideals.

In another letter to Yamamoto, dated 21 May, Sōseki apologized for sending the beginning of the novel later than he had promised. Fortunately, however, Tanizaki's work which should have ended on the 20th was to continue until the 24th. Sōseki assured Yamamoto that he would write one section a day, and indeed he was faithful to his promise. Thus *Light and Darkness* began to be serialized in both the Tokyo and Osaka *Asahi* newspapers on 26 May. Since Sōseki collapsed on 22 November and died on 9 December, the novel was broken off on 14 December; for there were twenty-two sections remaining after his collapse. It is said that at the time readers found it strange to be reading a novel in the newspaper after its author had died, since normally only the works of living authors were serialized.

Unlike the winter and early spring of the year, the summer and early autumn of 1916 were pleasant for Sōseki; we have his comments in several letters that his last summer of life was, strangely enough, his most enjoyable one. Some commentators have even seen in this a foreshadowing of Sōseki's early death, for there is a widespread belief in Japan that a person has a brief period of great energy immediately preceding his death.

The summer of 1916 represents the peak, not only of Sōseki's career as a novelist, but also as a poet of *kanshi*, or Chinese verse. He stated that the process of writing *Light and Darkness* in the morning so tired and so depressed him by his delving into the ugliness of man's soul that it required a cleansing of his own soul. He felt this could be best performed by his writing Chinese poetry. And again we find, in comparing these poems with *Light and Darkness*, a startling contrast. Perhaps it can also be said that this contrast between Sōseki's Chinese poetry and *Light and Darkness* is a continuation of the duality which we see in the two correspondences mentioned previously. For we find in Sōseki's *kanshi* an elevated tone and a deep searching for peace of soul that immediately reminds one of his humility towards the two young Zen priests. Two of these poems, dated 21 August and 6 October respectively, are significant in revealing his attitude towards religion. The former is especially important since he mentions *Light and Darkness*, albeit rather obliquely. The translations* follow :

> Though seeking solitude, not yet towards the turquoise hills have I gone.
> I live among men but my feeling for the Way suffices.
> Of light and darkness, mutually bound, three times ten thousand characters,
> While I fondled and rubbed my stone seal, have freely emerged.

> Not for Christ, nor Buddha, and not for Confucius :
> In the narrow lanes I sell my writings just for my own delight.
> I have plucked and gathered how many fragrances in crossing the garden of art?
> I have wandered leisurely around how many turquoise hills and pools in the poetry thicket?
> Within the ashes of burning books, books first know life.
> Within a world without law, law first understands rebirth.
> Strike and slay the godly men, for at the place where every trace of them is lost
> The empty void will clearly show the wise and foolish.

Interestingly enough, three of the poems showing this religious mood most clearly are his last three, written on 13, 19, and 20 November respectively. The translations follow :

> At himself he laughs, within the narrow world the man of mighty dreams.
> With the closed vault distant and vague, he soon forgets his soul.
> The nine o'clock morning sun on the pink peach gorge,
> A ten-foot patch of coral in the turquoise sea at spring.
> As the crane soars into the clear void, its exquisite feathers are calm.

* For the translation of these poems I have been aided by the paper of a former student of mine at Harvard University, Elling O. Eide. The translations in his paper were revised by Professor J. R. Hightower of Harvard University, and I have incorporated most of his revisions in my translations. I am responsible, however, for the final English versions as they appear here. The poems are filled with Zen paradoxes and allusions to the Chinese classics which it would be tedious to unravel here.

As the wind blows over the magic herbs, the medicinal roots
will sprout.
To lengthen my life never to the Isle of Eternity have I gone
forth.
Not to age indeed you need only to nurture the One Truth.

Great stupidity is as hard to attain as one's purpose is hard to
achieve.
Five decades' springs and autumns are but as a moment's
breath.
Contemplating the Way, without a word, I simply enter into
quietness.
Composing poems—a verse or so—alone, I seek purity.
Far, far beyond the heavens the forms of the departing clouds,
And in the soughing of the wind the sound of the falling
leaves;
Suddenly I look out the still window over the empty blankness,
And from the Eastern Mountains the moon emerges, to light
up half the river.

The path to Truth is lonely, distant, and difficult to find;
But I wish to embrace a cleansed heart and tread the past and
present.
In the turquoise waters and turquoise hills what is there of
the self?
All heaven and all earth : these are without artifice.
In the faint evening light the moon withdraws from the grass;
The blurred autumn voice of the wind is in the forest.
Eyes, ears, both shall I forget; my body too shall I lose;
And in the void, alone, I'll chant the white cloud song.

How then did Sōseki culminate his work as an artist in this last
mammoth novel, *Light and Darkness*? At first reading this work may
appear commonplace, for it certainly cannot be denied that it treats
lives and events which are ordinary in the extreme. Yet Sōseki has
achieved an extraordinary work while thus utilizing the most ordinary
material.

The action of the novel covers some ten days during which Tsuda
Yoshio, a company official, enters the hospital for treatment of a fistula
and after the operation goes off for a few days to a hot spring to re-

cuperate. This is practically the entire substance of the external action of the novel. Quite obviously, therefore, Sōseki's attention is directed towards the workings of the minds and hearts of the principal characters. For around Tsuda revolve five persons who are related to him in various ways: O-Nobu, his wife; O-Hide, his younger sister; Mrs Yoshikawa, the wife of the president of the company where he works; Kobayashi, his 'friend' from school days; and Kiyoko, his former sweetheart who is now married.

The main theme of the novel is the operation which is performed on Tsuda, and its outcome. Komiya Toyotaka, the foremost critic of Sōseki and author of the definitive biography, was the first to point out the symbolic significance of the opening section which deals with the necessity of Tsuda's undergoing an operation. Komiya states, and all succeeding critics have agreed with him, that while Tsuda must undergo an operation on his body, he must also undergo a much more basic and far-reaching operation on his soul. There can be no doubt that Sōseki intended this interpretation, for without it *Light and Darkness* becomes merely another 'medical' novel, much as Anthony West has caricatured Tanizaki's important work *The Makioka Sisters* (*Sasameyuki*) in his often-cited *New Yorker* book review.

The necessity for the operation is clearly indicated and Tsuda dutifully undergoes it, that is, the physical phase of it. The spiritual operation cannot be performed so simply, and there are certain critics who feel that the major aspect of it was yet to be treated at the time the novel was broken off. I feel, however, that there is ample proof in the section which exists to state that Tsuda's operation was already begun and, indeed, that he was responding to treatment. Of course, it is possible to say anything about how the novel would have ended, but all such speculation, while interesting to indulge in, is still gratuitous.

It is, I think, profitable in an analysis of this novel, to see the five major characters who revolve around Tsuda as each performing a part of the operation. And yet it must be remembered that the five have, in varying degrees, their own 'illnesses' which must similarly be treated. We can see these five characters as constituting a hierarchy of value from dark to light, to use the standards of the novel itself. At the end of the spectrum nearest to Tsuda in the 'darkness' of her soul is O-Nobu, who is of course also closest to him physically. In the second position on the road to 'light' stands Mrs Yoshikawa, who displays at every turn a worldliness and a sense of her social superiority which could hardly be termed humble or directed towards religion but who still makes a rather astute appraisal of Tsuda's essential cowardice and vanity. At a stage somewhat more advanced stands Tsuda's younger sister, O-Hide, who brings to bear in her excoriation of her brother and sister-in-law a penetrating mind and a highly evolved morality, but who, at the same time, is not wholly free from self-righteousness and an inability to forgive, and who is eaten away by jealousy of O-Nobu's freedom. Beyond the half-way point between 'light' and 'darkness' stands Kobayashi, who, though he is in abject poverty and practically begs for assistance from Tsuda and O-Nobu, displays a depth of compassion towards all suffering humanity and a quasi-prophetic insight into Tsuda's true problem. He further acts as a catalyst in speeding up the action between O-Nobu and Tsuda. At the very end of the spectrum, bathed in light, stands the beautiful figure of Kiyoko, 'the child of purity' as the Chinese characters of her name could be rendered. Significantly, also, Kiyoko appears towards the end of the work, and we thus have moved along in one direction from the 'darkness' of Tsuda's 'unoperated' condition to Kiyoko's naturalness, calm, and forgiveness.

I shall begin, then, with an analysis of the position that O-Nobu occupies in the novel, and especially of her function *vis-à-vis* Tsuda. There is a fierce controversy over her role : the pro-O-Nobu faction, the major proponents of which are younger critics such as Ara Masahito* and Etō Jun, see O-Nobu as a woman maligned and consider the major culprit responsible for such defamation to be none other than her creator, Sōseki himself, for they accuse him of 'stacking the cards against her'; the anti-O-Nobu faction, which includes the late Komiya Toyotaka, see O-Nobu as the feminine counterpart of Tsuda, suffering almost as acutely from the disease of egoism as Tsuda himself. Those favouring O-Nobu have pushed the controversy quite openly into the realm of value by attaching the adjective *kindaiteki*, or 'modern', to O-Nobu; conversely, her detractors within the novel, Mrs Yoshikawa and O-Hide primarily, and outside the novel, Sōseki and the anti-O-Nobu group, are described as *hōkenteki*, or 'feudal'. Thus, O-Nobu, much more than Kiyoko, has become a symbol : to those critics who approve of her, of individualistic integrity, courage in the face of the deadening and stultifying opposition of centuries of traditional, family- or class-centred ethics; and to those critics who indict her she has become a symbol, together with Tsuda, of the egoism that eats at the moral fibre of man

---

* Ara was born in 1913, but he still can be considered as belonging, spiritually if not chronologically, to the group of younger critics.

in no matter what century and in no matter what land, of that egoism which Sōseki sought to overcome, or perhaps more accurately, to exorcise, through his philosophy of *sokuten kyoshi*.

The major point of conflict lies, I believe, in the different emphasis—and therefore, in a sense, value—which each camp places on the will. For O-Nobu is manifestly a woman of will, a will so strong that her emergence in a Japanese novel of 1916 gives the lie to the all-too-facile assessments of the Japanese woman delivered by both native and Western authorities. Consider for a moment O-Nobu in contrast to O-Tama of Mori Ōgai's justly famous *The Wild Goose* (*Gan*), the serialization of which was concluded a scant three years earlier, in 1913.* Their psychologies are strikingly different. And yet it is not that there have never been other strong-willed women in Japanese literature, both modern and classical—the five heroines of Saikaku's seventeenth-century *Five Women Who Loved Love* (*Kōshoku gonin onna*) could hardly be termed timid or self-effacing—but rather that O-Nobu *does* typify a modern woman who employs all her energies for clearly-defined individualistic goals, and not for just a momentary passion, as is true of almost all of the other strong-willed women in Japanese literature. Rather than 'passion', 'dynamism' is the more appropriate term to describe the basic characteristic of O-Nobu's psyche. She is ever a woman in motion—physically, emotionally, and intellectually. Even her occasional pauses, or rests, are to be interpreted more as part of her strategy to recoup her strength, or regroup her forces for new enterprises.

From her first appearance in the novel in Section 3, where we see her playing the coquette by striking a graceful pose to look at some non-existent sparrows building a non-existent nest (at least Tsuda does not see a trace of either, and the reader is at that moment seeing, or not seeing, the universe through his eyes) until her last appearance in Section 167, where she almost convinces Tsuda that she should go to the station to see him off on his journey to the hot spring, she displays a force of character, a vitality, an energy that all but enlist the sympathies of the most rigidly traditional and conservative reader who would normally view her exceedingly unsympathetically, and who, upon concluding the novel and not having to view her in action any longer, may actually revert to the unsympathetic appraisal that was latent in his mind throughout his reading of the novel. O-Nobu reminds

---

* The novel is set in 1880 but O-Tama's psychology would still have been appropriate for a female character in a novel set in the early years of this century.

me of such heroines of popular Western fiction as Scarlett O'Hara, who moves through *Gone With the Wind* with the same vigour and unquenchable vitality—in short, with the same dynamic will. And just as not one of the millions of readers of the American work begrudges his admiration of Scarlett O'Hara's strength so too do I feel that all who read *Light and Darkness* must, of necessity, admire O-Nobu. The keen blade of the will ever commands attention, and even respect, for it is the very stuff of personality, the very core of being. Concern over the direction of the will, or its employment in the world of objective reality, must always be secondary to simple recognition and approval of the existence of the will. And yet, secondary though it may be, such concern does arise, and with it great diversity of opinion. It is here that the two camps emerge and face each other on the battlefield of value : for it is one thing to approve of the manifestation of naked will, as against non-will or the void, but to approve of its every employment is quite another.

It cannot be denied by the most ardent of O-Nobu's admirers that her actions are scarcely motivated by altruism or that her will is employed for sheer self-gratification. Her major goal, namely the forcing of her husband to love her, and her alone, is sought by methods which may appear to be a glorification of the individual as opposed to the family or class but which, on closer analysis, reveal themselves as crassly selfish.

From certain statements of Kobayashi, which he makes to her when he comes to receive from her the overcoat which Tsuda promised him, and from certain veiled references by O-Hide, O-Nobu suspects that Tsuda is still emotionally attached to someone else, as indeed he is to Kiyoko, who suddenly on the eve of their engagement broke off relations with him and married, shortly thereafter, a man named Seki, who never appears in the novel. (Significantly, and thus perhaps not coincidentally, his name means 'barrier', and he is indeed the barrier to any resumption of love between Tsuda and Kiyoko.) This suspicion of O-Nobu's is reinforced by the memory of an afternoon shortly after their marriage when Tsuda mysteriously burned some trash, including a packet of old letters, in the garden. Once roused, O-Nobu's mind, usually alert, becomes an exquisitely sensitive antenna to gather more information on which to base her actions. She accepts the challenge almost with eagerness, and moves forth to do battle. It hardly requires intelligence for her to realize that Mrs Yoshikawa and O-Hide are her arch-enemies, who are conspiring her undoing, but what she must still determine is the link between them and the woman who still has a hold on her husband's affection and who is thus the obstacle to his loving her, O-Nobu, undividedly and fully. Though O-Nobu is outnumbered, her strength would probably be sufficient in the struggle if she could only rely on her husband's loyalty—she obviously cannot rely on his undivided affection. Yet Tsuda is disloyal, and it becomes patently clear that he will not divulge any information that would help her. She thus finds herself in the position of defending a fortress that has already been given over to the enemy by its commandant. In one memorable scene she begs Tsuda to help her, and for a moment becomes all the more appealing by showing herself to be in such desperate need. I quote from Section 149 a part of the conversation between them, on one of her visits to him at the hospital :

She suddenly cried out :

'I *want* to trust you. I *want* to put my mind at ease. I want to trust you more than you can imagine.'

'Are you saying I can't imagine?'

'No, you can't possibly. Because if you could, you'd have to change. Since you can't imagine, you're as unconcerned as you are.'

'I'm not unconcerned!'

'Well, you certainly aren't sorry for me and you don't have any pity on me.'

'What do you mean by feeling sorry for you or having pity on you?'

After he had in effect rejected her criticism, he was quiet for a while. He then faltered a bit as he attempted to evade the issue.

'You say I'm not concerned about you—no matter how much I actually am. Because you can be sure that if there's reason to be I will be. But if there isn't, what am I supposed to do?'

Her voice trembled with tension.

'Oh, Yoshio, listen to me!'

He said nothing.

'Please tell me I don't have to worry, I beg of you. Put my mind at ease and rescue me, because I have no one else to turn to but you. I'm helpless, and I'll die if you turn me aside. So please say I can put my mind at ease. Just one word will do, but please say I don't have to worry.'

The 'one word' which O-Nobu wishes to hear, namely that Tsuda loves only her, is of course not forthcoming, and she must continue her struggle alone.

I have said enough to show that O-Nobu is courageous, that her opposition to her sister-in-law's involvement in her and her husband's affairs and to her husband's benefactress's condescension has considerable justification, and that her lack of support from her husband makes her plight almost pathetic. All of this is clearly on the credit side and goes a long way towards explaining the attitude of the younger critics with regard to her. And yet it is just as clear that she is really concerned about no one but herself, that her love of Tsuda, although wholly genuine, is simply the major weapon in her arsenal to force him to love her. Her entire behaviour in the novel is shot through with an egoism that simply cannot be passed off as individualism. For I am certain that however much such critics as Ara Masahito oppose the sacrifice of the individual to the family or class they too recognize that there are other important human relations in addition to the one existing between husband and wife. Surely O-Hide's and Mrs Yoshikawa's involvement in Tsuda's affairs cannot be dismissed merely as an outlet for their own sexual frustration in their marriages, as Ara implies.

My position in the O-Nobu controversy lies, therefore, somewhere between the two groups, but somewhat closer to that of the older, 'feudal' faction, for I cannot countenance such gross misuse, as the younger, 'modern' faction indulges in, of the important term 'individualism' to distort or conceal blatant selfishness.

With the above outline of O-Nobu's character, it is now easier to assess her role in the operation which is being performed on Tsuda's soul. It is interesting to observe how almost all of the Sōseki critics, Komiya included, overlook this healing function of O-Nobu. This is undoubtedly so because of the extremes of the positions taken for or against her : those in favour of her are so concerned with combating her detractors that they do not see that she is able to help Tsuda to an awareness of his own sickness, the gravity of which both groups recognize; those opposed to her see her egoism as so deep-dyed and so closely allied to Tsuda's that they feel she is wholly unable to assist in his recovery. They hold that she is too 'dark' herself to emit any 'light' whatsoever.

If there is any contribution which a Westerner can make to the seemingly exhaustive commentary and interpretation of this last great novel by Sōseki, it is precisely in this area of the definition of O-Nobu's positive role in Tsuda's spiritual operation. I think that only a Westerner can be sufficiently removed from the everlasting and dreary alternation of the two value terms, 'feudal' and 'modern', to be objective in his assessment.

Although O-Nobu is sick with the same disease as Tsuda, the symptoms are entirely different. Also, I definitely do not think that her case is as serious as her husband's. Within the terms of the symbolism of the novel in Section 1 she is even less susceptible to becoming 'tubercular' than Tsuda, for 'being tubercular' is tantamount to hopelessness. These two factors, then, provide that margin of light which enables O-Nobu to lead Tsuda. It is a case of 'the partially blind leading the almost totally blind', which is hardly an impossibility.

O-Nobu's egoism and Tsuda's differ qualitatively primarily in that O-Nobu is still 'open' whereas Tsuda is almost completely 'closed'. Such openness is magnificently revealed in the section which I have just quoted, where O-Nobu is not afraid to bare her soul, to admit her weakness (she who is so strong), and to beg for help, whereas Tsuda retreats ever further into himself, and shows at every turn his affinity with Sunaga of *Until After the Equinox*, Ichirō of *The Wayfarer*, and Sensei of *Heart*. It is interesting that even when Tsuda and O-Nobu are at their most egoistic, as in the most famous and most dramatic scene in the entire work, their open quarrel with O-Hide at the hospital, this basic difference in their symptoms is especially obvious. O-Nobu exults in the warfare, and comes to grips with her enemy almost immediately, whereas Tsuda is so closed as to be unable even to fight vigorously. He does not even listen to O-Hide's strictures; O-Nobu listens intently, if only to refute her sister-in-law's position. The quarrel only wearies him; it refreshes O-Nobu, and not only because she emerges from it as the acknowledged victor. She is open to outside influences, be they beneficial or harmful, creative or destructive. Tsuda is closed, and the poison in his system can find no outlet. Of course if he is completely closed, he will be unable to receive any influence at all, even from his wife. Happily, however, there is still a narrow slit through which some outside stimuli may enter.

Tsuda, then, is able to gain greatly from a comparison of his spiritual condition with that of his wife. He can see in her the first stages of recovery through which he will have to pass if he is to emerge from darkness. The very least that is required of him is that he become as open as O-Nobu, and I feel that there is ample reason to believe that her influence in this regard is already working on him, albeit slowly and subtly. For he can hardly remain wholly indifferent to her endless acts to bind him more closely to her and extort his love. Every evasion, every retreat or hesitation, every closing up on his part, such as the one we have seen in the face of her plea, brings him closer to the moment when he will have no place to retreat to, when he will either have to open up or seal himself in forever in the utter darkness of his soul. O-Nobu's very existence, then, is a challenge he cannot indefinitely spurn.

Yet another area where O-Nobu can heal him, or at least assist in the healing, is in her shaming him into action and out of cowardice by her own formidable courage. How long can Tsuda continue in the knowledge that his wife is the stronger, and more courageous, and still maintain his self-respect? It is here significant that Tsuda has such keen desire for social approval that the constant taunts of cowardice, from Mrs Yoshikawa particularly, must ultimately prod him to acts of courage—especially so, since his wife, whatever other failings she may have, is not lacking in that virtue. And indeed we must interpret his going to the hot spring to meet Kiyoko as the first halting steps towards a removal of that damning stain on his character.

Before I leave O-Nobu to move up one degree closer towards light in my analysis of Mrs Yoshikawa, I must touch upon the central problem, which I have hitherto only alluded to, namely that of love. O-Nobu's love of her husband is a greedy, self-seeking one, a posturing, coquettish one all too frequently, but the basic emotion, however mangled and distorted, is still very much alive within her. She is not cut off from that life-giving process, and indeed her involvement in love may explain in large measure her vitality and dynamism.

What, then, is the effect on Tsuda of O-Nobu's active participation in love? This question is doubly important since Tsuda is certainly the major object of that love. The main effect is that in the course of the novel Tsuda becomes acutely aware of the difference between loving and being loved, of the difference between performing ten thousand little acts to please another person and of being the person who receives those acts. O-Nobu is in no way successful in her goal of forcing Tsuda to love her but she unconsciously sets in motion the process which might ultimately bring about precisely the same result : for if Tsuda reflects sufficiently on the difference between O-Nobu and himself, and sees why it is that Kiyoko fled from him, he will be able to love, or, in other words, he will be healed. For to learn to love is to be freed from the prison of the self. It is the only known antidote to the poison of egoism.

Thus O-Nobu's role in Tsuda's spiritual regeneration is a considerable one, and she is definitely not the cause of his problem as both Mrs Yoshikawa and O-Hide contend. Of course certain peripheral aspects of Tsuda's condition may have been aggravated by his marriage, but it is perfectly clear that the basic symptoms were amply present long before he even met O-Nobu, and most likely even before he knew Kiyoko. This fact neither Mrs Yoshikawa nor O-Hide can see because they do not wish to see it, and because it is so much more convenient for them to place almost the entire blame on O-Nobu. (It is in the 'almost' that the reader sees *their* margin of light.) Naturally both Kobayashi and Kiyoko exonerate O-Nobu completely as the carrier of Tsuda's disease because they have known him so thoroughly prior to his marriage to her.

I turn, therefore, to this group of four, two of whom are basically in sympathy with Tsuda although they do criticize him, often severely, and two of whom have detached themselves from him so completely as to be able to make a devastatingly objective appraisal of his character. I begin with Mrs Yoshikawa, since, as I have said, she stands next, after O-Nobu, on the road to light.

Sōseki must have derived special enjoyment in his creation of this lady of the *haute bourgeoisie*, for she, too, like O-Nobu, breaks the mould of the Japanese woman—this time of the elderly Japanese woman of means. Indeed throughout my reading of the novel I had a mental picture of a French, English, or Russian *grande dame*, instead of a Japanese woman. If she had been a member of the aristocracy, instead of the *bourgeoisie*, I could almost have substituted Proust's Duchesse de Guermantes, who is an exact fictional contemporary of Mrs Yoshikawa, as indeed Proust is of Sōseki. Mrs Yoshikawa's freedom of action, her lack of reserve in her relations with Tsuda, her meddling officiousness, her wit and banter which emerge from a life of complete leisure—all of these again would hardly seem to be in keeping with the image that we normally receive of the wife of a Japanese capitalist during the early years of this century.

The first meeting between Mrs Yoshikawa and Tsuda in Section 10 is prefaced by a passage in Section 9 in which Sōseki describes eloquently the motivation for Tsuda's visits. It superbly sets in relief Tsuda's basic problem of egoism and serves to underline the type of relationship existing between him and his employer's wife :

He finally jumped on the streetcar running in the opposite direction from his house. Since he knew quite well that the Yoshikawas were very often not at home, he was aware that he might go there and not necessarily be able to see them. He knew further that even if they should be at home, the occasion might be inconvenient for them, and he would only be sent back without seeing them. Nevertheless, he had to pass through the gate of the Yoshikawa home from time to time. He would do this partially out of politeness, partially out of personal interest, and finally out of simple vanity.

'Tsuda is a special friend of Yoshikawa.'

Sometimes he liked to assume this pose and look at himself. He also liked standing before the world thus burdened with so important a friendship.

And yet if Tsuda is vain in desiring to be known as a special friend of the Yoshikawas, Mrs Yoshikawa is just as vain in accepting and basking in Tsuda's adulation. She thoroughly enjoys her role of Lady Bountiful dispensing advice and charity to her impoverished tenants from her ample store. Since Tsuda is a handsome young man of twenty-nine (we actually first learn his age when she banteringly asks him) her role becomes that much more pleasant; indeed at times she even appears to be flirting with him, secure in the knowledge she cannot possibly be rebuffed, for Tsuda 'knows his place' and is perfectly content to be thus condescended to by her.

The formal relationship between them is twofold : as I have already indicated, Mrs Yoshikawa's husband is president of the company in which Tsuda works and he is also a good friend of Tsuda's father in Kyoto; it was this link which led to Mrs Yoshikawa's arranging the meeting between Tsuda and Kiyoko. Since she failed in her attempt to bring about their marriage, she continues to feel responsibility for Tsuda (and in a sense for Kiyoko too, but this is not fully shown) although both of them have since married different people. While she enjoys meddling in and managing other people's affairs, we must admit that her intentions are the very best. She fully believes that her actions are altruistic and that she is actually being very useful in her various schemes for Tsuda's betterment. Her vanity, therefore, is not at all as complex or as deleterious as Tsuda's. Indeed in their two characters we can see the essential difference between vanity and egoism, which Sōseki is endeavouring to make, the one being naïve (for all Mrs Yoshikawa's external sophistication) and almost healthy, the other being deep-seated and malignant.

Mrs Yoshikawa makes one of her characteristically quick assessments of the causes of the unhappiness which Tsuda manifests on his visit to her : Tsuda is responsible for part of his unhappiness (as indeed he is, although not in the way that she imagines), and O-Nobu is responsible for the remainder. That is to say, Mrs Yoshikawa feels that since Tsuda is still attached emotionally to Kiyoko he is unable to be happy with O-Nobu. She holds that O-Nobu's responsibility is rooted in her selfish, calculating nature which militates against her becoming the kind of wife who would make Tsuda happy. Mrs Yoshikawa's hostility towards O-Nobu is shown from the first meeting with Tsuda in Sections 10 and 11, when she searches for adjectives to explain why O-Nobu seems older than Tsuda, although she is really seven years younger. I quote from Section 11 :

'Well, she's so mature. And she's such a remarkably clever person. In fact I don't think I've ever met such a clever person. Take good care of her now, won't you?'

From the tone of her voice there was very little difference between saying 'take good care of her' and 'watch out for her'.

Just to assess the difficulties in Tsuda's and O-Nobu's marriage is hardly enough for such a practical-minded, bustling woman as Mrs Yoshikawa. She must set about to correct those difficulties, and she is not slow in devising schemes which she feels will do precisely that. Her next meeting with Tsuda is at the hospital where she then broaches both of them. (He is of course extremely flattered that the wife of the company president would actually deign to visit him, and she thus makes it impossible for him to refuse co-operation with her plans.) He must see Kiyoko once more and settle his relationship with her, once and for all, in a manly manner (*otokorashiku*, as Mrs Yoshikawa repeatedly emphasizes). This can be done if he avails himself of the opportunity to go to a hot spring to recuperate after his operation. There he will meet Kiyoko, who has gone to regain her strength after a miscarriage; she will of course know nothing of his real reason for going, and will think it all a coincidence.

Tsuda complies with Mrs Yoshikawa's request, although not without considerable reluctance, so that half of her plan is realized, or, at any rate, is to be realized. She then launches into a description of her proposed second operation, namely the 'education' (she actually uses the Japanese term *kyōiku*) of O-Nobu. With marvellous condescension she tells Tsuda how she intends to make O-Nobu a 'wifelike wife' (*okusan-rashii okusan*). She is supremely confident that she possesses the wisdom and authority necessary to discipline this recalcitrant, overly clever, impudent young woman who has dared to defy her. It is most unfortunate that since the novel is incomplete we shall never know how the battle between these two wilful women is concluded. However, it is certain that neither will give in easily.

Since I have already indicated that I think Mrs Yoshikawa is wrong in placing any very large blame on O-Nobu for Tsuda's spiritual malady, I shall not comment further on her views concerning O-Nobu. Her views on Tsuda, however, deserve additional commentary, for she is precisely correct in contending that his unwillingness to accept the fact of Kiyoko's rejection of him is one facet, and an important one, of his distress and marital unhappiness. As I have shown, O-Nobu provides an object lesson in courage for Tsuda, but it is Mrs Yoshikawa who actually prods him into action. It is ironical (and Sōseki is wholly aware of his having produced such irony) that these two women, who in their goals are diametrically opposed and outright enemies, should unconsciously co-operate, and complement each other, in their influence on Tsuda. Mrs Yoshikawa badgers him into 'acting like a man', and O-Nobu, while opposing all such badgering, brings about the same result.

I now turn to Tsuda's younger sister, O-Hide, who, despite her self-righteousness, is clearly Mrs Yoshikawa's moral superior, and thus yet one step closer to light. If O-Nobu affects Tsuda by her mere existence, and Mrs Yoshikawa by her half-humorous taunts and jibes, O-Hide affects Tsuda by her stinging excoriation. As I have stated, she firmly believes Tsuda to have changed radically since his marriage to O-Nobu, and thus she condemns her sister-in-law more than her brother; but nonetheless much of what she says is valid, if we overlook her initial bias.

The crisis which brings to a head the always indifferent relationship between O-Hide and her brother and his wife is a matter of money. Tsuda has always been spending beyond his means, largely to impress O-Nobu, in front of whom he has consistently exaggerated the extent of his financial resources. The deficit in his budget was, until the time that the novel begins, made up by sums of money which his father sent from Kyoto. It is clear, however, that his father is now annoyed with his son's spendthrift ways and will not send him any more. With the added expenses for his operation, Tsuda is indeed in a quandary. O-Hide learns of his embarrassment and brings him a certain amount on her visit to the hospital. It is this act which arouses the emotions of both donor and recipient, and which involves O-Nobu too when she arrives on the scene.

This quarrel is the climax of the novel. For sheer emotional intensity it has few equals in Eastern or Western literature. That such a common-place event as a money matter between sister and brother should have been exalted and transformed into a piercing flash of insight into the soul of man, that his baseness and ugliness should have been so brilliantly exposed, represent the triumph of Sōseki's psychological method, and indeed of his entire literary art. Here, as it were, all of Sōseki's 'cards are on the table', and *Light and Darkness*, which moves more often in accordance with the inward processes of man, for a few brief sections explodes into action, with much of the tension that has built up dispelled by the blast.

If we set aside for the moment any consideration of O-Hide's own spiritual state and look only at her indictment of Tsuda, we cannot but be struck with its deadly accuracy. As O-Hide asserts, Tsuda is indeed unable to be grateful for anything : not just for his sister's gift but for every spiritual and material endowment. Exactly as she says, it is a tremendous misfortune for Tsuda to be unable to accept the kindness of others, and it is not only 'as if' Tsuda were deprived of the ability to be happy but rather that such is his actual spiritual state. (I here have purposely separated Tsuda and O-Nobu even though they are of course linked as objects of O-Hide's wrath.) It is significant that Tsuda can accept O-Hide's indictment of him as being concerned only about himself 'with composure because he did not doubt that it was a statement of a general human characteristic rather than specifically of one of his own'. He truly feels that selfishness and lack of concern for others is the common state of all human beings, and thus, arch-conformist that he is, he sees no reason to change.

And yet if Tsuda were wholly unaffected by O-Hide's impassioned denunciation he would be an extraordinary individual indeed. The effect on him is extremely subtle but still considerable. Of course he does not agree with his younger sister's strictures, but he is also not entirely indifferent to them. As I have indicated in my discussion of O-Nobu, Tsuda is wearied by the struggle. In Sōseki's words, O-Hide, according to Tsuda, 'had neither charm nor nobility : she was merely annoying'. It is this annoyance with her that he will be unable to shake off and which should be relied upon to goad him into corrective action in the future.

O-Hide's gadfly function is reinforced by Kobayashi, the penniless socialist journalist. Even the severest critics of Sōseki have been unstinting in their praise of this remarkable character who appears to have strayed from the pages of an unpublished Dostoyevsky novel at the same time that he is, paradoxically, unmistakably Japanese. Every word, every minor action of his is so absorbing, so essentially new, so alive that it is only with the greatest regret that the reader can say farewell to him in Section 167 as he is about to go off to Korea.

No two individuals could ever be more different than Tsuda and Kobayashi. Tsuda is, as I have said, an arch-conformist; Kobayashi's every bone is violently non-conformist. Tsuda is calculating and suspicious; Kobayashi cares nothing about the results of his actions for he has absolutely nothing to lose, and he is suspicious of no one for he has nothing to defend. Tsuda is an egoist of the first order while Kobayashi yearns for the day when all human beings have banished egoism and its concomitant loneliness in a society of perfect love and justice. The banishment of loneliness for Kobayashi is not just an abstract ideal but a keenly felt personal need, for, as he laments to Tsuda in one of the most touching scenes of the novel, he himself is appallingly *sabishii* (lonely).

Kobayashi thus stands in direct opposition to everything that Tsuda represents, and he is not slow in verbalizing this opposition. He flays Tsuda as strongly as does O-Hide but without a trace of the latter's self-righteousness. His denunciation of Tsuda at times seems almost as merciless as O-Hide's, and yet the reader is quickly aware that he is not rejecting Tsuda outright but rather attempting to transform him into a person who will at once be able to banish his own loneliness and enter into true brotherhood with him. Ironically, Kobayashi is trying to make Tsuda his brother while O-Hide, despite her protestations to the contrary, is casting Tsuda off and breaking the blood ties of actual brotherhood.

And yet Tsuda does not respond any more readily to Kobayashi's criticism than he does to O-Hide's; finally even Kobayashi despairs and leaves with the prophecy that Tsuda will be changed forcibly by events even if he refuses to accept Kobayashi's advice. I think Kobayashi's prophecy is also Sōseki's intent. Tsuda will be changed by events, but one of those events, and an important one, is his entire relationship with this maddening, exasperating, and thoroughly incorrigible 'friend'.

Perhaps it will be thought that I am giving blanket approval to all of Kobayashi's actions and statements relating to Tsuda. It is true that he is a far more appealing character than O-Hide, his morality is not so rigidly legalistic, he is closer to love and thus to truth than O-Hide, but he is by no means without faults. He appears to have a kind of inverted vanity in his poverty and in his being a social outcast. Moreover, his excoriation of Tsuda is not only of Tsuda as an individual but of Tsuda as a member of the bourgeoisie. Yet egoism, and certainly Tsuda's, is independent of economic status. Nevertheless, Kobayashi firmly believes, and here he is a doctrinaire Marxist, although he is never so defined, that if Tsuda's economic margin were removed he would be in large measure healed. Precisely in this mistaken diagnosis do we see the darkness in Kobayashi's soul which places him at one remove from Kiyoko, who stands, by common consent, at the pinnacle of the moral hierarchy of *Light and Darkness.*

While Sōseki's death deprives us of a conclusion to the novel, the 188 existing sections give us well-rounded portraits of five of the six major characters. Whatever else Sōseki might have written, the main lines and even most of the details of the personalities of Tsuda, O-Nobu, Mrs Yoshikawa, O-Hide, and Kobayashi are drawn so as not to allow any dispute as to their roles in the work. (As I have shown, the dispute about O-Nobu does not concern who or what she is but rather the value that is to be attached to her actions and personality.) It is only in the case of Kiyoko that we are lacking in sufficient material to describe her role with any precision, for she makes her appearance only in Section 176, at the very end of the novel.

Nevertheless so great is the economy of Sōseki's style that many things can be said about Kiyoko with the reasonable certainty that they would not have to be revised if we miraculously could acquire the remainder of the novel. Her actions reveal a soul that is pure, natural, and calm. She neither attacks nor condones Tsuda. Her physical beauty is but the complement to her greater spiritual beauty. This beauty informs her every motion so that we find Tsuda looking transfixed as she peels an apple.

I have been taken to task by several Japanese critics for having written, in a general study of Sōseki made thirteen years ago, that I felt Kiyoko might work Tsuda's salvation even as Sonia works Raskolnikov's in *Crime and Punishment.* Yet I see no reason to change my position except to add, as I have attempted to do here, that the other four major characters all will have a share in Tsuda's spiritual regeneration. Indeed, I must reassert my position of attaching great significance to Kiyoko's personality because I feel that in many ways she holds the key to the entire novel and even more to the entire art and thought of Natsume Sōseki.

Surely it cannot be an accident that Kiyoko's beauty, selflessness, and serenity should be the last creation of Soseki's pen. Surely it cannot be dismissed as sentimentality that even as his last poem, which I quoted earlier, should be so lofty, ethereal, and transcendental, so too should his last piece of prose have attained the same exalted state.

Even if it is open to doubt as to whether Kiyoko will save Tsuda, it is in no way open to doubt that Kiyoko represents a state of blessedness. To the reader who has toiled and suffered through five hundred pages of egoistic hell the figure of Kiyoko at the end can only be interpreted as a sign to him that all hope is not yet lost, that the gates of hell may yet be broken, and that the imprisoned spirits may yet rise to a purer, nobler realm.

Light and Darkness ends with Kiyoko's smile. The very last sentence that Sōseki ever wrote is: 'Tsuda returned to his own room, while trying to explain to himself the meaning of her smile.'

Indeed Sōseki's entire artistic life may be represented as a progression from a view of man as ridiculous to a view of man as infinitely precious, from a standpoint of satire verging on cynicism to one of the deepest compassion, or, in symbolic terms, from his nameless cat's impudent grin to Kiyoko's beatific smile.

V.H.V.

Tokyo, Japan
Sōseki's centennial year, 1967

❧❧❧TUTTLE CLASSICS❧❧❧

TUTTLE CLASSICS

HEARN, Lafcadio　ラフカディオ・ハーン

In Ghostly Japan　霊の日本　0-8048-3361-2 (4-8053-0749-8 for sale
in Japan only)

Kokoro　心　0-8048-3660-4 (4-8053-0748-X for sale in Japan only)

Kwaidan　怪談　0-8048-3662-0 (4-8053-0750-1 for sale in Japan only)

INOUE, Yasushi　井上靖

The Counterfeiter and Other Stories　ある偽作家の生涯、他
0-8048-3252-8

The Hunting Gun　猟銃　0-8048-0257-2

ISHIKAWA, Takuboku　石川啄木

Romaji Diary and Sad Toys　ローマ字日記、悲しき玩具
0-8048-3253-6

KAIKO, Takeshi　開高健

Darkness in Summer　夏の闇　0-8048-3325-7 (4-8053-0644-0
for sale in Japan only)

KAWABATA, Yasunari　川端康成

Beauty and Sadness　美しさと哀しみと　4-8053-0394-8

The Izu Dancer and Other Stories　伊豆の踊り子　0-8048-1141-5
(4-8053-0744-7 for sale in Japan only)

The Master of Go　名人　4-8053-0673-4

The Old Capital　古都　4-8053-0610-6

Snow Country　雪国　4-8053-0635-1

The Sound of the Mountain　山の音　4-8053-0663-7

Thousand Cranes　千羽鶴　4-8053-0667-X

MISHIMA, Yukio　三島由紀夫

After the Banquet　宴のあと　4-8053-0628-9

Confessions of a Mask　仮面の告白　4-8053-0232-1

Death in Midsummer and Other Stories　真夏の死　4-8053-0617-3

The Decay of the Angel　天人五衰　4-8053-0385-9

Forbidden Colors　禁色　4-8053-0630-0

Runaway Horses　奔馬　4-8053-0354-9

The Sailor Who Fell from Grace with the Sea　午後の曳航
4-8053-0629-7

The Samurai Ethics and Modern Japan　葉隠入門　4-8053-0645-9

The Sound of Waves　潮騒　4-8053-0636-X

TUTTLE CLASSICS

Spring Snow　春の雪　4-8053-0327-1
The Temple of Dawn　暁の寺　4-8053-0373-5
The Temple of the Golden Pavilion　金閣寺　4-8053-0637-8
Thirst for Love　愛の渇き　4-8053-0634-3

MIURA, Ayako　三浦綾子
Shiokari Pass　塩狩峠　0-8048-1529-1

MORI, Ogai　森鴎外
Vita Sexualis　ヰタ・セクスアリス　0-8048-1048-6
Wild Geese　雁　0-8048-1070-2

NAGAI, Kafu　永井荷風
A Strange Tale from East of the River and Other Stories　墨東綺譚
　4-8053-0266-6

NATSUME, Soseki　夏目漱石
And Then　それから　0-8048-1537-2
Botchan　坊ちゃん　0-8048-3703-1 (4-8053-0802-8 for sale in
　Japan only)
Grass on the Wayside　道草　4-8053-0258-5
The Heredity of Taste　趣味の遺伝　0-8048-3602-7 (4-8053-0766-8
　for sale in Japan only)
Kokoro　こころ　4-8053-0746-3
I am a Cat　吾輩は猫である　0-8048-3265-X
Inside My Grass Doors　硝子戸の中　0-8048-3312-5
The Miner　坑夫　0-8048-1577-1
Mon　門　4-8053-0291-7
My Individualism and The Philosophical Foundations of Literature
　私の個人主義、文芸の哲学的基礎　0-8048-3603-5 (4-8053-0767-6
　for sale in Japan only)
Spring Miscellany　永日小品　0-8048-3326-5
Ten Nights of Dream, Hearing Things, The Heredity of Taste
　夢十夜、他　0-8048-3329-X (4-8053-0658-0 for sales Japan only)
The Three-Cornered World　草枕　4-8053-0201-1
To The Spring Equinox and Beyond　彼岸過迄　0-8048-3328-1
　(4-8053-0741-2 for sales Japan only)
The 210th Day　二百十日　0-8048-3320-6
The Wayfarer　行人　4-8053-0204-6

TUTTLE CLASSICS

NIWA, Fumio 丹羽文雄
The Buddha Tree　菩提樹　0-8048-3254-4

OE, Kenzaburo 大江健三郎
A Personal Matter　個人的な体験　4-8053-0641-6

OOKA, Shohei 大岡昇平
Fires on the Plain　野火　0-8048-1379-5

OSARAGI, Jiro 大佛次郎
The Journey　旅路　0-8048-3255-2

SAWAMURA, Sadako 沢村貞子
My Asakusa　私の浅草　0-8048-2135-6

SETOUCHI, Harumi 瀬戸内晴美
Beauty in Disarray　美は乱調にあり 0-8048-3322-2 (4-8053-0747-1
　for sale in Japan only)

SHIGA, Naoya 志賀直哉
The Paper Door and Other Stories 襖、他　0-8048-1893-2

SUMII, Sue 住井すゑ
The River With No Bridge　橋のない川　0-8048-3327-3

TAKEYAMA, Michio 竹山道雄
Harp of Burma　ビルマの竪琴　0-8048-0232-7

TANIZAKI, Junichiro 谷崎潤一郎
Diary of a Mad Old Man　瘋癲老人日記　4-8053-0675-0
The Key　鍵　4-8053-0632-7
The Makioka Sisters　細雪　4-8053-0670-X
Naomi　痴人の愛　0-8048-1520-8
The Secret History of the Lord of Musashi and Arrowroot
　武州公秘話、吉野葛　4-8053-0657-2
Seven Japanese Tales　谷崎潤一郎短編集　4-8053-0640-8
Some Prefer Nettles　蓼喰う虫　4-8053-0633-5

TATEMATSU, Wahei 立松和平
Distant Thunder　遠雷　0-8048-2120-8

UCHIDA, Yasuo 内田康夫
The Togakushi Legend Murders　戸隠伝説殺人事件　0-8048-3554-3

UNO, Chiyo 宇野千代
Confessions of Love　色ざんげ　4-8053-0613-0